D1594667

IMPOSTER

BRADEIGH GODFREY

IMPOSTER

BLACK STONE
PUBLISHING

Copyright © 2022 by Dr. Bradeigh Godfrey
Published in 2022 by Blackstone Publishing
Cover and book design by Blackstone Publishing

The characters and events in this book are fictitious.
Any similarity to real persons, living or dead, is coincidental
and not intended by the author.

Printed in the United States of America

First edition: 2022
ISBN 978-1-6650-5518-5
Fiction / Thrillers / Psychological

Version 1

CIP data for this book is available
from the Library of Congress

Blackstone Publishing
31 Mistletoe Rd.
Ashland, OR 97520

www.BlackstonePublishing.com

To Nate
Because you always see the real me

PROLOGUE

She's in a hospital. She knows that. There are many other things she doesn't know—her name, or why she's here, or what day it is. But she's aware of the scratchy hospital gown she's wearing, the stiff sheets and antiseptic smell, and the click of shoes on linoleum floors.

Her head hurts. The pain has existed as long as she can remember, a gnawing in her skull that waxes and wanes but never disappears, and she wants to ask someone for help, to make it go away, but she doesn't know how. Words float through her mind like dandelion seeds on a breeze. She wants to reach out and capture them in her fist, stuff them in her throat, somehow form them into sentences. Into meaning.

But she can't reach for anything; her hands are tied down, her wrists encircled with soft bindings fastened to her bed. They don't hurt—only her head hurts—but the constraints are confining, stifling, and there's nothing she can do but twist her body and cry whenever the memories come: snow; darkness; fear bubbling in her chest. *He's following us.*

Outside her room, a familiar voice echoes, and she cocks her head to listen. Yes, she's known this voice all her life. Footsteps come closer, the voice draws near, and she sucks in a breath as recognition sparks.

It's her sister. *Finally.* Relief swamps her body, floods her limbs, and she relaxes against the mattress. Everything is going to be okay. Her big sister is here. She looks up, eager to see her. Their eyes meet, and she freezes.

Blind terror lights her up like a flash burn, white-hot. She rakes her legs across the sheets and twists her wrists against the restraints, trying to wrench herself free.

This is not her sister. It has her sister's face, her hazel eyes and red-gold hair, her chin and nose and lips, and when it speaks it has her sister's voice, calm and capable. But this is a stranger, a counterfeit. It's wearing her sister like a suit, like a second skin, which means her real sister is somewhere else, skinless and faceless and voiceless.

It leans forward, this thing that is not her sister, looming over her.

She's desperate to escape, scrambling to a corner of the bed, but her hands are bound and she can't get away and she gasps for air and wishes she had words to call for help, to make this thing vanish and never return.

Her mind fills with a red haze of fear, but one thought remains, bright and glass sharp.

I need my sister.

There's something I need to tell her.

PART ONE

CHAPTER ONE

In her years as a pediatrician, Lilian Donaldson had held thousands of babies. She'd counted their tiny fingers and toes, examined their soft fontanelles and delicate skulls. She knew how to soothe them, how to swaddle a newborn, and how to make a six-month-old giggle. After four years of medical school, three years of pediatric residency, and eight years in her own busy practice, she should have been an expert.

And yet she still felt utterly incompetent when it came to her own baby.

Four-month-old Abigail lay on the blanket in the middle of her beautiful nursery, Lilian kneeling next to her. She rechecked Abigail's hips, grasping her baby's knees and pressing down, then out, the Barlow and Ortolani maneuvers she must have performed ten thousand times.

Was that a clunk? If Abigail's left hip was slipping out of her socket, it could signify congenital hip dysplasia and cause pain and dysfunction if untreated. And firstborn female babies were more likely to have hip dysplasia, a fact Lilian had often used to quiz her medical students.

Sighing, Lilian rocked back on her heels, gazing at her daughter. Abigail was beautiful, with apple-round cheeks, deep blue eyes rimmed with thick lashes, and a perfect rosebud mouth. If a baby like this had been brought into Lilian's office, she would have told the parents that their little one looked absolutely perfect.

But as Lilian studied her baby—her own, delicious baby—she couldn't shake a vague sense of unease. A whisper from the past, warning her to be on guard, to be watchful. Just because the baby *looked* fine didn't mean she *was* fine.

Abigail started fussing, finding her fist and pressing it into her mouth.

"Are you hungry again?" Lilian murmured, picking Abigail up and settling into the rocking chair. The silent house felt suffocating, like a plastic bag over her face, preventing her from taking a full breath.

Unfastening her nursing bra, Lilian glanced out the window through the partially open curtains. A few snowflakes drifted in the dusky sky, and Lilian shivered. The last thing she wanted to do on a night with negative thirty-degree windchill was head outside, but she had promised Caleb she would do this, after some discussion.

"I can't deal with my sister on top of everything else," she had told him, to which he gently suggested it might help—as if all of Lilian's issues would magically disappear if she just reconciled with her sister.

"You could use a night out," he'd said, to which she responded that she didn't need a night *out*, she needed a night *in*. She needed a night of uninterrupted sleep—impossible with a nursing baby—not an uncomfortable dinner with the sister she hadn't spoken to in two years.

"She's in a good place right now," he'd said next.

Lilian had told him that he couldn't possibly know that from a fifteen-minute conversation after a chance encounter at Starbucks.

"If you won't do it for her, do it for me," he'd said at last, and that's when Lilian had finally agreed. Because she owed him this.

In Lilian's arms, Abigail was doing the thing where she was hungry but refusing to nurse. The hungrier she got, the harder she cried, which made it even more impossible to latch. The baby's wails, her frustrated mouth and red little face, made Lilian's entire body stiffen with anxiety. If Abigail didn't nurse well, then she wouldn't sleep well. The whole schedule would be thrown off and she'd be even crankier the next morning.

Just as panic began rising inside Lilian's head—*I can't do this anymore!*—Abigail took a deep breath and latched. Then came the rhythmic tug and release on her breast, and Lilian exhaled.

Soon after, she heard the door from the garage open into the kitchen.

"I'm home!" Caleb called, his voice echoing from downstairs.

Thank God. She'd made it through another day alone. And though she wasn't looking forward to this evening, she knew Caleb was right: it would be good to get out of the house.

Caleb bounded up the stairs and burst into the nursery, still wearing his scrubs, his hospital badge swinging, his blond hair messy. Sometimes he looked more like a boy playing at being a surgeon than a thirty-nine-year-old associate professor of Orthopedic Surgery in one of the top hospitals in the country. Lilian smiled in spite of herself.

"Sorry I'm late!" he said. "Rob needed help with the grant he's submitting, Nina needed to talk about a patient. You know how it goes."

Lilian did know, though her life as a busy academic physician had taken on a hazy, dreamlike quality. Her maternity leave, which had already been extended an entire month, was set to end in two weeks. She grimaced. Returning to work meant facing the mess she'd left behind.

Abigail popped off Lilian's breast, turning her head to give her father a milky grin.

"There's my baby girl!" Caleb said, kneeling to place his hand on Abigail's head. "Did you hear your daddy's voice? I missed you all day, peanut."

"Go ahead and take her," Lilian said, rolling her tense shoulders. "I should change my clothes, anyway."

Caleb lifted Abigail onto his shoulder and patted her back in a practiced rhythm. He was an excellent dad, loving and gentle, and as involved as he could be, given his long hours at work. But watching them, Caleb cradling Abigail as he spoke in his sweet daddy voice, brought back that niggling sense of unease.

"I'm worried about her left hip," Lilian said. "Will you check it?"

Caleb glanced at her. "Didn't you just take her to see Asha? Did she notice anything?"

Dr. Asha Ramachandran was their pediatrician and Lilian's former residency classmate. Yes, Lilian had taken Abigail for her four-month wellness check last week. And no, Asha had not noticed anything unusual. But had she checked closely enough? *Really* checked?

"Just try it for me," Lilian said. Maybe his orthopedic surgeon hands would pick up something Asha hadn't.

Caleb sent her a worried look but nodded. He laid their daughter down and took each of her squishy little knees in his big palms. Pressing downward at the hips, his forehead furrowed in concentration as he listened and palpated.

"Seems fine," he said.

Exasperated, Lilian got out of the rocking chair. She put her hands over his and guided him through the maneuver again. "Don't you feel that little click on the left? Just . . . there?"

"No, I don't." He sounded completely sure, but something still whispered at the back of her mind.

"But—"

"Lily," he said slowly. "What's going on?"

Lilian stiffened. Of all people, Caleb should understand why she would be worried about missing a diagnosis, about ignoring signs of something potentially devastating. He should understand why she couldn't trust herself.

But he didn't have to live with her mistake. Not the way she did. Lilian kept the memory tight against her chest like armor, feeling the weight, the girth, those sharp edges each time she took a breath. It kept her honest. It kept her on her toes.

"I'm not being paranoid, if that's what you mean," she said in a tight voice. "I know I'm just a lowly pediatrician, but please don't patronize me."

The worry on his face blossomed into hurt. "If you're worried, let's get an X-ray. Then we'll know for sure."

"And expose her to unnecessary radiation?" Lilian imagined the invisible rays penetrating Abigail's tiny body, snipping and splicing her DNA, making changes that, decades later, could cause cancer. Not likely with one X-ray, but why take the risk? "I'll keep monitoring it."

Caleb picked Abigail up again, kissing each of her cheeks "We are going to have the best time tonight, aren't we, Abby girl? Mommy's going out with Aunt Rosie, and we'll watch the game together."

Aunt Rosie. A confusing title, given that Rosie had never even met Abigail. But it vibrated deep in Lilian's chest—a longing she hadn't realized existed.

"There's a bottle of breast milk in the fridge," Lilian said. "I don't think I'll be gone that long, though."

"Take as long as you need," Caleb said, glancing over at her. His smile couldn't hide the concern in his eyes. "I'm proud of you for doing this. I know Rosie doesn't deserve it—"

"It's fine." Lilian didn't want to rehash what had happened between her and her sister. She had agreed to one dinner with Rosie. That was it. It didn't mean they would become close again, but Lilian wanted, at the very least, to know that her baby sister was all right. That was her job, as the older sister. Her parents' words drifted through her mind: *Take care of Rosie, Lilian. Make sure she doesn't get hurt. You're responsible for her, do you understand?*

A flash of color outside distracted her, and Lilian turned toward the window. A canary yellow Volkswagen Beetle had pulled into their driveway.

"I can't believe she still has that car," Caleb said.

"She's always loved it," Lilian said as memories flooded her mind. The morning of Rosie's sixteenth birthday. Lilian, a fourth-year med student, had come home for the weekend. Their mom made Rosie's favorite breakfast, Belgian waffles with Nutella and sliced strawberries. The three of them had been sitting at the scuffed kitchen table when a series of honks from the drive sent them scurrying to the front door. And there it was: the vintage yellow Bug Rosie had been talking about for months, their dad standing next to it with the biggest smile on his face, holding up the keys.

"Why don't you take the Land Rover?" Caleb said. "It's icy tonight."

"It'll be fine."

It seemed incredible that Rosie had managed to keep her car when she'd thrown away almost everything else related to their childhood, including Lilian, and at a time when Lilian had needed her sister the most. The old Bug their dad had salvaged and rebuilt couldn't be worth much—but if Rosie had cared enough to keep it all these years, maybe she hadn't lost sight of what really mattered: family. Imperfect, but still worth preserving.

For the first time since Rosie's phone call two weeks ago, Lilian felt a modicum of hope. They could never regain what they had lost, but maybe tonight could be a new beginning. Lilian hadn't been blameless in everything that had happened, either.

Yes, maybe Caleb was right: if Lilian fixed things with her sister, she might begin to heal in other ways, too. She could get back to her regular life, to a version of herself that she recognized.

"Have a nice time with your sister," Caleb said, leaning in to kiss Lilian's cheek. "Be safe."

CHAPTER
TWO

Rosie had made reservations at a restaurant in Greektown, which Lilian thought was too far to drive on such an icy night. But Rosie had insisted. The restaurant was a spot they used to frequent as a family, for celebrating birthdays, graduations, and anniversaries. At nine and a half years old, Lilian had sat on the cracked faux-leather seat of the corner booth, sipping her Sprite as her big, burly dad squeezed her mom's delicate hand and made the announcement that would change the course of Lilian's life. She wondered, now, if her parents had been scared; they were already struggling to make ends meet. They must have known that adding another child would strain an already-tenuous marriage. But all she remembered from that night were the smiles on her parents' faces and the excitement bubbling in her stomach. *I'm going to be a big sister.*

As Rosie drove through Lilian's neighborhood, she chattered in a high-pitched, nervous voice. "So fancy here in Wilmette! Can you imagine what Dad would think? Seeing that one of his daughters ended up as a north-sider? He would've died of shock."

And just like that, the glowing memory of her parents' smiles on that long-ago night was replaced by the image of her parents in their matching caskets, their graying skin, and waxy lips. Lilian flinched; Rosie flushed and went quiet. As they drove in silence, Lilian kept sneaking glances at her sister, catching shadowy glimpses when they passed a streetlight. The last time she'd seen her sister, two years ago, Rosie had been so thin she looked skeletal, her hair short and greasy, her movements twitchy. Lilian had wondered if she was on something.

Now she looked fresh-faced and glowing in her red pea coat and mustard yellow scarf. A younger version of Lilian: long, strawberry blonde hair, wide-set green eyes. Had they looked so much alike, growing up? With their age difference, it hadn't been as apparent. Now, looking at Rosie was like looking in a mirror with a ten-year time delay.

"Abigail sure is adorable," Rosie said, breaking the silence.

"Thanks," Lilian said.

She had briefly introduced Rosie to her daughter but hadn't let Rosie hold her, citing risk of infection in the winter months. Caleb had given Lilian a raised-eyebrow, worried-husband look, but hadn't said anything.

Rosie shifted the car into a higher gear and the vehicle shook. Lilian involuntarily reached for the door handle. Snow had started to fall in earnest, streaking across the windshield. Traffic slowed to a crawl, and Rosie sighed as she downshifted. Lilian shivered; the Beetle's tiny heater barely kept up with the freezing temperatures.

"Caleb looked good," Rosie said, glancing over. "How's he doing?"

"Really great."

"Still busy with work?"

"Yep." Lilian braced herself for the question she knew would come next.

"And how's work for you?"

Lilian hesitated, considering her answer. "I've been on maternity leave since Abigail was born."

"For four months?" Rosie said, her lips parting in surprise. "Lucky you."

"I wanted to soak up every moment with her," Lilian said, which was only partially true. But she wasn't ready to discuss the real reason for her extended leave with Rosie; even thinking about it was painful.

Earlier today, she'd broken one of her cardinal rules and checked an online review site, where patients could anonymously review physicians. Three new reviews had been posted—all negative. One in particular had blindsided Lilian.

This is the doctor who missed someone's cancer diagnosis so you can bet I am NOT going back there again.

A swift pang of guilt brought the memories back to the surface. A tiny, black-haired girl with a raspy cough, a desperate mother, an angry father. *My daughter is dying because of this piece-of-shit doctor.*

Lilian blinked away a sudden rush of tears and tried to squelch the memory. "How are you?" she said, changing the subject. "You look great."

"Things are good." Rosie flashed a quick smile as she accelerated, the car shuddering again. "I love my job—it's seriously my dream, Lil. The agency is amazing. Everyone's at the top of their game. I'm learning so much."

"That sounds like a great fit for you," Lilian said, recalling what Rosie had told her about her position as a graphic designer for some big-name ad agency downtown. "You've always been creative."

And Lilian had encouraged that creativity, hoping that if she kept Rosie occupied with painting and sketching and crafts, her little sister would stay oblivious to the tension in their home, the constant worry about money, the arguments between their parents. Creativity, she'd told herself, was a sign of a happy kid. A sign that Lilian, even as a teenager, was taking good care of her sister.

"I'm seeing someone new, too," Rosie said, her eyes fixed forward as she navigated the snow-covered road. "Actually . . . I moved in with him recently."

Lilian's response popped out before she could stop herself: "That seems fast."

"We've been together nine months. Since April."

Lilian nodded, keeping her expression carefully blank. Rosie didn't have the best track record when it came to relationships. "Tell me about him."

Rosie smiled, a flash of sunshine in the darkened car. "He's great. Smart and funny and kind. His name's Daniel. Daniel Connors. He's a professor at the University of Chicago. Actually, he's on sabbatical this year writing up his research. He's *amazing*."

Lilian's protective big-sister senses were tingling. Rosie always seemed to fall for significantly older men; in college she'd had a tumultuous affair with one of her professors. Yes, she was twenty-eight now, but it still made Lilian uneasy. "A professor, huh?" she said.

Rosie shot her a glance, eyes narrowed. "Don't make that face."

"I'm not making a face," Lilian said, but she smoothed her features into a neutral expression anyway.

"Yes, you are, you're making that disapproving face you always make—anyway, it's not like I'm his student."

"I'm just concerned, that's all," Lilian said. Never mind the professor thing, this Daniel Connors could be in his forties or even fifties. God, she hoped he wasn't in his *sixties*.

"Well, don't be. He's not that much older than me—stop being weird about it." Rosie's lips tightened. "Besides, I've been doing fine without you, Lilian. I don't need you to mother me."

Don't you? Lilian wanted to ask. That had always been the tension between them, growing up: Lilian had practically raised her little sister, for the first twelve years of Rosie's life until Lilian finally moved away for med school. And even then, Rosie had called her every day for months, begging her to come back home. She'd call Lilian whenever anything went wrong, laying the problem at her feet, expecting her to step in and fix things. But when Lilian tried to give advice or help, Rosie would ignore it and do whatever she'd wanted to do in the first place.

Lilian took a deep breath. It had taken less than an hour for them to slip right back into their old roles, like dollhouse figurines. Big sister, little sister. She wondered if they could ever just be sisters. Or even friends.

"Girls, knock it off," Lilian said in a deep voice, mimicking words their dad must have said hundreds of times during their growing-up years. She glanced over and saw Rosie grinning fondly.

"'You sound like two cats scratching at each other in the back alley,'" Rosie said in a singsong voice, mimicking their mom. Her smile faded, and Lilian caught a glimmer of tears in her eyes. "I miss them so much."

"Yeah," Lilian said quietly, wishing she could say, *I've missed you, too.*

They lapsed back into silence, listening to the hum of the engine, watching the windshield wipers clear away the snow. What do you say to a sister you don't know anymore? *You hurt me. I need you. I'm scared.*

Later, Lilian promised herself. A conversation would be a good start. Apologies—on both sides—would be even better.

"Want to see a picture of Daniel?" Rosie asked. With one hand on the steering wheel, she dug in her pocket—almost drifting into the other lane, which made Lilian gasp—then handed her phone to Lilian. Lilian caught a brief glimpse on the screen of Rosie and a man with dark hair.

"Shit!" Rosie said, slamming on the brakes. Lilian lurched forward, the seatbelt tensing across her shoulder. The phone clattered to the floor as the Beetle swerved, losing traction. Lilian's right foot jammed down, searching for a nonexistent brake pedal.

An instant later, Rosie righted the car. The brake lights of the car ahead drifted forward until they were almost invisible in the thick falling snow.

Lilian let out a shaky breath. "Maybe we should find somewhere closer to eat," she said, her heart still pounding. "We don't need to go all the way to Greektown."

"No, I've been craving saganaki," Rosie said. "Besides, this conversation is too important to have in a car." Her mouth tightened. Something dark flitted across her expression. "It's a matter of life and death, sis."

Goosebumps lifted on Lilian's skin at her sister's tone—grim and almost menacing—but a spark of irritation followed. Life and death? She tried not to roll her eyes. Rosie had a habit of hyperbolizing for dramatic effect, but this wasn't funny.

Before she could speak, Rosie coughed out an awkward laugh. "God, your face! Quit freaking out," she said, patting Lilian's thigh in a gesture that felt mildly condescending. "I'll explain everything at the restaurant. Look—traffic's letting up."

The cars around them increased speed, everyone accelerating in a collective need to reach their destinations despite the ice and snow. They were Chicagoans; they scoffed at southern cities that shut down for a skiff of white on the roads. Of course, most of them weren't in a vehicle with well over two hundred thousand miles and no antilock brakes.

Lilian twisted her gloved hands in her lap; they felt empty without her baby, and her chest fluttered with worry. Caleb had once propped Abigail up on the sofa when watching football, and Lilian had a sudden image of her daughter, facedown, struggling for air. She sent him a quick text: *How's it going?*

Less than a minute later, a selfie of him holding Abigail arrived, her fat little cheek smooshed against his shoulder. *We're good, Mommy! Have fun!*

Lilian exhaled.

"Everything okay?" Rosie asked.

"Yep," Lilian said. They were really moving now, passing the lights of the city on their right, the vague blackness of the lake to the left. Perhaps too quickly. She glanced over at the speedometer. Sixty-five miles per hour. "I think you can slow down, Rosie."

"I'm okay." Rosie tightened her hands on the wheel, then glanced behind her, to her left.

"But it's icy tonight. We don't need to rush."

Rosie glanced behind her again, and Lilian thought she caught a flash of panic on her sister's face. Rosie moved into the right lane, then looked over her left shoulder a third time. Nervous, Lilian twisted to see what Rosie was looking at, but she saw nothing but other cars, zipping down the road with them.

Then she caught a glimpse of the driver behind them in the left lane: a man, his face shadowed. An uneasy feeling spread in her stomach.

"Can we slow down?" Lilian said. "You're driving too fast."

Rosie smiled, but it didn't hide the fear in her eyes. "Relax, sis, I'm just trying to get us to dinner."

She glanced over her left shoulder one more time, and her smile faded into pure terror.

"Rosalie Jane," Lilian said, worry sharpening her voice. "What in God's name is—"

A jolt.

Everything happened at once: metal crunching, tires screeching, the world spinning. Lilian's seatbelt strained against her shoulder as her head snapped forward, then sideways into her window. A thousand sparks of light exploded in her vision as the safety glass crumbled.

Then it all went black.

CHAPTER
THREE

Time fragmented into flashes of awareness, like a scene illuminated by a strobe light. Her eyelids, heavy and leaden. A high-pitched squeal in her ears. Throbbing in her head. A sharp ache in her right shoulder.

Lilian forced her eyes open. The night sky seemed too close, the stars falling, drifting toward her, landing on her shoulders and face. No, not stars, she told herself. Snow.

"Hello?" she whispered. Her voice sounded like it came from underwater. The only answer was the shrill ringing in her ears and the frayed sound of her own breathing.

She looked down at her hands, at the shattered glass on her lap, on her seat. With effort, she turned to the left. Her vision blurred and refocused: a slumped body in a red pea coat, the driver's seat much too close to the steering wheel. She couldn't see the face, only a familiar strawberry blonde tangle of hair. *Just like mine*, she thought absently, wondering who the person was. Why they were here, together.

Footsteps crunched through asphalt and snow toward the driver's side. "Oh God, oh God, please God, no." A man's voice, thin and trembling. Lilian tried to lift her head to see him, but he said, "Don't move. I—I'm calling 911. It's going to be okay. Everything is going to be okay."

A pause, then the same voice, louder now, "Yes. There's been a car accident on Lake Shore Drive. We need an ambulance. Right away."

Lilian closed her eyes and drifted.

* * *

"Open your eyes for me now. Come on."

Lilian did, blinking as light flashed across her field of vision. Then it was gone, and above her she saw a ceiling of square industrial tiles. She couldn't move; a rigid backboard pressed against her spine. A hot, buzzing storm of doctors and nurses surrounded her, calling to each other, asking her questions. It felt like being in the center of a tornado, or inside a beehive.

"On my count. Three, two, one." In a single smooth movement, she was shifted horizontally onto a softer surface. Her clothes were cut off, leaving her exposed and shivering. Crumbles of safety glass tumbled across her skin, onto the bed and floor.

"Caleb," she whispered through an aching throat. She tried to turn her head but couldn't—a rigid cervical collar restricted her movements.

A nurse paused and took her hand. Her blond hair was gray at the roots, her eyes crinkled with compassion. "He'll be here soon, okay?"

Another woman entered Lilian's field of vision, gloves on her hands, pausing in the middle of a task. "Can you tell me your name?"

"Lily," she whispered, then corrected herself. Only Caleb called her Lily. "Lilian . . . Lilian Donaldson."

The woman nodded—a doctor, Lilian told herself. She looked familiar. Dark brown skin, curly black hair in a tight bun. "Do you know today's date?"

Lilian squeezed her eyes shut, mentally grasping for the information. "No," she said.

"Do you know where you are?"

"In a hospital."

"That's right. Do you know what hospital? And what city?"

I don't know. She sucked in a panicky breath. How could she not know where she *was?* Or *why?* She forced herself to focus. She could figure this out. If she recognized people here, then this was Caleb's hospital. She'd rotated here as a resident, too. "Chicago. I used to come here. Work here."

The doctor nodded. "Do you remember what happened tonight?"

Lilian closed her eyes and tried to sift through the haze and fear to grasp something solid. *Sitting in a rocking chair, looking out a window filmed by gauzy curtains, watching snowflakes drift through the air.*

Her breasts tingled and she remembered her baby. "Abigail," she said, her eyes popping open. The doctor's eyebrows lifted in confusion, and Lilian rushed to clarify. "My baby Abigail. She'll need to nurse soon—I need Caleb. I need Caleb to be here."

The doctor nodded, then patted Lilian's shoulder. "He will be."

Minutes passed, and the commotion died down. The trauma team continued to work with calm efficiency, and still, Caleb didn't come. Lilian's stomach knotted. Something flitted in the back of her mind, a vague sense that she should be worried about someone else, too.

But before she could demand answers, she was whisked out of her room and down a long hallway. The jostling of the bed sent a sharp stabbing pain from her head into her neck. The bed was heaved around a corner and into a dark room.

"You're getting a CT, girlfriend," a warm voice said. "Try and relax."

Relax, sis. A strangled, hysterical laugh bubbled out of Lilian's chest. If Rosie were here, she'd say that Lilian didn't know how to relax.

Rosie.

The thought of her sister brought a confused swirl of feelings. Betrayal, loss, love. A sharp tang of fear. Lilian hadn't seen Rosie in years. Right? But no; she sensed something more recent.

Lilian took a deep breath and closed her eyes.

* * *

After what felt like an eternity, she ended up back in the room where she'd started. Alone. The pain in her head had faded to a dull ache, but the high-pitched ringing in her ears was more noticeable in the silent, empty room.

Caleb still hadn't come. Her chest tightened, like she was sucking air through the tiniest of straws. The beginning of a panic attack, she knew, and she forced herself to take long, slow breaths.

The immense round light on the ceiling looked like an alien eye peering down at her. Its shiny surface reflected a distorted version of her face: pale skin, limp hair, frightened eyes. A baby cried somewhere close by, and her breasts tingled again. Raised voices echoed in a distant room. Beyond that, sirens.

Finally, solid footsteps echoed in the hallway, coming toward her.

"Hello, Lilian," a man's voice said. "My name is Sanjay Kumar. I'm one of the attending physicians from trauma surgery."

The name seemed familiar, but she couldn't place it. "Do I know you?" she said, embarrassed by her confusion.

"I work with Caleb, and I believe we've spoken on the phone about one of your patients." Dr. Kumar walked to the head of the bed. He reached for the brace around Lilian's neck and released the strap. "You have a nasty concussion and some bumps and bruises, but otherwise you're okay."

Lilian turned to look at him, stretching her neck. A day or two's growth of black stubble dotted his cheeks and chin; a few gray streaks highlighted the black hair at his temples.

"Where's Caleb?" She waited, her heart frozen in her chest, for him to answer.

"On his way," he said. "Do you remember what happened tonight, Lilian?"

Lilian tried again to think, to conjure up the memory. She had an excellent memory, always had. She'd been the fourth-grade spelling bee champion for her entire district. This felt like a similar kind of pressure, like standing on a darkened stage in front of a microphone, palms sweaty, mouth going dry, as she prepared to spell *onomatopoeia*.

"I was home with my baby—with Abigail," she added, to show that she knew her child's name. Surely that should count for something.

The image of her daughter's nursery came to her mind. Soft pink walls, sheer white curtains. Looking out the window at the snow. A yellow car pulling into the driveway.

She exhaled, frustrated. "Why am I here?"

"You were in a car accident," Dr. Kumar said.

Lilian's heart lurched. Had Caleb been hurt? When they kept saying he was on his way, did they mean in an ambulance? "What happened to Caleb?"

"He wasn't in the car with you," Dr. Kumar said. "Do you remember who was?"

A jumble of images flooded her mind. Looking in a mirror, seeing her own face but with long hair, the way she'd worn it years ago. Snow, streaking horizontally across a black sky. The musty smell of vinyl upholstery.

A professor?

You're driving too fast.

It's a matter of life and death.

Lilian sucked in a breath. "I don't know what happened," she said, her voice high-pitched, hysterical.

Dr. Kumar nodded. "It's normal to lose some memories after a concussion. Most of it should come back eventually."

A silent scream rose in her throat. Lilian Donaldson did not lose memories. She still remembered the Krebs cycle from way back in college biochem. She could diagram the brachial plexus and identify the most common sites of injury in a pediatric population. And yet, when she tried to remember what had happened just hours before, it was like someone had passed an eraser across the page of her mind. She could make out faint shapes, ghostly words. Nothing distinct.

"Was someone in the car with me?" she demanded. Abigail? Nausea rushed over her. Was the accident Lilian's fault? Had something happened to her baby?

Before he could answer, Lilian heard another set of footsteps rushing into the room. A familiar voice sent warmth flooding through her body.

"Lily? Lily, are you all right?" Caleb's arms came around her, and she burst into tears.

"You weren't here," she said, through sobs, "and I don't know what happened and I was all alone . . ."

He kissed her forehead, whispering, "It's okay, you're okay."

"Where's Abigail?" She pulled away, squinting as she focused on his face. He looked haggard, older than he had ever looked before.

"With my mom. She's fine, Lil. God, I was so worried about you. Sanjay"—Caleb straightened up—"she's okay, right?"

"A concussion and some bruising," Dr. Kumar said. "But I need to talk to you both about something else."

"What's going on?" Caleb asked.

Lilian struggled to sit up, the room spinning. Caleb sat next to her on the bed, one arm around her shoulder. Together they waited, expectant, as Dr. Kumar sat in a chair opposite them.

He leaned forward, elbows on knees. Lilian held her breath.

"Lilian doesn't remember who was in the car with her tonight," he said, looking at Caleb. "Do you know who it was?"

"Yes, her sister," Caleb said, sounding surprised, as if he had just remembered this information.

Lilian gasped. "My sister?" A glimmer of memory: climbing into Rosie's canary yellow Bug. A body slumped against a steering wheel. "Where is she? What happened? Is she okay? Is she—"

Dead? The word, unsaid, seemed to echo in the room. *I can't lose her,* Lilian thought, panicking. She couldn't go through that kind of loss again; couldn't plan a funeral and pick out a headstone and stand in a cemetery next to a gaping hole in the ground.

Then Dr. Kumar spoke, and Lilian's heart shattered.

CHAPTER
FOUR

Lilian had been in Sanjay Kumar's shoes before; the bearer of bad news to worried family members. She had watched some drop to their knees, sobbing desperate prayers, while others sat in stunned silence. Lilian fell into the latter group: frozen, unable to do anything but blink as the trauma surgeon listed her sister's injuries. Each statement felt like a load of bricks being piled on her chest.

Rosie's spleen had ruptured. She had sustained significant neurovascular trauma to her right leg. It might need to be amputated. She had arrived with a GCS of three, the lowest possible score in the coma scale: no motor response, no verbal response, no eye opening. The CT of her head had revealed a massive epidural hematoma—bleeding between the outer membrane covering the brain and the skull. Neurosurgery was performing a craniotomy, cutting through Rosie's skull to relieve pressure on her brain from the collection of blood.

Lilian might have spent the last decade of her career teaching and treating common pediatric complaints, but she could read between Dr. Kumar's carefully chosen words. She knew how to interpret the firm set of his mouth, the hollow look in his dark eyes.

Rosie might not make it out of surgery alive.

* * *

Caleb wanted to take Lilian home immediately, but Lilian refused. *She is my baby sister and I'm not leaving her.* Instead, she waited in the surgeon's lounge near the OR while Caleb checked on Rosie.

A kindhearted social worker from the emergency department brought Lilian graham crackers and a plastic cup of cranberry juice, but she felt too nauseated and dizzy to eat much. The same social worker then rounded up a breast pump, and Lilian gratefully took the opportunity to pump enough to ease her aching breasts. She hoped Abigail was sleeping, that Caleb's mother, Nancy, hadn't put her to bed on her stomach, that she wouldn't suffocate in her sleep. She resisted the urge to call and check in; it was nearly two o'clock in the morning.

Her mind kept drifting back to the day six-year-old Rosie fractured her collarbone. She'd launched herself off a dresser, pretending to fly, and Lilian had been across the room, too far away to catch her. She could only watch, helpless, dreading the inevitable crash. But for one split second, Rosie was suspended in the air, pigtails flying, pink fairy wings fluttering behind her. Weightless; ethereal.

Then she hit the floor and screamed.

Lilian imagined Rosie's skull, shaved and draped as the neurosurgeon sliced through bone, through the layers of meninges wrapping her brain. If she lost her sister now, just when they'd managed to reconnect, she would never have a chance to set things right between them. Lilian's stomach roiled with nausea, and she rushed to a nearby garbage can. She made it just in time, vomiting acid, slick and burning. She wiped her mouth and sat on the floor, head on her knees.

I'm seeing someone new.

The memory of Rosie's words made Lilian sit upright. Rosie's boyfriend. They had recently moved in together; he must be beside himself with worry. An image rose in her mind of a graying professor in a tweed jacket with patches on the elbows. Steadying herself on a nearby chair, she stood and poked her head out of the doorway. Fluorescent lights hummed above her, illuminating a long, sterile hallway with a bank of computers at the end.

The social worker, Monica, was sitting at a computer, forehead furrowed in concentration as she stared at the screen.

Lilian headed toward her, and Monica looked up. "Can I help you?"

"My sister has a boyfriend," Lilian said. "I don't have his phone number, but I was wondering if someone could try to track him down?"

The social worker flushed. "I'm so sorry—I meant to tell you earlier." She ran her hands over her face; she looked exhausted. "The police on scene at the accident called him. He's supposed to be on his way. He might even be in the ED waiting room, they were going to let me know if he got there but it's been such a crazy night—"

"I can go look for him," Lilian said. She knew how it could be in a busy emergency department, especially in the middle of a snowstorm.

"Hang on," Monica said, glancing at the screen. "Yep, there's a message saying he got here—ugh, an hour ago. I'm so sorry I missed that. The triage nurse told him to wait there."

"Thanks for your help," Lilian said, mustering up a smile for one of the unsung heroes of the hospital. "If my husband comes looking for me, can you tell him where I went?"

"Of course," Monica said, giving a brief smile before turning back to her computer.

Lilian followed the signs toward the emergency room, her shoes echoing in the empty hallway. As she approached the ED waiting area, the low murmur of voices grew louder. Then she was in the middle of a crowded, chaotic waiting room filled with worried family members, sick patients waiting to be taken back, fussy babies, people talking on their phones. For an instant she felt like she should be pitching in to help, taking care of some of these pediatric patients, but she shook herself. She was one of the worried family members, not a staff member.

Over at the check-in desk, a red-faced husband demanded that his wife be taken back immediately. The triage nurse looked harried and a little frantic, and Lilian didn't want to bother him with one more task.

"Daniel Connors?" she called into the room, trying to make her voice heard over the din. "Is anyone here named Daniel Connors?"

Scanning the crowd, she pressed her fingers to her throbbing temples. She couldn't remember much about him—but Rosie had shown her a picture, right? She recalled a brief glimpse of a man with brown hair.

"I'm Daniel Connors," someone said to her left.

Lilian turned, blinking hard to clear her double vision. "Daniel? I'm Rosie's sister, Lilian. I just found out that you're here."

Squinting, she focused on his face. First, she noticed his startling blue eyes. So clear they were almost translucent. Next, she took in the rest of him: wavy brown hair that looked like he'd spent the last hour running his hands through it, a square jaw dusted with five o'clock shadow, rumpled T-shirt, and jeans. Thirty-five at the oldest. A snippet of conversation floated through her memory: *He's not that much older than me*, Rosie had said. Definitely not the aging academic Lilian had conjured up with her big-sister worries.

"Thank you for coming," he said, his voice shaky. "How is she? No one could tell me anything."

Lilian hesitated before answering. "She's in surgery."

"But she's all right? She's going to be all right?"

The desperation in Daniel's voice made Lilian's throat tighten reflexively. How much information could he handle? He seemed close to his breaking point but keeping him in the dark wouldn't do him any favors, either.

Gently, she said, "She has a severe brain injury and a lot of other trauma. It's—it's serious."

His knees nearly gave out, but he steadied himself on a chair. "Can I see her? I need to see her."

Lilian understood; she had the same visceral, aching need to be with Rosie, to touch her face, to hold her hand. "Not yet. But let's head over toward the OR—my husband is supposed to give me an update soon."

He followed Lilian back down the hallway, their two sets of shoes echoing in the emptiness.

"I shouldn't have let her go tonight," he said as they walked, mostly to himself. "I was worried about the weather, but she wouldn't listen to me."

She was about to respond, to tell him he couldn't blame himself, when Caleb rounded the corner toward them.

"Caleb," she said, rushing over to him. The sudden movement made her head spin.

"Whoa there," he said, putting his hands on her shoulders. "You look like you're going to tip over."

"This is Daniel," Lilian said, "Rosie's boyfriend."

Caleb glanced up sharply, an appraising look on his face as he shook Daniel's hand.

"How is she?" Daniel asked. He had to look up a couple inches to meet Caleb's eyes.

"Her spleen's out and there's no other abdominal trauma. Her leg actually looks okay—I think she'll keep it. And the crani went well," Caleb said, referring to the craniotomy the neurosurgeon had performed. "They're closing now and then she'll go up to the neurotrauma ICU."

A wave of relief nearly knocked Lilian over. "When can I see her?"

Caleb shook his head, his jaw firm. "You need to get home. They promised they would call me with any updates."

"But—"

"Lily. There's nothing we can do here. And you need sleep or you won't be any use to anyone."

She knew Caleb was right, but she couldn't imagine walking out of the hospital, abandoning her sister. "I can't leave her," she said, her eyes filling with tears. "I can't leave her here all alone."

"I'll stay with her," Daniel said. His face crumpled, and for a moment Lilian thought he might lose control. But he cleared his throat before refocusing on Caleb.

Caleb nodded, looking relieved. "I'll call up and let them know you'll be coming." He turned to Lilian, taking her shoulders gently in both hands. "She won't be alone, okay? Let's get you home."

CHAPTER
FIVE

Cold winter sunlight slid through the half-closed shutters, casting narrow slices of light across the white duvet and sheets. For one blissful moment, Lilian thought it was any other Saturday morning. Caleb would be home from the gym soon with coffee and pastries from their favorite cafe. He would bring Abigail into bed when he arrived, and they'd snuggle together as a family while Abigail nursed.

Then the memories landed on her chest, knocking the wind out of her—a spinning car, the sound of crunching metal. The ambulance ride and the frantic hum of the trauma room. Rosie's injuries and her precarious condition. She'd caught a brief glimpse of her sister last night, coming out of the OR. A frail body in a huge bed, covered in tubes and wires and drains.

Panicking, she glanced at the alarm clock. Nearly ten o'clock in the morning—the latest she had slept since giving birth to Abigail. Her breasts were rock hard; Caleb must have fed Abigail a bottle so Lilian could sleep. But he'd said he would wake Lilian if anything happened with Rosie. She had made him *promise*.

Lilian stood, steadying herself against the headboard as a wave of post-concussive dizziness rolled through her. The morning light seemed too bright, too sharp. Her right shoulder ached, and she tugged over the neck of her nightshirt to get an eyeful of the seatbelt-shaped bruise forming there. After a few careful steps, she made it to her bedroom door, then walked down the hall and peered over the railing to the main floor below.

Caleb was pacing in the living room, his right hand holding a phone to his ear, his left arm cradling a sleeping Abigail against his chest. The sight of them nearly stole her breath away, her handsome husband and precious daughter. She vowed to never, ever take them for granted.

Caleb looked up at Lilian and stopped pacing. "Hey, Jeff, I better go, Lily's awake," he said into the phone. "Thanks for the update. We appreciate what you're doing. I'm sure we'll be by later."

Lilian made her way down the stairs, gripping the handrail to combat the dizzying feeling of descent. Caleb met her at the landing and gently pulled her against him. The presence of him—the clean cotton smell of his T-shirt, the rasp of his unshaven chin against her forehead—made her eyes prick with tears. Abigail, sensing her mother's presence, gave a sleepy cry.

"How you feeling this morning?" Caleb asked.

Dizzy. Sore. Scared. "I'm okay," Lilian said, taking Abigail and breathing in her sweet baby scent. "Who were you talking to?"

"Jeff Brockhurst—you remember him? He's covering the neurotrauma ICU this weekend. Come sit down, and I'll give you the update."

Caleb led Lilian to the vast leather sectional sprawling across the living room. They'd hired an interior designer after they'd bought the house, just over a year ago, and she'd filled the space with neutral colors and soothing textures. *It looks like a Restoration Hardware showroom in here,* Rosie had said when she'd picked Lilian up.

How could that have been only yesterday? Less than twenty-four hours ago, Rosie had stood in Lilian's entry, her coat and scarf the only spots of color in the room.

As Caleb ran through the update on Rosie's condition, Lilian lifted her shirt and nursed Abigail, who latched on eagerly. She'd missed her mama.

Rosie, Caleb said, had remained stable overnight, no major issues. If all went well, the plan was to try and get her off the ventilator today. Only then would the team be able to assess the severity of her brain injury. The impact from the accident, combined with pressure from the hematoma on her brain, would certainly cause neurologic damage—but how extensive? And would it be permanent? That, Lilian knew, was difficult to predict.

"We can go see her a little later," Caleb said.

"I'm ready as soon as I finish feeding Abigail."

Caleb gave Lilian a speculative look, as if trying to assess the severity of her concussion via his surgeon's stare. An ice pick of pain jabbed behind Lilian's left eye, but she tried not to flinch.

"There's no rush," he said, unconvinced. "Take a shower, eat some breakfast."

"I want to see Rosie."

"You got a nasty blow to the head, Lil. We can't push things, you know that. Besides, the police are coming over to talk to you."

Lilian straightened up, startling Abigail. "Police? Why?"

"They're investigating the accident, I guess. They said they had a few questions."

"And *then* can we see Rosie? Your mom will watch Abigail, right?" She needed to be with her sister, to touch her hands and see her face. Still, the thought of leaving Abigail made Lilian's stomach twist with worry.

"Lily, you need to be careful, okay? With your history . . ."

He trailed off, but Lilian knew what he was thinking: with her history, things were precarious enough already. A concussion could make everything worse, stealing away the hard-won gains she'd made over the past several weeks.

But other questions lurked behind his words, too: with Lilian's history, could Caleb trust her judgment? Could he trust her to stay in control, to make sound decisions, to avoid spiraling into anxiety and falling apart again?

Could Lilian trust herself?

She swallowed and looked her husband in the eye. "I need to see my sister."

*   *   *

When the police came, Lilian told them everything she remembered, which wasn't much: being on Lake Shore Drive, snow streaking across the windshield. Nothing specific. Even though she knew this was common after a head injury, it was still maddening.

The officers explained what they knew about the crash. Witnesses had seen a car pulling up behind Rosie's Beetle, in the left lane. Rosie had swerved into the right lane and hit another car, which set off a chain reaction on the slippery road. Nine other vehicles had been damaged, with multiple injured persons taken to nearby hospitals. Lilian was shocked by the scale of the pileup, but the police assured her there were no fatalities.

Several witnesses had called 911 to report the accident, and they all said the car that started it was a silver sedan with Indiana plates. Some said it had tapped Rosie's back bumper, others that it had simply gotten too close. Because of the snowstorm and darkness, no one had gotten a license plate number. Unless a reliable witness came forward with more identifying information, it was unlikely they'd find the driver.

The police also explained the reason why Rosie had been injured so significantly: her seatbelt had malfunctioned. If they'd taken Caleb's Land Rover, Lilian thought with regret, Rosie would have made it out with minor injuries.

The officers left behind the items they'd gathered from the crash site: Lilian's black Kate Spade tote and Rosie's purse, a fabric satchel made of mismatched, colorful squares. Inside it, Lilian found a hodgepodge of items: old receipts, lip balm, tampons, movie ticket stubs, and a leather day planner. They'd also found Rosie's phone at the scene, water damaged from the snow; they'd been able to make one phone call to Rosie's emergency contact before it died completely.

The cops found something unexpected, too. A small velvet box, tucked into a hidden pocket in the purse. Inside was an engagement ring: an emerald-cut center diamond in an ornate, vintage setting. Lilian wondered why Rosie hadn't been wearing it; if she'd been afraid of Lilian's reaction—which, she had to admit with a dose of shame, probably would not have been positive.

After the police left, Lilian told Caleb she wasn't waiting any longer. They needed to get to the hospital.

CHAPTER
SIX

The sights and sounds of the ICU were at once foreign and familiar—the hushed tones of the residents talking at the far end, the beeping of the monitors, the antiseptic smell. Caleb squeezed Lilian's hand as they entered. Three quick squeezes, their code for *I love you*. She squeezed back, appreciating the calm reassurance of his body next to hers, absorbing the fear radiating off her in waves.

As they walked into Rosie's room, Lilian sucked in a breath. This could not be her baby sister. This was a broken body in a green hospital gown, in a massive bed surrounded by monitors beeping and flashing, IV poles hung with translucent bags of fluid, tubes, and wires. Not the sister she'd taken swimming at the community pool each summer. *Time for more sunscreen, Rosie.* Not the sister she'd taught to tie her shoes. *Over, under, around and through.* That sister seemed like a distant dream.

But as she came closer, she could see it was still Rosie's familiar face, with her unfairly long eyelashes, that sprinkling of faded freckles on her cheeks. One of Rosie's eyes was swollen nearly shut, her cheekbone an angry red. A deep gash on her nose had been repaired with black sutures. Her hair hung long and stringy across the left side of her head.

The right side had been shaved to the scalp, a curve of staples set precisely into her skin. Lilian's stomach churned.

Then she noticed something that made her shoulders sag in relief: Rosie had been extubated. "She's breathing on her own," Lilian said.

Caleb came up behind her. "She's doing great."

Lilian moved the sheet and found Rosie's hand. She took in the pulse ox on Rosie's index finger, her scratched pink nail polish, the blood along her cuticles. Rosie's eyelids fluttered.

"Hi, sis," Lilian said, slipping two fingers into Rosie's palm.

Rosie's fingers tightened, just slightly, and Lilian's breath caught. She knew it could be a reflex, but it still felt significant. Like Rosie was in there, listening.

A flicker of memory from the moments before the accident: *This conversation is too important to have in a car. It's a matter of life and death.*

Goosebumps rose on Lilian's arms. She had dismissed that statement as typical Rosie theatrics. But now she wondered.

"What did you need to tell me?" Lilian whispered, leaning in and searching her sister's face.

Rosie gave no response, not even a flutter of her eyelids. Somehow, she'd irrationally hoped that Rosie would respond. But her sister's expression was as blank as the white sheets covering her body.

"I'm so scared for her," Lilian said, leaning against Caleb.

"She's young and healthy," Caleb said. "She had that epidural hematoma evacuated as quickly as possible."

"I know," Lilian said. Still, an icy current of fear ran through her. She'd seen remarkable improvements in her patients after head injuries— improvements so vast it bordered on the miraculous. But she'd also seen patients who didn't improve, who remained in a coma or a vegetative state. The ones who developed pneumonia or some other infection that led to sepsis and death. Rosie could go either way.

A young resident in blue scrubs entered the room, and Lilian looked up.

"I'm Adam Curtis, the senior resident on the unit today," he said. He shook Caleb's hand. "Hello, Dr. Kartchner, Mrs. Kartchner."

Lilian tensed. She'd received dozens of invitations addressed to Dr. and Mrs. Kartchner over the years, and it had always bothered her, the ease with which her professional title was dropped while Caleb's was never forgotten.

After a beat, Caleb spoke up. "Lilian's a pediatrician."

Lilian half expected him to continue with the words he always used when introducing her to anyone in the medical field: *My wife is the reason I didn't fail anatomy in med school. She graduated #1 in our class, you know.* Or at the very least, for him to explain that she was faculty in the pediatrics department, that she supervised her own medical students and residents.

But he didn't, and she told herself it didn't matter.

Adam flushed and said, "Sorry about that, Dr. . . . ."

"Donaldson," Lilian supplied, shaking his hand. "It's no problem— call me Lilian. I'm Rosie's sister."

Caleb spoke. "Adam, can you give us an update? I talked with Dr. Brockhurst this morning, but he didn't give me all the details."

Adam cleared his throat, and Lilian felt a brief flash of empathy for him. Discussing a patient with two family members who happened to be physicians could be nerve-wracking. But he did a good job, answering Lilian's many questions about Rosie's labs, and imaging, her vital signs and physical exam. It was too early to know much about her brain injury yet—and that was Lilian's most pressing concern.

Adam finished his list by saying, "Her hemoglobin dropped so I'm giving her two units."

"Okay, I'll sign the consent for the blood transfusion," Lilian said.

"No, it's fine," Adam said. "Her husband already did that."

Lilian tilted her head, confused. "My sister isn't married. Daniel is her *boyfriend*." Or her fiancé, depending on what Rosie had decided about the ring. "As her sister, I'm the medical decision maker, not him."

"Sorry—the intern did the consent and must have assumed he was the husband." Adam's eyes flashed with annoyance, and Lilian pitied the poor intern who would be scolded later. "You're okay with the transfusion, though?"

"Of course." That wasn't the issue. Daniel didn't have the legal right to make medical decisions for Rosie. Although, Lilian had to wonder, did *she* have that right? She hadn't seen her sister in two years. Daniel was the man Rosie was planning to marry.

Unless, Lilian realized, she'd already married him, and that's what she'd been planning on telling Lilian at the restaurant. It was possible—and unsettling to realize how little she knew about her own sister.

"Are there other family members?" Adam asked. "Your parents, other siblings?"

"I'm her only sibling, and our parents are deceased," she said.

Caleb squeezed Lilian's hand, silently transmitting support. The two-year anniversary of her parents' death had been just three weeks ago, between Christmas and New Year's. The entire holiday season had felt heavy, arduous, like she was dragging behind her the weight of all the Christmases of her childhood. The smell of Mom's cinnamon rolls baking in the oven; Dad singing along to *White Christmas* with Frank Sinatra; little Rosie leaving milk and cookies for Santa. But also: the strain in Mom's eyes as she watched her husband pour himself yet another drink; Dad getting louder and more belligerent as the day went on; the knowledge that every single present had been put on their parents' credit cards and would only cause stress over the next few months. Love and loss, disappointment and grief.

On the anniversary of their death, she'd spent the entire day in bed. Thank heavens for Caleb, who had taken the day off to be with her and help with Abigail.

"I'm sorry to hear that," Adam said, shaking Lilian out of her memories. "Do you know if your sister has any medical problems? Was she taking any medications? Any substance abuse?"

An image of Rosie filled Lilian's mind, the way she'd been after their parents' death: her gaunt, skeletal face; her twitchy movements, and her erratic behavior. "Perhaps some history of drug or alcohol abuse in the past. I don't think she's been using anything recently. Did you get a tox screen?"

He nodded. "All negative. Any family history of medical problems? You mentioned that your parents passed away . . ."

"They died of carbon monoxide poisoning," Lilian said. Again,

Caleb's hand tightened on hers. It was still difficult to say the words, to remember the senseless tragedy of their death. A massive snowstorm had knocked out their power; Mom must have cracked the door on the old gas oven to warm the kitchen, just as she'd done so many times in Lilian's childhood and forgotten to turn it off. The batteries in the carbon monoxide detectors were dead, the detectors themselves so old they didn't emit any alert as the batteries died.

Lilian cleared her throat, refocusing on Adam's question. "My parents were pretty healthy. Our dad had high blood pressure and possibly some early-onset dementia."

The dementia had only been noticeable in retrospect, when Lilian was trying to make sense of his failure to keep the carbon monoxide detectors in working order. For months he'd been forgetting names, misplacing items, once getting lost on a drive to work. After their death, Lilian blamed herself for ignoring the signs, but she couldn't help thinking that if Rosie had been more available, more present, they could have taken better care of their parents together.

"Lily," Caleb said in a gentle voice, bringing her back to the conversation.

Lilian sat up straight, blinking. "I'm fine."

"Do you have any more questions for me?" Adam said. When Lilian and Caleb shook their heads, he excused himself, promising them that Rosie would get the best possible care.

As soon as he left, Lilian sank into a chair. She'd held it together as long as she could, but now the fear came rushing back, a white-crested wave that knocked her over and sucked her under. Her rib cage squeezed; she couldn't get enough air. She took rapid, shallow breaths—inhale, exhale, inhale, exhale—until her face prickled and went numb.

Caleb knelt next to her and rubbed her back. "Take a long, slow breath."

She did.

"And another," Caleb prompted.

Her vision began to clear; her face stopped tingling. "I'm okay," she said, but when she opened her eyes, she saw the worry on Caleb's face. A familiar expression; he'd been worried about her for months. She wished she could pinpoint the exact cause: was it the error she'd made at work, the one that had cost a beloved patient her life?

Or was it everything that came after?

"I think we should go home," Caleb said.

The gentleness in his voice made her jaw clench. She didn't want to be led away from her sister's bedside like a weak, shrinking thing.

"I want to stay with her," she said.

Caleb hesitated. "Then let's get you something to eat, okay?"

* * *

After forcing down a stale sandwich in the cafeteria, Lilian felt moderately better. Caleb wanted to check his OR schedule for Monday, so she headed up to Rosie's room alone.

Adam's questions had resurrected painful memories in Lilian's mind. In particular, the way Rosie had abandoned her after their parents' death. For years before that, their relationship had followed a predictable pattern: Rosie, inevitably in the middle of a crisis, would call Lilian, Lilian would drop everything to help her. Once Lilian had solved the disaster du jour, Rosie would turn prickly and annoyed, and push Lilian away. Rinse and repeat, month after month.

But around the time she'd turned twenty-five, Rosie had stopped calling. The more Lilian reached out, the more distant Rosie became.

I'm worried about you, Rosie, she'd press. *Are you okay? Please tell me what's going on.*

And Rosie's dismissive replies: *I'm fine. I'm an adult now. I don't need you to worry about me.*

It had been disorienting for Lilian—how did she relate to her sister if she wasn't taking care of her? By the time their parents died, they hadn't been close for a few years. Surely, Lilian had thought, they would come together and support each other through their horrifying loss.

But no, Rosie left Lilian to do everything: notify friends and family, plan the funeral, make all the arrangements, deal with the financial mess.

For the first time in her life, Lilian desperately needed her sister to come to *her* aid, and Rosie did nothing. She didn't even show up to the funeral service until it was halfway over. Still, Lilian had been overwhelmed with relief at the sight of her. Rosie was late, yes, but she was *here*.

Then she started walking down the aisle, and it was clear that she was drunk. Teetering on four-inch stilettos, wearing dark sunglasses like a celebrity on her way into rehab. Lilian's relief morphed into embarrassment, then white-hot anger. Couldn't her sister keep it together for *one day*? For the past week, Lilian had wanted to allow herself to fall apart and grieve, but no, she had to be the responsible one. She could barely look at Rosie through the rest of the service.

When it was over, Rosie came up to her with her arms outstretched and said in a voice thick with tears, "Sis, how did this happen?"

It felt like a rebuke—as if Lilian had *allowed* it to happen.

"Where have you been?" Lilian demanded.

Rosie faltered. "I—I couldn't get away."

Lilian's throat tightened until she thought it might seal shut. "There is no reason why you couldn't have helped me. Do you know what this has been like, doing all of this alone? Do you even care?"

Rosie's mouth hung open for a few seconds. "I—I'm sorry," she finally said.

Caleb had arrived then, putting his arms around Lilian's shoulders. He pulled her close and whispered, "Let's get through the rest of the services, okay?"

Lilian relented; this wasn't the time or place to hash things out. She invited Rosie to come to their parents' house later, where Lilian had planned a reception for family and friends, and Rosie said she'd be there. Once again, Lilian felt that sensation of relief, knowing she would have her sister by her side.

But Rosie never showed up. She didn't call, she didn't text. And when Rosie finally resurfaced, it had taken just one ten-minute confrontation to destroy their relationship for two years.

Since then, Lilian's intense regret had been offset by resentment. *You're going to abandon me? Fine. See if I care.* But as she walked into the neurotrauma ICU, the weight of that regret doubled and tripled, grinding her into the waxed linoleum floor. She would give anything to rewind time, to fall at her sister's feet and beg her to come back. Now it might be too late.

As she entered Rosie's room, she saw a man standing near the head of the hospital bed, facing away from her.

"Daniel?" Lilian said, glimpsing his dark, wavy hair. About time he got here; they had things to discuss.

He turned with a jerk, and Lilian gasped.

It wasn't Daniel. This man was older, early forties at least, with a long, thin face. Dark eyes under heavy brows. A ragged scar curved along the right side of his jaw.

Recognition flickered in Lilian's mind. She knew this face. She had seen him before; she was certain of it.

An image floated in her mind like a shadow, a wraith: Rosie in the driver's seat, glancing back and to the left. Following Rosie's gaze and seeing a man in the car behind them. Snow pelting the windshield, brake lights flashing, the crunch of metal.

"Who are you?" Lilian demanded.

The man's eyes widened, and he took a quick step around her. Before she could stop him, he pushed out of the room and rushed down the hallway. Lilian followed him, her heart racing.

"Wait!" she called as he burst through the double doors, twenty yards ahead of her.

He glanced back, his face ashen, then broke into a run. Lilian took off after him, stumbling through a wave of dizziness from the sudden exertion. She reached the double doors, stomach cramping with nausea.

"Watch out!" A pair of nurses pushing a hospital bed nearly slammed into her thighs, and Lilian jumped out of the way.

"Sorry," she gasped, and grabbed the handrail on the wall to steady herself. She stood on tiptoe as the nurses passed, straining her neck to see down the hallway leading from the ICU.

The hall was empty.

The man was gone.

CHAPTER
SEVEN

"What are you saying?" Caleb asked, his forehead wrinkling. "You think this guy caused the accident?"

That was exactly what Lilian thought, but hearing Caleb say it made her realize how illogical it was.

"I saw him right before the accident," she insisted. "I know I did."

"You didn't remember anything specific when you spoke with the police this morning."

"It came back to me—I saw his face and it came back to me!"

When Caleb had arrived, she'd been in a panic. Talking things through had helped her calm down, but now she felt frustrated and irritated with him.

"Okay, okay," he said, raising his hands. "You think he was driving the other car? What was it—a silver sedan with Indiana plates?"

"Maybe," Lilian said.

The memories of that night were a tangle, but she remembered that Rosie had been on edge, glancing over her shoulder. And she remembered that man's face. You couldn't fake that feeling of recognition, like a lock clicking open.

"Even if that were true," Caleb said carefully, "that doesn't explain how he ended up here. He somehow discovered which hospital Rosie had been taken to, then came to check on her?"

"Maybe it wasn't a coincidence—what if he was following us?" Lilian said. "Rosie seemed frightened. Maybe he was chasing her. Don't look at me like I'm an idiot, Caleb. You weren't there."

Caleb pressed his lips together and took a deep breath, trying very hard to be the calm one, the rational one—which Lilian resented, because it put her in the *irrational* role. This was the new Caleb, the version of her husband that had appeared two months ago, after what he delicately referred to as Lilian's *difficult time*. She preferred the old Caleb, who might have lost his temper but would have treated her like an equal.

When Caleb spoke, he sounded excessively patient. "No one else saw him, Lily. The clerk doesn't remember letting in anyone with that description."

The unit required a phone call to enter, but it was possible for a visitor to slip in with someone else. There were security cameras at the doors, but when Lilian had suggested reviewing the footage, the clerk had rolled her eyes—a gesture that meant *oh, boy, we got a crazy one on our hands*—and told Lilian, to dismiss her, that she needs a warrant to see the footage. Lilian's resolve had shriveled. She hadn't pushed it further.

"That doesn't mean *I* didn't see him, Caleb." It came out harsher than she'd intended. That ice pick of pain was back behind her left eye, worsening her irritation.

And yet, could she be sure he was the man she'd seen before the accident? The more she tried to grasp the memory, the more it floated away, like a sliver of soap in a bathtub.

But she *was* certain of one thing: she had seen him at Rosie's bedside. He'd seen her and fled. That was suspicious, all on its own.

Caleb reached over and linked their fingers together. Lilian had a distinct impression that he was placating her. "It's completely understandable that you'd be stressed right now—"

"I didn't imagine him, Caleb," she said, but her voice lacked conviction to her own ears.

"That's not what I mean," he said. "You've hardly slept. Your sister nearly died. And on top of that, you have a concussion. You might need to see someone."

Lilian bristled at the suggestion. "I don't need another shrink, Caleb."

"Not a psychiatrist," he said gently. "I meant a concussion specialist."

He squeezed her hand three times, but she didn't soften. She knew he loved her, but that's not what she wanted right now. She wanted him to *believe* her.

But how could he, when Lilian struggled to trust her own judgment? With good reason, she reminded herself. This had started long before a concussion scrambled her memories. Her judgment had failed her before, with disastrous consequences.

"Who do you think he was, then?" she asked. "The man I saw."

"He was probably lost, ended up in the ICU by accident, and you startled him."

A logical explanation, though it didn't explain the feeling that she knew his face. Still, she'd had a concussion. Could she trust her memory at all right now?

"You need sleep and time to recover," Caleb said. "Rosie is safe. She's getting the best care possible. Try to think positive."

Think positive. Lilian wanted to scoff at the idea, but she knew what Caleb meant. He didn't want her fixating on all the things that could go wrong. Even as he said it, a host of possibilities swarmed her mind: Rosie's kidneys could fail, she could develop a pulmonary embolism, she could have a stroke, she could get an infection in her lungs, in her bladder, in her brain—some nasty, hospital-acquired, antibiotic-resistant bug that would ravage her frail body.

"Just because she's getting the best care possible doesn't mean she's going to be okay," Lilian whispered. "What if something gets missed?"

Caleb's eyes blazed with sudden intensity. "Listen to me. Rosie is *not* Dasha."

"I know that, but—"

"No, stop. You need to let that go, Lily. It's in the past. And it has nothing to do with what's going on with Rosie now."

Lilian pressed her lips together, biting back a retort. This discussion always went the same way: Caleb telling Lilian she needed to move on; Lilian trying to explain why she couldn't.

How can you "move on" from the death of a beautiful little girl? How do you "get over it" when her grieving parents never will?

Dasha died of *cancer*, she wanted to shout at him. *And I missed it.*

Yes, her symptoms had been vague—her mother had simply said her two-year-old daughter didn't "look right," and she was the type of nervous first-time mom to bring her child in for every bump and sniffle. Lilian thoroughly examined blue-eyed, dark-haired Dasha, then gave her most reassuring smile and pronounced her "perfectly healthy." Dasha's mother brought her back twice more over the next few weeks with the same vague complaints, and both times Lilian found nothing of concern.

But later, frustrated by Lilian's inability to fix their daughter, Dasha's father took her to another doctor. By that point Dasha had exhibited more symptoms: bruising, extreme fatigue, weight loss. That pediatrician did exactly what Lilian would have done: he ordered blood work which revealed that Dasha had an aggressive childhood cancer, acute myeloid leukemia.

Dasha's father was furious, convinced that Lilian had been negligent. He not only sued Lilian and the entire hospital for malpractice, he ignited a media firestorm, so even though the hospital's attorneys and various experts assured Lilian that she had followed accepted standards of care, they settled out of court for a huge chunk of money. When Lilian learned the total, it made her sick.

Not that the money had made Ben Nichols any less furious about the death of his sweet little girl. His angry, haunted voice never seemed to leave her mind: *You killed my daughter, you fucking bitch.*

But even though her colleagues reassured her, over and over, that she wasn't to blame, Lilian couldn't stop the niggling doubt that perhaps she *had* done something wrong. She had been too rushed, too certain of her own judgment, and had missed subtle symptoms. Because no matter what, the bare facts were this: if Lilian had caught the cancer earlier, Dasha might still be alive.

Did Caleb honestly expect her to forget that?

Lilian forced herself to uncurl her hands from their fists. Her fingernails had left four neat half-moons on each palm. Taking a deep breath, she said, "We need to find Daniel."

Caleb nodded, looking relieved. "They're not actually married, are they?"

"I don't think so, but either way, I need to talk with him about Rosie. I'll see if the nurse got his phone number."

And maybe, Lilian thought, he might know something about this man with the scar.

CHAPTER
EIGHT

On Monday morning, the third day after the accident, Lilian woke to the sound of her phone vibrating on her nightstand. The light from the screen felt like a knife stabbing her eyes, which were extra-sensitive from the concussion, and she squinted. Caleb was calling.

"How are you feeling?" he said when she answered. He'd offered to cancel his schedule and stay home with her, but she'd waved him off. She didn't need a babysitter. Still, she appreciated him checking in.

"I'm okay," she said, putting a hand over her aching eyes. Somehow, she felt even worse than she had the first two mornings after the accident. "Any sign of Daniel?"

"He was there last night, the nurse said—but before you ask, no, no one got his phone number."

Lilian bit back her frustration; it wasn't uncommon for information to get lost during shift changes. But a prickle of unease crawled across her skin. Rosie had never made good choices when it came to men, starting in early adolescence and continuing through college and into adulthood. As much as Lilian wanted to believe that Daniel was different—he had certainly seemed heartbroken the night of the accident—she couldn't shake the sense that something was off with him.

"It's odd," she said. "Like he's avoiding us."

"We'll run into him at some point," Caleb said. Always the practical one. "Rosie had a good night. Still doing great off the vent. Oh, I stopped by David Kessler's office, too."

"You *what?*" Lilian sat up with a jolt. Dr. Kessler was the Chair of the Department of Pediatrics, and Lilian's boss. "Why would you do that?"

"Well," Caleb said, ever reasonable, "he needed to know that you won't be returning to work anytime soon, right? I told him about the car accident, your concussion, everything with Rosie. He understood completely, said to take all the time you need."

"And you thought this was something *you* ought to take care of, Caleb?" She didn't bother trying to hide the irritation in her voice. "Of course I'm going back soon! Why wouldn't I?"

Caleb would have been livid if the tables were turned, if she had stepped in and told *his* boss he needed time off. Plus, it showed a huge lack of awareness on his part regarding the complexity of a busy pediatric clinic. Her first day back was in two weeks, which meant her schedule would be filling up already; it would be a major inconvenience to her partners to cover.

"I was trying to help out, Lil—"

"What will they do with all the patients on my schedule?"

Caleb hesitated, and in that pause, Lilian understood. She didn't have a full schedule. The pause lengthened. The rock of dread sank in her stomach. Did she have *any* patients scheduled?

"Listen, there's no rush," Caleb said, the phone crackling with static. "You need to give yourself time to recover. No sense in returning to work until you're ready."

She wanted to say that she *was* ready—but she knew, intellectually at least, that he was right. Between the concussion, Abigail and her worries about Rosie, she was in no shape to spend hours in a noisy, crowded peds clinic. When she *did* return, it might be good to start with a lighter schedule anyway.

Still, a voice whispered in the back of her mind, *maybe her boss was hoping she wouldn't come back at all.* Maybe he'd figured out what Lilian had always feared: she wasn't as competent or qualified as everyone believed her to be. She'd been top of her class in med school and received outstanding reviews in residency, but what if she had somehow bluffed her way through it? People like her—a child of blue-collar parents, always skimming the poverty line—didn't grow up to be doctors. She'd managed to maintain the facade for a few years, but it was bound to crack. Deep down, she'd always known that.

And now everyone else knew it, too.

The baby monitor on her nightstand squawked, making Lilian jump. Abigail was awake, waving her tiny fists in protest at not being instantly fed.

"Hey," Lilian said into the phone, "I need to go get Abigail. Have a good day, okay?"

Feeling like a hundred-year-old woman, she carefully, carefully maneuvered herself to a standing position and waited for the vertigo to subside. Then she headed down the hall to the nursery. As she entered, she said, "Good morning, Rosie," then froze, realizing what she had said.

"Abigail," she corrected herself. "Good morning, *Abigail*."

The baby smiled—a huge, gummy grin that should have sent all sorts of warm, maternal hormones zipping through Lilian's bloodstream. But it didn't, and Lilian settled, uneasy, in the rocking chair, telling herself it had been a simple slip of the tongue.

Abigail did look strikingly similar to Rosie as a baby—the golden-red hair, the gumdrop lips. And Lilian had spent much of her life, beginning at age ten, caring for her little sister when her parents couldn't—or wouldn't. She remembered the weight of that, but also the joy, the sweetness of seeing her baby sister's eyes light up when Lilian peeked over the crib each morning, her chubby hands reaching to be held.

In Lilian's mind, her daughter and her sister occupied the same category: *small female I am responsible for.* Easy to mix up their names. But she also had to wonder if the concussion had shaken her more than she'd realized.

After feeding and changing Abigail, Lilian considered her next move in pinning down the elusive professor Daniel Connors. Even if he didn't want to talk to Lilian, she needed to talk to *him*. Rosie's phone still didn't work—Lilian had even tried the bag of rice trick—so she couldn't access the contacts. But, she realized, she did have Rosie's day planner. Maybe she had some information about Daniel in there.

In her bedroom, Lilian set the baby down in the center of the bed, then opened her nightstand to find the leather-bound notebook. She flipped through the pages, amazed at the colorful, intricate designs. Rosie had kept a record of everything: one page had an elaborate drawing of a bookshelf, each book she'd read carefully inked in; another page tracked the miles she'd run over the past year (nearly eight hundred); others detailed her water intake, her sleep, her menstrual cycle; still more were filled with inspirational quotes in hand-drawn typefaces.

Lilian touched the pages with her fingers, imagining her sister creating these miniature artworks. It looked like something Lilian might have scoffed at on Pinterest, certain that no one in real life actually made anything so elaborate. But seeing it in her sister's handwriting, imagining all the hours it must have taken, felt almost sacred. A window into Rosie's life over the past year—and a reminder that Lilian hadn't been a part of it.

As she scanned the calendar pages—doctor appointments, haircuts, trivia nights at a bar—her eyes caught on something. A note written on the page for March of last year, 2018.

Armory Shooting Range, 7pm.

The words danced and twisted on the page, and Lilian blinked hard. The same thing was written every Tuesday that month, and—she flipped forward a few pages—every week for months thereafter. Lilian had trouble imagining Rosie at a gun range. But then again, they hadn't spoken in two years. There were probably a lot of things she didn't know.

She turned more pages, hoping to find a page with phone numbers. If not Daniel's, then maybe one of Rosie's friends, perhaps, or a coworker? *A coworker.*

Lilian realized, with a jolt, that Rosie should have been at work today.

She hoped Daniel had thought to let them know, but she couldn't be sure. Regardless, they might have him listed as Rosie's emergency contact.

Rosie had said she worked for an advertising agency, but Lilian couldn't remember the name. Maybe she had something about it on Facebook. Like most twentysomethings, Rosie hardly used the site, but—luckily for Lilian—there it was, on her profile. *Graphic Designer at Baker Kline Callahan Advertising in Chicago.* Lilian punched that into Google, eyes burning with the effort of focusing, and found the phone number.

Before dialing, her eyes caught on Rosie's Facebook profile picture. Rosie at seven years old, with missing front teeth and her hair in two braids. The image made her heart ache, longing for the little girl Rosie used to be. Lilian would have been the one to braid her hair. She'd gotten Rosie ready for school, helped her with homework, fixed dinner, put her to bed, even attended her parent-teacher conferences—which might have raised red flags somewhere else, but teachers in their neighborhood school were glad to have someone, anyone, show up. And Lilian's parents, chronically overworked and underpaid, were simply not around much. Lilian had always told herself she didn't mind; as the older sister, that was her job. Soon enough, Rosie would be ready to be on her own.

When Lilian finally moved away for med school, she'd been desperate to shake off the weight of responsibility, to focus on her own future. It seemed like the right thing to do, at the time. But it had also been the first step on a road that eventually led her and Rosie to this point: where her sister felt like a stranger.

With a sigh, Lilian dialed BKC Advertising. Easier to focus on a task than to drift into memories of the past that could never be undone.

"BKC. How can I help you?" a cool voice answered.

"I'm looking for the supervisor of Rosie Donaldson. She's a graphic designer."

"Ah, that would be the Creative department. One moment please, I'll transfer you."

The phone rang again, then a man's voice answered: "Yeah?"

Flustered, Lilian said, "Um. Hi. Are you in the Creative department?"

"Yeah," the man said again, sounding irritated. "What do you need?"

Lilian took a breath and collected her thoughts. "My name is Lilian. My sister, Rosie Donaldson, was in a car accident and is currently in the hospital. I wanted to make sure her supervisor knows."

A long pause, then: "What the fuck is wrong with you?"

Lilian blinked. "Excuse me? Do I have the correct extension? I'm trying to find the supervisor for my sister—"

"This isn't funny. I'm hanging up now—"

"Wait!" Lilian shouted. "I'm not sure what's going on. Who is this?"

The man exhaled a long, exasperated sigh into the phone. "Fine. You want to do this? I know it's you, Rosie. I'm not sure why you're calling, but it's a violation of the restraining order so I'm going to have to call the police."

Lilian shook her head, stunned. This had to be some kind of misunderstanding. "I'm not Rosie, I'm her sister," she said, using the professional voice she used when calling insurance companies. "That's why we sound similar. Rosie told me she worked at BKC, and I was trying to let someone know she was in a car accident. That's it. I have no idea what you're talking about."

"You're her sister? I didn't even know she had a sister." The bite in his voice was gone, and now the man sounded worried. "Was she really in a car accident?"

"Yes. She's in the ICU right now."

"I'm sorry to hear that," he said, "I truly am. But she doesn't work here anymore."

That made no sense. "What? Did she leave? Do you know why?"

"Listen," he said, lowering his voice. "I always liked Rosie. I was on her side through the whole thing, but I could get in some deep shit if I talked to you—to anyone—about it. I wish her the best, though. I truly do."

"But—"

He hung up.

CHAPTER
NINE

Lilian dropped her phone and rubbed her temples with her free hand. Abigail was getting fussy, so she stood and walked down the hallway, bouncing her gently.

Why had Rosie lied about her job? Maybe she'd been trying to make Lilian think her life was better than it was—saying she had a career she loved, when in reality she'd been fired or laid off.

But a restraining order? That sounded serious.

She needed to get back to the ICU. Not only to check on Rosie, but to find Daniel. He must know more about whatever had happened at BKC.

Which meant Lilian needed to do something she hated doing. Something that made her palms sweat and her stomach swirl with anxiety. *You don't have any other options right now,* she told herself. *No matter how hard it is, you have to do it.*

She picked up her phone and called her mother-in-law.

* * *

When the doorbell rang a few minutes later, Lilian was pacing with Abigail by the front entry.

"Thank you so much for coming," Lilian said as she ushered her mother-in-law, Nancy, inside. A gust of frigid air accompanied her.

"Of course!" Nancy took off her coat and hat, revealing her sleek blond bob, cashmere twinset, and pearls. "How are you doing, sweetheart? You must be worried sick about your sister."

"I'm doing okay, thanks. I want to get to the hospital to check on her."

For the most part, Lilian liked Nancy; that wasn't the problem. It was more that no matter what she did, she felt like she could never measure up. Every time Nancy came over, Lilian was certain that she was meticulously cataloging her daughter-in-law's shortcomings. *Oh look, the sink is full of dishes. Oh no, Abigail isn't wearing socks. Oh my goodness, Lilian sends Caleb's shirts out instead of ironing them herself like a good wife should.*

"Call me anytime," Nancy said. "It is *very* stressful having a loved one in the hospital. You know I'm always happy to watch my grandbaby—even if you just need a nap."

She reached for Abigail, and Lilian balked. Even though Nancy had watched Abigail the day before and everything had been fine, it still felt wrong.

This was another reason she'd extended her maternity leave. The thought of leaving her baby at the hospital daycare had given her literal nightmares. In residency, Lilian had taken care of an eight-month-old who'd suffered a skull fracture after falling out of a highchair at daycare and a two-year-old who'd choked on a bite of chicken. She would never forget the sound their mothers made when they realized their children were dead—a keening, almost animal wail. It would echo in her ears forever.

Lilian knew, objectively, that daycare was safe, and that children could be injured just as easily under their parents' watch—but the fact remained that no one would be as vigilant with Abigail as Lilian was. What Lilian called "vigilance," however, her psychiatrist had gently suggested could be symptoms of her postpartum anxiety. He recommended she take more time off, give the meds a chance to kick in. But it had been several months now, and she still wasn't back to her old self. So maybe she wasn't going to get better. Maybe this was her new normal.

"Are you all right?" Nancy said, her hands outstretched.

Lilian realized she was clamping Abigail tightly against her chest. "Yes," she said, shaking herself. "I'm just—" She swallowed. "It's just . . ." She trailed off, unable to explain.

Nancy tilted her head, studying Lilian. "Caleb told me you've been having a hard time."

The thought of Caleb confiding in his mother about her made Lilian's insides wilt with embarrassment. She met Nancy's eyes, gray-blue like Caleb's, expecting to see judgment or disappointment. Instead, she saw something that looked curiously like compassion.

"It's hard for me to let anyone else watch Abigail," Lilian said. It felt like a confession, saying it out loud.

Nancy gave a gentle smile. "I remember feeling the same way, when Caleb was small."

"You did?"

Nancy nodded. "No one loves Abigail like you do, but I come pretty close. I'll follow your rules exactly, Lilian. I promise."

Lilian's eyes filled with tears. Slowly, she relaxed her grip on her baby. She appreciated Nancy's words—they were exactly what she needed to hear—but she couldn't help thinking about her own mother, who'd never had a chance to be a grandmother. Would she have been as hands-off with Abigail as she'd been with Rosie? Or would she have blossomed into a doting grandma, helping Lilian through these first tumultuous months? Lilian would never know.

"Thank you," she said, putting Abigail into Nancy's outstretched arms.

"Don't worry about a thing," Nancy said, patting Abigail's back. "Abigail and I will have a lovely time together. We always do, don't we, sweetie?"

* * *

Lilian took an Uber downtown; she wasn't ready to drive yet, not with her double vision and vertigo. Her knees bounced with impatience, the desire to urge the driver onward, faster. On the way, she called Caleb to tell him about her phone call with BKC, but he was in surgery, and she hated having conversations on speakerphone while his surgical team listened in.

When she reached the hospital, she hurried into the elevator, then down the hall—but where the double doors to the neurotrauma ICU should have been, a row of vending machines blocked the way. Lilian rubbed her temples, swallowing down a flutter of worry.

Was she *that* confused? *That* impaired? Her mind had been on Rosie, but a small voice whispered that perhaps she should see someone about her concussion, as Caleb had suggested.

"Are you lost?" a woman in purple scrubs said, pausing next to Lilian.

Lilian blinked and looked at her. "I'm looking for the neurotrauma ICU?"

The woman smiled. "Ah, that's up one floor. Take the elevator and you'll find it."

Just one floor. Anyone could have made that mistake.

Lilian thanked her, and went directly to Rosie's room, wanting to prove to herself that her sister was still there, alive and unharmed. Her heart rate quickened as she entered the glass-walled space, almost expecting to see the man with the scar again.

But the room was empty, just Rosie in the bed surrounded by monitors and IV poles. Lilian let out a shaky breath. She came toward her sister, taking in the changes since the day before. Rosie still had the neck brace and partially shaved head, a swollen nose, and a nasal cannula for oxygen. Somehow, though, she looked worse: her face was sweaty, her hair greasy. The muggy odor of sweat and urine rose from her body, turning Lilian's stomach. The sheet lay rumpled at her feet, exposing the dressing on her right leg, from her toe up to the knee.

Lilian blinked, looked closer. There was something on Rosie's right upper thigh that she'd never seen before. An old scar in the shape of a W or maybe an epsilon. Well-healed. Jagged. From some sort of accident? It made Lilian wonder about what other events in her sister's life she had missed.

Lifting the sheet, she covered her sister. She'd always hated when unresponsive patients were left like this, exposed in a way no one would want to be seen.

At the movement of the sheet, Rosie's eyes opened. Lilian gasped. Her sister's eyes were a vivid green—brighter than Lilian's, which were more hazel.

Rosie stared at Lilian's face, her expression lucid. Something in her eyes flickered. Recognition?

"Hi, sis," Lilian said. "How are you? To be honest, you look pretty terrible. Even worse than the time I did your makeup for your third-grade class performance."

Rosie blinked slowly.

"Dad said you looked like Pennywise the Clown," Lilian said, smiling. "Sorry about that."

Rosie continued to look at Lilian steadily, but then her right eye turned in. It was unnerving, but Lilian persevered, putting her fingers into Rosie's hand, like she had the last time she'd been there.

"Squeeze," she prompted.

Rosie did. A faint pressure at first, and then a firmer one.

"Let go now," Lilian said, and Rosie did. Squeezing fingers could be a reflex, but letting go on command? That was voluntary. She reached over and tapped Rosie's left leg, the one not in the dressing. "Can you move this leg?"

Rosie's mouth tightened, and her left leg shifted from side to side. Lilian's heart leapt in guarded excitement. Her sister was improving. Just three days after the brain injury and she was already following commands.

"Don't go getting cocky now," Lilian said, as her eyes filled with tears. "It's so strange talking to you like this, Rosie. I'm not used to getting so many words in before you jump into the conversation."

She laughed, shaky. Rosie was still staring at her with that off-balance gaze, her bright eyes glittering. Lilian's laughter died as she remembered the phone call she'd made earlier. If she had stayed in contact with her sister, she would've known what had happened with Rosie at work. She could have helped her.

"Oh, Rosie," she said quietly, smoothing Rosie's unwashed hair back from her sweat-slicked forehead. "I should have taken better care of you."

A memory filled her mind of Rosie at thirteen years old, with a severe sore throat and fever. Their dad was out of work, and they didn't have any health insurance, so no one had taken Rosie to a doctor. When their mother called Lilian and said that Rosie couldn't swallow, Lilian—then in her first year of medical school—had rushed home in a panic. She took Rosie to her school's free clinic, where she was diagnosed with strep throat and an abscess next to her tonsil. Lilian spent the weekend perched at her sister's bedside, caring for her while studying for an upcoming anatomy exam.

Over the years, she'd tried to explain to Caleb what it was like being an older sister. He didn't understand why she worried so much about Rosie, even when Rosie was an adult herself, even when Lilian couldn't actually do anything to help—but then again, Caleb's childhood had been very different from hers. He'd grown up in a wealthy neighborhood with a doting stay-at-home mom and a successful surgeon father. Lilian's parents had married right out of high school with a baby on the way. Her dad had worked long, hard hours at the auto mechanic shop; her mom had bounced between various minimum-wage jobs and unemployment. It hadn't been a terrible childhood, no abuse or neglect, but Dad sometimes drank too much, money was always tight, and Mom struggled with what Lilian now knew was chronic depression.

Someone had to pick up the slack, Lilian had told Caleb, or else Rosie wouldn't have been cared for. Even after Lilian moved out, Rosie would call with crisis after crisis: she'd gotten suspended at school, she'd gone too far with a boy, she'd been caught with alcohol at a party. Lilian always felt compelled to help. That mantle wasn't something she could shake off and leave behind. It was part of her, baked into her bones.

Slumped in the hospital bed, Rosie seemed worn out, her eyes drifting closed. Lilian sat down, held Rosie's hand, and let her thoughts drift back to the last conversation they'd had before the two years of silence between them.

A couple weeks after their parents' funeral, Lilian had returned to work, trying to reestablish a normal routine. A well-meaning friend had told her that grief would come in waves, like the ocean, and she should let them roll over her. But these waves were two stories tall and unrelenting, knocking her flat, leaving her struggling for breath. She would never again hear her dad rant about the umpire's terrible call at the latest White Sox game, or spend Thanksgiving morning helping her mom make six dozen of her traditional butterhorn rolls. Her parents hadn't been perfect, but they had always been there. She didn't know how to exist in a world where they did not. They were gone, and Lilian was drowning.

One evening, she'd been at work late, catching up on charting, when her medical assistant said she had a visitor. It was Rosie. Her sister looked even worse than she had at the funeral. Ripped jeans, a stained hoodie, greasy hair. Lilian could see a smattering of acne along her forehead and nose. She was picking at her cuticles, shifting her weight in dirty canvas sneakers.

"Nice to see you again," Lilian said in a flat voice, too exhausted, mentally and physically, to react to Rosie's presence with anything more than dull irritation. Losing her parents had been devastating. Being abandoned by her sister was almost worse.

"I'm sorry for not being there," Rosie said. "I've been in a really bad place and—and Michael left me, and—"

Lilian nodded, her heart sinking. Rosie was only reaching out because her boyfriend had dumped her. This had been her pattern for years; she'd meet a guy and become obsessed with him, then she'd run back to Lilian for comfort when he turned out to be married, or a sex addict, or on parole. "What can I do for you, Rosie?"

Rosie chewed on her lip before blurting, "I want my share."

Lilian sat back in her chair, stunned into silence. "Your share of what?"

"Of what Mom and Dad left us. Half of it is mine. When can I get it?"

"What they left—?" Lilian shook her head, incredulous. "They didn't leave us anything, Rosie. The house was mortgaged; they had no savings."

Which Rosie would have known if she'd been present for the past several weeks as Lilian struggled to unravel the tangled financial mess their parents had left behind.

Rosie shook her head. "What about the baseball? Mom's ring? I should get my share of those."

Lilian's face flooded with heat. How dare she? Their parents had only two possessions that were worth anything: their father's signed baseball from the White Sox's triumphant 1917 World Series win, and their mother's engagement ring, which had been their paternal grandmother's.

"First of all," Lilian said, her voice shaking with barely suppressed anger, "I would never sell those. Not in a million years. And second of all—" She stopped, swallowing a sob. "They're gone."

"What do you mean, gone?" Rosie asked, paling.

"They weren't in the house when I went through it. I'm assuming Mom and Dad sold them."

"I don't believe you," Rosie said, eyes narrowing. "They would never sell those."

Lilian snorted. Rosie had the audacity to be shocked, when she was planning on selling them herself? "Listen, if you want some of Mom's and Dad's stuff, I'd love your help going through—"

"I need *money*," Rosie snapped, stepping forward. "Not a bunch of old clothes and stupid fucking knickknacks. If there's nothing from Mom and Dad, then you can give me some, right?"

As Lilian gaped at her sister, everything clicked together. Rosie's twitchy, shifty movements. Torn cuticles, runny nose, bloodshot eyes with wide pupils. Drugs; maybe heroin withdrawal. Rosie had gotten herself wrapped up in something bad. Her boyfriend had kicked her out, and now she needed help.

Lilian's heart squeezed with that familiar mixture of responsibility and resentment. Once again, it was *her* job to get Rosie out of the mess she'd made. She mentally sorted through options: she would find Rosie a good rehab program; Rosie could stay with Lilian and Caleb until she was back on her feet.

"I'm not going to give you any money," Lilian started, "but I'll—"

Rosie stepped forward and slapped her hands down on Lilian's desk. "You have always been such a bitch, you know that? Always telling me what to do, always trying to run my life. And the *one* time I ask you—I know you have the money! You never cared about me, did you? Not ever."

Lilian stood in a rush, sending her chair careening across the floor behind her. "Wait a minute, I—"

"You think you're so much better than me?" Rosie leaned in, lips curled in a sneer. "You think you know what my life is like? You know *nothing*, sis. Fucking *nothing*. All I want is a little help from my big sister—"

"A little *help*?" Lilian said, nearly shouting. A hot flush of anger crept up her neck. "I had to identify our parents' bodies, Rosie. I called over a hundred people to give them the news. I picked out their caskets, chose the clothes they were buried in, planned the entire funeral, put the house up for sale. You should have been right by my side—"

"You like being in charge of everything," Rosie said, jabbing a finger at Lilian. "You're such a martyr, poor Lilian—"

"I wanted my sister!" Lilian shouted, tears in her eyes. "I wanted you there and you abandoned me, and now I can't even look at you without feeling sick to my stomach! Our parents *died*, Rosie. They're gone, and all you want is your share? That's all you care about?"

For a moment, Lilian thought she saw tears in Rosie's eyes, too, a wild, raw grief that surpassed even her own—like a wound flayed wide open. It stole her breath from her lungs.

"I *miss* you," Lilian said, her voice raw. "I've been so lonely without you."

Something blossomed between them then, their bone-deep connection as sisters resonating in the small room. The grief that weighed on Lilian's shoulders seemed lighter, simply by virtue of two sharing it instead of one. She started around her desk, wanting to put her arms around her little sister and hang on tight.

But then Rosie's expression shifted into something cunning and sharp. "I don't have time for this, Lilian. I need money. Now."

Lilian stopped, stunned. The tether of connection between them ruptured, and she felt it as physical pain, an elastic snapping back against her hands.

"Get out." She surprised herself with the words, flat and cold.

Rosie took a step back. "What?"

Lilian swallowed down all the pain of the past weeks—and months—without her sister. "Get out of my office. I don't want to see you anymore."

And she hadn't. For two full years.

Now she stared at her sister's face and tried to imagine what could have been going through Rosie's mind. If Lilian hadn't lost her temper, if she'd listened and tried to understand, maybe they could have pulled together, helped each other across the swamp of grief and loss. Then Lilian would have known exactly what had happened with Rosie and this restraining order at BKC, because Rosie would have felt comfortable confiding in her.

And, Lilian whispered to herself, maybe she could have confided in Rosie, too. She could have used a sister, especially after Abigail was born and her constant needs felt overwhelming.

The sound of footsteps startled Lilian. She looked up to see a man with dark hair standing in the doorway. Her breath quickened—was it the man with the scar on his jaw?

But no. It was Daniel. Relief rushed through her. *Finally.*

CHAPTER
TEN

Lilian wanted to pepper Daniel with questions about the man she'd seen in Rosie's room, about Rosie's issues at work, about whatever life-and-death matter Rosie had been fixated on.

But something made her hesitate. Maybe it was the way he was looking at her—that rock-tight jaw, the tension in his shoulders. She had a distinct impression that he'd been hoping to avoid her.

Because he'd been calling himself Rosie's husband, trying to edge Lilian out of her care?

"I haven't seen you since the night of the accident," Lilian said, aware that she sounded accusing.

"I've been coming mostly at night," he said, shifting his weight. *Cagey*, her dad would have said. "I can't sleep."

Indeed, he looked exhausted. As if a gust of wind off Lake Michigan would have knocked him over. His eyes were lined with fatigue, his face unshaven, his shirt wrinkled. Before even taking off his coat or setting his messenger bag down, he walked to Rosie's bedside and touched her face with the back of his hand.

"Hi, sweetheart," he whispered. "I miss you."

Rosie's eyelids fluttered, but otherwise she gave no response.

Despite her misgivings, Lilian's heart softened, just slightly. Perhaps the issue with the blood transfusion had been a misunderstanding.

She studied him. Average height, average build, jeans, and a T-shirt. Fairly nondescript, except for his eyes. Such a light blue, they were almost colorless.

"She opened her eyes earlier," Lilian said. "And she squeezed my hand."

"That's good."

He sounded close to breaking down. Lilian's heart gave another reluctant squeeze. She couldn't grill him with questions, not right now. It was clear he was barely holding himself together.

Remembering the engagement ring, she fished it out of her purse. "I think I should give this to you," she said, though she felt reluctant to hand it over.

Daniel turned, wiping his eyes with his hand. "Where did you get it? I assumed it was lost."

"The police found Rosie's purse at the accident site and brought it to me."

Daniel sank into the chair next to Lilian and opened the box. His eyes turned glassy as he looked at the ring. "Did she tell you about me?"

Lilian nodded. "A little. She said you met this past summer and moved in with you a month ago. She said I'd like you."

One corner of his mouth lifted, somewhere between a grimace and a smile. "She didn't tell you that I'd asked her to marry me, I take it."

That answered one of Lilian's questions: they weren't married *yet*. "No," she said. "But we didn't have much time to talk. I'm sure she was waiting for the right moment."

"Yeah."

But he didn't look convinced, and Lilian sensed he was holding something back. The way his body angled away, the way his eyes met hers only briefly. He didn't trust her, either—maybe because of what Rosie had told him about her, or maybe because he was worried Lilian wouldn't allow him to have a say in Rosie's care. He wasn't a relative, by blood or marriage. Legally, he had no right to be in this room at all.

"Can we talk about something?" she said.

He snapped the box shut and looked at Lilian. She thought she caught a glimpse of tears in his eyes before they darted away again. "Sure. What about?"

She decided to start with the simplest issue. "I think they've been asking you for consent to do procedures? Like the blood transfusion yesterday." As she spoke, she tamped down the irritation she had felt earlier.

"Was that a bad idea?" He sounded unsure, as uncomfortable with all of this as she was. Maybe more so. She'd been planning on reminding him that she was the legal medical decision maker, but now that she saw his face—his obvious concern for Rosie, his uncertainty that he had made the correct choice—she reconsidered. It felt wrong to shut him out of Rosie's care.

She shook her head. "No, it was fine. But I think there was a misunderstanding—they thought you were her husband. That's why they asked you."

Daniel's eyes widened in surprise. "I . . . I didn't mean to give them that impression."

"An honest mistake, I'm sure. But I think we should work together when it comes to any medical decisions."

"Of course," he said. "You know her better than anyone else."

A pinprick of guilt made Lilian cringe. She *should* have known her sister better than anyone else. "If there are any big decisions to be made, I'll call you to discuss them?" She held up her phone.

He pulled his phone out of his pocket. "And I'll do the same."

After exchanging numbers, he walked back toward the head of Rosie's bed. Lilian sorted through the questions on the tip of her tongue. What did he know about Rosie's issues at BKC? Did he know who could have been following them on Lake Shore Drive?

But it seemed awkward to launch into twenty questions with Daniel when she hardly knew him—and when he hardly knew her, either. She wanted to get a sense for him first, for his relationships with Rosie. Lilian couldn't forget Rosie's history of awful boyfriends.

"How did you and Rosie meet?" she asked.

"Um, at the Art Institute," he said. "You know that huge Georgia O'Keeffe by the stairs? *Sky Above Clouds?*"

Lilian nodded, remembering the painting, though she hadn't known its name. Even as a little girl, Rosie had loved it. Her eyes would always light up as it came into view: eight feet high and twenty-four feet wide, spanning the entire wall over the grand staircase.

"I noticed Rosie on my way in," Daniel said. "She was standing at the top of the stairs, looking at the painting, and I—I wanted to talk to her, but I didn't know what to say. When I came back down a couple hours later, she was still there. Sitting on a step, her chin in her hands, just . . . staring. She looked like she'd been crying."

Lilian imagined the scene: Rosie almost in a trance, her long hair cascading down her back, her green eyes glistening with tears. Had she been remembering all the time they'd spent there, she and Lilian? Or maybe thinking about her own artistic dreams, which had never been supported by their parents.

Daniel's gaze dropped to the floor. "I figured she wouldn't give me the time of day, but I couldn't live with myself if I didn't at least try to talk to her. So I went up and said hello." He shrugged. "We started talking, and—I don't know. Something clicked. We talked for a couple hours, right there on the top of the stairs. I was half in love with her by the end of our conversation. Lucky for me, she agreed to go to dinner with me."

Lilian wrapped her arms around herself as sadness rolled over her. If she'd been a better sister, she would have known all of this; Rosie would have called her to talk about the new guy she'd met. At some point, Lilian would have invited them over for dinner, excited to meet the man her sister was crazy about. Daniel and Caleb might have become friends. Rosie would have called Lilian in happy tears after Daniel proposed. Instead, her sister's fiancé was a stranger.

She had to wonder what Daniel knew about *her*, though. What Rosie might have told him. "Did—" She cleared her throat. "Did Rosie ever tell you why we hadn't spoken in a while?"

Daniel hesitated, his eyes sliding away from hers. Of course she would have told him.

"Never mind," Lilian said quickly. She could guess whatever Rosie said hadn't shown her own actions in a good light. "What do you do? Rosie told me you were a professor on sabbatical, at some university here in Chicago."

"I'm a postdoc at the University of Chicago. I'm taking this semester to write up my research, and Rosie started calling it my sabbatical." The corner of his mouth lifted in a half-smile, as if remembering a conversation between the two of them. An inside joke. "She likes to make me sound better than I am."

"A postdoc in what?" Lilian realized she might sound like she was interrogating him, and she forced herself to uncross her arms and try for a relaxed, nonconfrontational expression.

"Art history."

"Makes sense," Lilian said, nodding. That's why they'd hit it off at the Art Institute. She could imagine them discussing art trends and influences, all the things Rosie had prattled on about that Lilian had never understood.

Lilian's mind flashed back to her phone conversation with the guy at BKC, the man with the scar. She wanted to ask Daniel about it but didn't know how to bring it up. *Just ask*, she told herself.

But before she could, he spoke again.

"She's going to be okay, right?" he said, his voice strained. "You're a doctor, so you understand what's going on, these tests they're running, but all this medical terminology goes over my head. I keep asking everyone the same question—is she going to be okay—and no one is telling me anything concrete."

Lilian hesitated. She wanted to explain that no one could predict Rosie's outcome. Her medical care was mostly supportive at this point. Keeping her body working while the real healing happened on an invisible, cellular level.

But she also knew that Daniel needed something to hold on to. Some source of hope, however small. She did, too.

"You should talk to her," she said, remembering a study she'd read a couple years back. "When loved ones talk regularly to people with brain injuries, they recover faster. She might not respond, but she'll recognize your voice. It'll remind her what she's fighting for: to get back to you."

She sounded more certain than she was, and she knew she wasn't answering his question. But her words seemed to help: Daniel's tense jaw relaxed a fraction.

"I can do that," he said, and turned back to Rosie.

Lilian stood. He needed space, and she ought to get home to Abigail. But she hesitated.

"There was a man here yesterday," she said. "In Rosie's room."

Daniel's head jerked up. "A man? What do you mean—like, a visitor?"

"I don't know who he was. Forties, dark hair. He had a scar right there." She traced a finger along the right side of her jaw, then shivered. "When I came in, he ran off."

Daniel's eyebrows pulled together. "That's strange."

"He doesn't sound familiar to you?" Lilian asked.

"No," he said, shaking his head.

Lilian hesitated again. Her next words were on the tip of her tongue: *I think he was following us right before the car accident.*

But then she forced herself to take a deep breath. Her questions about her sister's past were insignificant compared with the uncertainty of the present. Rosie was unresponsive in the ICU, fighting for her life. It would be cruel to bring this up with Daniel right now, when he was already overwhelmed and scared.

She took one final look back as she left Rosie's room. Daniel was holding Rosie's hand, talking to her in a quiet voice. Lilian couldn't hear what he was saying, but the sight made her smile for the first time since the crash.

* * *

Over the next few days, Rosie seemed to be stabilizing, but Lilian couldn't banish the low-level, simmering anxiety that hung like an invisible cloud around her. She visited Rosie every afternoon, and Daniel was always there when she arrived. He'd update her on any changes, and then he'd leave. Lilian sensed his exhaustion growing every time they spoke. She wouldn't be surprised if he sat by her bedside all night, staring at the glowing monitor, counting Rosie's respirations and pulse rate, as if they would cease if he took his eyes off them for a second.

Lilian understood. She put all her mental energy into focusing on her sister's recovery. Keeping track of all the medical issues, the myriad consultants and therapists and techs who came in and out of Rosie's room, was a full-time job in and of itself.

On top of that, Lilian was still dealing with the lingering effects of her concussion. Whenever her mind drifted back to the night of the car crash, to the face she might or might not have seen in the car behind them, she forced herself to forget about it. It had been a hit-and-run, like the police said. The man in Rosie's hospital room had simply been lost, like Caleb had said. Rosie's issues at BKC had nothing to do with any of that.

Most of the time, she believed it.

CHAPTER
ELEVEN

Ten days after the accident, Lilian headed to the hospital for her daily visit, her hands tingling with a mixture of anticipation and dread. Today, a new consulting doctor would evaluate Rosie to determine if she qualified for a specialized brain injury rehab program. If she did, that was wonderful news, a sign that Rosie would recover. If not . . .

No. Lilian wouldn't allow herself to consider that possibility. Rosie *had* to get better. There wasn't any other option.

When she stepped off the elevator, Daniel was waiting in the lobby—he'd wanted to be present for this discussion, too. He looked up at Lilian and jumped as if he'd seen a ghost.

"What?" Lilian asked, alarmed.

He shook his head. "Sorry, it's just—" He swallowed. "You look so much like her, at first glance. It caught me off guard."

Lilian looked down at herself. She had on a gray sweater, fitted black jeans, and ankle boots. "Rosie would never wear something this boring," she said.

A ghost of a smile crossed his lips. "That's true."

She'd never seen him smile before, she realized. It brightened his face, revealing a shallow dimple in one cheek. He wasn't in his usual rumpled T-shirt and jeans, either. He had on a collared shirt and gray slacks. His dark hair was neatly combed. For the first time, Lilian felt like she was seeing the man Rosie had fallen in love with.

But she still didn't feel comfortable around him.

"How's your postdoc going?" she asked.

"Slowly."

"It must be difficult balancing that while dealing with Rosie's condition," she said, as they reached Rosie's room.

"My adviser understands. I'll probably need to extend my fellowship, but that's fine. I don't want to be anywhere but here." His eyes darted toward Rosie's open door; he was probably as anxious as Lilian to hear the results of the consult.

"Well, thanks. For being here so often." The words came out awkwardly, but Lilian meant them. "Should we go in?"

He nodded, and Lilian followed him into the room. Her hands tingled with nervousness, and she took a long, steadying breath before crossing the threshold.

Inside, a woman in a long white coat stood at Rosie's bedside.

"Oh, hi," she said, straightening up. "I'm Dr. Melissa Rao, from the TBI service. Thanks for meeting me here. You must be Rosie's support system."

Lilian and Daniel introduced themselves, then settled into chairs to hear Dr. Rao's assessment. Lilian's feet tapped a restless rhythm against the floor, and she smoothed her hands down her thighs, trying to calm herself.

"She's doing very well," Dr. Rao said. "If she continues to stabilize, medically, we should be able to bring her to rehab early next week."

"That soon?" Lilian said, surprised. It was good news, but difficult to wrap her head around. Since the accident, Rosie had done nothing but lay in a hospital bed, dependent on nurses to take care of her every bodily function. She had a catheter to drain her urine. A feeding tube in her nose. She had to be turned and repositioned every two hours to prevent bedsores. And in a week, she'd be ready for rehab? Lilian wanted to believe it, but it seemed impossible.

"Can you tell us more about the rehab hospital?" Daniel asked.

Dr. Rao explained that Rosie would receive three hours a day of intensive therapy, focusing on everything from transfers and walking, to dressing and grooming, to communication and swallowing. She could spend up to a month there, but that was only the beginning of a long road to a destination that could not yet be predicted. Rosie might be able to go home, with lots of support from caregivers, or she might have to go to a long-term care facility.

Daniel nodded, but Lilian felt frozen to her chair, unable to respond. She knew she ought to be celebrating right now: her sister could learn to walk again, to dress herself, to communicate! Indeed, Dr. Rao was smiling like she'd just announced the winning Powerball numbers. But deep down, something inside Lilian shriveled and died. However irrational, a part of her had been hoping for a miracle. Hoping that one day Rosie would wake up, like a character in a soap opera, rub her eyes and ask what had happened. Back to normal.

Instead, reality smacked Lilian in the face like a two-by-four: this would be a long, arduous process. Hours of therapy, teams of specialists, and even then, Rosie might never be as she once was.

"I need to ask a few questions about Rosie's home situation," Dr. Rao said, glancing from Lilian to Daniel. "Have you discussed the plan for Rosie after discharge?"

"No," Lilian said, dazed. She hadn't begun to think that far in advance. All her energy had been focused on getting Rosie through the next day, the next night. She had no idea if Daniel had considered it, either.

"If Rosie can go home after rehab," Dr. Rao said, "who will be her primary caretaker?"

Me, Lilian thought immediately. *That's my job.*

But then she remembered Daniel, sitting just inches away. His body had stiffened, but he didn't say a word. She couldn't meet his eyes, afraid of what she'd see there. He obviously loved Rosie; he'd proven his dedication over the past week. But caring for a brain-injured woman long-term was a serious undertaking. Did he understand the depth of that responsibility? There was no guarantee that Rosie would recover to the point where they could have a typical relationship again. It would be a kind-ness to decide for him, she told herself. And it was her responsibility, both legally and morally, to take care of her sister.

Addressing Dr. Rao, she said, "I need to discuss with my husband, but I'd like to take her home with me."

CHAPTER
TWELVE

"You want to bring her *here?*" Caleb said, incredulous.

"I want to at least consider it," Lilian said.

They were in bed that night, Caleb reading *The Journal of Orthopaedic Trauma* and Lilian with her laptop, reading an article about long-term outcomes after severe traumatic brain injury. Because of her post-concussive headaches, she could only look at the screen on her computer if she turned the brightness all the way down. She shouldn't have been looking at the screen at all, she knew, but she needed something to occupy her mind.

Abigail was blessedly asleep in her crib. Even still, Lilian could feel the tension in her neck and shoulders from worrying that Abigail could wake up and need her mother at any moment.

"Lily, you have a lot on your plate already. The baby, your concussion, your own . . ." He trailed off, and Lilian knew what he was thinking: *your mental health.* Caleb shook his head. "You want to add being a full-time caretaker to your sister? I thought you wanted to go back to work."

"It's not about what I want. It's about what's best for Rosie."

Maybe she shouldn't go back to work, after all. Caleb made almost triple her salary; they would be fine without her income. Her department would probably be glad to get rid of her. Just today, a new review had been posted about her online.

> Dr. Donaldson used to be my son's pediatrician, but I couldn't in good conscience continue seeing someone who'd missed such a crucial diagnosis. I lost trust in her, her staff, and the entire clinic. Much happier with our new doctor.

It might be a relief to walk away from the whole mess. Setting aside the malpractice suit, there were other things she would be glad to leave behind. The paperwork, the endless charting, the hassles with insurance, the pressure from administration to see more patients in less time. Still, she loved connecting with children and their parents. And could she really walk away from her career? Her identity as a pediatrician? All those years of training and experience, wasted.

Not that all those years had helped Dasha Nichols much.

She shook her head, refocusing. "I have legitimate concerns about sending my sister home with Daniel. He's not from around here—I don't know what his plans are when he finishes his postdoc."

He hadn't said a word after their conversation with the rehab resident. At the time, Lilian had told herself that his silence meant he was grateful that she had decided for him. Now, she wondered if she'd steamrolled over him.

You always think you know best, Rosie used to say.

"The other option is to find a nice facility for Rosie," Caleb said.

"A facility?" Lilian's voice lifted into a shriek. A cold, sterile place filled with strangers? "Absolutely not. Are you serious?"

Caleb breathed out an exasperated sigh. "I said it was an *option*. You're struggling as it is—that's a fact, Lily, not a judgment—and you want to add more stress? I'm sorry, but that makes me seriously question your decision-making ability."

The blood drained from her face, and she turned her back toward him. What could she say to that? His words cut to the heart of her self-doubt. Could she make a good decision about this? Could she trust her own judgment? Maybe not.

She forced herself to consider what life would be like with Rosie here, all the time. It was too early to know exactly what kind of care Rosie would need, but no matter what, Lilian would have to coordinate it. Doctor's appointments, therapy sessions, medications—all on top of caring for Abigail, which Lilian already found overwhelming. She couldn't blame Caleb for being concerned. *She* ought to be concerned, too.

It didn't take much of a leap to understand the reason she wanted to bring Rosie home. She was trying to make up for her failures as a physician. For the ways she'd failed her sister, too.

"Let me talk with Daniel about it," Lilian said. "He needs to be part of the discussion."

Caleb nodded, apparently satisfied, and Lilian pulled out her phone to text Daniel.

I'd like to talk more about Rosie's discharge plans after rehab. Can I come by your place tomorrow?

She needed to see where her sister had lived, if returning there was even an option, and if Daniel wanted to be involved. If he didn't, at least she could make a plan moving forward.

Her phone vibrated with Daniel's response: *Sure. I'll be back from the hospital around noon, just let me know.*

He sent his address, on Everett Avenue in Hyde Park, a historic South Side neighborhood full of museums and universities, big trees, and old buildings. Lilian could imagine her sister there. Maybe it was the right place for Rosie, after all.

Lilian set her laptop on her nightstand and lay down, feeling simultaneously wired and exhausted. She was acutely aware of Caleb's warm body a few feet away, the rustle of the pages in his hands. In the past, before Abigail was born, he would have set down the journal and curled behind her. His hands would have roamed over her body; she would have felt him getting aroused. Lilian didn't really want to have sex tonight, but she wouldn't have said no if *he'd* wanted to. She missed his touch. She missed being desired by him.

"I can't stop thinking about what happened," Lilian said. "Why the crash happened."

"Hit-and-run on a snowy night—probably happens all the time," Caleb said absently.

Lilian nodded; she'd already told Caleb everything she'd learned about Rosie's issues at BKC. The restraining order. Not only that—the weekly visits to the gun range. He had listened, his forehead wrinkling in concern. At first, she'd thought he was worried about a possible threat to Rosie, but when he spoke, it was clear he was focused on *Lilian*. Worried she was being obsessive, once again, seeing potential disasters in ordinary, unconnected events.

Maybe he's right.

A vicious little thought, but one she couldn't ignore. Ever since her mistake with Dasha Nichols, Lilian had been terrified of missing something crucial with another patient—or, after Abigail was born, with her own baby. Her compulsive worrying was a coping strategy when she felt out of control—she knew that from the therapy sessions she'd done. Now, everything with Rosie felt out of control, too; was it any wonder that her mind was buzzing with worries again?

Still, she couldn't drop it. "I want to go talk to the police about the crash," she said.

"I'm not sure what that will solve," Caleb said. "The accident happened, it's over and done with."

"I want to know who caused that crash."

"Why?"

"Because she's my sister," Lilian snapped, sitting up in a rush. "If it was a hit-and-run, I want the driver arrested. I want him found and punished. My sister is never going to be the same again, and someone needs to be held accountable. Can't you see that?"

Caleb held up a hand. He set the journal down, and she felt a brief flash of triumph. "Whoa, there, Lily. I'm sorry—that's not what I meant. I'm just saying that it's not going to change the outcome. But if you want to review things with the cops again, that's fine. I'll go with you sometime next week."

Next week. That seemed like an eternity away.

Lilian flopped against the bed again, even more frustrated. He was appeasing her. Telling her what she wanted to hear.

With a huff, Lilian stood, grabbing her laptop.

"Where are you going?" Caleb asked.

Lilian didn't look back. "I can't sleep."

* * *

It was probably good she had left the bedroom, because Abigail had a terrible night. She was cutting her first tooth—her bottom gum red and swollen—but even with a dose of Tylenol, she wouldn't sleep unless Lilian held her.

Abigail's fussiness and discomfort were probably just teething, but what if it was something else? Taking Abigail out of her footed sleeper, Lilian checked her tiny fingers and toes, just in case there was a hair tourniquet around one. She checked Abigail's temperature over and over—99.5, 99.2, 99.8, not even a real fever. During the day, she might have been able to think more rationally, but exhaustion ratcheted up her anxiety, and loneliness compounded it. As the hours ticked by, she paced the room and tried to ignore the clamoring voices in her brain that told her something was wrong with her baby, terribly wrong; that if Lilian didn't find it and fix it, something even worse would happen.

That's enough, she told herself. *My baby is safe, and I am safe. Time to think about something else.*

Taking a deep breath, she resumed pacing, forcing her thoughts to the conversation with Caleb about bringing Rosie home. She felt good about the plan to talk with Daniel, but something Caleb had said was stuck in her mind: *I'm sorry, but that makes me seriously question your decision-making ability.*

That rankled. During their first years together, Caleb never would have questioned her. He'd needed her, back then. He was the one who'd turned to her for help. Without Lilian, he likely would have failed anatomy. Even though no one in the entire class could rival his dissection skills, he couldn't memorize worth a damn.

After he'd bombed the first anatomy test (which Lilian had aced), he'd asked her to study with him. She'd reluctantly agreed, worrying that he'd slow her down. But her ability to create catchy mnemonics, combined with his intricate colored pencil sketches, helped both of them. Studying together soon turned into more, and within a few weeks they were inseparable, night and day. When Caleb's father passed away three weeks before they were to take the first part of their boards, Caleb always maintained that Lilian was the only reason he hadn't failed. Even in residency and beyond, he'd ask her to remind him about basic physiology or pharmacology. He counted on her, and she liked it. It was what made their partnership work.

But neither of them had been prepared for the upheaval in their relationship after Abigail's birth. Even the sleep deprivation of residency couldn't compare to life with a newborn. Caleb wanted to help, but Lilian didn't know what to tell him, how to communicate the vast changes in her body and mind. Was it normal that she constantly worried about something terrible happening to Abigail? What about the thoughts of Abigail facedown on the mattress, suffocating? Abigail falling off the changing table and bashing her head on the hardwood floor. Abigail choking, turning blue; her tiny fingers jammed in a drawer; her thigh getting stuck in the slats of her crib and twisting, breaking her femur.

As a pediatrician, Lilian had seen all of this. She knew it was possible. No one was immune to tragedy. Wasn't she being a good mother by safeguarding against it? Didn't *all* mothers worry about their babies?

It all came to a head one day when Abigail was two months old. Caleb came home after a night on call to find Lilian sitting wide-eyed in Abigail's bedroom, staring at their sleeping baby and counting the seconds between her breaths. Lilian admitted she hadn't slept at all the night before—too terrified to take her eyes off her baby in case she stopped breathing.

Caleb immediately called a psychiatrist friend. Soon Lilian was in Dr. Evan Samuelson's office, detailing her symptoms and accepting a prescription for medication and a referral for therapy. The official diagnosis was postpartum anxiety, but Evan believed some of these issues could be traced all the way back to the Dasha Nichols case. Lilian felt like a failure and a fraud and a horrible mother—not to mention a shitty doctor for not even recognizing her own problems. But Evan said healthcare workers were notoriously terrible at identifying mental illness in themselves.

"It doesn't mean that you're weak, or unstable, or broken," Evan had said. "You're still just as strong and capable. This is a temporary setback, and we'll get you through."

But in the two months since, Caleb had treated her like a glass figurine, something delicate and fragile, to be kept out of reach so it wouldn't break. His intentions were good; he loved her, he wanted to take care of her. But the fact remained that he didn't see her as an equal. He didn't quite trust her anymore. Even worse, Lilian struggled to trust herself. Especially on a night like tonight, with Abigail wailing no matter what she did.

By two a.m., Lilian was almost delirious with fatigue and worry. She regretted all the times she had spouted platitudes like "sometimes babies just cry!" to the exhausted mothers of her patients. She hadn't understood what it was like to watch your baby suffer, unable to help.

A memory spiked, unbidden. A toddler curled in a hospital bed. A mother, twisting her hands in worry. *Something isn't right, Doctor.* Raised voices echoing down a darkened hallway. *I don't trust a goddamn thing you're saying.* A desperate father, lunging toward Lilian, his face a mask of fury. *I will fucking kill you, bitch.*

Lilian tried to shove the memories away. That was over and done with; it had nothing to do with Abigail. Light from a distant streetlamp filtered through the gauzy curtains, illuminating the room in a bluish glow. Bleary-eyed, she walked to the window and looked out.

There was a car in her driveway.

Lilian stiffened, blinking. Their house, at the end of a cul-de-sac, was often used as a turnaround point for lost drivers. But this car wasn't moving. A plume of exhaust curled around the back end. She squinted.

A silver sedan.

Lilian brought a hand to her mouth. Her pulse raced, her breaths fast and shallow.

A flash of light from inside the car made her jump. A camera? A phone screen?

"Caleb," she said. Her voice came out sounding froggy, and she tried again, louder. "Caleb! There's someone in the driveway."

Abigail startled, wailing. Lilian rushed downstairs, hoping to get a closer look. The make and model of the car. Any damage to the front bumper. The license plate.

Hurry. Hurry.

"Caleb!" she shouted. "Someone's watching the house!"

She heard him wake with a muffled shout. His footsteps pounded down the hallway upstairs. A small voice in her head told her to wait for him, but she didn't. She threw open the front door.

The car was pulling out of the driveway.

She stepped onto the front porch, heedless of the bitter cold, of Abigail shrieking in her arms. Staring into the darkness, she watched as the car sped away in a cloud of exhaust and squealing tires.

Caleb came up behind her. "What's going on?" he said, breathless.

"That car," she said, pointing a shaking finger. "It was in the driveway, watching the house."

Caleb's shoulders relaxed. "Probably just someone turning around, Lily."

Lilian shook her head. She hadn't been fast enough to catch many details, but she had caught a glimpse of the license plate: blue sky, green trees, a red bridge.

"It was a silver sedan. With Indiana plates." She spun around to look at him, heart in her throat. "We need to call the police! Right now, before he gets away—"

"Slow down," Caleb said, taking her by the shoulders. "Take a deep breath, okay? I'm not sure where you're going with this."

She was shaking with fear and exhaustion, Abigail's piercing wails reverberating in her ears. "The car that hit my sister's! Don't you get it? He was watching our house."

"Lily, take a deep breath—"

"I don't need a fucking breath!" Lilian's voice echoed in the cold night air.

Abigail had gone silent.

Lilian glanced down to see her baby's face screwed up in silent fury. Holding her breath. Not making a sound. Lips turning blue. Pure terror jolted through Lilian's body, but before she could react, Abigail sucked in a shuddering breath, then let out a piercing, animal wail.

Relief rushed into Lilian's body, and she nearly collapsed. "You're okay," she said, her voice shaking. "All right, you're all right. Everything is okay, sweet girl."

"She's okay?" Caleb sounded terrified. He led her into the house and shut the door behind her.

Lilian nodded, tears springing to her eyes. "Rosie used to do that," she said. Her whole body was trembling. "Once she held her breath until she passed out."

In an instant she was ten years old again, left alone with her baby sister, panicking as Rosie's cries intensified. After one long, ear-splitting wail, Rosie had fallen silent, her mouth open in a soundless scream, her eyes wide with terror. Her lips turned dusky, her eyelids fluttered shut, and she went limp in Lilian's arms. She would never forget the helplessness and despair in the seconds before Rosie gasped and started crying again.

Caleb wrapped his arms around her, and Abigail and they bounced together in the dark, quiet house, calming their baby. Lilian closed her eyes and leaned against him, the solid mass of his chest and arms encircling her. Soon Abigail settled against her chest, and Lilian's heart settled into a normal rate. Carefully, she pulled away and faced her husband.

"Caleb," she said in a whisper, so she wouldn't disturb Abigail. "We need to call the police."

He ran his hands through his hair, exhaling. "There have to be thousands of silver sedans with Indiana plates in Chicago—"

"It's not a coincidence," she said, shaking her head. "I refuse to believe that."

"Okay," he said. "But without a license plate number, what can the police do?"

She didn't answer, because she knew he was right. It was past two in the morning, the silver sedan was long gone, and she had nothing substantial. And yet, she couldn't dismiss the conviction that all of this was related. The car crash, the man with the scar on his jaw, Rosie's trouble at work, and now this car in their driveway. Somehow, it was all connected.

Caleb gently took Abigail, and she followed him inside and up the stairs. She watched him lay their sleeping baby in the crib, then allowed him to take her hand and lead her into their bedroom. He tucked her in, kissed her forehead, and told her to get some sleep.

Long after Caleb drifted off, Lilian lay awake, staring into the darkness. *A matter of life and death*, Rosie had said. The words echoed in Lilian's mind, getting louder as her fear grew. But beneath the fear, a fierce determination burned. She had to find out what Rosie had planned to tell her. She couldn't fix her sister's injuries. She couldn't undo the accident or erase the last two years they'd been apart, but she could find out who'd hurt Rosie—and why.

PART TWO

CHAPTER THIRTEEN

MyPsychJournal.com

Welcome, Rosie, to your online therapy journal.
You have chosen to share your entries with your therapist via
our secure network, but remember that you can change your
privacy settings at any time. Happy journaling!

JANUARY 10, 2018

Hi. My name is Rosie and I'm a liar.

I feel like that confession should be answered by a chorus of voices: "Hi, Rosie."

But this isn't like AA. There aren't any fellow liars sitting in a circle with me, shifting their weight and calculating how long it's been since their last tumble off the honesty wagon.

No, it's just me and this blank page and the harrowing memory of all the ways I've fucked up every important relationship in my life.

I've never kept a journal before. I feel kind of like a twelve-year-old at sleepaway camp for the first time, unlocking my diary and writing by flashlight while my bunkmates sleep. Not that I ever went to summer camp, and not that this is a physical journal with a lock and key—Dr. Vasudevan suggested this online journal, so I can do my homework and she can review it prior to our sessions.

Dr. V is a tiny woman with black hair and black eyes and a take-no-shit attitude, like those little birds with sharp beaks and claws that attack hawks who get too close to their nests. Small but fierce. The walls of her office are covered in diplomas from fancy universities, and over on a bookshelf I spotted three different textbooks she's authored. So: she's a badass, which is exactly what I need. She said today that my job is to Engage With The Process (that's how she talks, emphasizing some words like they're capitalized, which makes her sound even more intimidating), so that's what I'm trying to do. I'll be totally frank: I don't see how this will help. Nothing has helped before, but I'm committed to getting better.

That's what I keep saying, over and over, because maybe if I say it enough times, I'll believe it.

I am committed to getting better.

I am committed to getting better.

I am committed to getting better.

Maybe I shouldn't write that (the part about not believing this) if I know my shrink is going to read it, but she told me to be honest. We need to Work On Honesty, she said. Which is a nice way of saying "I know you're a liar."

I am a liar.

Anyway, Dr. V said we'd explore that in future sessions. Today's homework was simply to register for an account and write.

Write anything, she said. Anything at all. Just get comfortable with The Process. Soon enough we'll dive into Deeper Territory, don't worry.

Dr. V likes to talk about The Process, about Cause and Effect, Actions and Consequences, Memory and Reality.

Today she spent half the time going on and on about how our sense of "self" is basically a collection of memories. She started rambling about neurons and synapses and totally lost me, so she simplified.

Memories are pathways in our brain, she said, like the tracks made by a sled on a snowy hill. Even when the sled is gone, those tracks remain. But every time we review those memories, we connect them with other experiences and emotions, so it's like a child sledding down the same tracks, over and over again, taking a slightly new route each time, or veering off in an unexpected direction. Two people can live through the same event and have totally different memories.

No matter where the sled ends up, she told me, if we follow the tracks back, we can understand Where We Started. As we explore the memories of our actions, we can understand not only the consequences but also our reactions to those consequences.

(Have to admit, I'm terrified of what could happen as we do this. But, like I said, I'm committed to getting better).

So here I go.

What were your actions, Rosie? What were the consequences? What really happened?

CHAPTER
FOURTEEN

Rosie and Daniel's building loomed over Lilian as she approached, stroller in tow: an imposing brick and stone structure topped by wide penthouse-style windows and a snow-covered roof.

She was still shaken from seeing the car in their driveway last night, but her conviction hadn't wavered. The car crash had not been an accident; someone had targeted Rosie, and Lilian needed to find out who and why. She hoped Daniel could point her in the right direction.

An icy gust of wind whipped down the street, and Lilian headed inside. She struggled through the heavy front door with the stroller, and as she came into the lobby, she saw the doorman over at a desk in the corner, arguing with a delivery guy. Lilian shifted her weight, hoping to get the doorman's attention, then heard the elevator ding behind her.

Daniel emerged, looking like he'd just come out of the shower, his hair damp and curling.

"Lilian!" he said, brightening. "I saw you come in—our window overlooks the street—so I figured I'd come down and help you." Daniel walked over, crouching down to stroller height. "This must be Abigail.

Hi there, pretty girl." He smiled at Abigail, his clear blue eyes lighting up, his dimple showing—the first full, genuine smile Lilian had seen him give. "She's gorgeous, Lilian. Wow."

Abigail sent Daniel her biggest, gummiest smile. Lilian couldn't help smiling, too. It was cliché, sure, but there was no better way to a mother's heart than charming her children. "Thank you. This building is lovely. And thanks for coming down."

"No problem," Daniel said, straightening. "Here, let me push the stroller."

Lilian followed Daniel into the elevator—vintage-looking on the outside, modern on the inside. When they exited on Daniel's floor, she took in more details: the parquet floor and crown molding in the hallway, the craftsman-style doors to each apartment. She could imagine her sister here, and how she'd love the rich history and classic aesthetics of this place.

"This is me," Daniel said. He let Lilian push the stroller through while he held the door open.

Small but bright, the apartment had warm oak floors and big picture windows. Lilian caught a glimpse of the street below, a sliver of the lake in the distance.

"Can I take your coat?" Daniel asked, and Lilian gave him her coat and scarf.

He hung them on the coatrack, next to a robin's egg blue trench Lilian recognized; Rosie had found it at a thrift store years ago. Its presence made it seem like Rosie was here now, like she would pop out to greet Lilian at any moment. Her heart squeezed painfully.

"May I?" Daniel asked, holding out his hands to Abigail.

Lilian stiffened. She didn't like other people holding her daughter— she worried that they would drop her, hurt her by accident. But Abigail looked at Daniel and smiled again.

"Sure," Lilian said, handing her over.

Daniel cradled Abigail against his chest, looking so comfortable that Lilian figured he must have nieces or nephews. "Come sit down," he said, motioning to the living room.

As she entered, Lilian studied the room, hoping for glimpses of her sister's life. On one wall hung two paintings she recognized as Rosie's, from her college art days. Several funky, colorful throw pillows tumbled across the black leather sofa.

Then, on another wall, Lilian saw a painting that brought a rush of emotion to her throat. "Oh my God," she said, walking toward it.

Renoir's *Two Sisters*. It brought back dozens of memories of the times Lilian had taken Rosie to the Art Institute on free admission days. Rosie had loved exploring the museum, treating it like her own personal treasure trove, but this painting had been her favorite.

This reproduction wasn't as vivid as the original, but it was still beautiful, and deeply familiar. The older sister with her ruby-red hat, the younger sister with her flushed cheeks, the river scene in the background. Rosie, as a little girl, had pretended it was a picture of the two of them, Lilian and Rosie.

Another picture caught Lilian's eye on a nearby bookshelf. A framed photograph of Rosie and Daniel, sunlight glinting off their faces, the wide expanse of Lake Michigan glistening behind them. Rosie was grinning at the camera, but Daniel was staring at Rosie, captivated.

Below that sat a picture of Lilian and Rosie together at Rosie's twenty-fifth birthday dinner, three years ago. The last birthday dinner they'd spent together before their parents died, before everything fell apart. Arms linked, identical smiles on their faces. Lilian bit her lip, wishing she could rewind time back to that day. She would keep hold of her sister, never let her drift away.

"Can I get you anything to drink?" Daniel asked, behind her. "Coffee or tea or . . ."

"I'm fine, Daniel, but thanks."

He seemed nervous as they sat, Lilian on the black sectional, Daniel, still holding Abigail, on the ottoman. "You said you wanted to talk about something?"

Lilian exhaled. She wanted to tell him about the car in her driveway, but figured she'd start with the practical issues first: Rosie's discharge. This apartment was so full of Rosie's presence that it seemed wrong to send her anywhere else. But taking care of Rosie would be a huge undertaking. Lilian wouldn't blame Daniel if he didn't feel up to the task.

"We haven't talked much about Rosie's future," she said. "About the best place for her after discharge from rehab."

"You said you want to take her home with you." He said the words carefully, as if trying to feel Lilian out.

"I know, but—" She cleared her throat. "Is there a possibility that you would want to take Rosie back home?"

"Of course," he said immediately. "Of course, I would take her back home. I mean—I assumed you wouldn't want that."

"Why?" Lilian wondered if her earlier distrust of him had been so apparent and felt a twinge of guilt.

"She's your little sister. You want to take care of her. But—" He swallowed, his voice rough. "She's the love of my life, you know? That hasn't changed."

Lilian understood. If Caleb had been injured, even before they were married, she would have felt the same way. "Let's talk more with the rehab team before we make any decisions—we don't know yet how much care she'll need. But we can plan on that for now."

He glanced down at Abigail. "Did Rosie look like this when she was a baby?"

Lilian swallowed, her throat thick with emotion. "Yes. She did."

"I hope this doesn't sound weird, but I was really looking forward to having children with her."

"It's not weird," Lilian said. It was sweet, actually. "Had you talked about it together?"

He nodded, still gazing at Abigail. "Rosie said she wanted at least three, maybe four. I told her that was fine with me, but maybe we should start with one at a time."

Lilian smiled, remembering Rosie and the dolls she'd carefully tended as a little girl. "That sounds like Rosie. She always wanted a big family." She paused, taking in Daniel's serious expression as he watched Abigail, the sadness in his eyes. "Are you holding up okay?" she asked.

He glanced over, surprised. "Me? Oh. I guess so."

Lilian wasn't convinced. "It's difficult being the support person. You need to make sure you take care of yourself, too."

Her words felt trite, inadequate. She was echoing things she'd said to parents of her patients in the past—and also, she realized, words similar to those Caleb had said to her. But she worried that Caleb's held a subtle undercurrent of judgment. *You're barely handling things as it is.*

Daniel bounced Abigail, who was getting squirmy. "I'm okay," he said. "I just want Rosie to get better."

"I do too," Lilian said, hoping he understood that "better" might not mean "back to normal." She wasn't even sure if *she* truly understood it, yet. After spreading a blanket on the floor, she took Abigail from Daniel and laid her down on her back. Abigail kicked her legs and cooed. Lilian glanced back up at Daniel, and hesitated; now she needed to ask the other questions on her list. Talking to Daniel was the first step in unraveling whatever events in Rosie's life had led to the car crash.

"I've been meaning to ask—do you know what happened with Rosie at BKC?"

A muscle in Daniel's jaw twitched. "Why?"

"I called to let them know about her accident, and the person I spoke with made it seem like there had been some kind of problem with Rosie. He mentioned a restraining order?"

Daniel's face clouded with anger. "That was *not* Rosie's fault. Who did you talk to?"

"I don't know—some guy who answered the phone. He said he'd get in trouble if he told me." He'd also said he had been on Rosie's side, Lilian reminded herself.

"Yeah, he probably would. Get in trouble, I mean. The boss's son was involved." Daniel ran a hand through his hair, agitated. "She was blackballed by the entire advertising community. She couldn't even get freelance gigs."

Lilian leaned forward as his words sunk in. Why had Rosie lied to her, making it seem like she had her dream job? "What happened?"

"It was before we met, so I don't know all the details. Just that she was being harassed by her manager, Trevor Callahan. Inappropriate touching, disgusting jokes. Eventually he pressured her into having sex. She went to HR, but his dad's a partner in the company—Baker Kline Callahan, you know." His blue eyes flashed. "Rosie was reprimanded. She refused to back down. They fired her."

Lilian's protective older-sister senses flared. "How did they get away with that? That's got to be illegal." It explained why Rosie hadn't been honest about her job, though. She hadn't wanted Lilian to know she'd been out of work; maybe hadn't wanted to explain the backstory, either.

"She wrote an online article about him, exposing what he'd done. I was proud of her—it wasn't easy for her, going public about it—but then a few weeks ago, cops showed up at our apartment with a restraining order. Apparently Trevor said *she* had been harassing *him*."

Lilian bristled. This Trevor Callahan sounded like an asshole. Enough of an asshole to try and get rid of the problem by causing the car crash? She thought of the man she'd seen in Rosie's hospital room, his lean face and thin scar. Leaning forward, she said, "Do you know what he looks like?"

"I never met him. If I ever do—" His fists clenched, and then he shook his head, the anger fading from his face. "I don't know what I'd do. Probably glare at him *really* hard. But I hate what he did to her." He met Lilian's eyes. "Why all the questions about Trevor?"

Lilian bit her lip, hesitating. Her skin burned at the memory of Caleb holding her shoulders last night, his soothing voice. *Take a deep breath.* The way he'd squeezed her hand three times as he led her up to bed. *I love you.* That should have been reassuring, but his eyes had given him away: *My wife is paranoid.* She couldn't handle anyone else looking at her that way.

"I'm worried he might have had something to do with the accident," she said, hedging.

"Wow." Daniel looked stunned. "Are you serious? Why?"

She reminded him about the man she'd seen in the ICU, conjuring his face in her memory, as she had so many times before.

"What if that was Trevor?" she said. "What if he hit Rosie's car on purpose, then showed up the next morning to check on her?" Maybe out of guilt, she thought. Or to finish the deed.

Daniel sat back, taking that in. "I don't know. Rosie gave me the impression that he's the kind of guy who manipulates people but is too cowardly to actually confront anyone."

Lilian digested that. Even if Trevor wasn't dangerous, he sounded like he was used to getting his way. A man with a reputation to uphold, the son of a founding partner of the company . . . It made her uneasy.

Abigail squirmed on the blanket. "I better get going," Lilian said. "Abigail will need to eat and nap soon."

Daniel picked Abigail up as he stood. "Thanks for coming by, Lilian. I don't have family or even many friends here, so it's been . . ."—he hesitated, shifting his weight—"lonely. These past couple weeks."

She studied him, his ease as he held Abigail, his apartment bursting with signs of his life with Rosie. He'd been at the hospital every day; he'd accepted Lilian's decision to take Rosie home with her, but then he'd jumped at the chance to do so himself when offered. A lesser man might have slunk away, grateful to shake off that responsibility. Rosie had picked a good one this time.

"We're in this together," she said, and she meant it. "I'm glad my sister has you on her side."

* * *

As Lilian exited the elevator into the lobby, pushing Abigail's stroller, she saw the doorman back at his station.

"Hello there, Miss Rosie," he said in a jovial voice. He was a big guy with ruddy cheeks and a name badge that said MARTY. "Haven't seen you in weeks, dear. I love the new haircut. And who is this little one you have with you today?"

"I'm Rosie's sister, Lilian," she said, pausing. "I was visiting Daniel this afternoon. Rosie was in a car accident and has been in the hospital for a while."

Marty's face paled. "I apologize, miss! I had no idea. Daniel's seemed down lately—I guessed maybe they'd broken up, which I thought was too bad. They're a lovely couple. Just lovely. I'm sorry to hear about the car accident. Truly sorry. Will you give her my best wishes for a speedy recovery?"

"I certainly will," Lilian said. "Thanks so much."

As the doorman opened the door for her, he said, "This didn't have anything to do with that guy who was watching her, did it?"

Lilian froze, her heart in her throat. "Wait, what?" She jerked around to face him. "What guy?"

Marty flushed. "Sorry, I may be speaking out of turn. But Miss Rosie asked me a couple times if I'd seen anyone hanging around the building. Said she thought he mighta been watching her."

Lilian's pulse pounded in her ears, and she leaned forward. "Did she mention his name? Or what he looked like?"

"No, I can't say she did." His face scrunched up as he thought. "But this one evenin' a couple weeks ago, she was lookin' around like a scared rabbit, and I asked her if everything was okay. 'No, everything is not okay,' she said. I remember because she said she was meeting her sister for dinner—hey, was that you?"

"It was." Lilian's hands tingled. "Did she say someone was watching her that day?"

She held her breath, wanting to grab Marty by his shoulders and shake him until he spat out the information.

"No," he said. He tapped the side of his head. "But I got that sense, you know."

Lilian released a lungful of air.

A sense. Not exactly proof, but something—or someone—had frightened her sister that night.

CHAPTER
FIFTEEN

MyPsychJournal.com

Welcome back, Rosie. Happy journaling!

JANUARY 18, 2018

I had my second appointment with Dr. V yesterday. This isn't going to be easy, that's for damn sure. It shouldn't be hard to sit in a quiet room and talk for an hour, but it feels like she unzipped my torso from navel to throat and rummaged around inside my organs. Everything hurts.

Before I left, Dr. V asked me what I'm hoping to get out of our sessions. I thought for a minute, and then I told her that I wanted to learn how to form healthy and lasting relationships. I want to be close to someone, more than anything, but I don't know how to do that without hurting myself or the person I love.

Dr. V nodded, her black eyes glinting. That is a Very Important Goal, she said in that capital-letter voice of hers.

So. My homework assignment this week is to write about how my childhood affected my ability to form healthy relationships as an adult.

Or my inability, I guess. I told Dr. V that my childhood was great, that it has nothing to do with my issues, and it's true. My childhood was fine. My teenage years, though, were total shit. By the time I hit thirteen, I was engaging in "risky and reckless behavior," as my school counselor used to say. I explained to Dr. V that the problems started around that time, so that's where we should focus, but she still wanted me to go back even further. To where that sled started, I guess.

Write about your Earliest Memories, she said. Write the sights, sounds, and emotions of the Touchstone Moments of your first decade of life. (So cliché, right? Honestly, Dr. V, I'm a little disappointed.) But I've committed to this process. So here I go:

Three years old, walking down the sidewalk on a sweltering summer day. Bare feet scorching on the hot cement, heat shimmering in the air. My ankle hurts from a bee sting—I remember the prick, then the pain, the burning—and I'm crying. My sister is walking next to me, holding my hand, telling me I'm so, so brave. Her hand feels warm and capable. We're going to have a Popsicle when we get home. I think to myself, someday my hand will be that big.

Five years old, first day of kindergarten. I have a new lunchbox and I'm wearing a pink jumper and black Mary Janes. I pose on the front porch, one hand on my hip, for a picture. Then we're off, me and my sister, and I'm skipping down the sidewalk and swinging my lunchbox and crunching the early fall leaves under my feet.

Eight years old. It's dark outside, snowing. I'm in the bedroom I share with my sister, and we've made a fort out of sheets and blankets. She's strung Christmas lights around the room, too, and it's cozy and magical inside. We're listening to a CD—*August and Everything After*, Counting Crows; she knows all the words to every song—and I'm drawing a picture of a horse. I color the horse's mane and tail in rainbow stripes, careful to stay inside the lines.

There you go, Dr. V. Analyze that.

CHAPTER
SIXTEEN

Lilian had a plan: today she would go straight to the source and confront Trevor Callahan at BKC. It wasn't going to be easy. Her hands shook, thinking about showing up at his office, unannounced, prepared to lie through her teeth to finagle a meeting with him.

But before she did that, she'd make a stop to see Rosie. Earlier that morning, her sister had been moved to a step-down unit, in preparation for her transfer to the rehab hospital. She was medically stable, which was great news, and able to stay awake for a few hours at a time. She wasn't able to talk or follow directions yet, but Lilian hoped that would happen soon.

This floor had a vastly different feel from the ICU. Nurses chatting at the station and in the halls, visitors milling about, patients sitting in wheelchairs in the halls or watching TV in their rooms. After the purgatory of the ICU, the noise and movement seemed almost chaotic. But there was *life* here, and seeing it, Lilian's anxiety receded by a fraction. No matter what happened with Trevor Callahan, she felt better knowing that her baby sister was progressing.

As she made the turn into Rosie's new room, Lilian expected to see her sister lying motionless in bed, like usual. But as she entered the doorway, she stiffened. Rosie was in restraints—soft, padded cuffs circling her wrists, attached to the bed rails, that only allowed her to move her hands a few inches.

The restraints didn't seem to be bothering Rosie—she was gazing out the window, her face turned away from Lilian—but they bothered Lilian. There was something inhumane about tying a patient down, even though she knew, in her doctor-brain, that restraints could be a safe and effective option when a patient was agitated.

But Rosie had never shown a hint of agitation before, and she certainly didn't look agitated now. Lilian approached, and Rosie's head turned. In a split second, Rosie's expression changed from serene to terrified.

Her eyes flashed with fear, and she jerked away from Lilian, twisting her wrists like she was trying to escape the restraints.

"It's okay," Lilian said, trying to sound soothing. "It's all right, Rosie."

Rosie squeezed her eyes shut and shook her head, back and forth, over and over again, her face twisted with fear. Her feet scrambled across the sheets as if she wanted to run away. She looked terrified and uncomfortable, and all Lilian wanted to do was make her feel better, to take this all away from her. Panicking, her heart pounding, she spun on her heels, wanting to speak with whoever had ordered this.

A nurse walked in, took in the situation. She sighed, "Here we go again."

"Why is she restrained?" Lilian demanded.

The nurse glanced at her with a weary expression. "Rosie has been yanking at her tubes and lines all day. She pulled out an IV earlier and nearly got her catheter out. She was quite the agitated little lady."

The nurse turned her back to Lilian as she walked over to Rosie's bed and checked the bag of urine hanging from the side. Lilian took a breath; she knew the importance of keeping the nurses on your side, but she also wanted them to see her sister was a human being, not just another task on the list.

"Thank you for taking care of her," Lilian said. "Looks like the restraints may be making things worse. Can we get them off?"

"If I take those off, she'll hurt herself, and I have too much to do today to be replacing catheters and NG tubes," the nurse said. "I can give her something to calm her down, though."

Before Lilian could protest or even ask what medication she was giving, the nurse pushed a syringe full of liquid into Rosie's IV, then turned and left.

Lilian shook her head, frustrated. This nurse was probably overworked—this wasn't the ICU; the nurses here had a whole roster of patients—but no one had contacted her about the restraints, or the agitation, or the new drug. She made a mental note to speak with the physician in charge.

As Lilian walked over to Rosie's bedside, the medication had already started taking effect. Rosie continued to twist her wrists against the restraints, but her movements slowed, and her legs relaxed.

Lilian shifted her weight, feeling unsettled. For the first time since the accident, Rosie looked like a stranger. Not because of her partially shaved head, or the incision on her scalp, or the fading yellow bruises around her eyes and nose.

No, there was something different today. An unfamiliar, feral look in Rosie's eyes made Lilian shiver. She almost wanted to leave, just to break contact with that uncanny stare.

"How are you doing today?" Lilian tried to keep her voice calm, even though her heart was racing. Somehow this was worse than when Rosie was unresponsive. "I'm sorry, these restraints must be terrible for you."

She settled in a plastic chair next to Rosie's bed, searching her mind for something to talk about, something that might help Rosie relax. Her mind flashed to the reproduction in Rosie's apartment. Renoir's *Two Sisters*. "Their" picture. It had to mean something that Rosie had displayed it in the middle of her living room.

"Remember when we used to go to the Art Institute?" she said, crossing her legs. "You liked the miniature rooms, remember? We'd always go see those first, for you, and we'd see *Two Sisters* last."

As Rosie grew up, she could spend hours at the Institute, scouring obscure galleries full of ancient artifacts or staring at *The Old Guitarist*, searching for the painted-over ghosts of the young Picasso's prior attempts. Even though Lilian never understood the fascination—she preferred the Museum of Science and Industry, or even the Museum of Natural History she loved to watch her sister, bouncing on her toes in excitement, eyes glowing with interest.

"There was this one time we went, when you were maybe six or seven," Lilian said, opening her eyes. Rosie was still staring at her, grimacing. "I gave you a giant lollipop to keep you quiet on the L ride downtown. When we got to the museum, you refused to take it out of your mouth."

She laughed softly, remembering the feeling of Rosie's hand in hers, small and sticky, as they stopped in front of *Two Sisters*. For the first time, Lilian actually studied the painting, tried to take it in. The older girl seemed to be looking into the distance, wishing she could join whatever was happening outside the frame. And yet, her hands were folded sedately in her lap, as if she'd resigned herself to sitting on this bench, by this river, with her basket of fruit and her rosy-cheeked little sister while the summer afternoon rolled on without her.

The older girl's wistful, watchful gaze—keeping her sister close while longing for more—had echoed deep in Lilian's soul. She'd been recently accepted to a summer program for high school students interested in medicine, and the thought of spending the summer learning about anatomy and physiology made her heart sing. The only problem was she wouldn't be able to watch Rosie. Surely, she had told herself, her parents would understand that this was a huge opportunity. She deserved to focus on herself, on her future, for a few weeks, didn't she?

But the next night, just as she'd opened her mouth to ask, her dad had put his hand on her shoulder and said, "Mom's having a hard time again, Lil. We're gonna need you to be extra helpful for the summer, okay?"

And so she'd swallowed it down: the yearning, the hope that she could have something of her own. She knew it would be months before her mom felt better, and even then, nothing would change, not really. Rosie's small, sticky hand would always be clamped inside her own.

"We had the best time that summer," Lilian said to Rosie, her eyes blurred with tears. "Remember? We'd go to the library and the pool every week. You practically wallpapered our room with your drawings."

That was true, but there had also been endless afternoons in their hot, stuffy house. Rosie, bored and irritable, would whine and throw tantrums. Lilian, exhausted from keeping her sister occupied, would shout at her to cut it out. In a few intense moments, she'd even slapped Rosie. Lilian remembered the wave of guilt that would follow, how she'd hug her tear-streaked sister and promise that it would never happen again. *She's just a little girl,* Lilian would berate herself, *You need to be in charge.* The guilt would follow her for days. Weeks, even.

Rosie seemed even more relaxed now, almost too relaxed. Her hands hung, slack, from the bed rails, and her knees fell apart under her sheet. She stared at Lilian, open-mouthed, and Lilian wondered what was going on in her sister's mind. How much had she understood? How much did she remember?

Rosie's brow winkled. Her lips twitched. And then she said one word: "You."

"Me," Lilian said, smiling. She started to tear up again, but this time with hope, gratitude. *She knows me*, Lilian thought. *She's coming back to me.*

Rosie shook her head, her mouth tightening. Lilian leaned closer, holding her breath in anticipation, and Rosie looked her straight in the eyes.

Carefully, distinctly, Rosie said two words.

"Get out."

* * *

Hands shaking, Lilian called Daniel. "Have you seen Rosie today?" she asked as soon as he answered. She'd left Rosie's room in a rush. She couldn't stop replaying her sister's words. *Get out.* Her ribs felt like they were fracturing.

"No, I couldn't come by this morning. Had to go to the office. Is everything all right?"

Lilian had made it as far as the lobby near the elevators. She stopped and took a breath. Outside the window, a bank of low clouds swallowed the tops of the tallest buildings.

Was Rosie remembering their last argument, two years ago? Lilian had said those exact words to Rosie. Had their relationship, in Rosie's injured brain, been reduced to that single conversation?

"She's been moved to a step-down unit, which is good," Lilian said, trying to keep her voice steady. "And she spoke to me."

"What did she say?" Daniel asked.

Lilian coughed, hesitating. There was no reason she couldn't tell Daniel, but shame burned her cheeks. Her own sister had ordered her to leave. *Get out.*

"She said, 'You,'" Lilian said awkwardly. It was true—albeit not the entire truth. "I know it's not much, but it felt like a big deal."

"Absolutely," Daniel said. "I'm on my way—I'll be there in an hour."

As she hung up the phone, Lilian took a steadying breath. When Rosie saw Daniel, what would she say? Would she welcome *him*?

* * *

When they entered Rosie's room, she wasn't alone anymore. Dr. Melissa Rao, the brain injury fellow, was standing by her bed. "Oh, hi," she said, glancing up. "Just came to check on Rosie. I'm not happy about these restraints. They're only going to make things worse."

"That's what I thought—" Lilian started.

A high-pitched shriek interrupted her. It was Rosie, staring at Lilian with fear-widened eyes. Her feet scrambled against the sheets as she pulled herself to the far corner of her bed.

Lilian raised her hands in what she hoped was a calming gesture. "It's okay, sis. I brought Daniel—"

Another shriek from Rosie echoed through the room. "Go 'way," she whimpered.

Lilian looked at Daniel, whose face had gone white, and then at Dr. Rao. "Am I doing something wrong?"

"Of course not," Dr. Rao said. "Agitation and confusion are common after a brain injury. I think we should step outside the room, though. Let Rosie calm down."

Lilian nodded, and she and Daniel followed Dr. Rao out.

In the hallway, Lilian folded her arms tightly across her chest, holding herself together. Rosie's response had rattled her to her core. "I've read about agitation," she said to Dr. Rao, "but this seems extreme."

Dr. Rao waved a hand and gave her a reassuring smile. "Oh, no. Believe me, I've seen much worse. It's actually a good sign. Rosie's at a Rancho 4 right now, which is a great time to bring her to rehab."

"Rancho what?" Daniel asked. His voice cracked on the last word— the first time he'd spoken since walking into Rosie's room. He seemed shaken to the core.

"It's a scale we use for cognitive functioning after traumatic brain injury," Dr. Rao explained. "Rosie has progressed from a Rancho 3—inconsistently responding to stimuli—to a level 4, which is characterized by confusion and agitation. I know it's upsetting for loved ones. But it will improve, I promise. For now, the best thing we can do is create a calm, soothing environment. Lights off, low voices, limited visitors. I'm sure Rosie was just overstimulated."

Lilian took a deep breath. She felt out of her depth here, relying on a fellow to give her medical information. She was supposed to be the one in charge, the one dispensing knowledge to eager trainees. None of her experience in pediatrics had prepared her for this.

"I should go, anyway," she said, glancing at Daniel. Her next task loomed: meeting Trevor Callahan face-to-face. She'd decided not to tell Daniel her plans. He had enough on his plate, worrying about Rosie. "You can visit without me."

"Okay," Daniel said, though his eyebrows knit together in the worried expression she was now all too familiar with.

"Plan on Rosie coming to rehab tomorrow," Dr. Rao said. "She's going to do awesome!"

Dr. Rao excused herself, and Lilian headed down the hall. The image of her sister's terrified face flashed through her mind. *Get out.* Yes, it might have been the agitation talking. Rosie might have been overstimulated. But she hadn't screamed at anyone else to leave.

Rosie's response had felt specific to her. Personal.

CHAPTER
SEVENTEEN

Lilian pulled her scarf tighter against the icy wind as she hurried down the busy sidewalk. Her destination rose ahead: the building that housed the offices of Baker Kline Callahan. It wasn't called the Hancock building anymore, she reminded herself, but she would always think of it that way, with its distinctive lattice exterior tapering up to the iron sky above.

Inside the lobby, a few tourists took selfies in front of a massive sphere-shaped sculpture made of thousands of tiny lights. Opposite that was a check-in desk, where a woman with short platinum hair sat.

Lilian headed in that direction, hefting the cardboard box she'd grabbed from her car. This was part of her plan, which now felt silly and juvenile.

There's no way this is going to work, she thought.

Still, she smiled at the receptionist and did her best. "I have a delivery for Trevor Callahan at BKC. I need to give it directly to him, no one else."

The receptionist gave her a quick up-and-down glance. Lilian had tried to look professional; she had on a pencil skirt, suit jacket, and heels. She'd even put on lipstick.

She held her breath as the receptionist turned to her computer and picked up the phone. This was where things could easily go south. If Trevor Callahan wasn't in the office, if he was occupied in a meeting, or if he sent down an assistant, Lilian would be stuck. But luck was on her side. The receptionist spoke into the phone, then smiled at Lilian.

"He'll be right down. You can wait there," she said, motioning to the middle of the three elevator banks.

Lilian thanked her. Once in place, she balanced the box against her hip and tried not to look nervous. She was standing on tiptoe, watching the elevator doors open and close, when someone stepped in front of her.

"You have a delivery for me?"

Lilian took a step back. All her breath left her in a rush.

"You're Trevor Callahan?" she said, oddly disappointed. He was Lilian's height, with small blue eyes, ginger hair, and a face full of freckles. It would have been so easy, so *clean*, if he'd been the man she'd seen in Rosie's hospital room that night. The man with the scar on his face and a cold look in his eyes.

Still, she reminded herself, he might have information.

"Yes," he said, holding out his hands. "Can I sign for the delivery? I was in the middle of something."

Lilian held the box against her body. "I need to talk to you. My name is Lilian Donaldson," she said. "I'm Rosie's sister."

His eyes sparked with sudden recognition. Gripping Lilian's arm, he pulled her roughly toward a wall. "You need to leave. I should call security right now."

A flash of hot rage made Lilian's cheeks flush. "Is that what you did to my sister? Throw her out of the building? Silence her so you wouldn't lose your job?"

"*Silence* her?" Trevor said, leaning in close enough that Lilian could smell his stale coffee breath. "Clearly, you don't know anything about what happened."

"I know that you harassed her, and when she went to HR, you had her fired. Not only that, you made sure she would never get another advertising job in this city." Her raised voice attracted glances from a few passersby. Let them stare, she thought. He deserved it.

He rocked back on his heels. "Is that what she told you? I mean, I knew she wasn't exactly an honest person but, man, that is really something." He jabbed a finger at Lilian. "No, you know what? This is not on me. She didn't get fired, she quit. And if she can't get another job it's her own fault—she skewered BKC in that article she wrote. It went viral! A goddamn PR nightmare. Of course no one wants to hire her."

"So you took out a restraining order against her?" Lilian said, making a mental note to look up the article later. Daniel hadn't mentioned that it had gone viral. "Just because she made you look bad?"

He scoffed. "That's not why I got a restraining order. She wouldn't stop pestering me about a second article—"

"What do you mean, a second article?" Lilian shook her head, confused.

"I don't know—that bitchy website wanted more from her." He waved a hand, like he was shooing away a bug. "She kept showing up here, waiting for me when I left work, hanging around my apartment. *That* was harassment—she said if I thought the first article was bad, the next one was going to ruin my fucking life."

His last words echoed in the lobby; every head turned in their direction. Trevor's cheeks reddened, and he took a step back, breathing heavily.

Lilian lowered her voice. "When was the last time you saw my sister?"

"A few weeks ago," Trevor said, sounding like a sullen kid. "Before I filed the restraining order."

"Where were you on the night of January eleventh?"

At that, he blinked. "What? I have no idea."

Lilian took a step forward, wanting to drag the information out of him. "The night of Friday, January eleventh. Where were you?"

Trevor gave her a long stare, his face unreadable. "We're done," he said, stepping back. "And if you show up here again, I'll call the police."

CHAPTER
EIGHTEEN

MyPsychJournal.com

Welcome back, Rosie. Happy journaling!

JANUARY 24, 2018

Today's session with Dr. V didn't go so well. She'd read my journal entries before I showed up, those "touchstone moments," and when I sat down, she steepled her fingers and stared at me with her gleaming, black, birdlike eyes.

You are Not Being Honest, she said in that capital-letter voice. She looked like a fussy principal staring at me across her big oak desk, threatening to send me home if I didn't tell her the truth.

That bugged me, and I started to protest, but she interrupted me.

It is absolutely crucial that you are Honest In This Journal, she said. No one else is reading it but the two of us. If you're not honest with yourself, about what really happened, then none of this is going to work.

I was seriously pissed off. She was dead wrong, and how dare she imply that I was making it all up? What did she expect? Some deep, dark, disgusting secret that would explain why I'm so messed up?

I stood—ready to storm out of there, I was that angry—when she stopped me.

Do you know what a memory is? Dr. V asked.

Her voice, so quiet and serious, made me pause.

She said lots of people think memories are like photographs or videos filed away in our brain, an exact reproduction of the event, but that's not true at all.

A memory is a Story We Tell Ourselves, she said. It's not *what* happened, it's how we *feel* about what happened.

That made sense to me, and I sat back down.

Then she said something that hit me like a stun gun. I'm going to try to write it exactly as she said it, so I won't forget:

Sometimes memories are so painful that our brain chooses to remember them differently. Instead of fear or sadness or shame, our brain tells a different story. Then, over time, that story becomes more real than the actual events. Remembering is actually *re-remembering*. Recalling the last time you brought back that memory. Each time, a new track is laid down. Like the sled in the snow.

My homework this week is to write about what really happened during those touchstone moments. Interrogate Your Memories, she said. Find the Story Behind the Story.

So here I am, interrogating. I'm thinking about being three years old, with a bee sting on my ankle, hobbling down the sidewalk to our house. Five years old, on the first day of kindergarten. Eight years old, in the blanket fort in our bedroom with fairy lights twinkling and Counting Crows playing. I don't know why I didn't see it before, but all those memories are with my sister. Were my parents even around?

The bee sting: I remember my mom opening the front door as Lilian carried me inside. Mom held her arms out to me; I wouldn't go to her. I squeezed my sister tighter.

First day of kindergarten: My parents must have already been at work. Lilian walked me to school and all the way into the classroom.

She would have been a sophomore in high school; she must have been late that day.

In the blanket fort: I remember raised voices echoing from the kitchen; a crash like glass breaking; Mom crying. I remember Lilian turning up the volume on the music as I colored my rainbow horse.

So that's the Story Behind the Story, Dr. V. I'm guessing that's what you were getting at. Lilian was my constant, my safety net, my buffer against my parents' fucked-up relationship. When I think back to my early childhood, everything involves Lilian. She's braiding my hair, helping me with my multiplication tables, putting me in time out, reading me a Dr. Seuss book for the sixth time in a row. She disciplined me, comforted me, praised and supported me.

Then, when I was twelve years old, she left me. I don't think I can ever forgive her for that. She just left me there. Entirely alone.

CHAPTER
NINETEEN

Lilian arrived home to utter chaos—Abigail crying in Nancy's arms, refusing to take a bottle, exhausted from missing her nap. After feeding her and putting her to bed, Lilian finally had a chance to digest her confrontation with Trevor Callahan. She'd assumed, when Daniel said Rosie had written an "online article," that she'd put it on a blog or something similar. But a *viral* article? Lilian needed to read it.

Pulling out her phone, she googled Rosie's name. There it was: "A Man's Guide to Getting What You Want—and Getting Away with It," by Rosie Donaldson, published on a website called Lilith.com.

Lilian's vision blurred and she turned the brightness on her phone all the way down. Rosie had organized the article as a set of "tips and tricks" to her hypothetical male reader.

Step One: Be a powerful man. You'll need money, influence, or fame—better yet, all three.

Step Two: Identify someone who looks up to you, someone whose future you hold in your hands.

Step Three: Make your target believe they are special.

Step Four: Slowly push the boundaries of appropriate physical touch.

Rosie went on to describe not the incident with Trevor Callahan, but her affair as a freshman in college with her professor. Lilian knew much of the story already; she'd been appalled when Rosie had told her about it, a couple months in. She remembered telling Rosie she needed to end things right away, that she had no business getting involved with a professor in his forties, and definitely not one who was married.

Now, reading Rosie's words, she saw the experience from a different angle. The professor had clearly groomed Rosie, used her, and discarded her; he'd manipulated her into keeping the whole thing quiet, too.

That's Step Five, by the way, tell your target that the relationship is too precious to be public knowledge. No one will understand what we have, you'll say. But it wasn't until something similar happened, years later, that I recognized this pattern.

After that, Rosie described what had happened with Trevor Callahan. She didn't use his name, but she did say he worked at a large advertising agency in Chicago. This part was more along the lines of what Daniel had told Lilian. Rosie had just been promoted to her dream position as a graphic designer, after working her way up from an entry-level role as a junior production artist. She was thrilled that her manager, the son of one of the founding partners, thought she had talent. But one evening when they both stayed late to work on a project, his attention turned sexual. She described how he touched her, how he flirted and laughed, and, when she tried to move away, said, "I thought you wanted to take the lead on this project, Rosie. I was hoping to put in a good word to my dad about you. Unless that's not what you want?"

I was sick to my stomach, I didn't know what to do. I've read
about women freezing up during a sexual assault, but I didn't
think it would actually happen to me.

Lilian's own stomach turned as she read about Trevor Callahan
unbuttoning his pants, sliding Rosie's skirt up to her waist, and—

She stopped, too sickened to go on, and ashamed of the way she'd
reacted to Rosie's college experience. If she'd really listened to her sister,
if she'd tried to understand what had happened, could she have spared
Rosie the trauma of repeating her abuse?

After taking a few deep breaths, she skimmed ahead to Rosie describing the humiliation of going to Human Resources and being shut down.

Step Six: Make your target appear unbelievable and unstable
if they speak out about what happened.

Rosie wrote about how she felt forced to quit; soon after, she discovered she'd been blackballed.

Here's the kicker, powerful men excel at identifying wom-
en who are damaged in some way. When you've been hurt
enough times, you start to believe that *you* are the problem.
And that you deserve it.

She then described a man she'd dated before she started working at
that agency, and how the toxic nature of that relationship damaged her
confidence, isolating her from friends and family and wearing down
her self-esteem until she believed he was the only person in the world
who loved her.

That description could have applied to any number of Rosie's boyfriends, Lilian thought, until she reached the next part.

It wasn't until after my parents passed away and he tried
to prevent me from going to their funeral that I recognized

what he'd done to me. I left him three weeks later, and I still believe it was the bravest choice I've ever made. I had no friends anymore, and my only living family member, my sister, wanted nothing to do with me. I had nowhere to go, so I stayed in women's shelters until a social worker helped me land an apartment and a job. I worked my way up through the ranks of the company, proud of what I'd accomplished. But then I met my new manager at the ad agency, and the cycle started again.

Nauseated, Lilian set the phone down. Once again, she'd blamed her sister instead of the real perpetrator. If only Rosie had *told* her—but no, Lilian shouldn't have lost her temper. She shouldn't have let Rosie walk out of her office.

Why hadn't she chased her down? She should have thrown her arms around her little sister and promised that she would take care of her, no matter what.

Squeezing her eyes shut, Lilian kissed Abigail's downy head. The scent of her skin transported Lilian back to a time when her sister had been this tiny, this helpless. The voices of their parents echoed in her mind, heavy with disappointment: *It's your job to keep your sister safe, Lilian.* She'd failed in the worst way possible. She so easily could have helped Rosie. She would have been glad to.

But Rosie had asked for money, not help, Lilian reminded herself. Maybe because she didn't feel she could trust Lilian with the truth. If Lilian had been less judgmental, less quick to find fault, would Rosie have felt comfortable confiding in her?

Lilian read on, her eyes burning with tears.

I refuse to remain silent this time. Why should I, the victim, be the only one to bear the consequences? These "relationships" are like fungi—they flourish in dark, hidden, quiet spaces. So I decided to shine a light. And I decided to get really fucking loud.

And Rosie had been heard; another Google search confirmed what Trevor had said: the article had gone viral, all over Twitter and Facebook. Multiple articles had been written in response, some of them dismissing or deriding Rosie, others lauding her bravery. Even though Rosie hadn't mentioned the name of the professor, someone on Twitter had figured it out and shared it, Niall Lawrence. Ditto Trevor Callahan. The ex-boyfriend's identity was still a mystery, though.

Nearly two dozen former students of the professor had come forward to state that they'd had the same experience. It even came out that the school administration had buried a rape accusation, years ago, from another student. The school couldn't ignore the public pressure, and the professor had been forced to resign. His wife had left him.

Lilian found an article about this and scanned it until she found the professor's response.

> I may have engaged in a few consensual relationships with students over the years, but I didn't force anyone. I'm not a rapist. Rosie Donaldson twisted what happened and used it to get her fifteen minutes of fame. She gets applauded, and I lose everything. She ruined my life. That is the real crime here.

Lilian shook her head, anger rising inside her. The classic protestations of a good old boy who'd finally gotten his comeuppance. As horrified as she was about the experiences her sister had had, she was proud of Rosie for coming forward. For being brave and speaking out.

Then something else occurred to her, and a slow shiver worked its way down her spine.

The article spotlighted three men. Trevor Callahan, who'd been terrified of Rosie writing another article detailing his inappropriate behavior; Professor Lawrence, who'd lost his career and his marriage. And the unknown ex-boyfriend.

Rosie's article had been published in November of last year and had gone viral over the next few weeks. The car accident had happened the second week in January. Trevor had taken out a restraining order against

Rosie just a few weeks before that, Daniel had said. Professor Lawrence had resigned at the end of December.

And the ex-boyfriend? Rosie's article might have shown him how to find her again. It had included a picture of Rosie sitting on the front steps of her apartment building. He could have tracked her down.

Her sister's past was still hazy, still filled with questions, but these three men stood out crystal clear. Lilian closed her eyes as a wave of emotion rolled over her, anger and love and guilt. She rocked Abigail and listened to her baby breathing, in and out, felt the rhythm of her heartbeat, like a butterfly caught in her tiny chest. She almost felt like she was back in her childhood bedroom, memory after memory layered against this moment. She was ten years old and holding her newborn sister, she was fourteen and tucking Rosie into bed, she was eighteen and comforting her after a nightmare. All those past versions of herself seemed to whisper the same words: *Don't worry, sis. I'm going to take care of you.*

This article had brought her one giant step closer to doing just that.

CHAPTER
TWENTY

By the next morning, Lilian had hit a dead end. She'd found a picture online of Niall Lawrence, Rosie's professor. He was a broad-shouldered, fiftysomething man with deep blue eyes, a classically handsome face, and wavy salt-and-pepper hair. Not the man Lilian had seen in Rosie's room, though she supposed he could have hired someone to watch Rosie, maybe even to follow her.

The idea of a hired hit man seemed absurd, but she had to consider it. Trevor Callahan could have done the same thing. He had a wealthy, influential father who might have wanted the whole mess with Rosie to go away. Carlson Callahan, Trevor's dad, was easy to find online; he looked like an older, rounder version of Trevor. He clearly had massive influence in the advertising community—Lilian found pictures of him at charity galas, various product launches, and even on the red carpet at premieres of films for which his company had done the advertising.

But Lilian didn't know much about the ex-boyfriend. She vaguely recalled that his first name was Michael, but she couldn't remember his last name—if she'd ever known it. She'd never met him. But maybe Rosie had posted about him on Instagram, back when they were dating? A twinge of guilt reminded Lilian that she hadn't even looked at her own sister's Instagram in years.

When she pulled Rosie's account up on her phone, the pictures took her breath away. Rosie at Grant Park in the summertime with a group of friends, Rosie on a cruise ship in a short, silver dress, Rosie sitting on a beach in some tropical place. But for the past two years, she had rarely posted.

Lilian continued scrolling back in time, to the months before their parents' death. Rosie had posted more then, but they were mostly pictures of either herself alone, or—even further back—with friends. Maybe she'd deleted the pictures of Michael after they broke up?

But then, she saw something that made her heart stutter in her chest.

It was a picture of Rosie in a dark restaurant, sitting next to a man, his arm around her shoulders. The caption:

Happy birthday to @mikeylikesit So glad I could spend it with you, babe.

Their faces were mostly in shadow, catching the light of the candles on the table, and Lilian zoomed in on his.

He wasn't the man she'd seen in the ICU, that was clear right away. This man was startlingly handsome—light blond hair, chiseled jaw— and he knew it too, based on his cocky expression. He looked like a man used to getting what he wanted. He had bright, almost turquoise blue eyes; Rosie always had a thing for men with blue eyes. Lilian thought back to the picture of Professor Lawrence. He had blue eyes. So did Trevor Callahan, and Daniel, for that matter. Their dad's eyes had been blue, too, Lilian reminded herself.

What about the man with the scar? Did he have blue eyes? She hadn't seen him long enough to be sure.

She clicked on his handle, which led her to a private account with the name Michael Sorenson and the navy and orange C from the Chicago Bears' logo as his profile picture.

"I have his full name," she said to herself, her heart pounding with excitement. "That could be helpful . . ." But, she realized with a sinking feeling, if he wasn't the man she'd seen in Rosie's room, why would the police investigate him? Yes, it sounded like he had been controlling in the past, but she had no evidence that he'd had any recent contact with Rosie.

Unfortunately, Rosie's phone was still dead, which meant her contacts were inaccessible. But Lilian did have a phone number for Rosie's college roommate, Brynne. She and Rosie had stayed close after college, too, as far as Lilian knew. Worth a shot.

After putting her cranky baby down for a nap, Lilian sat cross-legged on her bed and called Brynne, hoping she hadn't changed her phone number in the past few years.

"Hello?"

"Hi, Brynne," Lilian said. "This is Lilian. Lilian Donaldson. Rosie's older sister?"

"Lil! How are you? It's been forever." Brynne's voice—chipper and friendly—brought back the memory of her face: dark curly hair, freckles, a generous smile.

"I'm fine, thanks. But listen—I need to talk to you about Rosie. She was in a car accident two weeks ago."

Brynne gasped. "Oh my God. Is she all right?"

"Not exactly. She was pretty badly injured."

"I'm so sorry." Brynne sounded horrified. "What happened? How is she doing?"

Lilian explained about the accident and Rosie's condition. When she finished, she said, "When's the last time you heard from Rosie?"

"Oh, it's been a while," she said. "A couple years."

That was disappointing; Brynne wouldn't be much help for more recent information. Still, Lilian had a question for her. "What happened? You two were so close."

"Oh, she drifted away when she started dating some guy a couple years ago, I can't remember his name. She basically disappeared off the face of the earth."

The controlling ex-boyfriend, Lilian thought. "Was he named Michael?"

"Yeah, that sounds right," Brynne said. Then her voice lost its warmth. "I only met him once. We went out to dinner together—me and my boyfriend with Rosie and Michael. I didn't like him. Or how he treated her."

The hairs on the back of Lilian's neck stood up. "How so?"

"Like, I remember that Rosie wanted to order fish, but Michael said he hated the smell, so she changed her order to chicken. And then she wanted another glass of wine but he told her she'd had enough."

"Go on," Lilian said, her heart dropping.

"It was the way he did it that caught my attention," Brynne said. "Rosie would say something in this tentative voice, then look at him to see if it was okay. Michael would frown and shake his head, and Rosie would change her mind. It was weird, because Rosie was never like that. She always had this big personality, right? But around him she became so . . . so timid, and I hated watching her change for him."

"I can imagine." Lilian had trouble picturing her bright, sarcastic, colorful sister as this careful, submissive creature.

"I remember the thing that really bothered me, though. It was our waiter—he was flirting with both of us, me and Rosie, but waiters do that, right? My boyfriend didn't care, but Michael got upset. He started yelling at the waiter, telling him to stop gawking at Rosie. It was scary, actually."

"What did Rosie do?"

"Oh, she tried to placate him. And then Michael grabbed Rosie's arm—hard enough that she winced. I was worried about letting her leave with him, to be honest. But she wouldn't listen to me."

Lilian closed her eyes, imagining a handprint-shaped bruise on her sister's arm. She wondered if Michael had apologized the next day, had promised it would never happen again, had begged Rosie to forgive him. She'd never been impressed with any of Rosie's boyfriends, but none of them had been this bad.

Or maybe they had, and Rosie hadn't told her because she didn't think Lilian would listen.

Swallowing down a pang of guilt, Lilian said, "She broke up with him two years ago, right?"

"Yes, the first time."

"Wait, what?" Lilian said, remembering Rosie's article. She'd written about breaking up with Michael a few weeks after their parents' death. "The first time of what? Are you saying they got back together?"

"They broke up not long after your parents passed away, but she was back together with him just a few weeks later. I didn't hear from her again until they broke up for good, a couple months after that. At least, I think it was for good. We haven't been close since then."

Lilian caught an edge of hurt in Brynne's voice. She couldn't blame her. Lilian knew how it felt to be shut out of Rosie's life. It would make anyone reluctant to give her another chance.

But Lilian wasn't just a friend—she was Rosie's *sister*. She should have done whatever it took to keep her close.

"Do you remember when she broke up with him, that last time?" Lilian asked.

"About a year ago, I think?"

Lilian bit her lip. A few months after that, according to Rosie's day planner, she'd started going to the gun range on a regular basis. Maybe a coincidence. Maybe not. But it gave Lilian a bad feeling, wondering if her sister had felt the need to protect herself—from Michael, or from someone else.

"This might sound like a strange question," Lilian said, "but do you have any idea if Rosie knew a man with a scar on his face? A long, thin one along his cheek. Maybe another ex-boyfriend?"

"What? No. I've definitely never seen her with someone like that." Brynne paused. "What's going on, Lilian?"

Lilian took a deep breath. She didn't want to get into everything with Brynne, but she had to give her some explanation. "Before the car crash, Rosie was worried about someone watching her—her doorman said she'd asked him to keep an eye out—"

Her phone beeped, and she pulled it away to look at it. Caleb was calling. "Brynne, my husband is calling. I need to go," she said, grateful for an excuse to end the conversation. "But I really appreciate the help."

"Of course. Keep me posted on how Rosie is doing, okay?"

"Will do." After hanging up, Lilian transferred to Caleb's call. "I need to talk to you about Rosie," she said in a rush.

"That's why I'm calling," Caleb said. "She talked to me today!"

She nearly dropped the phone. "Rosie? My sister, Rosie?"

"Who else?" he said, laughing. "I stopped by her new room in rehab, and she was sitting up in bed, working with the speech therapist. She looked right at me and said 'Hi, Caleb.' I about fell over. Then she gave me shit about the Sox beating the Cubs in the Crosstown Classic."

"That's amazing," Lilian said, relief washing away the tension she'd felt only moments earlier.

"It was just fragments of sentences, but still incredible, right?" Caleb said. "Listen, I know you'll want to come see her, so I already called my mom to see if she can watch Abigail. She'll be there at noon."

"Thanks," she said, touched by the gesture. "Maybe we can get lunch afterward?"

He hesitated, and Lilian imagined him checking his schedule. He seemed to be even busier than usual lately.

"I have a short break around one o'clock," he said eventually.

"Great, see you then!" she said, and ended the call.

They used to meet for lunch every week, back when Lilian was working. They'd swap stories about their patients, complaining about hospital administrators or the unwieldy electronic medical record system. A few times, they'd even locked Caleb's door and had breathless, hurried sex that left them with a smile on their faces for the rest of the day.

Today's lunch wouldn't be anything like that. But they would have something to celebrate. If Rosie had started to communicate, she might be able to explain what had happened before the crash—although, Lilian reminded herself, Rosie's memories of that night would likely be even more jumbled than her own.

At the very least, she could shed some light on the questions circling Lilian's mind. Who had been hanging around her building? What was this life-or-death matter?

Soon, Lilian would have answers.

CHAPTER
TWENTY-ONE

MyPsychJournal.com

Welcome back, Rosie. Happy journaling!

JANUARY 31, 2018

Dr. V didn't talk much about my journal entry at our last appointment. I asked her what she thought about it—the story behind the story— and she asked me what *I* thought about it. Typical shrink move.

I told her it made sense to me, how a happy, sweet little girl could turn into an angry, self-destructive teenager: because of deep feelings of abandonment. Then I told her about my teenage years, which were basically a lot of alcohol and drugs and sex. Dr. V listened. I cried, which I haven't done in a while. Crying usually leaves me feeling embarrassed and disgusted, but not this time. I felt raw, but clean.

Side note: I've been doing some reading about sibling relationships like mine and Lilian's. Lots of juicy stuff there, and I want to talk about it with Dr. V at our next visit (hint, hint, Dr. V). Apparently, when the younger sibling bonds with the older one instead of their parents, it causes all sorts of abandonment issues when the older one moves away (as I know, obviously). And when an older sibling takes on a parent role, they grow up to be compulsive caretakers, high achievers, desperate to be seen as competent and capable.

That explains a lot about Lilian. To be honest, I never thought about what it must have been like for her. And yeah, I recognize how self-centered that is, but I thought she liked taking care of me, liked being in charge—even after she moved out she was always calling, checking on me, offering advice I didn't want.

That was something else I read about: as adults, these siblings have complicated relationships, sometimes intensely close, sometimes distant. That rang true, too. It's been a year since I last saw my sister, and I miss her so much my bones ache. But every time I think about contacting her again, I remember the look on her face when she ordered me out of her office. It was more than disappointment, more than disgust—I could handle both of those; I'm disappointed and disgusted by myself, too.

No, this was betrayal. Like I'd stolen something precious from her. I can't face her until I've figured my shit out.

Anyway. My homework this week from Dr. V is to write about how abandonment affected my relationships as an adult. Because that's the heart of my issues—after Lilian left me, I was desperate for something, or someone, to fill the void.

Pick one relationship, Dr. V said, and Examine It With Clarity.

So here I go:

The first time I walked into my Fundamentals of Design lecture, my first semester of freshman year, I noticed the professor watching all the girls as they walked in. He had these intense blue eyes, and he seemed to be sifting through the girls, then dismissing them. I didn't want to be dismissed. When his eyes met mine, I held his gaze, letting my lips part. His eyes swept over me, getting stuck on my legs and then my chest before returning to my eyes. I knew I had him.

It only took me a few visits to his office hours, pretending to be confused about some concept we'd discussed in class, and soon we were in a full-fledged affair. My roommates and my sister were horri-fied. I remember Lilian saying, "Rosie, he has a wife and family! How can you do this to them?" But I didn't care. I was happy, and of course, now I realize why: I had found someone to fill that void. I feel sick about it now. What does this say about me? That I'm the kind of person who doesn't care who she hurts as long as she gets what she wants.

When the semester drew to a close, Niall said we had to break it off. His wife was getting suspicious. By then I'd learned this was his pat-tern, a new girl each semester. But I didn't want to join the ranks of his discarded lovers. After three days sobbing into my pillow and drinking way too much cheap booze, I made a plan. He could throw me away, but I wouldn't let him forget me.

I had pictures of us together in bed. I cropped my face out—I didn't want to be dragged into an investigation—but it was clear I was a student. I sent copies to the Dean of Students, along with a letter saying that Niall had coerced me into having sex in exchange for a bet-ter grade. That was a lie. He never forced me to do anything—I was the one who initiated our relationship. I just wanted to pay him back for dumping me.

But guess what? Nothing happened to him; the university covered it up. They chose him over me.

And that, my dear Dr. V, didn't help with those feelings of aban-donment.

Looking back, it's easy to see that what came later can be traced to this, my first "adult" relationship: my desperate, frantic need to be loved; the power differential between us; my reaction after he left. Not only the devastation of being abandoned, but my desire to get some sort of revenge. Maybe if I had recognized it at the time—hind-sight being twenty-twenty and all that—I could have prevented myself from repeating the same pattern, just with different men.

Maybe I could have prevented myself from falling into something much more dangerous.

CHAPTER TWENTY-TWO

Lilian's shoes clicked on the linoleum floor as she hurried down the hall to Rosie's room. The brain injury rehab unit was locked down, for the patients' safety, and Lilian had been buzzed in. She passed a therapy gym on her right, full of therapists and patients walking, or going up and down stairs, or working on their balance. A full kitchen was off to one side, where a therapist sat at a table with a young man, encouraging him to stack cups with his weak arm.

Before this, Lilian had never paid much attention to what happened to patients after they left the regular hospital and went to rehab. An entire building focused on helping them reach their maximum potential seemed like a miracle.

She rounded the corner into Rosie's room, hoping to see her sister as Caleb had described: sitting up in bed, awake and alert. Instead, Rosie was curled on her side, the room darkened. A young woman in scrubs sat next to her; the sitter the rehab team had ordered, replacing the restraints that had so agitated Rosie. This was all part of brain injury protocol—a low stimulation environment, lights dimmed, voices down, no television.

"I'm Rosie's sister," Lilian said quietly.

"I'm Dawn," the sitter said. "I recognize you." She nodded at a framed picture on the nightstand, the photograph of Lilian and Rosie together, from Daniel's apartment. He must have brought it from home—a thoughtful gesture.

"How is she doing today?" Lilian asked.

"She was awake earlier, but after speech therapy, she fell asleep. She has PT soon, so it would be good for her to wake up again."

"I don't mind sitting with her if you want to take a break," Lilian said to Dawn.

Dawn smiled. "That would be great. Thanks."

After she left, Lilian came around the side of the bed and sat next to her sister. Someone had shaved the rest of Rosie's hair, and her staples had been removed. Daniel had brought some clothes and shoes from home so she could do therapy. Rosie looked more like a person and less like a patient, even though her short, buzzed hair reminded Lilian of a lead singer in a punk band.

There were no monitors attached to Rosie, no IVs, not even a pulse ox. No Foley catheter, which meant Rosie was going to the bathroom on her own. The NG tube remained in her nose, but hopefully Rosie's ability to eat and drink by mouth would improve and that could come out soon. Progress in a medical setting could be measured by the loss of wires and tubes over time, and this was major progress.

"Hi, sis," Lilian said. She reached out and touched Rosie's hand. "How are you feeling today? Caleb said you looked great."

Rosie stirred but didn't open her eyes. "Sis?" she said in a sleepy voice.

"That's right!" Lilian said, heart leaping. "I can't tell you how good it feels to hear you say that."

Rosie's eyes opened, glittering green in the dim light. When she saw Lilian, her forehead furrowed. "Y-you," she said.

Lilian's smile faltered. Rosie had said the same thing at their last visit, right before telling her to *get out.* "I'm your sister, Lilian."

"No," Rosie said, shaking her head. Her legs, under the sheets, started moving in a restless motion. Her words came out jumbled: "No—not, not Lil—not Lilian."

Lilian knew she needed to back off. Something about her presence had upset Rosie again. When she said, "not Lilian," did that mean she didn't want Lilian there? She wanted someone else to visit her, but not Lilian?

Or maybe she didn't recognize Lilian.

But she had recognized Caleb. Lilian yearned for the same thing, for her sister to smile at her and say *Hi, Lilian.* But their relationship had been fraught for years; in Rosie's mind, they might still be estranged. She might still be angry at Lilian; based on what Brynne had said, she certainly had reason to be. Rosie had ended up back in a toxic relationship because Lilian hadn't helped her.

None of that explained the panicked look in Rosie's eyes, though. She was muttering something under her breath, and Lilian leaned forward, catching a few words: *Look like . . . sister . . . watching me . . . who are you.* Not enough to make sense of anything she was saying.

"It's me—your sister," Lilian said. "I'm here. I've been here practically every day."

Rosie shook her head, the stubble on her scalp rasping against the pillowcase. Her face contorted in a grimace that looked like pain—or maybe fear. She continued mumbling, words spilling out of her, but Lilian couldn't make sense of it.

"What's wrong?" Lilian asked. "Does something hurt?" She reached out a hand to touch Rosie's shoulder.

Rosie slapped her hand away. "Don't!"

Lilian stood in a rush, knocking her chair over. At the sound, Rosie scrambled backward to the far corner of the bed, pulled her knees into her chest, and put her hands over her ears. She stared at Lilian with eyes wide with fear. In an instant, Lilian was in their childhood bedroom, a thunderstorm raging outside, five-year-old Rosie curled in a ball next to her, shaking and terrified. *Lightning is just nature's fireworks, little sis. You're safe.*

Then she blinked and she was back in the hospital, her hand stinging from Rosie's slap.

"I'm sorry," she said, her heart pounding. She felt out of her depth;

Rosie didn't want her here, yet Lilian wanted desperately to stay. To help her sister somehow. "Are you okay? Should I get the nurse?"

"Stop," Rosie whispered in a shaky voice.

"All right," Lilian said, hoping she sounded soothing. This was all part of the process of recovery, she reminded herself. There would be steps forward and backward, but Rosie's overall trajectory would be positive. Lilian just needed to be patient.

She reached into her purse for her phone, planning to text Caleb. But Rosie sat up with a jolt and Lilian startled, nearly dropping the phone.

"Rosie?" Lilian said, a twinge of worry in her stomach.

Her sister's eyes glinted with a new, primal emotion. Not pain or even fear. No, this looked like hatred. The hairs on the back of Lilian's neck rose. She felt frozen in place, trapped by the intensity of her sister's emerald gaze.

And then Rosie spoke, her words knife-sharp: "Who the fuck are you?"

* * *

Lilian left the room in a rush, hoping to find a doctor she could talk to. On the way out, she nearly ran into Daniel.

"Lilian," he said, taking a step back. His smile faded as he took in her expression. "What's wrong?"

Lilian put her hands to her cheeks, still disturbed. "Rosie's okay," she said, and he visibly relaxed. "But she's—I don't know. Caleb visited her earlier and she recognized him. They had a conversation. But now . . ." She trailed off, unsure how to explain her sense of unease.

The physical therapist, a tall guy with a two-day beard and a tidy man bun, stepped around them with the wheelchair he was pushing. "Excuse me, guys. Time for Rosie's PT."

After the physical therapist went in, Lilian faced Daniel. "How has she been with you? Does she recognize you?"

Daniel shook his head, a pained expression on his face. "Not yet. But I haven't seen her today."

"Let's go in there together before she leaves for therapy," Lilian said, and he nodded.

When they walked into the room, Rosie was sitting on the edge of her bed, her back to them. She had lost weight, Lilian saw, which was more noticeable with Rosie in an upright position. From behind, her shaved head and delicate shoulders gave her an almost childlike appearance. The physical therapist had placed a bright pink belt around her waist—a gait belt, used to steady Rosie during transfers and walking. The PT, whose ID badge said Eddie, sat on a stool in front of her.

"Hi there," Daniel said, and Rosie's head swiveled around. The expression on her face—narrowed eyes, tight mouth—sent a chill down Lilian's limbs.

"Who the fuck are you?" Rosie said.

The same words she had said to Lilian, now directed at Daniel.

Eddie, the physical therapist, said, "This is your fiancé, remember? The man you're going to marry?" He gave Daniel an apologetic look. "It's Daniel, right? She seems a little irritable today."

"No worries," Daniel said, but his voice sounded tight, like he was trying not to show how much it bothered him.

"Not Daniel," Rosie said, then started mumbling again, her words too quiet, too jumbled, to understand.

"Of course it's Daniel," Eddie said to Rosie, unperturbed.

Rosie shook her head, faster and faster, until her entire body trembled. Eddie reached a steadying hand to her waist.

"You're all right," he said. "Now push up with your left leg."

But Rosie was too agitated, words bubbling out of her mouth, now loud enough that Lilian could hear: "Not Daniel, not Lilian." Her voice rose in a rhythmic chant. "Not Daniel, not Lilian, not Daniel, not Lilian."

Lilian wrapped her arms around herself, unsettled and uncertain how to react. She'd read about behavior problems after severe brain injuries: agitation and confusion, profanity, inappropriate sexual behavior, sometimes even violence. *It's important to realize that these behaviors are not under your loved one's voluntary control,* one article directed at family members and caretakers had cautioned. *These are a result of the brain injury.*

But this felt personal. Rosie had singled out Lilian and Daniel for her aggression, and there had to be an explanation.

"Sorry, guys," Eddie said with another apologetic smile, "but this is upsetting her. Maybe come back later, yeah?"

As soon as they left the room, Lilian pulled out her phone and sent Caleb a text, saying she wasn't going to meet him for lunch. She had more pressing issues to take care of now.

She glanced over at Daniel. "I want to talk to the doctor," she said.

CHAPTER
TWENTY-THREE

MyPsychJournal.com

Welcome back, Rosie. Happy journaling!

FEBRUARY 7, 2018

Today Dr. V started off our session by saying that she wanted to push back about something I wrote in my last journal entry—the part about how I lied, claiming that my professor had coerced me into having sex in exchange for a better grade.

Was it a lie? she asked. Well, yeah, I told her. I wanted to hurt him, to get revenge on him for dumping me, though it didn't work.

Then she told me to Interrogate That Memory. Look for the Story Behind the Story. I tried not to roll my eyes, because I remember exactly what happened, crystal clear.

Who had the power? she asked, and I said it was me—I instigated the affair. But she kept pushing me to dig deeper, and as we talked, the memory shifted and flipped until all of a sudden, it hit me: he was a grown fucking fortysomething professor; I was his student, still a teenager, for God's sake. He knew exactly what he was doing. Probably had me pegged right away: a lonely, insecure girl looking for someone to latch onto. Maybe he'd never used those exact words—have sex with me and I'll give you an A—but his intention had always been clear: you take care of me, and I'll take care of you.

Anyway, that was a bit of a breakthrough. I'm still digesting it. Still a little pissed off at Professor Niall Lawrence, too. Not that any of this excuses what I did, but it puts it all into context.

After that, Dr. V talked about how a person's emotional health is like a marble inside a glass jar. Every time the marble hits the jar, it's exquisitely painful, like the marble is made up of raw nerve endings. If the jar is empty, even small movements—shifting, rebalancing—send the marble crashing into the glass.

When you're a child, your parents are supposed to fill your jar, to provide a cushion or a buffer in times of stress. But if you don't have that—if you haven't learned your own coping skills—you'll reach for something else to fill the jar. Alcohol, drugs, sex, gambling, overeating. Anything to cushion the blow of the marble against the glass.

Relationships, too. Even unhealthy ones, Dr. V said, can feel better than rattling around in an empty jar.

Then, for the first time since I started seeing her, Dr. V finally asked about Michael. I've been waiting all this time to talk about him, but every time I bring him up, she says we aren't ready for that. We're Laying the Foundation, she always says, arching one of her perfectly penciled black eyebrows. So I guess that means the foundation has been laid: she knows that I have issues; that I have a problem with lying and manipulating and hurting people I love. Michael included.

For this week's homework, she asked me to write about him. How we met, what attracted us to each other, how it all started. It's weird to think about him again, to allow myself to write his name. All my memories of that time are laced with shame and regret. But I know I need to do this. I need to face it.

Honestly, it was sort of a whirlwind when we met. I was twenty-five and I thought I was a "real" adult. I had my own apartment and a decent job. Lilian and I had drifted apart, mostly because I was sick of her always telling me what to do while at the same time treating me like the lowest person on her priority list. Her job, her marriage, all of it came before me. So yeah, once again: a void.

Enter Michael. Older than me, handsome, sensitive, and a little mysterious. On our first date, we talked for three hours at dinner and then spent another three hours just walking around downtown and talking. You know how most people go through life with an invisible shell around them, protecting their messy, delicate insides? He didn't have that. It felt like I was seeing to the core of him, right from the beginning, and because of that, I wanted him to see to the core of me, too. I remember that we ended up talking about our childhoods, and he opened up about some horrifying things that happened to him. Maybe that should have been a red flag, but at the time, I liked his vulnerability.

Wait. I'm trying to be honest in this journal, so I'll put it out there: I liked that he was damaged. More damaged than me.

Things progressed quickly after that. I'd never been with someone who accepted me exactly the way I was—he thought I was gorgeous, smart, funny, interesting. Unlike other men I've dated, he never said I talk too much, never implied that I'm too loud, too wild, too obsessive. There was this one time, about a month after we met, we had plans to see his favorite band, but I got working on a painting and lost track of time. When he came to pick me up, instead of being dressed and ready to go out, I had on old jeans and a paint-spattered T-shirt. I was so embarrassed, and I apologized over and over, but he just kissed me and said he loved how passionate I was. Even though he didn't have an artistic bone in his body, he understood that this was an intrinsic part of me. It felt like I was being seen—really understood and accepted— for the first time in a while. Maybe ever.

We moved in together within a couple months. We started making plans for a future together, for a house and some kids, and a dog. It was all so beautiful, so shiny and glittery and full of possibility, like a scene inside a snow globe. I wish I could rewind time and live in those early months, forever preserved in glass.

But it didn't last. Of course it didn't. And I don't know exactly how or why it went bad, and I don't know how much was my fault and how much was his, but I do know that I screwed up, big time. That's what I do.

So that's what I'd like to focus on now, Dr. V. Where did I go wrong? And how can I prevent this from happening ever again?

CHAPTER
TWENTY-FOUR

Lilian stood outside Rosie's hospital room and listened as her doctor questioned her. Yesterday, after Rosie's reaction to her and Daniel, she had spoken with Rosie's attending physician, Dr. John Kirkpatrick. A physiatrist specializing in brain injury rehabilitation, he'd promised to do a thorough evaluation of Rosie this morning.

She could hear his voice, deep and steady, running through questions to assess Rosie's orientation to person, place, and time—"Can you tell me your name? Do you know what day it is today? What month? Where are you?"—but Rosie's responses were muffled, unintelligible at this distance.

"Do you know who this is?" Dr. Kirkpatrick asked. Lilian couldn't see what he was referring to, but she leaned in, listening just outside the doorway.

Rosie mumbled a response, loud enough for Lilian to catch a few words: ". . . my sis . . . that's my sister, is my sis . . ."

Lilian sucked in a breath. Rosie recognized her?

"That's right, it's a photograph of your sister," Dr. Kirkpatrick said. "And what about this one?" he said, referring to something Lilian couldn't see.

"My *sister,* where the fuck is my sister is," Rosie snapped, then trailed off into something meaningless.

The doctor poked his head out of the room. John Kirkpatrick was about fifty, with a generous smile and a fondness for bow ties. "Thanks for waiting, Lilian," he said. "Why don't you come in."

Lilian followed him into the room, where Rosie sat upright in a chair near her hospital bed.

She attempted a careful smile. "How are you feeling today?"

Rosie's eyes flashed with alarm. "Go away," she said, her voice a warning growl.

"Who is this?" Dr. Kirkpatrick asked, pointing to Lilian.

"A fake, she's a fake, is a fake," Rosie said, then turned away, muttering to herself.

The words were like a hammer driving a nail into Lilian's bruised heart. *A fake.* A phony, a counterfeit. She knew Rosie didn't mean it that way, but her words cut directly to Lilian's internal struggle.

For months, maybe years, she'd had the nagging feeling that everything she'd accomplished—her medical career, her marriage, her beautiful home—had been a fluke. Somehow, she'd fooled everyone into believing that she deserved it, but the truth was bound to come out eventually. It had already started, with little Dasha Nichols, like the first crack in a dam. Soon the entire structure would crumble.

Lilian swallowed, hard, and told herself to focus on Dr. Kirkpatrick. He was holding out the photograph of Lilian and Rosie. "And who is this?" he asked, tapping the picture.

"That's my sis, I told you that my sis is my sister," Rosie said, then mumbled something Lilian didn't catch.

"What's her name?" the doctor prompted.

Rosie blinked, a flash of confusion in her green eyes. "My sister is my sister, that's my sis."

He motioned back to Lilian. "This lady looks like the person in the photograph, don't you think?"

"Not the same, is a fake is a fake . . ." Her words faded into a muddle of sounds.

"How do you explain that they look the same?" Dr. Kirkpatrick asked, sounding genuinely curious. Lilian got the feeling this wasn't something he often encountered.

"It's tryin' a trick me and watch me is a spy." Rosie's gaze dragged down Lilian's body, a suspicious glint in her eyes. "Get the fuck away from me away from me."

But Lilian wanted to go to her, to put her hands on her sister's cheeks, and force Rosie to look her in the eyes. *I'm your sister,* she would say. *I've known you since the day you were born.* She knew the noises Rosie made in her sleep, the way she chewed on her cuticles when she was anxious. She knew that Rosie liked chocolate chip cookies with walnuts but not pecans, that she hated mint flavor, and had used bubblegum toothpaste into her twenties.

Being denied by her one remaining family member felt like another rip in the fabric of her life. As if all their memories together—the nights Rosie crawled into Lilian's bed with a bad dream; the Valentine's Day boxes they'd made together; the speech Rosie had given at Lilian's wedding—were a lie.

The memory rushed into her mind: Sixteen-year-old Rosie in her pink maid of honor dress, standing in front of all their friends and family, saying, *I am the luckiest girl in the world to have Lilian as my big sister. She's my favorite person, my best friend, my first call in good times and bad. And I know that she would walk across fire for me.*

"Can we speak outside the room for a few minutes?" the doctor asked, his expression grave.

Lilian blinked back tears and focused on him. "Of course. Let me see how close Daniel is. I know he wants to be here for this discussion."

"Tell him to meet us in the family conference room."

She pulled out her phone and sent him a text. His response came within a few seconds: *Parking right now. Be there in ten.*

"Have you seen this?" the doctor said as they each took a seat in the conference room. He showed Lilian a notebook that had been tucked against his arm. "Rosie's been busy with the recreation therapist."

Lilian took the notebook from him. Her mouth fell open. "It's Renoir's *Two Sisters.*"

Rosie had created a rough pencil sketch of the painting, the two girls in front of a river. It wasn't a skillful drawing—full of shaky lines and stray marks—except for two specific areas: the older sister's eyes and the younger sister's hands. These had been rendered with painstaking precision: iris, pupil, and lashes for the older girl, ten tiny fingers for the younger one, her palms outstretched, as if in supplication.

"She liked to pretend this was a painting of us," Lilian said, tearing her eyes away from the drawing.

This had to mean something. Rosie was thinking about the two of them, trying to communicate their relationship, a shared memory, a common past.

Dr. Kirkpatrick nodded, his eyes drifting to the ceiling as he collected his thoughts. "The fact that she's sketching something that relates to you as sisters, the fact that she recognizes you in photographs but not in person is . . . interesting."

"What do you mean?" Lilian asked. It was never good to be the interesting patient. *Interesting* meant that the doctor hadn't seen your condition before. The best thing to be, as a patient, was *boring*.

Dr. Kirkpatrick stuck his hands in the pockets of his white coat. "Daniel was here this morning. Rosie called him a 'liar' and screamed at him until he left the room. It's unusual, the persistence in this specific aspect of Rosie's memory deficits."

Lilian flinched, imagining the scene and how that must have hurt Daniel. "What are we going to do about it?"

"That's what I'll cover when Daniel gets here. In the meantime, I have another question for you," Dr. Kirkpatrick said. "Have you seen the scar on Rosie's thigh?"

Lilian nodded. Jagged lines on Rosie's thigh, a well-healed scar that must have been made by something thin and sharp, like glass. "What about it?"

"My resident found something in her medical records. Rosie went to the emergency department with a laceration on her right thigh. She needed sutures."

"Okay," Lilian said, not understanding the point of this.

"The ED note said her boyfriend was with her. There was concern that he'd cut her. Branding, it's called. When someone carves their initial on someone else. It can be a sign of an S&M relationship that has gone too far."

"My God," Lilian said, stunned. An initial? "How long ago did this happen?"

"About two and a half years ago."

Not a W, she realized, thinking back. She had been looking at it upside-down. An *M*.

An image rose in her mind of Rosie's pale thigh, exposed and bleeding. What could possibly bring her little sister to allow something like that? Or had Michael forced her? Had he tied her down and carved a jagged letter into the flesh of the woman he was supposed to love, while Rosie screamed and begged him to stop?

Bile rose in her throat, acidic and hot.

"Apparently Rosie was intoxicated," Dr. Kirkpatrick said, "so she couldn't give a good history, and the attending thought the boyfriend was acting suspicious. But when she called a social worker, Rosie and the boyfriend left AMA."

Against medical advice. Had Michael brought her to the emergency department in a panic when he realized what he had done? Lilian had seen abusive parents do the same after beating their children. And, just like Michael, they would take their kids home as soon as they caught wind of the doctor's suspicions.

"My sister was in a bad relationship a couple years ago," Lilian said, trying to remain calm. Although *bad* was an understatement— that son of a bitch had *branded* her, Lilian thought with a flash of fury.

"So that's not the man she's with now . . . ?" Dr. Kirkpatrick said, and Lilian realized why he had brought it up. They needed to make sure Rosie wouldn't be returning to a dangerous environment.

"Absolutely not."

"Good." He glanced up as Daniel walked in the room "Have a seat, Daniel," Dr. Kirkpatrick said. His lips thinned. "We need to talk."

Daniel glanced over at Lilian, a question in his eyes. Lilian gave a small shrug. She had no idea what Dr. Kirkpatrick was about to say, but she had a feeling that it would change everything.

"I believe Rosie is presenting with Capgras syndrome," Dr. Kirkpatrick started.

The diagnosis rang a faint bell in the back of Lilian's mind, but she didn't recall any details from her med school lectures.

Daniel seemed equally confused, his forehead wrinkling as he asked, "Cap—what? What did you say?"

"Capgras syndrome," Dr. Kirkpatrick said again, pronouncing it slowly: *Cop-graw.* "A syndrome in which the affected person believes their loved ones have been replaced by identical-looking imposters."

"That's a real thing?" Daniel said. "It sounds like something from a soap opera. No offense," he added.

"None taken," Dr. Kirkpatrick said, smiling. "It's rare, but it can occur after traumatic brain injury, in other organic brain disorders, such as dementia, or in various psychiatric conditions. It's fascinating, actually."

Lilian fought a stab of irritation at his pleased expression. She knew he wasn't smiling because he enjoyed being the bearer of bad news, but because he had nailed the diagnosis. She remembered that feeling— but she hoped she had never made her own patients feel like this. Like their loved ones' life-altering diagnosis was a fun, albeit complex, problem to solve.

"But it doesn't make sense," Lilian said. "She recognizes me as looking like Lilian, but she doesn't think I *am* Lilian."

"Her ability to recognize faces is intact," Dr. Kirkpatrick said. "The disconnect is in the pathway that should lead to an emotional connection, the feelings of warmth and familiarity one experiences in that person's presence. Because Rosie knows your face but doesn't feel any connection to it, she assumes that you are somehow impersonating her sister."

Lilian shivered. "Why does she recognize me in pictures, then?"

"That's been described previously in Capgras syndrome. The mechanism isn't well understood, but it isn't unheard of."

"But Rosie doesn't think her brother-in-law is an imposter," Daniel said.

Dr. Kirkpatrick leaned forward eagerly. "That's common, actually. The patient often believes only her closest loved ones are imposters— spouses, partners, children. You are her only remaining family member, correct?" he asked Lilian.

She nodded, swallowing the familiar pang of grief. "Our parents passed away."

"And you're her fiancé?" He glanced at Daniel, who nodded, a pained expression on his face. "The two closest people in her life. Very typical presentation."

"That doesn't make sense," Lilian said, digesting this. "She's known Caleb longer than she's known Daniel."

Dr. Kirkpatrick leaned back, crossing one ankle on his knee. "We like to try and put the brain into boxes. Especially now that we can image it, get an MRI or a CT, point to the area with the tumor or bleed. But the brain is so much more complex than what you see on the screen. It's a wild thing—it doesn't care about our boxes. I've been in practice twenty years, and I still encounter things I've never seen before."

"So you've never seen Capgras syndrome?" Lilian said, latching onto that. He could be wrong—maybe this was something else entirely. Maybe Rosie needed *more* imaging of her brain, some kind of specialized therapy, a clinical trial?

"I've seen it in psychiatric disorders, such as schizophrenia, as well as in dementia. Not after a traumatic brain injury, though. That said, I've discussed this with several of my colleagues at academic centers around the country. They all agree with me."

"How do we treat it?" Daniel broke in.

Dr. Kirkpatrick turned to him. "Unfortunately, there's nothing much we can do, other than the excellent therapy she's already receiving. No medication or psychotherapy is proven to reverse this disorder. It's a fixed delusion."

Lilian exhaled a growing sense of despair. If Rosie was going to fling profanities at her, Lilian would rather it be because she fully recognized Lilian as her sister. Lilian could handle that; she wouldn't blame Rosie for being angry with her. But the lack of recognition, combined with the flinty suspicion in Rosie's green eyes, nearly flattened Lilian every time she walked in the room. She wanted her sister back—not a stranger. But then she realized that from Rosie's perspective, *Lilian* was the stranger. It began to dawn on her just how frightened her sister must feel.

A rush of hot tears pricked her eyes, and she dashed them away. "So that's it? She'll be like this forever?"

Dr. Kirkpatrick shook his head. "Not necessarily. The good news is that, unlike a person with dementia, Rosie has made incredible gains since her injury. It's possible that with time, she will recognize you and this will all be behind us."

He was giving them the best-case scenario. Which meant there was also a worst-case scenario.

"But . . ." Lilian prompted.

He tilted his head, acquiescing. "There are several documented cases of lifelong Capgras syndrome after traumatic brain injury."

Lilian's heart sank. "I can't—I can't imagine sending her to live with someone she believes is an imposter. She's terrified of me and Daniel. It would be cruel."

"I understand," Dr. Kirkpatrick said. "But Rosie has a few more weeks here. My main concern right now is that she has become distrustful of the staff here—the therapists and myself—because we keep insisting that you *are* her sister, that Daniel is her fiancé. She seems to think we're in cahoots with you two, and the paranoia is slowing her progress."

"What can we do about it?" Lilian said.

"Well, to start, we'll avoid discussing either of you for a while, and if you could keep your visits brief, that may help. I want to try an atypical antipsychotic, and our neuropsychologist will see her." He leaned forward, giving a sympathetic smile to her and Daniel. "Mostly, though, I think she just needs time. The brain is plastic, remember. Let it do its job."

Lilian had heard that phrase in her neurology rotation in med school. *The brain is plastic.* Meaning that it has the capability to grow and change, even in adulthood, even after injury. *Neuroplasticity.*

Much easier to believe in when it wasn't applied to your injured little sister.

"I—I need a minute," Daniel said, pushing his chair back so hard it screeched against the floor. Lilian caught a glimpse of his face as he exited the conference room—he was pale, his eyes watering.

Shit. Lilian had been focused on her own questions and emotions. But Daniel had just learned that his fiancée might never recognize him again—and he didn't have Lilian's medical background. He must be not only devastated, but overwhelmed.

"Excuse me," Lilian said to Dr. Kirkpatrick, and went to find him.

It took a few minutes, but she eventually found Daniel standing by a wide window near the elevator, looking out at the city below.

"Hey," she said, touching his shoulder. "You okay?"

He exhaled a burst of air and shook his head without answering. His face was expressionless, his eyes red, as if he'd wiped them too many times.

Lilian stood next to him, staring at the dark sky, the rows of street-lights and buildings reaching to the horizon. Whenever she looked over this vast city, she always thought about the millions of people out there, living their lives—their own joys and tragedies. Compared to all that, what had happened with Rosie was just a small blip.

But to Lilian—and to Daniel—it was everything.

At least they weren't alone, Lilian thought. At least they had each other.

"When I was twelve, my parents left me in charge of my little brother for a couple hours," Daniel said, and Lilian's eyes snapped to his face.

"You have a little brother?" she asked, surprised. She still didn't know much about him.

He nodded, not looking at her. "Jake was four years old and such a disaster. In the two hours my parents were gone, he managed to dump out an entire gallon of milk, spread a five-pound bag of sugar across the kitchen floor, and flush a bunch of matchbox cars down the toilet. And then while I was plunging the toilet, he got in the fridge."

Rosie had been similar at that age, Lilian thought, though her weapons of choice had been Lilian's nail polish and makeup bag.

Daniel pressed a hand flat against the window. "I looked up to see

Jake standing there, his lips turning blue. He was choking on a grape. I panicked—I tried to do the Heimlich, but it didn't work. Jake was still choking, and it went on for so long he passed out."

Lilian's heart slowed as she imagined a twelve-year-old Daniel, in charge of his brother, panicked and alone. She had personally lost two patients to choking on grapes. "Oh no, Daniel."

Daniel glanced at Lilian, taking his hand off the window. "Jake was fine. My parents came home at exactly the right time, my mom called 911, my dad did the Heimlich—the grape shot across the room. No one blamed me. But I had trouble sleeping for months after that. I'd lay awake at night, thinking about those moments when Jake was choking and I couldn't get him breathing again."

"You must have been terrified," Lilian said, remembering the time Rosie, as an infant, had cried so hard she'd stopped breathing. The blind panic, the crushing responsibility.

"Yeah, but that's not why I couldn't sleep. It was because I couldn't help my brother—I was useless." He stuck his hands in his pockets and turned back to the window. "I feel the same way now."

Lilian nodded. As an older sister, as a daughter, as a pediatrician, and as a mother, she had felt that same sense of impotence. Nothing she said to Daniel would lessen the weight he carried.

It was all so brutally unfair. Just when they thought Rosie was getting better, just when it seemed like she was turning the corner, they were slapped in the face with *this*: the person they loved with their whole souls might never recognize either of them again.

And someone was responsible for this. Someone had hurt her little sister—permanently injuring her, forever altering her life.

Her hands clenched into fists at her sides. For a brief moment, she imagined raising her fists and slamming them into the window, shattering it in pieces, feeling the cold snap of wind against her face.

Instead, she forced herself to spread her palms flat against her thighs. She felt useless, too, just like Daniel.

"I wish I remembered more about the night of the crash," she said.

"What *do* you remember?" Daniel asked, turning to her.

"Not much. Rosie picked me up in her Beetle. We were heading to a restaurant in Greektown. We made small talk. She said she had something she wanted to discuss."

This conversation is too important to have in a car. It's a matter of life and death, sis.

"What was it?" Daniel asked, his gaze intense. "What did she tell you?"

Lilian shook her head. "She wanted to wait until we got to the restaurant to talk. I thought she was driving too fast, she kept looking over her shoulder, and—that's all I remember. But I got the distinct impression that . . . that someone was following us."

Lilian's shoulders tightened involuntarily. She half-expected Daniel to dismiss what she'd said, to tell her that couldn't possibly be what had happened. Just as Caleb had.

Instead, he leaned forward, his eyebrows drawing together in concern. His pale blue eyes caught the light from the window. "Who was it? Did you see?"

Lilian shook her head, shoulders relaxing in relief at being taken seriously. "I don't remember. I might have looked, I don't know—I only have vague memories of a face in a car. That's it. But when I saw that man in Rosie's ICU room, I recognized him. I saw his face the night of the accident. I swear I did."

He appeared in her memory now, as he had so many times since that day. Dark hair, thin face, that curved scar along the right side of his jaw.

"He was the one driving the car?" Daniel asked.

"I don't know—my concussion jumbled things up," Lilian said. "But last week . . ." Taking a deep breath, she told him about the car in the driveway, the silver sedan with Indiana plates.

Daniel's face paled. "Did you call the police?"

"Caleb said we'd go to the police station sometime this week," she said, still frustrated by his lack of urgency. Even when she'd explained what she'd learned about Trevor Callahan and Niall Lawrence, and what Brynne had said about Michael, he'd looked at his schedule, sighed, and said he might be able to squeeze it in soon.

"Later this week?" Daniel's eyes widened. "I don't think you should wait any longer."

Lilian shrugged. "I don't think so either, but I'd prefer not to go alone."

"I'll go with you. We can go right now, if you want."

Lilian hesitated. She wanted nothing more than to rush to the police station and get answers, but the invisible thread connecting her to her daughter pulled tight. "I'm supposed to pick Abigail up from my mother-in-law in two hours."

"That's enough time," Daniel said. "Let's go."

Finally, she thought, someone who understood. Who wanted answers as much as she did.

She faced him. "Okay."

CHAPTER
TWENTY-FIVE

MyPsychJournal.com

Welcome back, Rosie. Happy journaling!

My appointment with Dr. V is tomorrow and I want to write more about Michael before then. I'm having trouble trusting my own memories because at the time, his behavior seemed sweet, protective. He drove me to and from work. He'd send flowers to my office, he'd meet me for lunch several times a week. He loved to buy me gifts and surprise me with them. A couple of my coworkers said he was being overbearing, but I liked it. It made me feel secure. Cherished.

He would choose my outfits, picking his favorite ones for when we went out together, or more conservative pieces for me to wear to the office. He didn't want anyone leering at me, he said. Again, I thought it was nice. No one had cared that much about me in a long time.

He was always checking up on me, making sure I came home on time. For example, once I stopped by a friend's place after work to see his new baby and Michael texted, asking why I was late. I'll admit that after a while it started to bother me, but I knew if I asked him to stop, he'd be offended. "I care about you, Rosie. I worry when you don't come home on time." Or he'd be jealous: "What were you doing with him? Do you have feelings for him?" It became easier to lie, to tell him my boss stopped by my office to talk, or that I was caught in traffic. But then he'd catch me in my lies, and that would start a whole new argument: "What else are you lying about? I can't trust you at all, Rosie."

And he was right, wasn't he? Why should he trust me? I've always lied to get out of trouble, ever since I was a teenager. And it's not like I knew what a healthy relationship looked like—my parents weren't a good example; I'd never made good choices in men. In some ways, Michael treated me better than any other boyfriend—he never cheated on me, he never abandoned me, he told me every day how much he loved me.

But there were other things I noticed, too. I started misplacing things, my keys, my purse, my phone, and part of me wondered if he was doing it, trying to rattle me, to make me distrust myself, but that seemed insane. Then I started missing texts from friends, invitations to go out to lunch or meet for drinks. I had issues with the calendar on my phone, with appointments being changed or deleted, so I was always showing up late or not at all—and not just to social things, but work events, too. I thought I was overtired, stressed out—in fact, that's what Michael said. He suggested that I cut back or even leave my job entirely. He was worried about me, and it was nice to have someone care.

See, that's the confusing thing about Michael. It's impossible to prove that he purposefully manipulated me. Once, when his birthday was coming up, I thought he said he wanted to spend the evening at home together, get takeout and watch a movie. But then his birthday rolled around, and he insisted that he told me he wanted to go out to dinner at his favorite restaurant, and why hadn't I made reservations? Didn't I care about him? Why was I so self-absorbed, so flaky and unreliable? And I don't know, maybe I had mixed it up. I do tend to focus on myself and forget about other people. But that kind of thing happened all the time, and sometimes I would get so frustrated that I'd start screaming at him, and it would always end with ME apologizing to HIM.

Honestly, I went overboard plenty of times. I have a temper, a bad one, and a couple of times I got so upset I threw things—plates, books, anything I could get my hands on. Once he ended up with a black eye from a vase I threw at him. I felt horrible about it, for hurting him, for losing control. I'm still ashamed of myself for that.

So I have to ask you, Dr. V, don't I bear some responsibility in what happened? I understand that he was manipulative and controlling, but I'm not blameless, either. I'm not some poor, abused little victim. I have my own issues, serious ones, and I'm so worried that I'm going to spend the rest of my life hurting people I care about.

Oh, and by the way, that birthday dinner? We ended up getting a table at his favorite restaurant, and the waiter flirted with me a little. Said my hair was "absolutely gorgeous." It was nearly down to my waist at the time, thick and wavy. I was flattered, and I flirted back, even though I knew it was a shitty thing to do to my boyfriend on his birthday. I was still pissed at him, and I wanted to get the upper hand, to rub it in his face: see, other men find me attractive. I don't need you. You're damn lucky to have me.

But then I woke up the next morning to see Michael, standing over me, holding my hair in his hands.

I used to braid it at night to keep it from getting tangled. And he'd cut the braid off, right at the nape of my neck, while I was asleep.

"Don't you dare flirt with another man in front of me," he said. I remember how his voice sounded: quiet, like a whisper against my skin, giving me goosebumps from head to toe.

But here is what confuses me: the way I felt in that moment, it wasn't as simple as fear. Or even anger. Yes, it scared me, but more than that, I respected it. Even appreciated it.

Because a man who cared enough to do that was a man who would never leave me.

And yet, he did leave me. I told that to Dr. V and she seemed surprised. It's true, though. The first time we broke up, it was Michael who did the leaving, so what does that say about me? He did some shitty things to me, but what I did to him . . . it might have been even worse.

CHAPTER
TWENTY-SIX

"To sum up," the police officer said, "there is clear evidence that another vehicle swerved into your sister's vehicle and initiated the collision sequence. Now, whether that happened accidentally or on purpose, I'm not able to say."

Lilian sat back, her mind whirling.

She and Daniel were at the police station, meeting with Sergeant Morgan, a car-crash forensics expert. He'd run through everything on the computer, talking about angles and skid marks and friction coefficients. Lilian didn't understand any of it, but she trusted that Sergeant Morgan did.

"And witness statements corroborate this?" she said.

"That's right," Morgan said. "A silver sedan with Indiana plates clipped the left rear bumper of your sister's vehicle."

"Jesus," Daniel whispered. He looked sick—and Lilian couldn't blame him. Watching the computerized model, the silver sedan hitting Rosie's yellow Beetle again and again, felt like a repeated kick to the gut.

"What do we do now?" Lilian said. "Is there any chance of finding the driver?"

Morgan turned to his computer. "I've run an analysis through the

Indiana Department of Motor Vehicles's licensing division. Witnesses'
statements were conflicting on the number of the license plate, but we
can be fairly certain there was a *B* or an eight at the beginning, and a
one or an *I* at the end. Within those parameters, and including the silver
sedan model from the past ten years, we have"—he paused and punched
a few keys—"nearly one hundred thousand possibilities."

Disappointment curdled in Lilian's stomach. "What if I had some
ideas about who the driver could have been?"

"That would be extremely helpful," Morgan said.

"Someone was following her—stalking her in the weeks leading up
to the accident."

Daniel shot her an alarmed look. "You didn't tell me about this."

"Your doorman mentioned it when I was leaving your building the
other day," she said. "Rosie asked him to keep an eye out for any men
hanging around. He said that the night of the accident, she seemed
scared."

Morgan's eyebrows raised. "Do you have a name?"

"Maybe." She told him about Rosie's article featuring Trevor Callahan, Professor Lawrence, and the controlling boyfriend, Michael
Sorenson, though he hadn't been named. Then she told him about the
man she'd seen in Rosie's hospital room.

"I *think* he was the driver of the car that hit us," she said, "though
I can't be sure, because of my concussion. But I recognized his face. I
know I did. And he definitely wasn't any of those three men."

Morgan leaned back, folding his arms across his chest and looking up
at the ceiling. "The most likely explanation is a regular old hit-and-run.
Snowy evening, slippery road; someone loses control and hits the car in
front of him. He's terrified—maybe in a state of shock—so he takes off.
Doesn't call the cops, doesn't want to get in trouble. But pretty soon,
the guilt starts eating him up. He can't stop thinking about the car he
hit, he somehow finds out which hospital they took the victims to, and
he goes there to see what he's done. Maybe wants to apologize, maybe
as some kind of atonement."

Lilian considered that. It was possible, but it didn't explain everything.

"What about the man hanging around our building?" Daniel said.

Morgan held up a hand. "Give me a second. The other possibility is that someone was following your sister, and they hit her car on purpose. Maybe out of revenge, or to shut her up. That article she wrote sounds pretty inflammatory. If the man you saw wasn't Callahan or Lawrence, it could still have been someone they knew or even had hired."

Lilian sat up straight, vindicated. So her hit man hypothesis wasn't totally crazy, after all.

"But," Morgan said, continuing, "an obsessive ex might be more likely to hang around her building, and that's someone she might not feel comfortable talking to her *current* boyfriend about. What do you know about this Michael Sorenson?"

"Not much," Lilian said, then told him what she'd learned from Brynne about Michael's behavior at the restaurant, and what Rosie had written about him in her article.

"All right," Morgan said, turning back to the computer. "Race? Age? Hair and eye color? Height or weight?"

She sat back, remembering the picture she'd seen of Michael on Rosie's Instagram. The chiseled jaw, the arrogant expression. "He's white. Somewhere around thirtyish. Blond hair. I don't know how tall." She remembered her sister's fondness for blue-eyed men. "Oh, and blue eyes," she added.

"Let's do a range from age twenty-five to forty, with blond hair and blue eyes, name Michael Sorenson." Morgan pressed a few more keys, then frowned. "Unfortunately, that's a fairly common name—there's a couple hundred listed. But with the other parameters . . ." He leaned back, smiling. "Now we're getting somewhere—that leaves only fourteen. Let me take a look at the cars they have registered to them."

He punched a few more keys, his forehead creasing. Lilian held her breath; this could be it. The answer she'd been looking for.

"No, sorry," Morgan said, and Lilian deflated. "None of them have a silver sedan. He could have borrowed or rented the car, I guess."

Or he might not be involved at all. Lilian exhaled a long, frustrated sigh. Another dead end.

"Now, if you had a name for the guy you saw," Morgan said, "the one with the scar? *That* might get us somewhere. But unfortunately, there's no way to search for that in the database."

Beside her, Daniel leaned forward, forearms on his thighs, shoulders slumped. "You're saying that whoever did this might never be caught?"

"I'm sure this is frustrating to hear," Sergeant Morgan said. "Believe me, I understand. Call me if you have any more information. But until then, it's very much a needle in a haystack."

CHAPTER
TWENTY-SEVEN

Lilian followed Daniel out the doors of the police station. The sun had set while they were inside, and it was dusky and bitter cold, the kind of Chicago freeze that cut straight to your skin. She tugged her scarf tighter around her neck.

"Do you want to grab dinner before we head back?" Daniel asked. "After all that, I could use some food."

She hesitated. She was supposed to pick up Abigail from Nancy's in thirty minutes. But despite the omnipresent tug toward her baby, she realized that she didn't want to leave yet. She was hungry, too, but the main reason went deeper. She wasn't looking forward to telling Caleb about the visit to the police station and what little they had discovered. He wouldn't say, *I told you so*, but he'd be thinking it.

Plus, didn't she deserve to do something for herself? That's exactly what she used to tell parents of her infants when they sat in her office looking exhausted and overwhelmed: take care of yourself so you can take care of your baby. And it would be good for Caleb to occasionally rearrange *his* life around their daughter.

"Let me see if Caleb can pick up Abigail from his mom's," she said.

* * *

She led Daniel south and west from the police department, down Dearborn to Jackson, past throngs of people heading home from work. They were just four blocks west of Millennium Park and the famous Bean sculpture, an area Lilian knew well. She had been in medical school when the Bean—actually called Cloud Gate—was constructed, and she remembered seeing it for the first time with Caleb. They'd been captivated by the sculpture, the way it reflected the lake, city, and sky in mirrored brilliance, the images somehow familiar and new all at once. They'd spent a good two hours there, trading cameras with eager tourists—no one had cellphones that took selfies back then.

That day seemed a lifetime ago, a sunny afternoon shimmering with excitement for their future. Nothing like today's frigid, gray evening. Lilian and Daniel walked in silence, each absorbed in their thoughts.

Caleb had agreed to pick up Abigail from Nancy's on his way home from work. He'd seemed rushed on the phone, so they hadn't had a chance to talk. He thought Lilian had wanted to stay longer with Rosie, and she hadn't corrected him even though a sliver of guilt pricked her heart.

"Here we are," she said, stopping. They'd reached Luke's, her dad's favorite place to bring his girls after a visit to Grant Park.

"After you," Daniel said, opening the door.

Inside was a cozy counter-serve restaurant, crowded with people and smelling of bread and spices. It brought back a rush of memories: Dad was usually in a good mood here, away from the stresses of work and home, treating his daughters to dinner.

"What's good here?" Daniel asked as they waited in line to place their order.

"I keep forgetting you haven't lived in Chicago very long," Lilian said. "You ever had an Italian beef?"

"No."

"Then that's what you should get." Lilian stepped up to the counter and placed her order: "Two Italian beefs. Both hot and wet."

"Do I want to know what that means?" Daniel asked as he followed Lilian toward the red-checked tablecloth covered tables.

She smiled but didn't answer. Soon they were wedged into a corner, each of them with a soggy sandwich bun piled high with fragrant, thinly sliced meat and topped with pickled peppers. Daniel eyed his as if he wasn't quite sure how to manage without everything falling out the end, then picked it up and took a bite.

"Oh, wow," he said as he finished chewing. "That's amazing."

"I can't believe you've never had an Italian beef," Lilian said, smiling.

"You have to admit they don't *look* very appetizing," he said, motioning to the greasy bun in front of him. "But I was wrong—I admit it."

Lilian took another bite, enjoying the savory meat and crisp crunch of the hot peppers between her teeth. "Where'd you grow up?" she asked.

"Northern California, in a little town a couple hours north of San Francisco. I did my PhD at UC Davis and then took the position here."

"What do you think of the Windy City?"

"I like it," he said, taking another bite. "Although I could do without this cold. After living most of my life in California, this feels like the Arctic to me."

Lilian smiled. "Your PhD is in art history, right?"

"Yes," he said. "It's not saving lives, but I enjoy it."

"I bet Rosie liked that about you. *Likes* that," Lilian corrected herself. She didn't want to talk about Rosie as if she didn't exist, even if Rosie didn't recognize her as her sister.

"We loved visiting little galleries around the city," Daniel said. "I told her she should talk to them about showing her paintings, but she always said she wasn't interested. She didn't know how good she was."

"Our dad wasn't the most supportive parent for a budding artist," Lilian said. "I wasn't around much during Rosie's high school and college years, but he was always telling her she needed a job that would pay the bills."

"He wasn't wrong," Daniel said. "Very few people can make it as a full-time artist, but Rosie has a lot of talent. I actually . . ."

He stopped talking and looked at the table.

"What?" Lilian asked.

He cleared his throat and looked away. "Sorry. It's hard to think about what we had planned together, before this happened. Anyway." He cleared his throat again. "We talked about when I finished my post-doc and had a permanent position somewhere, how I'd support us for a few years so she could focus on her painting. See if it went anywhere. I thought she could be an amazing art teacher, too, maybe have her own studio for lessons."

Lilian had the urge to reach out and put her hand over Daniel's, but she didn't, unsure if it would be construed as support or pity. "Maybe that can still happen," she said after a pause.

So many "maybes" after a brain injury. *Maybe* Rosie would paint again. *Maybe* she could recover enough to live independently. *Maybe* she would recognize Lilian and Daniel someday.

They lapsed into silence. And in that silence, Lilian felt a tickle of worry in the back of her mind about Abigail. *She's fine*, she told herself. Caleb was with her; she needed to trust him. Lilian took a bite of her sandwich, trying to force her thoughts away.

But would it hurt to check the app on her phone for Abigail's baby monitor? Of course not. One little peek, and she'd feel better. She picked up her phone and opened the app, watching as the black and white image came into view.

Someone was in Abigail's bedroom, near the changing table, but it wasn't Caleb.

Lilian stiffened. Her pulse quickened. With shaking fingers, she zoomed in, turning the camera to get a better view.

It was Nancy. Nancy in her pressed slacks and cardigan, tickling Abigail's belly. Lilian exhaled, telling herself to relax. Caleb must have called his mother and asked her to bring Abigail home and get her ready for bed. Lilian was grateful to Nancy, but that meant that Caleb hadn't done what he'd promised. A small thing, but it irritated her.

She flipped to the Find My Friends app, which showed her Caleb's location—he'd suggested it after Abigail's birth, when Lilian's anxiety was so high she'd panic if he was even a few minutes late getting home from work. Caleb's blinking blue dot was several blocks away from the hospital. Lilian zoomed in, but the area was full of high-rises; she couldn't determine the exact location. He could be in a restaurant, a department store, an office.

She sent him a text: *Where are you?*

Three dots appeared immediately, then disappeared. Caleb was weighing his answer, probably trying to come up with an excuse to placate his henpecking wife.

Another minute, then, finally, he texted: *Took the research team out to dinner. We submitted the grant. Wanted to celebrate.*

Lilian shook her head, exasperated. It was hard to be *too* upset with him; she had gone out to dinner, too. But she was eating a five-dollar sandwich and fries, whereas Caleb would spring for drinks, appetizers, steak entrees, and desserts for everyone.

She imagined his research team: Martina Sanchez, a respected PhD researcher in orthopedic trauma, a couple grad students, maybe a few residents or fellows. Definitely his research assistant Shaylie, a twenty-seven-year-old woman with shiny blond hair and a forehead so smooth you could ice skate on it.

Congrats, Lilian replied, weakly. *I'll see you at home.*

She flipped back to the baby monitor and watched Nancy, her pearl necklace visible even in the grainy video, cradling Abigail in her arms. She had a sudden urge to be home. Her breasts tingled; she would need to pump, since she hadn't fed Abigail, and if she waited too long, she'd leak.

"Everything okay?" Daniel said.

"Oh, yeah. Sorry," Lilian said, pocketing her phone. "Just checking on my baby girl."

Daniel took another bite, chewed, and swallowed. "This car crash . . . Lilian, I know there's probably nothing we can do to find out who was responsible. But a silver sedan with Indiana plates hit Rosie's car, then showed up in your driveway in the middle of the night. I can't believe it was a coincidence."

The rush of gratitude that went through her surprised Lilian. Daniel believed her. Not only that, he wanted to help unravel the truth.

"I wish there was some way of identifying that guy I saw in Rosie's hospital room. He has to be the missing link." She glanced at Daniel, who had a strange look in his eyes. Almost like a lightbulb had flicked on inside him. "What is it?"

"What if it wasn't Rosie they were after?" he said.

Lilian shook her head, confused. "What do you mean?"

"Maybe we've been looking at this the wrong way. Rosie picked you up at your house. The man in the silver sedan might have been watching *you* and decided to follow the car. Then he shows up in *your* driveway in the middle of the night. You're the common denominator." He paused. "Is there anyone who wants to hurt you, Lilian?"

His eyes, such a clear blue it almost hurt to look at them, met hers. The memories slammed into Lilian with so much force that she couldn't breathe. A tiny girl, a sobbing mother. A furious father: *I will fucking kill you, bitch.*

"It's possible," she whispered. "I had a patient named Dasha Nichols. Two years old. Such a pretty little girl."

CHAPTER
TWENTY-EIGHT

Lilian stopped, her throat tightening. Saying Dasha's name felt like swallowing glass, but it was a good pain. Like a penance.

Daniel waited, not saying anything, until she went on, telling him about Dasha's visits to her clinic for seemingly minor complaints. Three visits within the span of one month, and each time, Lilian found nothing of concern.

She remembered the third visit so clearly. She'd agreed to overbook Dasha into an already packed clinic because Galina, Dasha's mother, had sounded so worried on the phone. Then Lilian had walked into the clinic room to see Dasha laughing and playing with a stuffed animal, looking for all the world like a normal, happy kid. So Lilian swallowed down her impatience, smiled, and went through the entire examination for a third time. And once again, she told Galina to call her with any more concerns.

But Galina didn't call, and she didn't bring Dasha back.

"Two months later," Lilian told Daniel, "I was sued for malpractice—Ben and Galina had taken Dasha to another pediatrician, who diagnosed her with leukemia."

"Oh no," Daniel said, his eyes wide.

Lilian nodded, her stomach clenching with the memory. "The hospital's attorneys reviewed everything. They said Ben and Galina Nichols didn't have a case. But then the story got picked up by the local news, and it got so much worse."

She'd turned on the TV one morning to see a tearful Ben Nichols holding a news conference, begging for "Justice for Dasha." Protestors started to show up at the hospital, chanting and waving signs as Lilian walked in and out of work, screaming insults and obscenities. Because of the fallout from all the bad press, the hospital eventually agreed to settle with the Nichols family out of court, though it took months before it was all resolved.

"I have colleagues and friends who have been sued," Lilian said to Daniel, meeting his eyes again. "I'm not unique. But it was about a year after my parents died. I'd had the falling out with Rosie, and I guess I couldn't handle losing anyone else. I became obsessed with doing everything right, with not missing anything again."

She'd started ordering more tests for her patients: blood work, X-rays, ultrasounds. At night she stayed up late with her laptop, researching rare ailments, desperate to never make a similar mistake. She should have been more careful, more attentive. She should have *listened* more to Galina. She shouldn't have been so rushed, so eager to label her an overly protective first-time mom and move on to patients with "real" problems.

To make matters worse, negative reviews about Lilian started to appear online. Several referenced Dasha's delayed diagnosis, questioning Lilian's skills, citing circumstances that Lilian could not remember. Still, it nagged at her—maybe they were right? When she was a new intern, terrified that she would make a mistake and kill someone, her senior resident had told her to "fake it till you make it." But maybe she had *never* made it. Maybe she had *never* been good enough, and she'd somehow made it this far without anyone noticing.

Over time, she stopped getting new patients, and Lilian figured her reputation was the problem. Some of her patients asked to switch to other pediatricians. And the bad reviews kept piling up. "Try to ignore them," her colleagues said. "They don't define you." But behind their words, Lilian sensed a new wariness. An erosion of the respect they had once held for her. If all these patients believed this about Lilian, it couldn't be completely false. Right?

"But worse than any of that," Lilian said to Daniel, shaking herself out of the memories, "was that Dasha kept getting sicker, spending weeks in the children's hospital. I used to pull up her chart, just to check on her. One day it said *Palliative care only. Hospice consulted.*" She looked down at the napkin in her hands. "She had just a few days to live, so I did something I shouldn't have."

By then Lilian was a few months pregnant, and life felt fragile, uncertain, and scary. Her parents were dead. She hadn't seen Rosie in well over a year. Dasha was dying. She'd started having vivid, horrifying dreams of her baby being born deformed, and even though her obstetrician reassured her that these types of dreams weren't uncommon, they rattled her. For some reason, in her grief-drenched mind, Lilian thought that if she could see Dasha one more time, if she could say goodbye, maybe she could lay some of her fears to rest, too.

When she finished her work that evening, she walked over to the children's hospital. She didn't go into Dasha's room—that wouldn't have been appropriate—but she peeked in the door for one last glimpse of her sweet patient, curled on her side in bed, a few tufts of black hair visible on her little head.

She'd only stayed for a few seconds, tears building in her eyes, before turning away. She got just a few feet down the hall when she was stopped by a man's voice, shouting her name.

It was Ben Nichols, with Galina. They had aged a decade in the past year, and Lilian's heart sank. Galina looked frail and haunted, clinging to her husband's hand like she might fall over without it. Ben's hair had gone completely gray, and exhaustion lined his face. But when he saw Lilian, his eyes flashed with fury.

"What the fuck are you doing here?" he demanded, heading toward Lilian. "What did you do to my Dasha?"

Lilian faltered. "Nothing. I—I was just walking by—"

"You killed my daughter, you fucking bitch," Ben interrupted. "I don't trust a goddamn thing you're saying. Stay away from her."

Lilian wanted to tell them that her heart ached for them every day, that she was so incredibly sorry for not catching the leukemia earlier. It might not have changed the outcome, but what if it had?

"I feel terrible about what happened—" she started.

"*You* feel terrible? *You* do?" Ben gave a bitter laugh. Galina, next to him, tugged on his arm, but he got right in Lilian's face. "Fuck you, Doc. *Fuck you.*"

Two nurses—one man, one woman—hustled over, stepping between Lilian and Ben.

"All right," the male nurse said to Ben. "Let's calm down, Dad."

"Calm down?" Ben shouted, his face red. "My daughter is dying because of this piece-of-shit doctor and you're telling me to *calm down*?"

Galina fell to the floor, sobbing. Lilian's heart shattered—she wanted to join Galina on the floor, wailing at the injustice of it all. She'd lost so many patients over the years, and while she knew her sorrow could never compare with a parent's grief, she carried them all with her, every lost child etched on her soul forever.

The female nurse took Lilian by the arm and steered her away. Lilian recognized her as a nurse she'd worked with as a resident. "You shouldn't be here, Dr. D," she murmured.

"I know," Lilian said, tears streaming down her face, "I just—"

"You need to go," the nurse said.

"I will fucking *kill you*, bitch!" Ben shouted, lunging for Lilian. He got one hand on her wrist before two security guards tackled him, slamming his head against the linoleum floor.

As Lilian finished the story, she looked down at the napkin, now shredded to bits. Daniel, who had remained silent, pushed another napkin in her direction. After she took it, she realized her cheeks were wet with tears.

"I think about them, about Ben and Galina, all the time," Lilian said, wiping her eyes. "I know they'll never forgive me. Ben, especially." She looked up at Daniel. "I used to see him places. Ben, I mean. After

Dasha died. He'd be in the parking garage as I left work. He never said anything, but he'd watch me. Even after we moved to Wilmette, I'd see him around. At Panera, at Trader Joe's. I have no idea how he found out where we lived, and I never told anyone about it."

"Why not?" Daniel said. The first words he'd spoken since she'd started the story.

She shook her head. "I don't know. Maybe because I didn't think he was dangerous? No—that's not true. He scared me. I think I didn't tell anyone because I didn't want him to get in trouble. I figured I'd already done enough to hurt him, and maybe I deserved a little discomfort, a little fear. That probably sounds ridiculous—"

"No, it makes sense." Daniel said, rubbing the five-o'clock shadow on his chin. "When was the last time you saw him?"

Lilian thought back. "I was coming out of Target one evening. End of December, I think—all the Christmas stuff was on clearance. I was out of diapers, and Caleb wasn't home, so I took Abigail with me. Ben was sitting in his car in the parking lot, watching me."

She shivered at the memory of his face, shadowed in the dark cab of his truck. Someone else had been in the truck with him—maybe Galina?—but it was too dark to see. Ben's eyes had followed Lilian as she'd walked to her car, loaded her purchases into the trunk, clicked Abigail's car seat into its base, and driven away. The entire time, her whole body shook with terror.

She had tried to tell Caleb, when he got home that night. *Remember Ben Nichols?* she had started.

And Caleb had sighed and said, *Lily. You've got to put this behind you.*

She'd swallowed it down and tried to follow his advice. A few days later, she'd made plans to go to dinner with her little sister, and after that, all her attention had been occupied with the aftermath of the car crash.

Daniel cleared his throat. "Lilian," he said gently, "we need to tell the police."

"I know," Lilian said, though she didn't want to.

He got out his phone, tapped the screen, then set it on the table between them, faceup. He'd pulled up Sergeant Morgan's direct line. "Do you want to? Or should I?"

Hesitating, she stared at the phone. Calling would mean reliving the whole story. It would mean she'd have to tell Caleb. It would also mean dragging Ben Nichols into a police investigation, and he'd already been through hell. He probably had nothing to do with the crash.

But what if he did? His last words to her echoed in her mind: *I will fucking kill you, bitch.*

She picked up the phone.

CHAPTER
TWENTY-NINE

MyPsychJournal.com

Welcome back, Rosie. Happy journaling!

FEBRUARY 15, 2018

My appointment with Dr. V was yesterday and I'm still keyed up and frustrated. I think she's drawing her own conclusions about my relationship with Michael, and I'm not sure she's right. I guess I should be glad she's putting more of the blame on him, but it feels like a cop-out to pretend like I didn't play a huge role in what happened.

A memory is a Story We Tell Ourselves, she said, emphasizing those words, her dark eyes gleaming at me, giving me shivers. What story are you telling yourself, Rosie? Is this story easier to accept than what really happened?

I don't know. I don't know what she's talking about. We spent some time talking about memories and how they're affected by emotions, and she asked me what emotions I feel when I think back to that time with Michael. I think she expected me to say "fear" or "powerlessness" or something like that, but nope.

It's guilt.

So now she wants me to write about what precipitated our breakup. The first one, anyway. The one that happened a few weeks after my parents died.

But first, I should back up. I think I mentioned that when we moved in together, we got a dog. Bowie was a rescue mutt with spiky fur around his face that reminded me of David Bowie's character in Labyrinth. I used to watch that movie with Lilian; it scared me to death, the part about the baby being kidnapped. But she'd tell me not to worry; if the Goblin King ever took me, she would come and rescue me. Anyway—I loved that little dog. He'd sleep in our bed, right between us, and snuggle with me while we were watching TV in the evenings. There's something about the complete, unconditional adoration of a dog, right? I assumed Michael felt the same way.

When Bowie got sick—losing weight, acting lethargic, then vomiting—we took him to the veterinarian together. He was in kidney failure, and he had to be admitted for a few days to the animal hospital. It was terrifying, and Michael was right there with me through it all, supporting me, worrying with me. Eventually the vet figured out that Bowie had eaten some raisins—they're toxic to dogs. I was confused. I'd never given Bowie raisins. But then Michael admitted that he had. He felt awful, and he swore he had no idea that raisins could hurt a dog. The vet said it was a common mistake, and that Bowie should be okay.

A couple weeks later I had to go on a short trip for work, just three days, and when I came home, Bowie was gone. Michael said he had run out the door after a cat and never came back. He'd put up signs around the neighborhood, checked at all the local animal hospitals and shelters. I was heartbroken, Michael apologized profusely, and I believed him when he said it was an accident. I had no reason not to.

But later that night, he said something else: "If you hadn't left me for three days, the dog would still be here."

For a second, I thought maybe he had done it on purpose. He was punishing me. But that seemed absurd, and the most likely explanation was that if I had been home, Bowie wouldn't have run off, or if he had, we would have been able to find him together.

Fast forward to a couple weeks after my parents' death. I was a mess—I couldn't eat, couldn't sleep, could hardly function, and it was all compounded by the fact that, after my sister called me with the news, I didn't hear from her at all. No calls, no texts, nothing—I had to find out about my own parents' funeral from the fucking obituary, which I guarantee Lilian wrote, all by herself. Even though I hadn't been close to my parents or sister in a while, it was such an earth-rattling feeling, knowing that I was alone in the world. I started drinking too much and taking prescription pain pills left over from some dental work I'd had. Michael took care of me, held me at night while I cried. I was so grateful for him.

Until I found Bowie's collar in a safe in his closet, along with the braid of my hair.

When I saw that, I knew he had gotten rid of my dog on purpose. And I also knew that he wanted me to find the collar—he used my birthday as the code for the safe, he always did. He wanted me to know that he could do anything to me, could take anything away, and I would stay with him, no matter what.

Before my parents' death, I would have lashed out. That's probably what he expected: a knockdown, drag-out fight that would end with me apologizing to him for losing my temper. Then he could be the magnanimous one and forgive me. I don't know if it was the death of my parents or the pain pills making me feel a little invincible, but this time, I decided that I wouldn't get mad—I would get even.

I walked down to the drug store and bought a bottle of syrup of Ipecac. The next morning, I put some in the fruit and spinach smoothie he had every day for breakfast. He spent the next couple hours vomiting so hard he couldn't leave the house. I did the same thing the next day, and the next, until he was so dehydrated and miserable that he wanted to go to the emergency room. That's when I calmly opened my medicine cabinet, pulled out the syrup of Ipecac, and set it down in front of him. The expression on his face was pure, unadulterated shock.

I'm sick to my stomach right now, just thinking about that. I know it was awful. I know it was cruel. But in that moment, all I felt was vindication. I'd wanted to punish him, and I had. So there you go, Dr. V. I'm just as bad as him. Maybe worse.

The next day, I came home to find that he'd packed all his things, cleared out his side of the closet, and left. But here's the kicker: you'd think I would be glad he was gone, but I wasn't. I remember sinking to my knees in the middle of the floor and sobbing until my throat was raw—completely devastated, but not in the hyperbolic way most people use that word. Devastated like a small coastal town after a Category Five hurricane. Flattened.

That's when I went to see my sister—we've already talked about that, in other sessions. You know what happened. I was a mess, I'd run out of oxys and I was desperate for something—anything—to numb the pain. My parents died, Michael abandoned me, and then Lilian told me to get out of her life.

People talk about hitting rock bottom? I hit granite. Over the next few weeks, I lost so much weight my clothes hung on me. One night I drank too much and carved Michael's initial into my thigh with a razor. It felt good, at first, that pain—clean and cold. But then it wouldn't stop bleeding and I panicked. I didn't know who to call, and I didn't have any friends left, so I called Michael.

He came for me. He took me to the ER; they stitched me up. I could tell the staff was suspicious of him, so we left before they could get someone in to question either of us.

After that, he came home. It was such a fucking relief to have him back, to no longer be a bundle of exposed nerves rattling around in my empty jar. It's easy to judge people for staying in a dysfunctional relationship, but unless you know the blind terror of being abandoned, you can't comprehend the urgent need to keep someone with you, no matter the cost.

And that cost would get even steeper. For both of us.

CHAPTER
THIRTY

"What are you doing up so early?" Caleb asked as he walked into the kitchen.

Lilian looked up from her laptop, bleary-eyed. He was dressed to go to the gym: running shoes, shorts, hoodie. She glanced at the digital clock on the microwave: 5:04 a.m. She'd come down to the kitchen hours ago, unable to sleep after feeding Abigail.

"Just some research," she said, rubbing her gritty eyes.

Caleb grabbed his fancy French press from the cupboard. "Oh yeah? On what?" He craned his neck, looking at the notebook in front of her, filled with her messy scrawl.

Lilian flushed. Calling it "research" was generous. It had been three days since her visit to the police station with Daniel. Sergeant Morgan had put them in touch with a detective, who'd taken Lilian's statement about Ben Nichols and said he'd look into it. She hadn't heard back from him.

As each day passed, her worry grew. Last night the anxiety had felt like teeth, like claws, so sharp she launched out of bed, desperate for something to occupy her mind. Just a short time ago, she would have lain awake ruminating about Abigail, wondering if she ought to get out of bed just to check and make sure she was still breathing.

But a new, more urgent fear had taken over.

She'd filled half a notebook with everything she remembered about the car crash, and everything she remembered about Ben and the times she'd seen him watching her. After that, she'd switched gears to her other obsession: recovery after a traumatic brain injury. Determined to figure out some way to help her sister, Lilian had gone down a rabbit hole into the neuroscience of facial recognition.

She hadn't learned anything new about Capgras syndrome, but she'd read about something called the *butcher on the bus* phenomenon—the overwhelming sensation of recognizing a face outside of its normal context, of knowing someone is familiar but not knowing why or how. The brain always tried to make connections, she knew, but that didn't mean the connection was correct. So the man with the scar on his jaw was probably someone she *had* seen before, in a different setting. He could have been one of her patients' fathers, or a fellow patron at the grocery store. There was no objective evidence he was involved in the car crash at all.

Which should have been a relief, but it just made Lilian even more nervous about Ben Nichols. Before the anxiety could bite her again, she closed her notebook, shut her laptop, and sent a reassuring smile in Caleb's direction. He knew about all of this, of course. She'd told him everything, and he had listened, but since then, he'd seemed even more worried about her. Worried and distant, as if he might break her with one wrong move.

"I'm learning everything I can about brain injuries," she said. "It makes me feel like I'm doing something to help Rosie."

Caleb nodded, but he looked pensive. "You want some?" he asked, holding up a package of his favorite dark roast blend.

"No, thanks. I think I'll go back to bed and try to catch a couple hours of sleep before Abigail wakes up."

"Hang on," Caleb said.

Lilian turned. He stood staring at her, hands on his hips, lips pursed. "What?" she asked.

"You're doing that thing. The same thing you did before. When you obsess about things you can't change, spend all your time researching—"

"No, I'm not," she said automatically. This was nothing like that. And even if it was— "I'm just covering all the bases, Caleb. Making sure I'm not missing anything."

Caleb pressed his lips together, weighing his words. Always so careful with her, this new Caleb. So thoughtful and concerned. "Are you taking your meds?"

"Yes." She thought back. "I think so. Most days, anyway."

He took several long breaths before speaking. "This is important, Lily, especially now. You need to take them *every* day."

She paused, taking in the man her husband had become in the past few months. Worry had etched new lines into his forehead and around his mouth. She wanted to tell him that this was different, but he was right to worry: a concussion could worsen mental health issues.

"I'll take them right now," she said.

His eyes followed her as she walked across the kitchen, opened the cupboard, took out the prescription bottle, emptied the capsule onto her palm, and washed it down with water. She fought the impulse to open her mouth and show him her tongue, the way patients on her psych rotation had.

"Happy?" she said, forcing a smile.

In response, he studied her, a wrinkle of concern forming between his eyebrows. "You need a break. You're visiting Rosie every day, taking care of Abigail, up all night worrying. Let my mom watch Abigail for a day so you can rest. Take a nap, go to a yoga class, meet a friend for lunch. I don't know—but you're obviously overwhelmed—"

"What do you mean?" she said. Exactly what was so *obvious* to him? And he wanted her to take a break? He'd been working sixty to eighty hours a week for months—maybe *he* should take a break. "I know I'm struggling, Caleb, I am well aware of that, but I thought you of all people would understand why. My sister is injured, and Ben Nichols was following me around, and—"

"Which is exactly why you need a break," he said, then shook his head. "Lily, you have to admit that things were rough even before the car accident. For a while, now. Sometimes I don't know where my wife went."

His words echoed between them. She didn't know what to say. Sometimes she wondered where that wife had gone, too.

"Come here," he said, taking her hand and tugging her close. She put her arms around his waist, her cheek against his chest. He smelled like old workout clothes and morning breath, but underneath that was the scent of the man she had loved for fifteen years.

It should have felt reassuring. But a seed of unease had taken root inside her. For the first time, she wondered if Caleb didn't think she *could* come back.

CHAPTER
THIRTY-ONE

"This is Detective Berenson. Is this Lilian Donaldson? I'm calling to follow up regarding Ben Nichols."

"Yes," Lilian said, her heart speeding up. She was walking into the rehab hospital for her daily visit—a brief check on Rosie, and a lengthier update from the nurses and doctors. Now she hurried over to a chair in the lobby and sat. "Did you find him?"

"Yes, ma'am, I spoke with him myself." The detective's South Side accent brought back memories of her father. "His wife left him six months ago. He lost his job soon after that; sounds like after the little girl died, he'd been struggling at work and his boss got fed up. To be honest, he seemed angry, looking for someone to blame. He was pretty hostile."

He paused, then coughed. "But. He says he was visiting his brother in LaGrange on the night of the accident. The brother confirmed that they were alone in his home together. That's not the most solid alibi in the world, but I've also confirmed that Mr. Nichols does not have a silver sedan registered to his name. Of course, he could have rented a car, and I'm checking out rental car companies in the area. Unfortunately, I don't have much else to go on at this time."

She nodded, grateful but dazed. Across the lobby, a large family group carrying balloons headed across the lobby into the elevator. They were talking and laughing; probably excited to bring their loved one home. Lilian put a finger to her ear and spoke into the phone, "What should I do now? He could still be watching me."

"Does your home have an alarm system?"

"Yes."

"I recommend that you keep it armed at all times. Keep your doors locked. I told Nichols that watching you in public places is considered harassment and intimidation. If you see him again, call me right away. We'll want to document it, in case you'd like to file for a protective order."

"I will," Lilian said, shaken by his stern tone. "Thank you for everything you've done."

"My pleasure, ma'am. You have a good day now."

When they hung up, she set down her phone and allowed it all to sink in. Ben Nichols had lost his daughter, his wife, and his job. He had every reason to want revenge. Some might even say he was justified. Last night, for the first time in weeks, she'd checked to see if any more reviews had been posted about her. She'd found a particularly scathing one that ended with the words, *This doctor took everything from the Nichols family. She deserves to have everything taken away from her, too.* It'd been posted under an anonymous username, but she imagined Ben Nichols typing those words, alone, devastated, and angry.

Her scalp prickled, and she whirled around. The lobby was empty except for a receptionist at the check-in desk, but she didn't feel reassured. Ben could be anywhere. He could be watching her right here, right now.

Her chest tightened until it hurt, her breaths becoming fast and shallow. The start of a panic attack. Next would come the uncontrollable shaking, tingling in her face and hands, tunnel vision. She needed Caleb; she couldn't do this on her own. But as she fumbled for her phone, she remembered his words the other night: *You're obviously overwhelmed.* She didn't want to give him any more reasons to doubt her.

Without allowing herself to think, she dialed Daniel's number.

"Hey, Lilian. What's up?"

"The detective called me about Ben Nichols," she said, then told him about the phone call. Her voice wobbled at the end, and she forced out a shaky laugh. "Sorry. I don't know why I'm so freaked out by this."

"No need to apologize," he said. "It would frighten anyone. Where are you?"

The steady rumble of his voice made the tightness in her chest ease a fraction. "On my way in to visit Rosie. But now I can't stop thinking about Ben."

"I'm in the middle of a project for work, or else I'd come and meet you. Maybe we could talk about something else to distract you? Let's see." He paused. "Did I ever tell you about the squirrel bridges?"

"No." She closed her eyes and drummed her fingers on her thighs.

"You know the power lines that cross the roads in residential areas, that squirrels sometimes run across? When I was a kid, my dad told me those were put there to keep the squirrels safe. It made total sense, and I believed him for years, until I told a friend about the squirrel bridges, and he looked at me like I was nuts."

That made Lilian smile, thinking of Daniel as an earnest little boy. "When was that?"

"Oh, like a year ago."

Lilian burst out laughing. "I mean, it's not a bad idea. I always feel so bad for the dead squirrels."

"Well, that's the thing. Apparently, squirrel bridges really do exist in some places. I know this because I spent an entire weekend researching them to prove to my friend I wasn't nuts."

"Tell me about these bridges," she said, and he did. As he spoke, her muscles relaxed. Her vision cleared. *I'm okay,* she told herself.

And yet she sat and chatted with Daniel for another fifteen minutes before taking the elevator up to see Rosie.

* * *

As Lilian entered the brain injury unit, she spotted Rosie in the therapy kitchen, finishing up a session with the occupational thera-pist. They were standing at the counter, the OT holding a gait belt around Rosie's waist, steadying her as Rosie stirred a pot of what looked like spaghetti.

Dozens of memories sprouted in Lilian's mind: *What should we make for dinner tonight, Rosie?* Nine times out of ten, Rosie would shout *S'ghetti!* She always wanted to pour the noodles into the pot, which had given Lilian a mini heart attack every time the boiling water nearly splashed on Rosie's hands.

Did Rosie remember that? Lilian wondered. Had she asked to make this specific meal? Or maybe the therapist often used this task to practice motor skills, balance, and executive function while sequencing a complex task. Rosie's physical gains had far outpaced her cognitive recovery—she still couldn't communicate clearly, and just yesterday, the occupational therapist had reminded Lilian that Rosie would need constant supervision after discharge.

Which brought up another question: If Rosie believed that Daniel and Lilian were imposters, was it in her best interest to go home with either of them? Daniel was still planning on taking her home, Lilian knew, but Rosie wouldn't allow him to get near her, so he hadn't received much hands-on training. Dr. Kirkpatrick had adjusted her medications and was hopeful that would help with her agitation and paranoia. But Lilian's research into Capgras syndrome had confirmed that no therapy or medication could alter Rosie's belief.

Even more disturbing, Lilian had learned that in rare cases, individuals with Capgras syndrome could become violent toward the "imposter." Some had even killed their loved ones. As horrifying as that sounded, it made sense. If you truly believed you were being held captive—by the KGB, or a serial killer, or a cult—wouldn't you do anything to escape? Those individuals had been charged with murder, but in all the cases Lilian had read, they'd been found not guilty by reason of insanity. That didn't mean they walked free; they were admitted to secure psychiatric facilities, presumably for the rest of their lives.

Shivering at the thought, Lilian watched as Rosie carefully drained the pasta, her brow furrowed in concentration. After scooping a serving of noodles onto a plate, she flashed the therapist a triumphant smile.

In moments like this, Lilian could almost believe that a facility might be the best place for Rosie. She'd be cared for by professionals, people she could learn to trust. But that would feel like she was deserting her sister, once again, and that made Lilian sick to her stomach.

When the therapy session ended, the OT took Rosie back to her room. Lilian hung back, waiting until the therapist was gone before she entered. She'd keep her visit short, she promised herself, but she could never leave without talking to Rosie. The room was dark and silent, the curtains closed. Rosie was in bed with the blanket over her head. When Lilian's footsteps echoed in the room, she pulled the blanket off and looked up.

Lilian braced herself for Rosie to scream and swear at her, but she simply stared at Lilian, eyes wide and unblinking. The new medication must have kicked in.

"Where are my mom and dad where are they where'd they go—my mom and dad?" she said. Her face was all cheekbones and angles now, accentuated by her short, buzzed hair. It gave her a haunted look.

Lilian had been through this with Rosie already, many times, but it still hurt to say the words. "They died, remember?"

"I know who killed them—I know—killed them I know." Rosie's voice was flat, expressionless. Probably another effect of the medication; Lilian wasn't sure she liked it. Still, she seemed more fluent than ever before. "*You* did it *you* killed them I know you're a spy you're watching me—who killed them."

Lilian swallowed past the lump in her throat. "No one killed them, Rosie. It was an accident."

"I know that," Rosie snapped, looking and sounding just like she had as a teenager whenever Lilian tried to explain something. That sullen, annoyed glare.

Back before Rosie could communicate, when she couldn't remember anything, it was easy to imagine that the real Rosie was trapped inside, waiting to be set free. The body in the hospital bed was Not Really Rosie. But this person had Rosie's voice, Rosie's mannerisms, and many of Rosie's memories. Earlier this week she'd repeated the phrase *New York pizza sucks* in a dead-on imitation of their father's voice.

Lilian had to come to grips with the facts: this *was* Rosie now. This was the new reality of their relationship as sisters.

Her gaze caught on the sketchbook on Rosie's bedside table—another sketch of Renoir's *Two Sisters*. This one was more confident, capturing a general impression of trees, the river; the older sister's coat, and the younger sister's hat.

The little sister held something in her outstretched palms—several small, cylindrical objects. Almost like cigarettes or short, stubby cigars, although Lilian knew that couldn't be right. When she searched her memory, she couldn't recall what the younger girl held in the original painting.

Rosie whirled around and sat bolt upright.

"Don't look at that—mine—it's mine don't touch it," she said, snatching the sketchbook away.

"I'm sorry," Lilian said, oddly disappointed. The drawing was a window into her sister's mind, the only real glimpse Lilian had gotten since the crash.

Rosie stuffed the sketchbook under her pillow, then fixed her eyes on Lilian again. "What do you want stop spying me—watching me," she said. Her mouth twisted in an odd grin, and Lilian's scalp prickled. "Stay away not Lilian stop spying."

Lilian wanted to protest, to say, *Of course I'm Lilian*, to verify her credentials as Rosie's older sister. But she knew none of that would help. Acknowledge the patient's confusion, she had read recently in an article about Capgras.

"I know you're confused right now—"

"Not fucking confused," Rosie said, her voice sharp as a slap. "Get out—now."

Biting back a response, Lilian stood and left the room. Out in the hallway, she leaned against the wall, her eyes blurring with tears. Nothing she could say or do would convince Rosie that she—Lilian—was her sister, or that Daniel was her fiancé. Nothing she could say or do could make Rosie trust either of them.

But maybe there was another way to communicate with Rosie. Something Lilian hadn't tried yet.

CHAPTER
THIRTY-TWO

Lilian walked down the hall to the rehab dayroom, pulled out her phone, and dialed the number the nurse had given her.

Betty, the nurse, answered on cue. "Hello, Lilian? Rosie's right here. Let me give her the phone."

Lilian didn't know if this would work, but she'd read that some Capgras patients could recognize their loved ones' voices on the phone—something about bypassing the visual pathways in their brain that led to the confusion. It was worth a try.

"Hello," Rosie said, her voice flat and tinged with suspicion. The same voice Lilian had just heard in her room.

"It's me, Lilian."

A long pause.

"Sis?" Rosie's voice, in that one word, held an ocean of feeling: hope, familiarity, loneliness. "Sis where are you why'd you leave—why'd you leave me all alone?"

She sounded like a frightened child, like she had when Lilian moved away from home, and Lilian's vision blurred with tears. Closing her eyes, she drifted back to that long-ago day when she'd loaded up her car to head off to medical school, so excited about the future that she thought she might burst. But as she drove away, she'd glanced back at the house, and there it was, the sight that sent a pang through her chest: Rosie's small, pale face in the window, her eyes red from crying.

A similar feeling filled Lilian's chest now, as she imagined how abandoned Rosie must feel, believing that the people she loved most had deserted her.

"I'm so sorry," Lilian said, her throat thick. "I—I've been away. But I've been talking to your doctors and nurses."

"Going to visit me soon—come here and visit me?"

Lilian closed her eyes, wishing she could go straight to Rosie and put her arms around her. Wishing that Rosie would allow that. "Yes. I will. But I can't come right now, okay?"

"But *why*?" Rosie said. "Why'd you leave me all alone—and why I'm all alone?"

"I didn't—"

"You always leave me you *never* stay you left me you left me you left—" She broke off, her breath hitching in a sob that Lilian seemed to feel in her own body.

"I'm sorry—I've missed you so much." Hot, stinging tears filled Lilian's eyes again. She didn't know if Rosie was referring to Lilian leaving for med school, their argument two years ago, or Lilian being replaced by an "imposter." Maybe all of the above.

When it came to that argument, though, this could be an opportunity to find out what had prompted it, from Rosie's perspective.

"Can you tell me about Michael, Rosie? Can you tell me what happened with him?"

"Is he here?" High-pitched, panicky. "I don't want to see him please sis don't—don't let him come here please don't let him—"

"I won't," Lilian said, trying to sound soothing. "You're safe here." She paused, waiting until Rosie's rapid breathing slowed, then tried a different direction. "You know it's almost time for you to leave the hospital, right?"

"I want to go home this isn't my home."

Lilian paused. This was the heart of the conversation. "And where is home, Rosie?"

"Where I used to—with Daniel where our apartment in the park—no. Hyde Park." Her voice brightened, as if she'd just remembered. "You see the lake from the window sis and I love it there can I go there again please?"

Lilian smiled sadly. "What if Daniel can't take care of you? Where would you like to live, then?"

"I don't know nowhere else or maybe—with Mom and Dad—I don't know."

"Remember, Mom and Dad died, Rosie."

"Oh." Rosie's voice caught. "Yeah I know I—I know they did."

Lilian pressed her free hand to her forehead, massaging away the ever-present tension. "I'm not sure exactly what's going to happen, but I want you to feel good about it. If it were up to you, you would want to live with Daniel again. Is that right?"

"Yes do you know Daniel—the real Daniel—haven't seen him in so long and where he is and why he left me—the one who comes here I don't like." Rosie sounded like she was on the verge of tears again.

"I've been talking to him, too. He loves you. He misses you."

"Does he want me to come—home does he want me home with him?" Rosie's voice lifted with hope.

Memories of Daniel and Rosie's apartment filled Lilian's mind: Rosie's paintings on the walls, her blue trench hanging on the coatrack, Daniel saying *She's the love of my life.*

"Yes, he does."

She didn't need to carry on this conversation any longer, but she couldn't seem to let go. She clung to the phone, relishing the connection with her sister. In this moment, Rosie knew Lilian. She recognized her. And Lilian wanted more.

"How are you feeling?" she asked, settling onto the sofa. "There have been a lot of changes for you lately. I'm sure it's been scary and hard."

"I hate it," Rosie said flatly. "I hate not knowing what's—I'm scared all the time and Lilian—Lilian you need to know there's a man who comes to see me and he—everyone says he's Daniel and everyone thinks he's Daniel but he isn't he is *not* so they're liars too—they're *all* liars and I try to tell them and they don't care they won't listen—"

"I know—"

"And there's a Lilian too a Lilian who isn't you but she looks like you—they're watching me—they scare me sis and everyone here lies to me all the time where are you? Why haven't you come to see me I miss you."

"I know," Lilian said again. "But listen, Daniel and I have been talking and we've come up with a plan."

She hoped he would still be okay with this. If not, she would re-adjust.

"A plan?" Rosie repeated. "For me?"

"You know the man who comes to see you who says he's Daniel? He's going to take you home."

Rosie gasped. "He's a liar sis he says he's Daniel but he's not him I swear he's not him I promise he's not him—"

"It's okay," Lilian said, hoping she sounded reassuring. "Daniel— the real Daniel—and I know him. We trust him."

A pause. "You do? Why would you—are you sure are you—everyone here lies to me but you won't lie to me sis right?"

"I would never lie to you," Lilian said, aching to go to her sister, to talk to her in person. She hoped she was doing the right thing. "He'll take care of you until Daniel and I get there. Okay?"

"No but I—no but you don't give a shit what I think." Rosie again sounded like a surly teenager. It took Lilian back to those years, when she'd feel whiplashed by the extremes of her sister's behavior. Rosie would call, begging Lilian to come home, and Lilian would drop everything. But when she arrived, Rosie would storm off to her bedroom, slam the door, and shout at Lilian to leave her alone.

Once, after that had happened, Lilian came back into the kitchen to see their mother sitting at the table, her hair in a messy ponytail, look-ing exhausted and worried. *I don't know what to do with her,* she had said. *You were so much easier.*

"Daniel and I will be there as soon as we can," Lilian said, blinking away the memory.

"You promise because he scares me I'm scared where—where are you? Why haven't you come to see me I miss you—don't lie to me ev-eryone here lies to me all the time nobody listens to me—you promise?"

Lilian held her breath for a few seconds before answering. She hated doing this to her sister, especially now, but she couldn't think of another way to get Rosie to go home with Daniel without being frightened.

"I promise," she said.

* * *

That night, long after midnight, Lilian was in Abigail's bedroom, nurs-ing her back to sleep. Since her conversation with Rosie, a huge weight had lifted. Lilian had discussed the arrangement with Caleb and Daniel, and they were all in agreement: Rosie would go home with Daniel, Lilian would help as much as possible, Caleb and Lilian would pitch in financially. It was the best possible scenario, given the circumstances.

Abigail drifted off to sleep, and Lilian wished she could relax, too. But she felt the old restlessness scratching at her. Anxieties swarmed around her head like gnats. She wanted to reach up and swat them away. Worries about Ben Nichols, about Rosie's past, about Abigail, about her relationship with Caleb. *Nothing's wrong*, she told herself, but she won-dered if she would ever truly relax again.

Sighing, she leaned her head against the rocking chair's cushion. Outside, the wind moaned, and the house creaked. Based on the fore-cast, the temperature would hit record lows tonight.

Right before she closed her eyes, she saw the camera for the baby monitor move.

She froze, staring into the gritty darkness. The monitor, as usual, was across from her on Abigail's dresser, but it wasn't pointed at the crib. It was angled halfway toward Lilian—but no, she told herself, it hadn't *moved*. She must have bumped it earlier.

With a long exhale, she forced her limbs to relax.

But then the camera panned to Lilian and stopped.

Her heart skipped a beat. Lilian instinctively reached for her phone, but it was on her nightstand in the bedroom, where she'd left it.

The app controlling the baby monitor must have malfunctioned. Or maybe Caleb had woken up and decided to check on her without having to get out of bed. *That must be it,* she told herself, but she still felt shaken.

"Caleb," she whispered, staring into the black eye of the camera. "Is that you?"

The camera moved again. Back and forth, side to side, as if shaking its head.

No.

A shiver ran down Lilian's legs. Only she and Caleb had access to the app. *And Nancy,* she realized. She had helped Nancy download it several weeks ago when she'd come to babysit Abigail. But Nancy would never be awake in the middle of the night, checking the app.

Lilian's breath caught. Someone was controlling the baby monitor. Someone was watching her.

"Who are you?" Lilian said, louder this time.

No movement from the camera. A gust of wind howled past the window.

"You're watching me, aren't you?" Lilian whispered.

This time, when the camera moved, it was in an up-and-down motion.

Yes.

Lilian's pulse whooshed in her ears, almost deafening her. She could feel it thrumming through her body, in her arms and legs, fingers and toes. She took a long, shaky breath. "Why?"

No movement from the camera.

"Do you want to hurt me?" Lilian whispered.

The camera looked like a mouth, a black, gaping maw that might swallow her whole.

It moved—up and down.

Yes.

CHAPTER
THIRTY-THREE

MyPsychJournal.com

Welcome back, Rosie. Happy journaling!

FEBRUARY 21, 2018

We had a good session today, me and Dr. V. We spent most of the time discussing healthier ways of coping with uncomfortable emotions. But I'm still having trouble wrapping my head around something. She kept calling Michael my "abuser" and I kept correcting her. I hurt him, too, I told her. I don't have any moral high ground here. It was a mutually abusive relationship.

But then she got serious, her black eyes glinting at me as she peered over her glasses. "Is it easier to think of it that way, as mutually abusive?"

I told her of course it's not easier. God. I hate that I acted that way—I'm ashamed of myself.

Then she said: "If Michael had never hurt you, would you have hurt him?"

No. I don't think so, anyway.

Then she softened her voice. "Abusers rarely, if ever, have any genuine desire to change. Look at you here, right now, doing all this work. Can you imagine Michael doing this?"

I almost laughed at that. No, Michael didn't think he needed to change. I was the one who was paranoid, hysterical, violent, crazy. Even his apologies were meant to shift the blame away from himself.

"Abuse is about control and power. Period. Answer me this, Rosie: Who had the control in your relationship with Michael?"

I struggled to answer that, because yeah, he did a lot of manipulative stuff, but I'm the one who finally did something awful enough to make him leave. Doesn't that mean I had the power?

Then Dr. V said that Michael left me because he was trying to regain control. By walking away, just weeks after my parents died and my sister told me to get out of her life, he took away my last safety net. He was banking on the fact that I was so grief-stricken, so lonely, that I wouldn't be able to cope without him.

He was right.

I told Dr. V how, after Michael came back, I found out he'd blocked Lilian's number in my phone. That's why I hadn't gotten any of her calls or texts after my parents' death. That should have made me leave him, but by that point, it didn't even matter anymore. I had screwed things up so badly with my sister that I felt like there was no hope of ever fixing things with her. And I was just so grateful that Michael had forgiven me. Without him, I would have been totally alone.

And we all know I can't handle that.

Dr. V told me at the end of today's session that I have made incredible progress. So much progress, in fact, that after next week's session, she wants to drop our sessions to once a month. That sent a warning flare through my mind: is she abandoning me? But no, she said this is a sign that I'm improving. I don't need her as much; I'm learning to change my thought patterns, interrogate my memories, and create my own buffers.

I'm not so sure about that. But one thing I know about Dr. V is that she wouldn't lie to me. So maybe . . . maybe I'm getting better.

CHAPTER
THIRTY-FOUR

Caleb called the police about the baby monitor. Lilian had woken him up, shrieking about someone watching her, and he'd panicked. When they both calmed down, Lilian explained what had happened, and Caleb didn't hesitate.

The Wilmette Police Department took it seriously, too. Two uniformed officers arrived and searched the house and perimeter. They didn't find anything, but they took a statement from Lilian about everything: the accident, the car she'd seen in the driveway, Dasha's tragic death, and Ben Nichols's threats. Lilian asked them point-blank if this could all this be part of a revenge scheme.

Not likely, they said. Apparently Wi-Fi-controlled monitors were prone to hacking. Most of the time it was harmless, the cops assured Lilian, just idiot kids playing a prank or trying to access your home network. But after Lilian pushed them again, they agreed to contact Detective Berenson with the Chicago PD and talk to him about Ben Nichols.

After that, Caleb called their security system and demanded that a technician come out immediately. The technician arrived a few hours later, looking like he'd just rolled out of bed. After checking their system and assuring Caleb and Lilian that it was secure, he recommended more cameras along their exterior and entrances, and getting rid of any interior cameras not connected to the security system.

Which meant no more baby monitor.

As soon as Target opened, Caleb bought an old-school radio monitor. No video capabilities, which made Lilian's chest constrict with anxiety. What if Abigail got herself wedged in a strange position and suffocated, or tried to climb out of the crib? Never mind that she wasn't even five months old yet. Something terrible could happen. Lilian needed to watch her baby.

And yet, she couldn't take the risk of someone *else* watching her and Abigail, too.

* * *

"What's on your mind, Lilian?" Daniel asked. They were at a hot dog place near the hospital, getting a quick lunch after visiting Rosie.

Lilian hesitated before answering. The events of the past twelve hours had blurred together. After bringing home the new baby monitor, Caleb had called his mother and asked her to come over, despite Lilian's protests. He'd canceled his morning clinic, but he had a surgical case that afternoon that he couldn't miss.

I don't need your mother to watch me, Lilian had said.

Caleb had pinched the bridge of his nose. *Just do it for me, please, Lily. I can't spend my entire day worrying about you.*

A low blow, and one that had set off suppressed fury. She'd countered that it would be better if she dropped Abigail off at Nancy's house, so she could take a nap at home. Caleb hadn't liked it, but he'd acquiesced.

After Lilian dropped Abigail off at Nancy's, though, she headed to the hospital. It wasn't just a "screw you" to Caleb. There was no way she could sleep in that house—not after what had happened last night. At the rehab hospital, she checked on Rosie and touched base with the resident taking care of her. And now here she was, eating lunch with Daniel. She knew she probably looked as exhausted and drained as she felt.

"I—" She almost swallowed down the words, almost tried to brush everything off. But Daniel's eyes met hers, calm and steady, and it all spilled out. "Someone was watching me on the baby monitor last night."

His eyes widened in shock. He set down his hot dog, spilling pickles and peppers across his plate. "Jesus, Lilian. Are you okay? How are you feeling?"

She took a long, shaky breath. In all of the furor surrounding the incident—the police and security system investigation—she had been asked dozens of questions.

Are you certain you saw the camera move, ma'am? Any chance it could have moved on its own? Who has access to the app controlling the monitor? Has Ben Nichols contacted you since the last time you saw him?

And the questions that had bothered her most, delivered by the police after Caleb mentioned her "mental state": *You're currently being treated for anxiety? Are you taking your medications as prescribed?*

But no one, not even her husband, had asked her how she felt about all of it.

"I'm scared," she said. "Home is supposed to be a safe space, right? I feel invaded, naked. Someone was watching me for who knows how long. What were they doing, getting off on the sight of me nursing? It makes me sick."

"I don't blame you," he said. "Do the police have any leads?"

"Not really. They said it was probably kids playing around. But I—" She swallowed. "I can't shake the idea that it could be Ben Nichols. I know that's crazy—"

"Not crazy," Daniel said firmly, and Lilian's chest flooded with gratitude.

Earlier that morning, one of the cops had given his partner a look, a subtle twitch of his eyebrows. It seemed to encompass the entire situation from his point of view: a sleep-deprived housewife with an overactive imagination. Did they think she had made it up? As if she *wanted* that kind of attention?

And even though Caleb had ostensibly done all the right things, she had the feeling his actions were more about appeasing her than protecting her from any real or imagined threats.

"You told the police about Ben Nichols, right?" Danial asked, bringing her back to the conversation.

"Of course. They're going to check him out." She took a bite of her hot dog, hardly tasting it. She'd lost her appetite.

They sat in silence, listening to the buzz of conversation around them, the noise from the street outside. Daniel seemed to be studying Lilian, his light blue eyes tracing her face, her eyes, her mouth. Lilian's cheeks warmed under his perusal, and she shifted her weight.

"You know what?" he said, his voice resolute. "We should go see a movie."

"What?" Lilian almost laughed, it sounded so bizarre. "I thought you wanted to go back to see Rosie this afternoon."

"I do, and I will later. But you"—he pointed at Lilian—"need a break. An actual, honest-to-God break from this situation. When's the last time you did that? You need a couple of hours in front of a funny, stupid flick, with a bucket of popcorn and a Coke."

Lilian hesitated. It sounded irresponsible, hiding from reality by escaping into mindless entertainment. It also sounded perfect.

Daniel leaned in, his eyes fixed on hers. A whisper of a smile curved his lips. "Come on, Lilian."

"Only if I can get Milk Duds," she said.

His eyes twinkled. "Deal."

* * *

The movie was, as Daniel had promised, funny and stupid. For those two hours, Lilian was able to forget everything outside the theater. And even though the volume seemed too loud and the screen too bright and her head pounded with lack of sleep and a post-concussion headache, she ate her popcorn and laughed at the crude jokes, and shared a box of Milk Duds with Daniel.

After that, though, she had to go home.

She picked up Abigail from Nancy's, thanking her mother-in-law profusely for the help. Despite Lilian's frustration with Caleb, she appreciated his mother's willingness to step in whenever asked. But her life was feeling increasingly fragmented: her life at home, taking care of Abigail, and her life at the hospital, visiting Rosie. She felt split in two, like she couldn't give her full attention in either situation. Something was bound to fall through the crack.

As she pulled into her driveway, she saw a short, stocky man in a dark suit standing on her front porch, ringing the doorbell. He turned, and she rolled down the window.

"Detective Berenson, Chicago PD," he called, showing a badge. His breath made a cloud in the cold night air. "Following up regarding Ben Nichols."

* * *

After inviting him inside, Lilian perched on the edge of the sofa. Abigail, in a bouncy seat a few feet away, squealed.

"Cute baby," Detective Berenson said, but he didn't smile.

"Thanks." Lilian's hands twisted in her lap. Might as well cut to the chase. "You said you wanted to talk about Ben Nichols?"

"That's right. The Wilmette PD called me about the hacking of your baby monitor last night. I didn't like the sound of that, so I decided to check on Nichols again." He paused, fiddling with the small notebook in his hands. "He's gone, ma'am."

Lilian's blood seemed to turn to ice. "Gone?"

"I went to his home, he wouldn't answer, so I knocked next door— it's a duplex. The lady who lives there said Mr. Nichols told her he was taking a last-minute trip out of state, wanted to know if she could pick up his mail." He coughed, a smoker's cough, raspy and deep. "I contacted his ex-wife and his brother, but both said they know nothing. In short, ma'am, I do not have any information regarding his current whereabouts."

Lilian's hands started to shake. Ben must have gotten spooked by the questions from the police. Which meant he must have something to hide. It also meant he could be anywhere.

"So that's it?" Her voice sounded high and panicky. "There's nothing else you can do?"

"No, ma'am, that's not what I'm saying," the detective said. "The Wilmette PD has their tech guy looking into who hacked the baby monitor. I've already checked car rental companies in the area for records of Mr. Nichols renting one on the night of the collision, but it's possible he borrowed a car. We're looking into it. I have a guy keeping tabs on Nichols's brother and ex-wife. Rest assured, we're not giving up yet."

"What do I do?" she asked, dazed. A dozen other questions were contained in those simple words. How would she keep herself safe? How would she keep her *daughter* safe? How would she continue to go about her daily life, caring for Abigail and visiting Rosie, knowing that Ben Nichols could be out there, watching her, lying in wait?

"Keep your security system armed. Doors locked. Stay in public places, don't go off somewhere in the boonies or whatever, okay? And call me if anything else happens that makes you nervous."

* * *

After thanking the detective, Lilian shut the front door and set the alarm system, punching in the numbers so viciously her finger hurt. The emptiness of the house pressed against her chest. Every time she blinked, her mind flooded with memories, swirling and shifting in a kaleidoscope of fear: Rosie in the car, looking over her left shoulder; Ben Nichols' face, twisted with anger; the baby monitor, moving in the darkness; the silver sedan in the driveway, surrounded by a plume of exhaust.

Racing back into the kitchen, she grabbed her phone and called Caleb. No answer. She left a terse voice mail: *Call me as soon as possible.* Then she sent a text with the same message.

Her Find My Friends app showed him still at work. His phone was probably on silent, buried under a stack of papers, or left in his office while he met with a colleague.

The thought of the way he'd looked at her just this morning made her stomach clench. The weariness in his eyes, as if she was just one more thing he had to deal with. *I can't spend my entire day worrying about you.*

Maybe he'd left his phone behind on purpose.

In a burst of agitation, she turned on the lights in the entry, in the hallway, and the office, each switch making a satisfying *snap* as she flicked it on. Then she turned on the TV in the living room, needing to be distracted from the ringing in her ears, the thud of her pulse, the ragged in-and-out of her breathing.

When she went upstairs with Abigail, she continued turning on all the lights: up the stairs, across the landing. She fed Abigail and put her to bed, then headed into her bedroom. Exhaustion hung leaden on her eyelids, but the panicky fluttering in her chest could not be ignored. The terrifying sensation of being out of control threatened—her chest was already beginning to tighten. She needed to get ahold of herself.

In a rush, she grabbed her lists, her notebooks, and her laptop. Rosie would be discharged in a week or so, and Lilian needed to focus on her sister, to make the transition as smooth as possible. For the next couple hours, she researched home health agencies, specialists in Capgras and related delusions, medications, and therapies. Anything to help Rosie. Anything to keep her mind off the pervasive sense of fear that she couldn't shake.

But even after an hour of feverishly writing, filling page after page with her almost illegible scrawl, she didn't feel any better. Another glance at her phone showed that Caleb hadn't responded; his location hadn't changed, either. How could he stay late tonight, after everything that had happened? How could he let his *work* take precedence over his wife?

A vicious, sneaky voice whispered that maybe he was staying late at work to avoid her. To avoid the entire situation.

Caleb had wanted a wife who would be an equal partner; he liked that they were both professionals, academics, on equal footing. He'd fallen in love with a different Lilian, a competent, confident version she'd somehow maintained for the first fifteen years of their relationship. Caleb hadn't signed up for a wife who needed daily medication to cope with the stress of caring for their child, who was avoiding going back to work because she didn't want to face the mess she'd left behind. A wife hiding in her bedroom, shaking and terrified.

Lilian set down her pen and leaned against the headboard, exhausted. The soft glow of the lamp on her nightstand created a shadow of her own head on the pages scattered in front of her. She'd never liked the saying that someone was "a shadow of their former self." A shadow wasn't an actual thing; it was, by definition, the absence of light, created by some interposing object. You can create a shadow, but you can't *be* one.

Holding her breath, she gazed down at her shadow, the slight point of her ears, the thinness of her neck, her familiar profile. A perfect reproduction of herself, but in negative. She wondered if this is what Caleb saw when he looked at her. A Lilian-shaped absence.

CHAPTER
THIRTY-FIVE

MyPsychJournal.com

Welcome back, Rosie. Happy journaling!

FEBRUARY 28, 2018

Today was a difficult session with Dr. V, one of those sessions that leaves me feeling like a scraped-out gourd. She started by suggesting, flat-out, that it's easier for me to remember what happened with Michael as a toxic and dysfunctional relationship than to remember it as it really was. If I accept that Michael was abusive, she said, then how will that affect how I see myself?

I didn't answer. I didn't know what to say.

Then she asked if Michael was ever physically abusive, and I said no, which is the truth. He never touched me in anger. He never even raised his voice. I'm the one who yelled, who slammed doors and threw things, who gave him a black eye.

But for my homework this week, Dr. V asked me to write about ways he made me feel physically unsafe, and now that I think about it, it's like a lightbulb has come on. The fact that he cut off my hair and poisoned my dog meant that I always knew he could hurt me, if he wanted to. Especially after we got back together. He knew that no matter what he did, I'd come crawling back to him. It was like the gloves came off. No more subtle manipulation, oh no—he just flat-out told me what to do. He wanted me to quit my job, so I did. He didn't want me spending time with anyone but him, so I didn't. He wanted control of the money, so I let him.

Dr. V also asked about sexual abuse and I told her no, he never raped me. But now I'm remembering dozens of times when he wanted to have sex and I went along with it because I felt like I couldn't refuse. Michael liked rough sex—I did, too, early on—but toward the end, yeah, he would sometimes go too far. It scared me. But what could I do? Just imagine how it would have gone if I'd tried to go to the police: "So your boyfriend chokes you during sex, and you used to like it but now it's too much. Well, have you told him to stop? No? How about you try that, little lady, and stop wasting our time."

Actually, now that I think about it, it was sex that finally got me to leave him, for good. He started talking about having a baby together, and I said I wasn't ready for that. But then my birth control pills went missing—I was used to "misplacing" things by then; now I'm sure he took them—and I couldn't get a new pack until the next month. So I told him we would need to use condoms for a couple weeks. But then I woke up in the middle of the night to realize that he was on top of me, already inside me, unprotected, and it was too late. He tried to explain it away by saying that he'd had a dream about having sex, that he was half-asleep and didn't realize he was doing it. But that was the wake-up call I needed; I knew he'd never give up until I got pregnant. I may be broken and needy, but I was smart enough to realize that we shouldn't bring a child into a situation like that.

But he never hit me, never left a mark on me, so after I left him, I felt like a fraud staying at that shelter with women who had been beaten black and blue, had bones broken and teeth knocked out by their boyfriends or husbands. On the other hand, I could totally relate to their fear that they would be found. I was terrified of Michael finding me.

Or maybe I was terrified that if he found me, I would end up going back to him.

He did find me, of course. I always knew he would—he's good at playing the long game. And what happened next . . . well, I wish I could say it surprised me. But it didn't. I'm just lucky it didn't turn out worse.

CHAPTER
THIRTY-SIX

A polar vortex swept through Chicago, coating the entire region in ice and snow, forcing Lilian to stay inside as much as possible, preventing her from visiting Rosie. The Chicago River froze over; an ice storm coated tree branches and power lines in eerie, translucent membranes. The windchill could cause frostbite within minutes. She couldn't in good conscience take Abigail with her to the hospital, and Nancy had escaped the bitter cold with a group of girlfriends on a cruise.

Lilian missed seeing her sister with a deep, gnawing pain she recognized from their years of estrangement. She called Rosie once on the phone, just to hear her voice, to experience even a momentary spark of connection, but it made Rosie so confused and tearful that it didn't seem fair to do it again. *Where are you sis—why did you leave me all alone?*

Lilian ended the call in tears, too, missing her sister so much it hurt to take a breath.

Thankfully, Daniel called every day to keep her updated. Rosie still didn't recognize him, but the earlier phone conversation with Lilian had helped—she kept repeating that her sister wouldn't lie to her, Daniel said, which made Lilian cringe with guilt. The doctor had increased her antipsychotic dose, which kept her calm in Daniel's presence. It flattened all her emotions, which Lilian didn't like, but it was necessary for the time being.

Caleb continued to work long hours, preparing to travel to London for a prestigious podium presentation of his pilot research. When he was home, he was sweet with Abigail and solicitous with Lilian—"Did you take your medication? Careful with your laptop; screens won't help your post-concussive headaches. You're keeping the alarm system armed, right?"—but they weren't connecting as husband and wife, not really.

When he worked late, Lilian would check his position on her Find My Friends app. Often, his blue dot was several blocks away from the hospital. Lilian knew there were multiple work-related explanations: a meeting with a colleague, dinner with a pharmaceutical rep. Still, she wished he *wanted* to be home.

It had been a week since Ben Nichols had disappeared, and the police still had no new information. The Wilmette PD hadn't been able to determine who'd hacked the baby monitor. Detective Berenson hadn't called with any updates. And Lilian hadn't seen anything suspicious, but she was still tense and anxious, jumping at tiny noises, having nightmares. The fact that Caleb didn't seem worried at all made it worse.

* * *

Three days before Rosie was scheduled to discharge from rehab, as Lilian sat on the floor with Abigail, helping her practice sitting up, her phone rang. It was Daniel.

"Hi!" she said, her voice too loud and eager in her quiet house. "How are you? How's Rosie?"

He gave her the update—today they'd practiced getting in and out of a car in the parking garage—and then the conversation turned to other things. He asked about Abigail, about how Lilian was surviving the polar vortex.

"I've missed seeing you," he said. "It's not the same here without you."

Lilian put the phone on speaker and set it on the floor, next to Abigail. "I've missed seeing you, too," she said, almost embarrassed by how much she meant those words. Her entire life had shrunk to these four walls, her baby, and phone calls from her sister's boyfriend. "How is it going with Rosie's discharge planning?"

"Good. The staff recommended a bunch of equipment, and I'm working on getting it delivered. We need a hospital bed. A wheelchair, a walker, equipment for the bathroom. That sort of thing."

The gravity of what Daniel would be taking on struck Lilian once again. He would need help for at least a few months, possibly even years, and she hoped he would accept it.

"Did they say anything about home health?" she asked. "An aide, or some therapists?"

"Actually, yes," he said. "I was hoping we could talk about that. I have some questions I want to run by you before I ask the staff. Are you going to visit Rosie anytime soon?"

"I can't," Lilian said, wincing. The disconnect from her sister felt like a fractured bone, achy and tender. "With the weather, it's not a good idea for me to take Abigail anywhere. Caleb's swamped at work and—"

"I understand."

Lilian sat back against the ottoman. The late afternoon sun filled the room with murky light; it would be dark soon, and it was only four o'clock. Caleb wouldn't be home for hours. Loneliness pressed against her chest, a heavy fist flattening her rib cage. And behind that, the ever-present anxiety, fluttering like moth wings.

"You could come here," she said, the words zipping out of her mouth before she could stop them. She cringed at the desperation in her voice.

"Would that be okay?" he asked. "I don't want to intrude—"

"It wouldn't be an intrusion. Honestly, I could use the company."

"I'll see you soon, then."

* * *

Lilian answered the door to see Daniel standing on her front stoop with snow on his head and shoulders and a bag of takeout in his hands. Behind him, a flurry of flakes filled the air; a new storm was rolling in.

"You didn't need to bring anything," Lilian said.

"My mother taught me never to go anywhere empty-handed," he said, stamping his snow-covered feet on the welcome mat. "I figured if I'm interrupting your evening, I might as well bring dinner. I hope you like Thai? I have massaman curry and lard na."

"Sounds delicious."

She led him into the kitchen, but seeing it from his eyes—dishes from last night still in the sink, baby bottles drying on the countertop—made her insides shrivel with embarrassment. She started tidying up, but Daniel stopped her.

"Don't worry about it," he said. "You don't need to impress me. I'm already impressed—this place is beautiful."

They settled on stools at the marble island, and Lilian put Abigail nearby in her highchair, then pulled out paper plates. They each took a heaping scoop of steaming white rice, fragrant curry, and noodles. On a whim, Lilian opened a bottle of red wine and poured two glasses. She hadn't had any alcohol in months, but she had nursed Abigail before Daniel arrived, so she should be fine for the next feeding.

It takes two to three hours for one drink to clear the bloodstream, she always counseled her patients' parents. Still, it felt like she was living on the edge. Maybe a good thing, she realized, if she learned how to relax a bit.

"You said you had some stuff to talk about," Lilian said after they started eating. "About taking Rosie home? Are you . . ." She trailed off, not sure how to say the words. *Are you having second thoughts? Are you certain you want to take this on?*

She wouldn't blame him if he backed out.

"I'm still planning to take her home with me," Daniel said, as if he knew what she was thinking. "But I've been looking into this specialized neuropsychiatric facility, where she can get a few weeks of more high-end, intensive care. I want her to have the best possible chance of recovery."

He told her about the specialists he had spoken with on the phone. The neuropsychologist and neurologist had been very impressive, and they had a high success rate for cognitive disorders with intensive therapy over a two- to three-month stay.

"It sounds great," Lilian said, sensing that there was a *but* coming.

"It's expensive," Daniel said, and Lilian nodded. Medicaid was paying for Rosie's hospital and rehab stay, but it wouldn't pay for anything out of the mainstream.

"Caleb and I are happy to pitch in—"

He lifted his chopsticks, cutting her off. "That's not the biggest problem. It's in California."

Lilian sat back against the stool. "Oh." The thought of Rosie so far away made the dull ache in her chest grow stronger.

"We don't need to make a decision right now," Daniel said. "I put Rosie's name on the waiting list, but we can always decline if it doesn't work out."

Lilian appreciated his use of the word *we*. "How long is the waiting list?"

"Typically six to nine months, but sometimes they'll have a cancellation and get people in sooner."

Six to nine months. Lilian relaxed slightly. She took another bite of curry, then a swallow of wine to cool her mouth. "So you'll stay here in Chicago until then?"

He nodded. "I'd never whisk her away without telling you. I would only do this with your full support."

Again, Lilian appreciated that he had never tried to take over Rosie's care, to usurp her role as Rosie's sister. "Can you give me some info on the facility?"

"I'll send you a link to the website," he said. "I know it's probably grasping at straws, but I want to do whatever it takes to help her."

Lilian felt the exact same way. She was beyond grateful for everything the rehab team had done for Rosie, but she wanted more. There *had* to be some kind of cure, right? She knew she was acting like the patients who used to frustrate her, who would turn to all sorts of alternative remedies when standard ones didn't give the results they wanted. But she now understood the desperate need to *try*. Even if it meant sending Rosie to California, even if it meant paying for expensive treatments out of pocket.

"When is the first payment due?" she asked Daniel.

"I had to put a little down to get her on the waiting list, but it's refundable." He took another bite of noodles, avoiding eye contact with Lilian. He didn't want to tell her—he wanted to take care of Rosie on his own, which was admirable, but not necessary.

"How much?"

"Five hundred," he said, "but it's fine. I put it on my credit card."

"I'm not letting you do that," Lilian said gently. "I want to contribute—Caleb and I both want to contribute."

A hint of color crept up Daniel's neck. Embarrassment. "Once I get a permanent position somewhere, my income will go up significantly. I—"

"I remember what it was like to be in training, Daniel." A postdoc didn't make much more than a resident physician, which was barely enough to support yourself, let alone pay for expensive medical treatments. "Let me transfer you some money."

He hesitated, then set down his chopsticks and turned to her. "Lilian, I appreciate that you want to help. I do. But I'm not comfortable accepting a handout from you. I know she's your sister, but she was going to be *my* wife."

Lilian studied his face. A good face; a kind face. His dark hair needed a trim; it fell over his forehead in thick waves, curling around his ears. The lines around his blue eyes had deepened, worry and lack of sleep etched onto his face. This had taken a toll on him. Lilian wondered what story her own face would tell about these weeks.

"What if we set up an account in Rosie's name," she said, "and you and I are both on it? That way I can deposit money and you can use it for Rosie as needed, and it will feel separate from your own account."

She and Caleb had talked about setting up a trust for Rosie, to provide for her in the future, just as they had for Abigail. He would be in full support of this plan, Lilian was certain.

Daniel still looked skeptical, but eventually he nodded. "It's still a ways off. In six to nine months, Rosie might be doing well enough that she doesn't even need to go."

"I hope so."

* * *

After they ate, they moved to the living room and sat on the sectional. Lilian finished her glass of wine, enjoying the warmth spreading through her body like thick, glowing sunshine. Abigail played on the floor in front of them, content and happy, while they talked.

She asked about his childhood, and Daniel told her about growing up in a small coastal town two hours' drive north of the Bay Area. He had two brothers—Andy was just a year younger; Jake, the one who had choked on the grape, was eight years younger. They both worked with their dad, who was a general contractor. Daniel had grown up working construction, being paid far less than minimum wage, but he'd learned basic plumbing and electrical work, which he said came in handy. He was the only member of his family who had gone to college, and they always gave him grief about that.

Dad would have liked this one, Lilian thought as he talked. Daniel was the kind of man her father would have related to—from a blue-collar background, not afraid to get his hands dirty. Dad had always been not-so-subtly judgmental of Caleb, who called someone *else* to fix things around the house.

Then Daniel asked about Lilian's childhood, and she told him stories about growing up on the South Side, visiting the Indiana Dunes in the summer, watching the White Sox play. She told him about spending so many years taking care of Rosie, and he said he understood the sense of responsibility an oldest child always carried.

As they talked, Lilian pulled a blanket from the back of the couch and tucked it around her legs. At some point, Abigail started fussing and Daniel reached down and picked her up. She settled against his chest and promptly fell asleep. Lilian found herself relaxing for the first time in weeks. Months, maybe. She had almost forgotten what it was like, having a grown-up conversation like this.

"Did you play any sports growing up?" she asked, after she'd finished telling Daniel about how her dad had coached her softball team for years.

"Yeah. Baseball, actually. Left field. Andy and I were on the high school team together—he was shortstop. Even as a sophomore, he was much better than me."

"Was your team any good?"

"We were all right. Would have been better that year if I hadn't kept us out of the state championship game."

"You did?" Lilian leaned forward, grinning. "Tell me."

"If you insist." He smiled and lowered his voice dramatically, patting Abigail's back. "It was the bottom of the ninth inning—"

"How come all baseball stories happen at the bottom of the ninth?" Lilian said.

"Shhhh, Lilian. It's my story." He lowered his voice again. "Bottom of the ninth and the other team, our rivals, the Bateman High Braves, were up to bat. We were up by one and there was one out left. They were back at the top of their batting order with two runners in scoring position—that's on second and third, Lil."

"I know, idiot." She smiled. "Keep going."

"The batter hit the ball to left field, and I went to catch it. But the sun was in my eyes, so the ball went over my head. I ran back and got it, but I was frustrated and overthrew my cutoff, which was Andy, of course, and two runners scored." His smile faded. "It was over."

"That sucks, Daniel. I'm sorry." Lilian felt like a much younger version of herself, a version who used words like *sucks*.

"Yeah," he said, patting Abigail's back again. "I felt like a moron, sitting through my coach's postgame speech, trying to ignore Andy's eyes boring into the back of my head. He was a great shortstop, and if I'd gotten the ball to him, he would've stopped the runner. We would've won the game, and everyone knew it. But really, that wasn't the biggest issue. I mostly dreaded facing my dad."

"Why?" Lilian asked. "Your dad sounded sweet when you talked about him earlier."

He huffed. "My dad's a hard-ass where baseball is concerned. He played in the minors for a couple of years. When I got home, I went straight to my bedroom, thinking I'd probably just quit the team, wouldn't play my senior year."

"Did he come up and talk to you?" Lilian remembered countless postgame debriefings with her own father; sometimes supportive, but often critical.

"He did," Daniel said. "I expected him to start ranting about how I should have spent more time on my cutoff drills, or how I had to stop wasting time on my candy-ass artsy stuff—he never understood my interest in the arts, of course—but he didn't."

"What did he say?"

"He said, and I can still hear his voice, 'Danny, you got frustrated today. You missed that catch and then you overshot your throw to Andy. That's an unfortunate mistake, son, but it's not a crime. It would be a crime if you let this define you.'"

Lilian smiled at his imitation of his dad's voice. "He sounds like a good dad."

"He is," Daniel said, a little reluctantly. "And then he said, 'If you learn nothing from all these years playing ball, I hope you learn this. It's nice to win games, especially when you make a great play. Everyone cheers, your coach is happy, you feel like a king. But you want to know the game that sticks with you, that teaches you what you're made of? It's the one you lose.'"

"That's good advice," Lilian said, missing her dad so acutely it felt like a physical pain in her chest. He hadn't been a perfect father, but he'd taught her to work hard and to be responsible. On the day her acceptance letter to med school arrived, he'd taken the whole family out to dinner, and had spent the entire evening beaming as he told every person in the restaurant that his daughter was going to be a doctor.

"So did you quit?" she asked, shaking the thought away. "Or did you play your senior year?"

One corner of his mouth turned up in a quick smile. "I didn't quit. I practiced my ass off and played awesome my senior year."

Lilian burst out laughing. Of course he had—this blue-collar, baseball-playing, art history–loving postdoc. Rosie was lucky to have him on her side.

Then she sobered, her thoughts returning to her parents. They'd still been alive for the whole debacle with Dasha Nichols and the malpractice suit; they'd been solidly on Lilian's side, of course, and Dad had ranted one Sunday evening after dinner (and after too many beers) that these assholes weren't going to keep *his* daughter down.

What would Dad think of her now?

"I quit the team," she said to herself.

Daniel turned, eyebrows knitting together. "What's that?"

Lilian sighed, shaking her head. "Medicine is just like your dad said—everyone's happy when you make the correct diagnosis, when you save the patient. But sometimes you can't. Sometimes you don't. That's as much a part of medicine as losing is in baseball." She raked a hand through her hair, wishing she could go back in time and do everything differently. "If the one you *lose* shows you what you're made of, what does that say about me? What am I made of?"

"I guess it says that you're human." Daniel's voice was thoughtful. "But don't let—"

"I know, I know, don't let that mistake define me," Lilian said. He was right. She'd carried the memory like armor, thinking it kept her on guard, kept her safe, when all it was doing was weighing her down. For the first time, she imagined how it would feel to drop the burden.

Daniel shook his head. "I think it will always define you. How could it not? But that's not necessarily a bad thing." He paused and stared at the ceiling, as if searching for his next words. "I haven't known you very long, Lilian. But I know that you're strong and compassionate, fiercely protective of the people you love, and you always do your best. It's clear to me what you're made of. I wish . . ." He hesitated, met her eyes. "I wish you could see it, too."

She almost felt like she could see it, reflected in his clear blue eyes. A stronger version of herself. Flawed, but wiser for it. A woman who maybe, someday, could get back in the game.

Her phone rang, startling her. She picked it up from the coffee table. Caleb.

"Hi," she said. "Everything okay?"

"Hey, Lily, there's been a big pileup on the Dan Ryan and we're getting traumas." He sounded rushed; voices echoed in the background. "Tobias was supposed to come on for me, but because of the storm he's stuck out in Naperville. You okay if I stay here overnight?"

"Of course," she said, glancing out the window. The snow blew in horizontal streaks across the black sky. "Be safe."

"I will. You stay home, okay? The roads are terrible."

"Will do."

She hung up and turned to Daniel. "Caleb's staying overnight at the hospital. The bad weather is causing a lot of accidents."

"I should get going, then," Daniel said.

Lilian bit her lip. The thought of being alone in her dark and silent house made her skin crawl. And Caleb had said to stay off the roads.

"Unless . . . well, maybe give the snowplows some time to get the roads cleared?" Her cheeks flushed. "I mean, if you want to. Don't feel like you need to rush out."

He held her gaze. "I'd love to stay."

CHAPTER
THIRTY-SEVEN

Soon it was time to put Abigail to bed. Lilian went upstairs, nursed her, changed her, and laid her in her crib. By the time she returned to the kitchen, Daniel had put all the dirty dishes in the dishwasher and was wiping her counters.

"You didn't have to do that," she said, even though she appreciated it. She couldn't remember the last time Caleb had so much as put his own coffee mug away.

He shrugged. "No worries."

They settled back on the sectional, each with another glass of wine. Lilian flicked on the gas fireplace. The wind howled outside, and she curled up with the throw blanket over her legs. For the first time in weeks, her worries about the car crash—about Rosie and baby monitors and silver sedans and angry Ben Nichols—seemed to fade into the distance. She felt warm, not quite tipsy, and comfortable.

Their conversation inevitably turned to Rosie. Most of their discussions about her had centered on the tangible: her progress in rehab, possible treatments, planning for discharge. But this time, Lilian could sense they were slowly testing the edges, the tender areas they'd avoided.

"You want to know the hardest part of the whole thing?" Daniel said. His voice had gone quiet, thoughtful. "I see Rosie every day, but I *miss* her. It's . . . bizarre. Disorienting."

Lilian nodded, his words resonating deep in her chest. She understood perfectly, this tension between two extremes. They'd lost Rosie, but they hadn't. Rosie was gone, but she was here. They were grieving her and getting to know her, simultaneously.

"I don't know how to feel," Lilian said. "I'm so grateful she survived—every single day I'm grateful—but I am so damn angry that she was hurt in the first place. Whether it was an accident or not, it should never have happened." Her hands curled into fists around the throw blanket as she remembered wanting to slam them into the window, after getting Rosie's diagnosis of Capgras. "And I *hate* that she doesn't know who I am."

Pain flickered in Daniel's eyes; he understood. "You know that feeling when you're in a crowded place—like a party, maybe—and you make eye contact with the person you came with? The person you'll be going home with; the person you're in love with. Somehow you got separated and now you're feeling a little lost in the crowd, but then your eyes lock and in that split second, you know exactly who you are."

He swallowed, his throat bobbing. "It won't ever be like that again. She doesn't recognize me, but I don't recognize her, either. Not really. She doesn't look like herself, she doesn't act like herself. And because of that I don't know who *I* am anymore, or how we fit together." He stopped, flushing as he glanced over at her. "I'm sorry—that came out wrong."

"Not at all," Lilian said. On the contrary, he had articulated something she'd been struggling to put into words. "When my parents died, it was awful. My entire foundation crumbled. But there was something clean about it. They died. We had a funeral. I grieved. This?" Her throat tightened with emotion. "Every single time I see Rosie, it's a death. Every time she doesn't know who I am, it's another death. I'm terrified that the future is going to be more deaths, over and over again, for the rest of our lives."

This was the heart of it, the truth that made Lilian cry in the shower most days. Despite all her progress, Rosie would never fully recover, not with her degree of brain injury. She would never be the woman Daniel had planned to build a life with. She'd never be the sister Lilian remembered, the sister she wanted to know again.

Daniel stared at the fireplace. "I don't—I don't know how to do this."

She could hear the unspoken message behind his words. He didn't know if he could be the man he wanted to be—a man who could selflessly care for Rosie, no matter the cost. It was the first real vulnerability she'd seen in him. Yes, she had seen him frightened and overwhelmed, but he had always been confident that he could take care of Rosie.

"Daniel," she said gently, "if, someday, it becomes too much, if it becomes too difficult, please let me know. Rosie would want you to be happy. Even if that means moving on without her."

"I—" He cleared his throat. "I don't want to move on without her. I don't know if I can."

"I know," Lilian said. But she hoped that if the time did come, he would consider it. "You've been an amazing support to Rosie since the crash. And to me. I can't imagine going through this without you."

It was true, she realized. Without Daniel, she would have been so alone.

Daniel's eyes, an almost translucent blue in the dim light, met hers. "Things are going to be different after Rosie discharges from rehab," he said quietly.

"Very," Lilian said.

After Rosie discharged, Lilian would visit her and Daniel. He would keep her updated on Rosie's progress. But she would miss talking to him every day—she already missed seeing him. Daniel had never dismissed her as paranoid or ridiculous; he'd gone with her to the police station; he'd brainstormed theories about who could have been responsible for the car crash. He'd been her only real friend through all of it.

"I better get going," Daniel said, looking around. "It's getting late."

Lilian glanced at the time on her phone, surprised to see it was past midnight. "I'll walk you to the door."

In the darkened entryway, Daniel pulled on his coat and scarf, and Lilian bent down to straighten the boots lined up by the wall.

When she stood up again, they were too close together. Close enough that she could smell him, could feel the heat from his body. She lifted her eyes to meet his, and he didn't look away. The only sound was the wind outside and the thump of Lilian's heartbeat. She knew she should take a step back. But she couldn't bring herself to do it.

Lilian didn't know what to say, how to articulate what she was feeling. She only knew that it would be another loss, watching him walk away, knowing that things were changing. Could she go back to her life as it had been, her dark and lonely days worrying about her baby and counting the hours until Caleb came home?

"Take care of yourself, Lilian," he said. He leaned down and brushed his lips against her cheek.

She put a hand on his arm. "Daniel, I—"

He stopped, their faces just inches apart. She caught the faint scent of wine on his breath, watched as his lips parted, as his eyes tracked her face, and settled on her mouth.

She didn't know who closed the remaining distance, if he made the move or if she did. She only knew that their lips met, that a small sigh of relief escaped from her. She didn't allow herself to think, she just allowed herself to feel his mouth on hers, the quiet whisper of his breath on her skin.

Then his hands moved up to cradle her face, and a spark caught. The kiss turned hungrier; deeper. A wave of warmth swept over her, and she ran her palms up to his shoulders. He tilted her head back and kissed her jaw, her neck, then returned to her lips for another long, fierce kiss before slowing and pulling away.

When they parted, they were both breathing hard. He studied her with a serious expression, two lines forming between his eyebrows. "Lilian, if we had met under different circumstances—"

"I know."

She could blame it on the darkness, on the storm outside, on the wine. Or she could call it what it was: two people who had been lonely for weeks, who had found something in each other, a connection that would never progress to anything else but wasn't any less real.

"Drive safely," she said, and he left.

CHAPTER
THIRTY-EIGHT

MyPsychJournal.com

Welcome back, Rosie. Happy journaling!

MARCH 8, 2018

My visit with Dr. V isn't for two more weeks, but I need to record something that just happened so we can talk about it at our next session.

I've mentioned my sister, of course. She's a doctor. A pediatrician. She's always been a high achiever, I mentioned that, too.

Well, this morning as I was grabbing coffee, a TV in the corner of the cafe was showing the local news and Lilian's name flashed across the screen. Apparently one of her patients died of cancer and they're saying she missed the diagnosis. She's being sued for malpractice.

It was like everything went into slow motion, all the sound fading around me. All I could hear was the sound of my own breathing. I couldn't stop staring at the screen, at my sister's name, at her picture, her professional smile, and her crisp white coat. After that, there was footage of the father and mother giving a teleconference. The father looked furious, the mother looked distraught, there was a crowd around them holding signs and chanting Justice for Dasha and all I could think about was Lilian. How awful this must be for her.

There was a time in my life when seeing that news story might have made me feel triumphant: See! Lilian's not perfect, either! I felt like such a fuck-up compared to her. It didn't help that my parents were always saying things like, Why can't you be more like Lilian? When Lilian was your age, she was taking care of you AND getting straight A's AND keeping the house spick-and-span. She never caused us a minute of worry.

So yes, I grew up with a lot of resentment toward my sister. But at that moment, I wanted to rush out of the cafe and find her, to throw my arms around her and hug her. I also wanted to find the parents who were suing her, to tell them there was no way my sister would have ever done anything to harm their daughter. I know Lilian. She's the most conscientious person you can imagine. And if she did make a mistake, it was just that—an *honest* mistake. I'm sure the guilt is destroying her.

I've been thinking back to when I was little, how I'd throw tantrums because I didn't want to go to bed, or I wanted grape jelly instead of strawberry on my PB&J, or some other stupid thing. Lilian would get so fed up she'd lose her temper, smack my hand or put me in time out. She'd feel so guilty about it afterward, crying and apologizing, trying to make it up to me. I could get her to do anything I wanted. I wonder if that's where it started, this problem with manipulating other people.

But that's not the point. The point is this: if Lilian did something that led to a child's death, even accidentally . . . I know my sister. This could ruin her.

I can't stop thinking about her. I almost called her today—I even pulled her up on my phone—but I stopped myself. I keep thinking about the last time we spoke, how she ordered me to stay away from her. My stomach twists into ropes just thinking about it.

If I could do something for her, to help her, it might prove that I'm different now. That I've changed.

More than anything, I need her to trust me. Because the things I have to tell her? They're hard to swallow.

CHAPTER
THIRTY-NINE

Caleb made it home at eight o'clock the next morning. Lilian was in the kitchen with Abigail, feeding her a breakfast of baby oatmeal mixed with pureed bananas. The storm had stopped overnight, and a beam of sunlight pierced the bay window overlooking their snow-covered backyard.

"Good morning," Caleb said, coming over to kiss Lilian.

She cringed—she couldn't help it—and turned her head so his lips landed on her cheek. Thoughts of Daniel and their kiss had lingered all night. Caleb noticed the movement, and his expression seemed hurt.

"I haven't showered," she said, by way of explanation. "And you must be exhausted."

But Caleb, as usual after an overnight shift, was more wired than tired. He wasn't ready to head upstairs and crash; he needed breakfast; he needed to decompress.

"How was your night?" he asked.

"Fine." Lilian paused, debating whether to tell him about Daniel. In the end, honesty—or partial honesty—won out. "Daniel stopped by. He wanted to talk about an idea he has for Rosie."

Lilian told Caleb about SNIC, the neuropsychiatric specialty unit

Daniel had found, about the six- to nine-month wait-list and the five-hundred-dollar fee.

"I told him I'd give him some money to help cover it," she said. "I know I should have talked to you first, but—"

"No, it's fine. Of course we'll help with the cost."

"He doesn't want to take our money," Lilian said. "I think he feels embarrassed that he can't pay for it himself." She thought back to the flush creeping up the back of Daniel's neck. The curl of his dark hair against his collar. Her own cheeks warmed.

"That's ridiculous," Caleb said, buttering his toast. "He can't pay for all of it."

"That's what I told him. But it still makes him uncomfortable, so I suggested that we create a joint account in Rosie's name, with both me and Daniel on it. That way I can deposit money as needed to help with things, and Daniel can use it for Rosie."

"Great idea," Caleb said. He turned, his voice deliberately casual. "So, Daniel was here for a while last night?"

"Yes. Why?"

Caleb shrugged. "No reason. It's just that you've been spending a lot of time with him."

"I've been spending a lot of time with Daniel because he loves my *sister*," Lilian said, emphasizing the word. "How many men would be there, in the hospital every day, for their girlfriend? A lot of husbands wouldn't do that, let alone boyfriends."

Caleb spread his hands in front of him. "Sorry, sorry. It's just . . . you've seemed far away lately, Lily. Distant."

"Distant?" Lilian stood, pushing her stool back. "You're working sixty, seventy, eighty hours a week. No—I'm not upset about last night," she said, before he could interrupt. "I'm glad you stayed and helped out. But you need to think about your priorities, Caleb. I know there have been times you said you were working late when you were going out to dinner."

His eyebrows pulled together. "You've been checking up on me? Honestly, Lil—"

"I wouldn't have to check on you if you came home when you said you would!" She threw her hands in the air, frustrated.

"Maybe I would come home if it was actually pleasant to be around you."

She sucked in a breath. "You don't want to be around me?"

"It's not that I don't want—" He stopped, and she waited for the calm, controlled version of her husband to appear, the one she'd known for the past several months. The one who took long, deep breaths before he spoke, who never raised his voice, who treated her like she was some delicate object.

Instead, his eyes flashed. "Look. I know you've been through a lot. You lost a patient, you lost your parents, you struggled after Abigail was born, then this accident happened. We've been bouncing from one crisis to the next. I have tried to be understanding, I've tried to be supportive, but no matter what I do, it doesn't help. You feel like a stranger, and we can't communicate and it—it's not working." He set his jaw. "*We* aren't working, Lilian."

Her eyes flooded with tears. Caleb never called her Lilian, and the sound of her name seemed to widen the gulf between them.

"What are you saying?" she whispered.

"I'm saying that I can't keep doing this," he said, and her heart fractured.

In a flash she imagined a world without Caleb: joint custody of Abigail; shuttling their daughter between two houses; communicating through terse text messages because they couldn't stand to speak to each other. Her hand rose to her throat, where all her words seemed to be lodged.

Caleb blew out a long, long breath. He looked exhausted, older than his years. "We can't have this discussion right now. I've been awake since yesterday morning."

"Okay," Lilian said, dazed.

He turned and walked away, up the stairs, and into their bedroom.

* * *

Caleb didn't emerge from their bedroom for hours, not until Lilian was coming out of the nursery after putting Abigail down for her second nap of the day. She couldn't stop replaying his words on an endless loop. *I can't keep doing this. We aren't working, Lilian.*

Turning, she studied him, dreading the conversation. He'd showered and shaved, put on jeans and a clean sweatshirt, but he still looked weary. She wondered how long he'd been keeping this inside, stewing on it. The worst-case scenario flashed through her mind: he'd fallen in love with someone else; he wanted a divorce.

Please God, she prayed, let him not be having an affair. She was willing to work through a lot to keep their marriage, but she didn't think she could get over that level of betrayal.

"Something happened last night," he said.

Lilian stiffened, thinking of Daniel. Wondering if Caleb somehow knew about their kiss at the front door.

But he continued, saying, "We had an entire family brought in after a car accident, mom and dad, two little kids. The mother and both children died. The dad had an unstable pelvic fracture, so I took care of him. After that, another trauma came in, but I wasn't needed. Since I was the only one available, I told the father what had happened to his family."

Lilian closed her eyes, imagining the scene. Her husband, exhausted from working all day and night, sitting down at this man's bedside. She imagined Caleb saying, in his gentle voice, *Your wife and children died. We did everything we could. I'm so sorry for your loss.*

She had always loved the way he talked to patients, the way he avoided jargon and spoke to people at their level. But she knew he would have been struggling to keep his composure. She also knew he would carry that moment with him for the rest of his life. The weight, the crushing responsibility. The impotence of giving everything and it not being enough. She thought not only of Dasha Nichols, but of the other patients she'd lost over the years. No matter how hard physicians worked, they were human, just as their patients were. Human minds and bodies could never be invincible. At some point, they would fail.

"The father—he was devastated," he said, his voice dropping. "I've given bad news so many times, but this was . . . God. I was a mess the rest of the night, couldn't concentrate. I even had to step outside for a while. I haven't cried since my father died, Lil, but last night . . ."

He trailed off. Lilian opened her eyes, moved closer to Caleb, and put her arms around him. This man. Yes, he could be infuriating but no one gave more to his patients.

"I'm so sorry," she said.

His arms tightened around her. "I kept imagining my life if I lost you and Abigail. It terrified me. Then I came home, and it seemed like you were a million miles away. And I realized that I *am* losing you. I've been burying myself in work so I didn't have to face what was happening." He pulled away to meet her eyes. "Lily, I promise, after I get back from London, things will be different. I just emailed my Chair and let him know I need to cut back some of my responsibilities."

The knot in her stomach loosened as the realization sank in: he wasn't leaving her. But then she shook her head. Caleb was on the verge of taking a huge leap forward in his career, breaking onto the international stage in his field. "You can't cut back right now. Your career—"

"My career will be fine. This"—he motioned between the two of them—"is my priority. Lily, I'm worried about us. I don't want to lose us."

She knew they needed to keep talking. She wanted to go deeper, to help him understand that there was more to the distance between them. The fact that he didn't respect her the same way he once had, that he'd dismissed her concerns on multiple occasions.

But she didn't want to say that right now. Instead, she took his face in her hands and kissed him. He felt so familiar, so *right*, and she deepened the kiss. He responded. They must have done this thousands of times over the past fifteen years, these same movements, in this same order: she reached under his shirt and ran her palms up his back; he fisted one hand in her hair; she pressed her pelvis against his; he slid his other hand up her back and flicked open her bra.

Then Caleb lifted her up, carrying her backward to their room, leaving a trail of clothing in their wake. They fell into bed, skin on skin, a tangle of need and want. Caleb did everything right, everything she liked, and the feeling of her husband, the weight of him above her, grounded her. But the closer she got to the edge, the more she struggled to focus.

Her mind flashed to the night before, to the press of Daniel's mouth on hers. She flushed, instantly heated, and wrapped her legs around Caleb's waist, pulling him deeper and deeper until they both came undone.

After, Caleb pressed his forehead against hers. "That was—God, Lily, you're amazing. I've missed this—I've missed us."

Lilian's throat constricted with guilt. As Caleb kissed her again, she tried very hard not to think of a pair of clear blue eyes in the darkness.

CHAPTER
FORTY

MyPsychJournal.com

Welcome back, Rosie. Happy journaling!

MARCH 21, 2018

Today's therapy session did not go as expected. First of all, Dr. V wasn't there. Apparently, she had to leave the country in a rush because of some kind of family emergency. When I heard that, I started to panic—I have a relationship with her, I need to see her, she's the only one who's ever been able to help me. But the person at the front desk said not to worry, one of her colleagues was filling in for her. I wasn't happy about it, but I agreed to at least meet this other psychologist.

My first impression was . . . not great. He doesn't have the gravitas of Dr. V, that's for sure. He's quite a bit younger, and he was wearing this hideous mustard sweater with a coffee stain on the front. He's sloppy, that's what I'm saying. I don't think that bodes well for a psychologist. Plus, I caught him looking down my shirt.

(And yes, I know he could read this, and so could Dr. V. Maybe he'll stop ogling his patients).

He didn't even give me a homework assignment, but here I am, writing, because that's what Dr. V always told me to do. If nothing else, I'm good at following instructions.

Dr. C—that's the new guy—spent the whole time asking random "getting to know you" questions, and I wanted to tell him to just read my chart. I'm sure Dr. V had all of this written down. But halfway through our session, I realized that maybe he knew what he was doing, because I was relaxed and comfortable with him.

After that, we spent a few minutes talking about my last journal entry, about my sister and her malpractice suit, and how I felt about it. And then we spent the rest of the time talking about abuse, and how I have a hard time thinking about what happened with Michael in that context. Why it's easier to pretend like it wasn't, in fact, an abusive relationship.

Dr. C said that even though Michael wasn't physically violent, he disregarded my autonomy as a human being, over and over again. He made me doubt my own thoughts and feelings. But if Michael was my abuser, does that make me his victim? Dr. C said that I get to choose how I want to think of myself, and many people who have been abused by their partner prefer to think of themselves as a survivor. It's empowering, he said.

I told him that I don't relate to either of those words. Victim. Survivor. They both feel uncomfortable, like I'm wearing a shoe that's too small on one foot, and a shoe that's too big on the other. "Victim" suggests that I had no agency; it dismisses my personhood—but then again, Michael violated me, against my will and without my consent. That's the very definition of a victim, so why should I be afraid of that word? On the other hand, "survivor" celebrates the fact that I was strong enough to get out, brave enough to leave, and that's great and all—but does it mean I was weak and cowardly all those other times, when I chose to stay? Fuck that. Michael was manipulative and controlling, and I am not responsible for his actions. But he didn't kidnap me and chain me in the basement. I own my choices. All of them—good, bad, and indifferent. Implying otherwise gives him the power. And I'll be damned if I ever allow that to happen again.

If I've learned anything from all this therapy, it's that Michael craved power. Which is why, after I left him, he was desperate to regain it.

That's the other thing I want to write about today: what happened when Michael found me. It took about a month, but one day I walked in the coffee shop near my new office building to see him sitting there, smiling. "Good morning, Rosie," he said. "How's the new job?" I lost my shit and told him he needed to stay the fuck away from me, but guess what that accomplished? Nothing, other than making myself look like a crazy person for yelling at a perfectly nice man for no reason. A similar thing happened when I got to the L station one day and he was already there, reading the paper and grinning like it was all a lovely surprise. "Oh hi, Rosie. So nice to run into you." Again, I freaked out, and guess what? I was told to leave and stop harassing the other riders.

But the worst was when I walked into my gym one morning to find him there, lifting weights and smirking. "Have a good work out, Rosie," he said. I knew damn well that he joined that gym to frighten me, to make it clear that he could get away with anything and there was nothing I could do to stop him. I talked to the owner, but he blew me off. "We can't kick out your ex-boyfriend just because you don't like seeing his face in the morning." Let's be honest: it's easy to blame a woman for overreacting when she's agitated and close to tears, especially when the man she's accusing never loses his cool, never gets upset, and comes across as trustworthy and harmless. Michael knew this, and he used it to his advantage.

I think I finally understand what Dr. V has been trying to explain, and Dr. C, too. All the things Michael did to me, they were motivated by a need for power and control. All the things I did to him—and I did some awful things, I realize that—were motivated by fear and anger. There's a difference. And maybe that's what makes me a survivor. I made some stupid choices, I allowed a terrible human being into my life, I treated him badly, too, but then I got out. And now I'm trying to change.

I can't imagine what would have happened if Michael had continued harassing me like that—maybe I would have gotten back together with him, just to get him to stop? Maybe I would have snapped and hurt him? I don't know. But I'm grateful he's gone, grateful that he gave up and moved on a couple months ago. I do feel guilty that he's probably victimizing some other woman now. The world would be a better place without Michael Sorenson in it, and sometimes I have dreams that he's dead, that he had a heart attack or was hit by a bus, that he's dying in front of me and I turn and walk away.

But like Dr. C said today, the best revenge is living my life, learning to be happy, and moving on.

CHAPTER
FORTY-ONE

"Where we going?" Rosie asked as Daniel pushed her wheelchair down the hall, away from the room where she'd spent the past three weeks.

It was Rosie's discharge day; her "graduation day," as the rehab staff called it. Five weeks of hospitalization—two in the regular hospital and three in rehab—were over. Nancy had decided to stay with a friend in Florida instead of coming straight home from her cruise, and Lilian, wanting to be there for Rosie, had bundled up Abigail and brought her along.

"You're going home," Lilian said, hoping her voice didn't betray the awkwardness she felt. It was the first time she'd seen Daniel since the night he'd come over, two days prior. Since he'd left her standing in her darkened entryway with his taste on her lips. She felt stiff and uncomfortable around him, unable to meet his eyes without her stomach flipping over.

Daniel, however, seemed relaxed, smiling as they rode the elevator down to the ground level. When the doors opened, he pushed Rosie's wheelchair across the lobby, through the sliding glass doors, and out onto the busy Chicago sidewalk.

Lilian had called Rosie on the phone that morning to reassure her about the discharge plan; she'd told her that the real Daniel and Lilian would be there soon. That promise—plus a cocktail of medications—had kept Rosie relatively calm. But she kept sneaking suspicious glances back at Daniel.

"Where we going where?" Rosie asked again.

"Home," Daniel said. "We're going home."

Rosie glared at him. Daniel had brought her a pink stocking cap and a scarf, but even still, the tip of her nose had turned red from the wind. "I want to live with Daniel not you—you fooled everyone but not me you don't fool me—I want to live with Daniel the real Daniel. You're not the real Daniel."

"I know," he said in an easy voice. His breath made clouds of smoke in the frigid air as he pushed Rosie's wheelchair down the sidewalk toward his car. "And I'll take good care of you until he comes back, okay?"

Rosie eyed him again, still suspicious. "I'll be watching you I know what you did so I'm gonna find it—what?" she snapped, glancing up at Lilian. "Stop spying on me don't look at me."

Lilian fell back, out of Rosie's line of sight and followed, pushing Abigail's stroller and listening to their conversation. Daniel seemed calm and confident, with no trace of the hesitation he'd displayed that night at her house. The memory of their kiss flashed through her mind again, followed by a guilty feeling in her stomach. She shoved it away. That was over and done, and it wouldn't do any good to bring it up—with either Daniel or Caleb. She was committed to working on her marriage, which meant her relationship with Daniel had to exist firmly within appropriate bounds. The less said about the kiss, the better.

When they reached Daniel's pickup, Lilian pulled out her phone. "Let me get a picture," she said.

Daniel knelt on one knee next to Rosie's wheelchair, his arm resting on the back. Lilian snapped the picture, then looked at it. Rosie was squinting into the sunlight, her body tense and angled away from Daniel. He was smiling, though, his dimple showing, his eyes shining with hope for the future. Something twinged in Lilian's heart, an emotion she didn't dare examine too closely. This was exactly why she needed the picture, she told herself: to remember that Rosie and Daniel were together, a pair, as they should be.

Daniel loaded the rest of Rosie's things into the back of his truck, then turned to Lilian. "Well, this is it. Want to come over?"

Lilian met his eyes, making her stomach pitch again, then shook her head. "Another day. I don't want to keep Abigail out in this cold. But let me know if you need anything, okay? Caleb and I are working on setting up the account for Rosie, but in the meantime, I'm going to Venmo you some money—"

"You don't need to do that—"

"I want to," she said. "Just text me your username. It'll help cover some of the extra expenses of having her home. And we should talk about hiring help so you can get out, okay?"

He nodded reluctantly. "Thank you. I appreciate it."

"Thank *you*," she said, and she meant it. "For taking care of my sister, for being here for her. For being my friend."

He gave her a long look, his face unreadable. "Thank you for giving me a chance," he said. "And thanks for being my friend, too."

And then it was over. He drove away with Rosie, off to their home together.

* * *

The next two days passed slowly. Lilian couldn't get away to visit Rosie—Nancy wasn't home yet; Caleb was preparing for his conference in London. She spoke on the phone with Daniel every day, though. It was so much easier to talk over the phone than it had been in person. He said Rosie's adjustment had been rough the first night but had improved since. He was confident she would settle into her new routine soon.

Lilian considered asking to speak with her sister on the phone, just to experience that spark of recognition in her voice, but she decided against it. Rosie always ended up confused and emotional after their phone calls, and Lilian couldn't do that to her. Or Daniel.

She missed Daniel more than she'd ever thought possible, but he wasn't hers to miss. Their friendship had one purpose only: to support

Rosie's recovery. As the rehab team had reminded Lilian, Rosie was just beginning the long road to recovery. It might take a few weeks to get used to this new normal, but Lilian would get there.

Then she got the phone call from Daniel.

* * *

"What do you mean, she got in?" Lilian asked. She was sitting on the floor with Abigail, playing with a stuffed elephant with a bell on its trunk. They had been doing this for a solid twenty minutes, and Abigail still laughed every time Lilian touched the bell.

"She got a spot at SNIC." Daniel sounded excited. "Hang on, I'll send a screenshot."

Lilian's phone buzzed, and she glanced at it to see a text from Daniel—a screenshot of an email. As she read the words, her eyes unexpectedly filled with tears.

Dear Mr. Connors,

We have had a cancellation, which has opened up a spot in our traumatic brain injury and complex neuropsychiatric residential treatment facility.

Let us know if you are still interested. The session would begin next week, and the first third of your tuition must be paid in full within the next forty-eight hours to reserve this spot.

Please respond at your earliest convenience.

Best wishes,
Sandra Kimura, LCSW
Intake coordinator
Specialized Neuropsychiatric Institute of
California (SNIC)

"Someone dropped out," Daniel was saying as Lilian put the phone back to her ear. "They want her to start next week!"

Lilian wiped her eyes with her free hand and tried to sound upbeat. "Wow. Next week?"

So soon. Lilian wasn't ready to let her sister go. She still hadn't gotten used to Rosie being at Daniel's. If Rosie went to SNIC, she would be thousands of miles away.

"I know it's sudden," he said. "More sudden than I expected—we just got settled here. But I don't want to give up this opportunity."

"Of course not," Lilian said. "But how will you make it work? For your fellowship, I mean?"

"I already talked to my adviser. He's fine with it. Well, not fine, but he understands, and he says he'll make it work. There's another postdoc who can take over the class I've been teaching. And I can use the time to finish the book chapter I'm working on."

"So you're planning on accepting the spot," she said.

He paused. "If you don't think it's a good idea—"

"That's not what I mean." She did think it was a good idea. She wanted Rosie to have the best possible chance of recovery, and everything she'd read about SNIC sounded wonderful. But the thought of her little sister all the way across the country in California made her feel queasy.

It wasn't just the physical distance—the emotional distance hurt more. Lilian wouldn't be there to see Rosie's progress. She would hear about everything secondhand. Maybe it was selfish, but Lilian wanted to be intimately involved; she wanted a seat at the table of Rosie's life. After their years of estrangement, she didn't want to hang around the periphery, waiting for crumbs of information.

"We won't do it if you're not one hundred percent sure," Daniel said.

"Rosie should do it," Lilian said firmly. "No doubt about it. I just wasn't ready for this quite yet." They needed to think things through— airfare, transportation of equipment. "How much do we need to pay now? A third?"

"A third up front and another third at check-in." He sounded reluctant.

"So that's what, ten thousand now and ten thousand when she arrives?"

"Yes. But I'll figure it out—"

"I'll send you the money," Lilian said. He couldn't float that kind of charge on his credit card. She and Caleb would need to move some funds around, but it would work. "When do you think you'll go?"

"I've started looking at flights. I'm thinking we'll fly in on Monday morning and check in that afternoon."

Just five days. Five days until her baby sister got on an airplane and left Lilian behind.

"That sounds great," Lilian said. Her eyes filled with tears again. This was the best thing for Rosie, she reminded herself. Daniel would be with her, and he would keep Lilian in the loop. And it was only for a month. She could probably even go out and visit.

"Lilian? You there?" Daniel's voice brought her back to the present.

She blinked her eyes to clear the tears. "Yes, I'm here. I'm just—I'm thrilled about this opportunity for Rosie."

CHAPTER
FORTY-TWO

MyPsychJournal.com

Welcome back, Rosie. Happy journaling!

I did something I probably should not have done.

My next session with Dr. V is in a week, and I need to discuss this with her. I'm writing it here so she can read it, so I don't forget to bring it up with her. Remember the malpractice suit against my sister, the poor little girl who died?

Well, I found the father. And I went to see him.

It wasn't hard to find his information online—he's still in the local news all the time. It sounds like he's not just trying to get a huge settlement out of the hospital, he's trying to ruin my sister's career. I found some scary comments on those articles, people who think Lilian deserves to lose her job, go to prison, even burn in hell because of what she did. I thought that maybe if I could talk to Ben Nichols, to show him a different side of my sister, he would back off.

Or at least tone it down. One article said he works at a paint shop in Oak Park, so I went there.

It didn't go well.

Ben wasn't in, but I met his brother, Jeffrey, who also works there. He seemed like a nice enough guy until I told him who I was. Then he got angry. He started spewing terrible things about my sister, saying she'd ruined his brother's life; she deserves to lose someone close to *her*. When I tried to leave, he grabbed my arm and got right in my face. He said he heard my sister was pregnant and asked me how would she feel if something happened to *her* baby.

I wrenched myself away from him, ran back to my car, and locked the doors, shaking so hard I couldn't drive for a few minutes. But after the fear wore off, something else consumed me. I didn't know Lilian was pregnant, and that news landed like a brick. My sister is going to be a mom, and even though I know she's not *my* mother, it still feels like I'm being replaced. Like she wants a new, perfect, unblemished person to take care of, someone who hasn't treated her terribly and taken her for granted.

God, I don't even know if that makes any sense. But every time I think of my sister with a baby, I feel that brick sinking in my stomach again. All this time I've been trying to make myself better, so I can show Lilian how much I've changed, but now I'm not sure what the point is. I can't undo what I've done. Years of dysfunction can't be magically healed with a few months of therapy.

All it took was one small revelation—that my sister is having a baby—and I'm spiraling, panicking, doubting everything I've learned. Lilian will always look at me as her fuck-up little sister. She'll never believe anything I say.

I'm on my own. And we all know I can't handle that.

CHAPTER
FORTY-THREE

Lilian wandered into her bedroom and sat on her bed, facing the window. A gust of wind rushed through the oak tree in her front yard, tapping the bare branches against the glass. The sound echoed in the silent house; Abigail was napping, and Caleb had left early that morning for London. He'd offered to cancel, but she'd told him of course he should go. There was no reason for him to stay.

She'd promised to stay inside with the security system armed, but thoughts of her own safety had been crowded out by new concerns. Rosie was leaving for California in four days, and Lilian ached to go with her.

Her gaze fell on her nightstand, where Rosie's leather-bound day planner had sat for weeks. Lilian picked it up, feeling the cool leather against her palms, thinking about her sister's hands touching this cover, these pages.

She'd looked at the journal before, hoping to find clues about who or what could have caused the accident. But this time she flipped through the pages looking for a glimpse of Rosie, of her life during the two years Lilian hadn't had a relationship with her. With Rosie leaving soon, it seemed even more vital to connect with her sister in whatever way she could.

She leafed through the calendar pages, carefully drawn in colorful ink and filled with Rosie's looping script. Haircut appointments, eyebrow waxing. Meeting someone with the initials ST for coffee, meeting KL for drinks. Starting in April, every Thursday evening had the same tiny writing: *Kerrigan's trivia night 9pm.*

Various doctor's appointments were scattered throughout, including one scrawled message about a session at the University of Chicago psychology clinic in January of last year. *Dr. Vasudevan—3rd flr Bldg 2. Arrive 15 min early.*

Lilian was glad her sister had seen a psychologist, maybe to work through the loss of their parents, the estrangement from Lilian, the damage from her unhealthy prior relationships. She hoped it had given Rosie some peace and healing.

Again, she noted the references to Rosie's weekly trips to the gun range. Not long ago, Lilian had been certain those had something to do with whoever had caused the car crash—that man with the scar, the face she would never forget. But maybe Rosie had simply been looking for a way to feel safer while living on her own.

Indeed, those visits tapered out around the time Rosie seemed to have met Daniel. On a Friday evening last April, Rosie had written *Meet DC at Green Parrot, 7pm.* And then the following weekend, *Dinner with DC, 8pm.*

Lilian's heart squeezed painfully as she thought about the two of them meeting, dating, falling in love. She was glad Rosie had found someone like Daniel. And yet . . .

Lilian, if we had met under different circumstances—

Shaking off the memories—the wine on his breath, the press of his lips—Lilian turned the page. She flipped forward, through the months. A music festival in late summer, a Labor Day weekend trip to Wisconsin with *DC*, a Halloween party at a favorite bar. Thanksgiving at someone named Emilie's place. *Bring Dutch apple pie*, Rosie had written. Their mother's specialty, with the crumble topping.

On December 1, Rosie had written *Move in day!* She'd also written what looked like a grocery list on the side of the page: *Milk, Eggs, Toilet paper, Red wine, Gummy bears.*

Lilian grinned. That was so Rosie—even as a twenty-eight-year-old grown woman, she still loved gummy bears.

Then she leaned forward, looking at another note. This one in pencil, near the bottom of the page.

MyPsychJournal.com
RosieAllDay
Renoir2Sisters#!

Lilian grabbed her phone and pulled up the website.

WELCOME TO YOUR
ONLINE THERAPY JOURNAL!

Click here to learn why thousands of satisfied customers are using My Psych Journal, the best source for online personal journaling. Your private online diary allows you to write knowing that your thoughts are safe and protected. You can choose to share with your therapist via our secure network, or keep your entries personal.

Lilian squinted. The light from her screen still hurt her eyes, even now, more than five weeks out from the concussion. She almost closed the website. If Rosie had written in an online journal as part of her therapy, it was none of Lilian's business. But this could be her only chance to get a glimpse of her sister's past, in her own words. That felt even more important now, with Rosie leaving so soon, going where Lilian could not follow. And maybe she could find something that would help in Rosie's recovery.

In the top right-hand corner of the website she found a place to enter in a username and password. She glanced back at Rosie's datebook. RosieAllDay was likely the username, and Renoir2Sisters#! looked like a password. She typed them in, then pressed enter.

It worked. At the top of the page, a blue banner read: *Welcome back,*

Rosie! It has been 306 days since your last entry. On the side bar was a list of all the entries Rosie must have made, beginning in January of the previous year.

Another twinge of guilt nearly stopped Lilian. This was Rosie's private space. Lilian had no right to read these posts. But again, the urge to understand her sister—to know the version of Rosie that had existed before the accident—was stronger.

She clicked on the first entry, January 6, one year ago.

Hi. My name is Rosie and I'm a liar.

* * *

Before Lilian even made it through all the entries, tears were rolling down her face. For the first time, she realized how her leaving for medical school had affected her little sister. For Lilian, it had felt like the natural order of things: she'd taken care of Rosie for twelve years, sacrificing her adolescence and even her college years; finally, it was her turn to live her own life. But for a twelve-year-old who had never slept a night in her life without her older sister ten feet away, it must have been beyond disorienting. Shattering.

Other aspects of the journal rang uncomfortably true—including what Rosie had written about sibling relationships like theirs, with an older one raising a younger one. It made sense that Lilian had always been obsessed with being responsible, with being perceived as competent—all the way through medical training and into her career. That had been her role in the family, and she'd taken it seriously. No wonder the mistake with Dasha had wrecked her.

Perhaps her older sister role had played into her postpartum anxiety, too, she realized with a flash of clarity. Abigail reminded her of Rosie. Long-buried memories flashed through her mind: nights when baby Rosie would wake up crying in her crib, when Lilian would spend hours trying to soothe her little sister so she wouldn't wake their parents. She remembered pacing back and forth in their bedroom until she thought she'd faint from exhaustion. *Why is she crying? Is something wrong? What if I get so tired I drop her? Please be quiet, baby, please be quiet.* That sensation of being out of her depth, struggling to stay in control, must have felt all too familiar when Abigail was born, even if she'd never consciously connected it to her sister.

More memories rose to the surface, these fueled by shame: the times Lilian had grown so frustrated with Rosie's toddler tantrums that she'd slapped her; the time she shut Rosie in the closet because she wouldn't stop screaming and Lilian couldn't take it one more second. All the times she'd resented Rosie for being the reason she couldn't hang out with her friends, or get a job of her own, or go away to college. The day she'd packed up her old Dodge Stratus, leaving Rosie sobbing as she watched in the front window.

It all made sense, everything Rosie had done, starting in eighth grade after Lilian left: the terrible teenage boyfriends, the partying and skipping school, even the affair with her college professor. She'd been searching for something to fill the void Lilian had left behind. That loss had forged Rosie's identity, her outlook on the world, her view on relationships. Better to be controlled and abused than to be alone.

Bile burned in Lilian's throat as she imagined her sister drawing a blade across her own skin, desperate to feel something other than emptiness. A rush of the familiar guilt followed: if Lilian had helped Rosie when she'd come to her, instead of losing her temper and throwing her out, Rosie's rock-bottom crash might have been prevented. And she wouldn't have gone back to Michael. Thank God she had been strong enough to get away from that man.

But the last journal entry worried Lilian: Rosie's reaction to finding out about the malpractice suit. Lilian wished Rosie *had* called her. Not only would it have been wonderful to have her sister by her side, it would have been smarter than trying to confront Ben Nichols, no matter how good Rosie's intentions had been. The way Ben's brother had treated Rosie made Lilian uneasy. She remembered Detective Berenson saying that Ben Nichols's alibi for the night of the crash had been his brother. Did *he* have a silver sedan with Indiana plates?

Something cold seemed to crawl across Lilian's skin. The journal entry had been written nearly a year ago, she reminded herself, but that didn't make her feel better. Ben Nichols had been watching her just a couple of weeks before the car crash, and there had been another person in his truck with him that night in the Target parking lot. Lilian was sure of that, though she hadn't been able to make out a face. Someone had been watching Rosie, too, around her building.

According to Detective Berenson, Ben Nichols was angry and hostile under questioning. He'd lost his job and his wife had left him, on top of the loss of his daughter. He blamed Lilian for destroying his life. Had Ben Nichols—and his brother—found a way to even the score?

There was one more journal entry left. After that, Lilian told herself, she'd call the detective and give him this information.

She pulled up the site on her phone again and, with shaking hands, clicked to the last entry.

CHAPTER
FORTY-FOUR

MyPsychJournal.com

Welcome back, Rosie.
Thank you for updating your privacy settings.
Your therapist will NOT have access to this entry.
Happy journaling!

APRIL 18, 2018

Dr. V still isn't back. Apparently her father is dying, so she's taking some time off to be with him until he passes. When I heard that, it snapped me out of the little self-absorbed spiral of chaos I was in when I wrote my last journal entry. Dr. V is facing a real tragedy—I know how it feels to lose a parent—and my worries about being replaced by my sister's baby can't even compare. I left a note with the secretary to send to Dr. V, because I do care about her. She's become important to me, and I missed seeing her.

But on the plus side, I got to see Dr. C again today.

He said he was worried about me—he'd read my last journal entry, and he wanted to make sure I was okay. I told him that I'm fine and he doesn't need to worry—I've calmed down since then. But I appreciated his concern. Dr. V definitely would not have reacted that way. She would've analyzed it, analyzed *me*, asked me to consider how the event related to my History of Abandonment Issues. She's smart and tough, and that's what I needed in a therapist, but I'll admit it—it was nice having someone be concerned about me.

By the way, my first impression of Dr. C—this sloppy, inexperienced nerd—was totally wrong. He's a great listener, kind and funny. Nice eyes, too. He said he wanted to talk about what I wrote earlier, how I said I can't handle being alone. He pointed out that I have been on my own, for six months now. I have a job I love, an apartment of my own, a new group of friends. I told Dr. C about them, how we meet at the shooting range every Tuesday and for trivia night at a bar every Thursday.

"Looks to me like you are handling it just fine," he said.

And I guess he's right.

Talking to him, I finally had the chance to tell someone about my sister, what I'd heard about her pregnancy, and my conflicting feelings, the weird sensation of being replaced. I told him that I wanted to reach out to her, but something kept holding me back.

I guess I'm worried that she'll be disappointed in me, that I need to meet some kind of standard before I'm worthy of seeing her again?

He said it's normal to have those feelings; subconsciously, I think of Lilian more as a parent than a sister, so it's understandable to feel unsettled by her having a "real" child. He also said he understood the feeling of never measuring up to someone else's expectations no matter how hard you tried. He said his dad was the same way—never satisfied with his son's efforts, even when he got a PhD. "I had to learn that my expectations matter more than someone else's," he said. I told him that Dr. V would call that an Important Life Lesson, and he laughed and said I sounded just like her.

Before I left his office, Dr. C stood and hesitated by the door, sort of awkwardly. I asked him what was wrong—I was worried that he was going to tell me that Dr. V wasn't coming back at all. But then he said that since he won't be my doctor anymore, we should meet somewhere off campus and talk. Maybe get dinner.

I wanted to be very clear about what was happening, so I said, "Are you asking me out?" I haven't dated at all since leaving Michael, and I'm a little out of practice.

His cheeks turned an adorable shade of red and he said, "That depends on if you're going to say yes or no."

He's not the kind of guy I usually go for—but maybe that's the point. Maybe I need to date someone who isn't my type at all. Plus, he has the prettiest blue eyes I've ever seen.

So I smiled and told him that if I went to dinner with him, I couldn't call him "Doctor" the entire time. He needed to tell me his first name. And he did.

So. Guess what? I have a date next week with Dr. Daniel Connors.

PART THREE

CHAPTER
FORTY-FIVE

Lilian sat, frozen in shock.

I have a date with Dr. Daniel Connors.

It wasn't possible. But she read the words again. And again. Over and over until the words blurred on her phone screen and nausea overwhelmed her.

Holding a hand to her mouth, she rushed into the bathroom, barely making it to the toilet before vomiting. She dropped her phone, sending it clattering across the floor, and retched, again and again, her stomach cramping as if trying to expel poison.

It wasn't possible. It wasn't possible.

Finally empty, she sat back and leaned against the wall, closing her eyes. *Dr. C.* Her stomach churned again, and she swallowed. Leaning over, she grabbed her phone from where it had landed. The screen had a new hairline crack, right across the center. A hysterical laugh bubbled out of her lips; she knew exactly how that felt.

With shaky hands, she did a search for the doctor Rosie had mentioned. *Dr. V.* She'd written her full name in her day planner, and it was unusual enough that it had stuck in Lilian's mind. *Dr. Vasudevan, psychology, University of Chicago.*

There she was: Saya Vasudevan, PhD, professor of cognitive psychology. A slight woman in her sixties with short, black hair and an imperious smile. Important enough to be ranked twenty-seventh in the International Psychological Review's list of the one hundred most influential psychological researchers of the century.

Lilian scanned down the list of other faculty at the clinic, looking for another name, hoping she didn't find it. As she reached the bottom of the page, her shoulders relaxed. No Daniel Connors.

But wait. At the very bottom, almost as an afterthought, she saw a link to the postdoctoral fellows. She clicked on that, holding her breath.

And there it was.

Postdoctoral Fellows, Neuropsychology Division: Lena McLean, Adam Kowalcyk, and Daniel Connors.

Lilian's hands started to shake. She stared at the name again, not wanting to believe it.

I'm a postdoc, he had said.

In what field?

Art history.

Had he hesitated before answering? She couldn't recall—but now her mind raced back through Rosie's journal, making connections. Dr. C was Daniel Connors. *Her* Daniel Connors, her friend. Her confidante. Her sister's boyfriend.

Swallowing hard, she continued reading his bio: *Dr. Connors received his PhD in psychology from the University of California, Davis, then accepted a postdoctoral fellowship at the University of Chicago to further his research in functional imaging of the brain in neuropsychological conditions.*

Lilian's hands trembled again—this time with anger. At herself, for not figuring this out sooner. At Daniel, for deliberately concealing it.

But why? Why not be honest with Lilian? His expertise could have been helpful, alongside his knowledge of Rosie's past history.

He must have been worried that Lilian would think it was inappropriate for him to get involved with his patient.

And it *was* inappropriate. Lilian scrambled to her feet, jammed her phone in her pocket, and returned to her bedroom, pacing back and forth. Daniel *knew* it was a major breach of professional ethics. If Lilian had known this from the beginning, she would have thrown him out of Rosie's hospital room so quickly he'd have landed on his ass. She'd already been wary of him—he must have picked up on that and concealed the truth so he could continue to see Rosie.

Which begged the next question: Could Lilian blame him? No matter what, it was clear that Daniel cared about Rosie. He had been at her bedside every day for weeks. He'd willingly dedicated the rest of his life to caring for her.

But if he could lie about something this important, what else had he lied about?

Lilian yanked out her phone and tried calling Caleb. She had no idea what time it was in London, but she got his voice mail. Not that he would have been able to help. She needed answers from Daniel himself. And not over the phone, either. She needed to see him face-to-face, to look him in the eye as he explained why he'd deceived her for weeks.

Taking a shaky breath, she typed out a text to Daniel: *Hey, can I come for a visit today?*

His response came within seconds: *That would be great. I need to run some errands, so if you could sit with Rosie for an hour or two, I'd appreciate it.*

Sure, she typed. *See you soon.*

Then she dialed Nancy's phone number. Her mother-in-law had returned from her trip two days ago and was desperate to spend time with Abigail. She said she was more than happy to come right over.

Minutes later, Lilian was speeding down I-90, her hands sweating as they gripped the steering wheel.

* * *

A gust of icy wind accompanied Lilian into the lobby of Rosie and Daniel's building. The doorman was the same one Lilian had met the last time she'd been there. Marty, she reminded herself as she looked at his name tag.

He recognized her, too. "Hello there, Rosie's sister," he said. "Welcome back. How is Miss Rosie doing lately?"

"She's doing well. She actually moved back home a couple days ago." She shifted her weight in her boots, anxious to get going.

"Ah, I've been off for a little while. Drove to Wisconsin to meet my first grandchild."

"That's wonderful!" Lilian forced a big smile. "Congratulations, Grandpa."

Marty gave her a pleased grin. "Thank you. That's wonderful about Rosie, too. So happy she's back home. You heading up to see her and Daniel now?"

"Yes, I am. I don't remember which floor they live on, though?"

"Eighth floor," he said, and then added, "Apartment 8A."

"Thank you so much," Lilian said, hurrying off.

"You're very welcome. And give my best wishes to your sister."

As Lilian rode the elevator, she readied herself to confront Daniel. If she met him with all her anger and frustration—which would be justified—he might get defensive, and she needed him to come clean with her. To explain why he hadn't been honest.

She found herself hoping that he had a good reason. But maybe that was because she had *liked* him. An inky feeling of shame accompanied that admission. Lilian had cared about him as a friend—as more than a friend. She had been attracted to him, had looked forward to spending time with him. And he'd been lying to her the whole time.

When the elevator opened on the eighth floor, she stepped into the hallway, then stopped. Blinking, she looked around, fighting a vague sense of disorientation.

Get it together, she told herself as she took a few careful steps forward.

This hallway felt unfamiliar because that last time she'd visited, her concussion symptoms had been worse. Confusion, blurry vision, headaches; she hadn't been able to look at her phone without getting dizzy and nauseated. This disorientation was a jarring reminder of how significant those symptoms had been.

And yet, as she walked down the hallway to apartment 8A, the uneasy feeling persisted. She wiped her sweaty palms on her jeans, then knocked. She heard footsteps, then the lock turning. The door opened.

Lilian blinked in shock, speechless.

The man standing on the opposite side of the door wasn't Daniel. But she knew him.

Dark hair.

Long, thin face.

A curved scar along the right side of his jaw.

"Can I help you?" the man asked.

Lilian wanted to take him by the collar and shake him, to demand he explain who he was and why he had been in the ICU, watching her sister. Instead, still dazed, she cleared her throat, and said, "The doorman told me 8A. I . . . I'm looking for Daniel Connors."

"What can I do for you?" he said.

Lilian blinked, confused. "Excuse me?"

"You said you needed Daniel Connors, apartment 8A." He squinted at her, hands on hips. "Have we met before? You look familiar."

Lilian stared at him. She had not imagined this face, this scar. It could not be a coincidence that he was here. "What the *fuck* were you doing in my sister's hospital room?" she demanded.

"Your sister?" His face drained of color. "Oh God."

Her mind filled with a thousand questions, and they all rushed out of her mouth in a furious jumble: "How do you know my sister? How do you know Daniel? What are you doing in their apartment?"

"What are you—*I'm* Daniel," he said, louder. "This is *my* apartment."

Lilian grabbed her phone from her pocket and flicked to the picture she'd taken of Rosie and Daniel on the day she'd left the rehab hospital. "If you're Daniel, then who is this?"

She turned the phone toward him, and his mouth fell open. Speechless.

He answered, stumbling over his words, "That's Michael Sorenson. Rosie's ex-boyfriend."

CHAPTER
FORTY-SIX

Lilian sat on the threadbare sofa in Daniel Connors's apartment as everything tumbled out.

"This doesn't make sense," she said, putting her fingers to her temples. Her head was spinning. "This can't be right."

"What?" Daniel said. He'd already confirmed that he was a postdoc in psychology at the University of Chicago, working under Dr. Saya Vasudevan. Lilian had asked for identification, and he'd produced it: a New York state driver's license, a University ID badge. He'd met Rosie when he was covering for Dr. Vasudevan. They'd started dating last spring and moved in together in early December. He even produced a copy of their apartment lease, with his and Rosie's names at the top.

Before answering, Lilian studied him: sweatpants, stained T-shirt, a hole in his sock. He did have blue eyes, she noted, though they were more gray. He had a nervous habit of running his fingers along the scar on his jaw.

The apartment was small, dark, and messy. No pictures on the walls, unopened boxes near the entry, as if he hadn't fully moved in. Papers spilled across a computer desk in the corner; coffee cups and takeout containers littered the kitchen counters.

This was the man Rosie had mentioned to Lilian during their car ride, all those weeks ago? *This* was where Rosie had lived? Lilian wasn't impressed. The setting alone stood in stark contrast to the apartment Lilian had been shown by the *other* Daniel Connors, the one who had been at Rosie's bedside for weeks.

She pulled up the picture on her phone again, the one she'd taken on Rosie's discharge day, and stared at the two of them: the tension in Rosie's posture, the smile on his face.

"You're sure this is Michael?" she asked, pointing to the picture.

"Well, yeah." He fidgeted with a loose thread on the cuff of his shirt. "Of course I'm sure. I've met him. Several times. He lives in the building."

She sucked in a breath—Daniel already knew this? "For how long?"

"He moved in a couple weeks after we did—Rosie was terrified when she found out."

"But I thought he'd stopped following her around . . ." She trailed off, thinking about Rosie's therapy journal. She hadn't seen Michael in a few months; she thought he'd moved on to someone else.

"When we started dating, he popped up again, showing up in random places, sending her flowers and gifts. After we moved here, Rosie saw him hanging around the building. But she never expected that he would actually move in." Daniel shook his head. "We went to management and asked them to break our lease, but they wouldn't. We were trying to figure a way around it. That's why we never really unpacked. That night you went out to dinner together, Rosie was going to ask if you could lend us some money to get out of the lease."

Lilian put her hand to her mouth, dazed. This must have been what Rosie had been meaning to tell her. *It's a matter of life and death, sis.*

She thought back to the picture on Rosie's Instagram, the one Lilian had assumed was of Rosie and Michael. But if the real Michael somehow had access to Rosie's Instagram account—if he'd known her password—he could have edited the photo caption. He also could have deleted any pictures of him.

"Did Rosie have any pictures of him here?" Lilian asked, needing to see with her own eyes.

"Uh, yeah," Daniel said, standing. He disappeared into the bedroom and returned carrying a cardboard box labeled ROSIE in familiar handwriting.

"I never unpacked her things," he said, shooting Lilian a guilty look. "You can take them whenever you want. There's a photo album in this box."

Lilian flushed with anger at the thought of this man abandoning Rosie while she relearned how to swallow, how to communicate, how to walk. There was something deeply wrong with him. But she had more important things to focus on right now. Daniel had pulled out a photo album and handed it to Lilian.

She opened the cover—*Rosie and Michael's First Summer*, it read on the front—and there he was, on every page. Posing with Rosie on the steps of the Art Institute near one of the bronze lions. Sprawled out on a blanket at an outdoor concert in Millennium Park. With Rosie at a busy farmer's market, each of them holding a giant tomato and laughing.

And then a picture Lilian recognized, the one she'd seen in the apartment of the man she had known as Daniel Connors. He and Rosie, standing in front of a glistening Lake Michigan, his arm around her shoulder.

Lilian's breath left her in a rush. She knew this face. She knew those eyes, bluer than the lake behind them. It was true, then. He had posed as Daniel Connors, and she had fallen for it, every twisted bit of manipulation, all his lies. Her fingers involuntarily touched her lips, and she nearly gagged at the memory of their kiss.

Thinking back, she remembered the police saying the officer on the scene of the accident had used Rosie's phone to call her emergency contact before the phone died completely. Maybe Rosie hadn't changed it after the breakup with Michael? And then at the hospital—had Michael overhead her calling the name Daniel Connors into the crowded waiting room and jumped at the opportunity?

But that didn't explain why she had seen *this* Daniel Connors's face on Lake Shore Drive right before the crash.

"Why were you following us on the night of the crash?" she blurted, before remembering that they were alone in his apartment, behind a solid oak door. He could be dangerous. No one would hear her if she screamed, and as she realized this, her hands tingled with fear.

Daniel jolted upright. "Following you?"

Lilian squeezed her hands into fists—maybe she shouldn't have confronted him directly, but the cat was well out of the bag now. "I saw you before the car accident," she said. "You were there."

Daniel sat, stunned speechless. Then he reached into his pocket—Lilian flinched, wondering what he was going for—and pulled out his phone. "I drove up to Madison that night, Lilian. I was at a friend's party. He got tenure. Look. I wasn't even in Chicago."

He showed her a picture on his phone—there he was, standing in a bar with three other men his age, each of them holding a beer and smiling at the camera. The time stamp was 7:32 p.m. the night of the crash; the location Madison, Wisconsin, a good two and a half hours drive from Chicago. Lilian mentally did the calculations: the crash had occurred just after 6:30 p.m.

"I didn't realize until the next morning that Rosie never came home," he said, pocketing his phone. "She didn't answer when I called her, so I called all her friends. No one knew anything, so I started calling around to hospitals. I didn't track her down until the next morning."

"But I *saw* you before the crash," Lilian said, her voice quavering with emotion. "I know I did, because when I saw you again in the ICU, I knew your face. I *recognized* you."

Daniel seemed baffled by this, fingers tracing his scar again. "I have no idea. I wasn't driving that car, Lilian. I don't even have a car."

Then something occurred to Lilian, and she thought back to that snowy night, to the moments before the crash. Rosie had told her she was seeing someone, that she'd recently moved in with him. He was a professor on sabbatical; she thought Lilian would like him. Then—the memory clicked into place, a key in a lock—she'd asked Lilian if she wanted to see a picture.

"Her phone!" Lilian said. "She showed me a picture of you on her phone, and then she swerved and I dropped it, and then—the crash. I don't remember anything else."

Her brain must have made a connection between his picture and those terrifying moments before the accident, when Rosie kept looking over her shoulder. That made sense, except: "Why did you run off when you saw me?" She recalled the look of fear in his eyes, the way he'd darted out of Rosie's hospital room.

Daniel's gaze dropped to the floor. "I talked with the nurse that morning," he said, flushing. "She told me that things were pretty bad, that Rosie might not make it—and when I saw you, I panicked."

She could see the entire story written on his face: he'd been overwhelmed and scared by Rosie's condition. He'd run away when he saw Lilian because what if she'd expected him to take responsibility for Rosie? He knew he wasn't up to the task.

"But you never came back?" She didn't even bother trying to hide her disgust. "You never wondered how your brain-injured girlfriend was doing?"

He blinked, surprised. "What are you talking about? You're the one who asked me to step aside. It would be better for her—that's what you said."

It was Lilian's turn to be shocked. "I have no idea what you're talking about."

"The letter!" His forehead furrowed in confusion. "Hang on—I'm questioning everything now." He stood and walked into the kitchen, dug around in a drawer, then returned with an envelope, out of which he took single piece of paper. "This wasn't from you?"

Mystified, Lilian took it from him and read the typed words.

Dear Daniel, this is Rosie's sister, Lilian. As you know, she has suffered a severe brain injury. Unfortunately, her doctors say she will likely never regain consciousness . . .

The letter went on to ask Daniel to please respect their family's privacy at this time and promised to contact him with any good news. It was signed Lilian Donaldson. Sickened, she put her hand to her mouth. Michael must have written it to make sure the real Daniel never showed up.

But that was no excuse. If Daniel really loved Rosie, nothing would have kept him from seeing her. Instead, he'd conveniently put her out of his mind, and whenever the guilt crept in, reassured himself that he'd done the right thing for Rosie.

Still, what could she expect from a man who'd asked his patient to dinner at the end of a therapy session? He wasn't just weak and cowardly—he had zero integrity whatsoever.

"How could you propose to her and then leave her when she needed you most?" Lilian said, her voice brittle.

Daniel glanced up sharply. "Wait, what? I didn't propose to your sister."

"She had a diamond ring in her purse, Daniel. An engagement ring. Who else would have . . ." Lilian trailed off as Daniel's eyes widened. She had a feeling she knew exactly where the ring had come from.

"I never proposed to Rosie," he said quietly. "The ring was probably from—"

"Michael," she finished. Had he delivered it to Rosie in person? Or sent it to her as a gift? Either way, it must have been chilling to receive. Like he'd been marking his territory, making his intentions clear. She shook her head, refocusing. "He showed up at the hospital on the night of the accident and said he was you. I had no reason not to trust him. And now he's taken Rosie home with him, just a few days ago."

"What?" Daniel said, lifting his hands in a calming gesture. "You need to repeat that. Start over and go more slowly this time."

Lilian did, running through all of it—from the night of the accident to Rosie's long hospital stay and her recent discharge, going home with the man Lilian now knew was Michael Sorenson.

"You haven't seen her around the building with Michael?" Lilian said, but when Daniel shook his head, she wasn't surprised. Michael would have been smart enough to avoid Daniel when he brought Rosie home, and she hadn't left the apartment since then. "Tell me what you know about Michael."

"I—" Daniel averted his eyes. "Well. Forgive the armchair diagnosis, but from a psychological perspective, I think he has antisocial personality disorder."

Lilian's blood ran cold. Mentally, she ran through what she remembered about the disorder: disregard for right and wrong, persistent lying, using charm to manipulate others for personal gain, a sense of superiority, a lack of empathy.

"Go on," she said. She wanted to rush to her sister's side and confront the man who had deceived her—but she needed information from Daniel Connors first. She needed to know what she was up against.

"Let me think," he said, running a hand through his hair, clearly agitated. "Rosie told me a little bit about him. I'm pretty sure he grew up outside of San Francisco with a single mom, no contact with his father. The dad was apparently some big shot CEO and married. He wanted nothing to do with Michael. Later on, Michael's mother got married. The stepfather was physically abusive; the mother became an alcoholic. Michael was a smart kid, though—he got into Stanford on scholarship, though I don't think he actually graduated. At some point, his biological father died and left him some kind of trust. As far as I know, he hasn't had to work since."

Lilian shivered, thinking about the happy home life Michael had described: a boy growing up playing baseball and learning to work with his hands.

He's not Daniel, Rosie had said, over and over again. *He scares me.* And Lilian had sent her home with him anyway, because Rosie had said the same thing about Lilian. Had she recognized him as Michael? With her brain injury, it could be difficult to know how much she understood.

Not that Rosie would have told Lilian—she didn't trust Lilian any more than she trusted "Daniel." And if the rehab staff heard Rosie ranting about Daniel being someone named Michael? Well, Rosie also ranted about Lilian being a spy. She hadn't trusted the staff either; she'd told Lilian that they were all liars. From Rosie's perspective, they were complicit with the imposters—not only the fake Lilian, but Michael posing as Daniel. Then they'd given Rosie medication to treat her "paranoia," keeping her calm enough to send her home with a sociopath. Not that she could blame the rehab team—they'd done their best.

Lilian had to wonder when Michael realized that he could use Rosie's brain injury to his advantage. It seemed like a risky gamble, but then again, what did he have to lose if it didn't work? At any point, if Rosie had identified him, he could have walked away and never looked back.

"Tell me about the behavior of someone with antisocial personality disorder in a relationship," she said.

"Charming and gregarious at the beginning. Flattering, even endearing." Daniel paused, shook his head. "But it's an act, of course. It's always an act. At the heart of sociopathy is an absence of empathy. These individuals play with emotions, manipulating people around them. They can be intensely cruel. Controlling. And they feel no remorse."

His words hit home. Lilian had firsthand experience with Michael's skill at manipulation.

"Is that why he wanted Rosie to come live with him?" she asked. "To control her?"

Or was it the money? Lilian had already given Michael thousands of dollars, with plans to give him thirty thousand more for Rosie's treatment at SNIC. He might have even forged the acceptance letter—there was usually a months-long waiting list, but somehow Rosie had conveniently gotten a spot? He must have been planning to take her to California, then disappear. Lilian shuddered, realizing how close she had come to losing her sister.

"Control is definitely a large part of it," Daniel said, hesitating.

"What's the rest of it?"

"I think he wants your sister to have a baby with him."

Bile rose in Lilian's throat. Back when Michael and Rosie were together, he had tried to get her pregnant without her consent. All those times he'd held Abigail—he'd looked like a natural, like he adored babies. Lilian had eaten it up. He'd asked if Rosie had looked like Abigail when she was little; he'd mentioned being devastated that he and Rosie might never have children together.

Daniel was right. Michael wanted a baby with Rosie. Something to tie her to him, forever.

Lilian had sent her sister home with a man who would rape her and force her to carry his child.

And Rosie had already spent several days alone with him.

CHAPTER
FORTY-SEVEN

Lilian hurried into the elevator and pressed the button for the ground floor. Her hands shook. She'd left Daniel's apartment in a rush, desperate to call the police, ignoring Daniel's frantic pleas to keep him out of it. But she didn't care about him; the only thing that mattered was getting Rosie away from Michael as soon as possible.

A text message flashed on her phone screen: *You still coming by today?*

She stared at the message, and at the name at the top of her screen: Daniel Connors. It took her a few beats to realize who had sent the text.

Less than two hours ago, she'd been ready to confront him for failing to tell her that he was actually Dr. C from Rosie's journal. She never would have guessed his true identity.

Another thought occurred to her, and she paused. What would happen if she *did* call the police? It would take a while before they actually showed up. When they did, Rosie would be terrified by a bunch of cops rushing into the apartment.

And Michael? She couldn't predict what he would do, if he were cornered like that, but what if it were something violent? What if he harmed Rosie?

On the other hand, he was already expecting Lilian. They'd made plans for her to sit with Rosie while he ran some errands. Once he was gone, Lilian could get Rosie out of the apartment and away from him. And she was *right here,* just a few floors away.

She tapped out a reply: *I'm in the elevator on my way up. Remind me what floor? The doorman was busy.*

His response pinged back: *Great, see you soon. It's 15.*

The elevator shuddered to a stop; she'd reached the first floor. Lilian hit the button to keep the doors closed. Then, taking a deep breath, she pushed the button for the fifteenth floor.

* * *

"Good to see you," Michael said as Lilian entered.

Lilian struggled to keep her face neutral. He looked like he always did, handsome and smiling, his eyes a startling blue, contrasting with his dark hair. But it all seemed false now, his body too relaxed, his smile too easy.

"How's Rosie?" Lilian said, forcing her own smile. She kept her tone light, casual.

"She's doing well. Like I said, the first night was rough; she didn't want to go to bed. Last night was better, though."

Lilian tried not to wince at the thought of Rosie going to bed.

"Where is she sleeping?" she asked, hoping her question didn't sound unusual.

"In the spare room. I didn't think she'd be comfortable sleeping with me yet, and she does better getting in and out of the hospital bed."

Just because they slept in separate beds didn't mean he hadn't assaulted her. The thought nearly made her retch, and Lilian swallowed hard.

Rosie was curled up in a chair by the window, holding a sketchbook and pencil, her back to Lilian. Her hair had grown out in a short pixie cut, obscuring the healed incision on the right side of her skull. With her leggings and tunic-style sweatshirt, she looked like a chic, artistic young woman on a cold winter morning.

Once again, Rosie had drawn Renoir's *Two Sisters.* Lilian walked closer, studying the drawing. Her sketch seemed more confident and de-tailed, especially the older sister's eyes and the younger girl's hands, her tiny fingers. Again, Rosie was drawing something in the girl's cupped palms, her pencil moving with quick, efficient strokes.

Lilian glanced behind her at the reproduction of the painting on the wall to remind herself of that detail. The younger sister's hands were clutching the edge of her older sister's basket of flowers—not out-stretched, not holding anything. Nothing in the picture looked like the small, stubby cylinders Rosie was sketching.

Not that it mattered—the meaning was clear. Rosie wanted her sister. She needed Lilian, even if she didn't trust her yet.

Lilian turned back to Rosie, her heart swelling with fierce protec-tiveness. "Hi, sis."

Rosie turned at the sound, a hopeful expression on her face. But when she saw Lilian, her eyes narrowed. "You're not my sister not Lilian," she said in a nervous voice.

"It's okay," Michael said, smiling. "You're safe, sweetheart."

Lilian almost gagged. No one would think him anything but the loving fiancé.

"It's nice to see you," Lilian said to Rosie. "I was hoping we could spend some time together this afternoon. How are you feeling?"

Rosie glanced at Michael, who gave an encouraging nod. She turned back to Lilian, still wary. "I'm okay," she said.

Lilian cleared her throat. "I have a couple hours before I need to get back to Abigail, so Daniel"—she hoped she hadn't stumbled over his name—"can take a break."

"That would be great," he said. "I need groceries and I have to pick up the dry cleaning. Rosie's still not ready for that, although we're think-ing about taking a drive through the city later tonight, right, Rosie?"

Rosie blinked at him, her eyes bright and wide. "I don't want to go with you I want to go with Daniel where is he—when is he coming to—you're not Daniel."

Lilian shivered at the words—the same things she'd heard her sister say so many times, but had discounted.

"I'm someone who loves you very much," Michael said, and goose-bumps rose on Lilian's shoulders.

"Anything I should do while you're out?" Lilian asked him. "Does she need any medications?"

He shook his head as he pulled on his coat. "No, just spend time together. Rosie, do you want anything from the store?"

Rosie shot him a glare, then turned back to her sketchbook. "Gummy bears," she said.

After the door shut behind Michael, Lilian counted to a hundred in her mind, then turned to her sister.

"I know he's not Daniel," Lilian said.

Rosie glanced up, eyes narrowed. "What do you want I'm not talking to you—I know who you are stop spying on me. Get away from me."

Lilian took a deep breath and tried a different tack. *This* was exactly the issue: Rosie didn't trust her enough to tell her about Michael. "I know I'm not your sister, but I'm friends with her."

Rosie perked up, though she still seemed skeptical. "You are?"

"We're very good friends."

"Can you ask her why she doesn't come visit me?" Rosie's eyes—angry, wary—filled with tears.

"She sent me to get you, to take you to see her," Lilian said, sickened by the feeling of lying to her sister. Then she decided to slide in the next information, hoping it wouldn't upset Rosie: "Lilian doesn't trust Michael, and she doesn't want you to live here with him."

The use of his name didn't provoke much of a reaction. Rosie scratched at the incision on her scalp, contemplating this. "I don't—I don't wanna live with him anymore I don't want to be here," she said. "Michael did a bad thing a very bad thing."

So she *did* recognize him as Michael. When had that realization happened? Here or at the hospital? But there was no time to discuss that now—Lilian needed to know about the *bad thing*, whatever it was.

"What did he do?" Lilian struggled to maintain composure. "Did he hurt you?"

"Yes."

Lilian's stomach dropped. Rosie continued, her voice gaining urgency. "He did a bad thing a very bad thing and it's here—I tried to find it but he's always around he's always watching me and I can't find—I can't look for it."

"What are you looking for?"

"I know it's here I know it," Rosie said, as if Lilian hadn't spoken. "You can find it if you look."

Lilian stood, worried enough to start searching. "What am I looking for?"

But Rosie was agitated, her words running together. "Michael did something bad a very bad thing and it's here—you can find it—I tried to find it but he's always here so I can't look for it but you can find it."

Lilian's breathing quickened. What could Rosie be talking about—something he had used to hurt her? Nauseated, she almost grabbed her sister by the arm. She would physically carry her out of this place if she had to.

"Rosie, we should leave now, while Michael's away. Once we're gone, we can talk about what Michael did to you." She tried to take Rosie's hand, but Rosie snatched it back.

"No!" she shouted. "Not leaving until you find it look for it."

"I don't know what I'm looking for!"

"Find it!"

Frantic, Lilian glanced around the living room. There was nothing to do but try and look—at the very least, it would appease Rosie. She turned over couch cushions. Nothing. She ran into the kitchen and opened cabinets, drawers, but didn't see anything unusual. Rosie followed her, using a cane for balance. She couldn't move quickly, and she huffed with impatience, urging Lilian onward.

In the bedroom, Lilian searched through the drawers, under the bed, in the nightstand. Nothing seemed out of order. Opening the closet, Lilian threw aside clothes, looked under shoes. At the back, her fingers hit something solid. She brushed aside the hanging clothes and leaned in.

A safe. Two feet wide, solid metal, with a combination lock.

"Do you know the combination?" she asked Rosie.

Rosie screwed up her face, confused, but the answer came to Lilian with a jolt: *he used my birthday as the code for the safe, he always did.*

September 23, 1990. 092390. Lilian entered the numbers, and the lock released with an echoing click.

Pulse pounding, she opened the lid.

Inside the safe was a handgun: black, metallic, ominous-looking.

Under the gun was a set of license plates.

Indiana license plates.

CHAPTER
FORTY-EIGHT

Lilian's hands shook. She didn't dare touch the contents of the safe. The one thing she knew about guns was to always assume they were loaded.

She pointed to the license plates and asked Rosie, "How did you know he did this? Do you remember?"

"You're not my—where's my real sister," Rosie said, suspicion settling into her expression again.

"I know, I know," Lilian said, fighting the rising hysteria. "But Rosie, listen. Witnesses to the car crash saw a silver sedan hit your car. That's what caused the accident. A silver sedan with Indiana plates, Rosie. It was Michael."

Afterward, he must have gotten rid of the car. When he'd come to her house, Lilian had seen an old blue pickup in her driveway.

Rosie shook her head, her forehead wrinkling in confusion. "No," she said.

Lilian squeezed her hands together, fingers interlocked, like a prayer. Her knuckles cracked. Every cell in her body screamed at her to run, to grab her sister, and haul her out of this place.

But if she did that, Rosie would panic. Lilian couldn't drag a frightened, screaming, disabled woman down the hall, into the elevator, and out the door.

Stay calm.

Keep *Rosie* calm.

"Michael was driving the car that was chasing you," Lilian said. "You were trying to avoid him. Do you remember?"

Rosie stared at the license plates with a blank look on her face. "Wrong," she said.

"No, I—"

"That's the *wrong* thing!" Rosie shouted, suddenly agitated. "Michael did something bad and it's here it's here I need to find it I have to find it please help me find—"

"This *is* a sign that he did something bad," Lilian said, trying to sound soothing. "We need to call the police and get him arrested, Rosie."

Hot, furious rage spiraled inside her as she thought about Michael. His smile, his eyes, his curated facade. All the ways he had made her feel supported and important and believed-in during her most helpless moments.

Worse than that: all the pain and terror he had wrought in her sister's life.

Lilian stood. She would get her phone from her purse and call 911. She would explain to the operator that she needed help, that this was a delicate situation with a frightened, brain-injured woman, and that the police needed to hurry and get here before Michael returned.

But Rosie seized her hand in a vice grip. "Keep looking," she said.

"We need to get out of here," Lilian said. Her heartbeat a frenetic rhythm in her chest. "Come *on*, sis."

Rosie withdrew as if slapped. "Not Lilian," she said, her green eyes glittering. "You look like Lilian but you're *spying* on me get *away* from me."

"I'm friends with your sister, remember?" Lilian tried.

"Not Lilian," Rosie said, backing toward the closet, her eyes wild, like those of a cornered animal. "Get away from me get away—"

"We don't have much time," Lilian said to her sister, pleading. "We need to go now."

A voice spoke from the bedroom doorway. "And where do you think you're going, Lilian?"

She whirled around, heart stopping. She couldn't breathe.

Michael stood in the bedroom doorway, his icy gaze taking in the scene: The bedroom, which Lilian had torn apart in her search. Rosie, shrinking against the closet. The open safe next to her—although Lilian couldn't tell if Michael could see it.

"Rosie wanted to take a walk," Lilian said in a light voice.

Michael shook his head, a sad smile on his lips. "I have to say, I'm disappointed, Lilian. I trusted you."

"Not Lilian," Rosie said, her voice high-pitched with terror. "She's not Lilian she looks like Lilian but she isn't Lilian."

Michael took a step forward, his eyes trained on Lilian's, his face bland and expressionless. "You're right, Rosie," he said quietly. "She's not Lilian at all. But you know who I am, don't you, sweetheart?"

"Michael did something bad," Rosie whispered.

He kept his eyes on Lilian, only on Lilian. "I feel terrible about what happened the night of the accident," he said in the same quiet voice. "I was trying to make sure you both got to the restaurant safely. I was worried about the weather."

"You were stalking my sister." Lilian pushed the words out through gritted teeth. "Were you trying to kill her? Or was this your plan all along—to permanently injure Rosie so she'd be dependent on you?"

Michael looked genuinely hurt. "Of course not. Her Bug is terrible in the snow. It lost traction—"

A burst of fury: "You hit her bumper, *Michael*! And then you drove away and left us there."

"I didn't drive away," he said, his hands spread wide in gentle supplication. "I would never do that. I stayed close by, I called for help—I was sick with worry."

For an instant, she almost believed him. His low voice was melodic, soothing. A vague memory floated through her mind: snow falling like stars around her; a man's voice, calling 911. *Michael's* voice.

Another memory: Rosie, the day after the crash, her head half-shaved, the craniotomy incision, the neat row of staples biting her scalp.

"She almost died," Lilian said as her eyes flooded with tears. "My baby sister almost died. And then you lied to me, to everyone, so I'd let her go home with you."

"You *wanted* her to come home with me," Michael said, his voice like a silk ribbon snaking between them. "You put on a good show as the concerned older sister, but I know you, Lilian. You never wanted to take care of her, not really. You thought she'd be a burden." His voice dropped lower. "You even told *me* to move on without her."

"That's not what I meant," Lilian said, faltering.

"You think *I* pretended to be someone else? What about you? Who were *you* lying to, all that time we spent together?"

"You used me."

His eyes dropped to her mouth. "You wanted it."

Lilian couldn't speak, couldn't breathe. She could do nothing but stare into the cold depths of his eyes as he took another step toward her.

"I could have had you that night," he said, his voice so low she felt it in her bones. "I could have backed you against the wall and taken you, right then and there, and you would have let me. *That's* the kind of person you are. The kind of person who lies to her husband, over and over. Who meets her brain-injured sister's fiancé for lunch, over and over. Who invites him to stay while her husband is gone for the night. Who fantasizes about him and doesn't feel an ounce of guilt."

Lilian couldn't tear her eyes from his. His intensity, the hypnotic sound of his voice, paralyzed her. Even from across the room, he held her as tightly as any vise.

Because he was right, wasn't he? She had done all of those things. She had justified it, telling herself she was spending time with him for Rosie's sake. That Caleb wouldn't care, because he was burying himself in work. That she *needed* a friend, someone who understood her, who believed in her. She'd felt waves of guilt and shame before, but never like this. This was a tsunami, barreling down at her, a thousand feet high.

The sound of quiet sobs broke the spell.

Lilian glanced behind her, at her sister. Rosie had pulled herself into a tight ball. She lifted her tearstained face to meet Lilian's eyes.

"I hate you," she whispered. "I hate you I hate you I hate you."

Gutted, Lilian sucked in a lungful of air. She whirled back to face Michael, fury flashing red across her vision, and froze.

Michael was blocking the only exit. His eyes flicked to the safe near Rosie, and Lilian knew that he had seen it, open.

She needed to get herself and Rosie out of there, alive.

"Let me take Rosie now," Lilian said, her throat raw with desperation. "I'll take her with me, and I'll never say a word to the police about your involvement."

His jaw tightened. "I can't let you do that."

"I'll leave today—you'll never hear from either of us again. You can keep the money—"

"This isn't *about* the money!" His eyes flashed, blue ice.

Lilian was losing him—he was getting angry. She switched tactics, softening her voice. "I know it's not about the money. You love my sister. You always have. But it's not easy to take care of someone with a brain injury, no matter how much you love them."

He tilted his head, listening.

Lilian continued. "You've been wonderful with Rosie, all this time. You've shown how much you love her."

"I do love her," he said.

"I know—"

"But it's hard," Michael said. His eyes glistened, and he wiped them with one hand. "She's so different. It's not what we wanted. We had such plans for the future."

Lilian took a step forward, spreading her hands wide. Maybe if she played her cards right, she could get Rosie out safely. "We both love Rosie. We both want what's best for her. Let me take her home with me, and I won't—"

"No!" Rosie shouted.

Lilian spun around.

Rosie stood, balancing herself with one hand against the closet door. In the other hand, she held the gun.

Pointed at Lilian.

CHAPTER
FORTY-NINE

"Put the gun down, Rosie," Lilian said, her voice shaking.

Lilian had never touched a gun in her entire life, but she knew Rosie had. Her sister had gone to the shooting range every week for months. Now, even with her poor balance, even with the fear crashing across her features, she clearly knew what she was doing. She held the gun in both hands, pointed it straight and steady at Lilian.

Panicking, Lilian reflexively tapped her pocket for her phone. *Shit.* It was in the living room, in her purse. She couldn't even call 911.

"Who are you?" Rosie said, eyes narrowing. "Where's my sister?"

A jolt of fear made Lilian blurt out the exact thing she should not have said: "I *am* your sister!"

"No you're *not you are not*," Rosie said, taking a step forward. "What did you do to Lilian?"

"Rosie, I'm—" Lilian stuttered, unhinged by the wild look in her sister's eyes. She sucked in a breath. "I know this is confusing and scary for you."

"I am *not* confused stop treating me like a fucking idiot where is my sister where is she?"

Lilian glanced over at Michael. His arms were folded across his chest, a smile playing on his lips as if this was all going according to his plan. If Rosie shot Lilian, it could be explained as a result of the Capgras delusion. Michael could say that Rosie had gotten scared, had turned on her sister. Lilian could imagine him calling Caleb to report what had happened, his eyes filling with tears, his voice full of compassion.

Caleb would believe him.

But that wasn't the worst of it. If Rosie shot and killed Lilian right now, Michael might get her for the rest of their lives. Lilian could not allow that to happen. She turned, staring down the barrel of a gun fifteen feet away, pointed directly at her face.

"Rosie, listen—"

"Don't talk like my sister," Rosie said, hand tightening.

Lilian stiffened, cursing internally. No matter what she said, there was no way she could convince Rosie of who she was.

"Michael did something bad," Lilian said.

Rosie's eyes flickered. "Not my sister you're not Lilian."

"I know," Lilian said, her entire body trembling. "But Michael did something bad, remember? You told me."

The gun wavered slightly in Michael's direction.

Michael spoke up, his voice gentle. "Rosie, sweetheart, she's not your sister. You know that. She's not Lilian."

"Not Lilian," Rosie repeated in a whisper, and the gun swung back over, to Lilian again.

Lilian took a deep breath and held it. She imagined Abigail growing up without a mother, imagined Caleb white-faced and grim at her funeral.

Then she thought about what Michael had done six weeks ago on icy Lake Shore Drive. What he might have done to Rosie in the past forty-eight hours.

But if Rosie couldn't trust her? If Rosie wouldn't listen to her?

Rosie's finger twitched on the trigger.

Frantic, Lilian glanced at the wall next to her, then at the window. The drapes were pulled tight. Dark enough? Maybe.

There was only one thing she could think of. It might not work. But it was her only chance.

Lilian reached out her hand, found the light switch, and flicked it off.

Darkness. Gray and fuzzy.

Michael's voice, outraged: "What the fuck—"

Rosie, hysterical: "I can't see I can't see I can't see."

Lilian took a breath, imagining the gleaming barrel of the gun. No idea where it was pointing now, but she only had a few seconds before all their eyes adjusted.

"Rosie? Rosie, it's Lilian."

A pause.

"Sis?"

The sweetness in her voice—the hope, the recognition—made Lilian's eyes flood with tears.

"I'm right here," she said.

A heavy footstep, then another. Michael's. Slow, deliberate. Echoing on the wood floor as the dark blur of his body edged toward the closet. Toward Rosie.

His voice, calm and soothing: "Rosie, sweetheart—"

"What did Michael do, Rosie?" Lilian said urgently. Desperately. "What did Michael do?"

She held her breath, her pulse thudding in her ears.

Then gunshots cracked: one, two, three.

A scream, a thud.

Silence.

CHAPTER
FIFTY

Lilian flicked the lights back on and blinked.

"Ohmygod ohmygod ohmygod," Rosie chanted, swaying, her gaze glued to Michael's body.

He'd fallen near the foot of the bed, half-turned on his side, cheek pressed against the wood floor. One shot had hit him in the chest, the other in his left shoulder. The third must have gone wide.

Lilian started shaking, a trembling that started in her feet and traveled up her body until her teeth knocked together. She couldn't take her eyes off Michael and the spreading circle of red beneath him. She waited for any signs of movement. Signs of life.

There it was: a flutter of his eyelids, a slight expansion of his chest.

A clattering noise made Lilian jump. She spun around to see Rosie. Her sister had dropped the gun, but she still stood, frozen, her hands outstretched, a dazed expression on her face.

"Michael did something bad," Rosie whispered.

Lilian took several steps toward her sister and kicked the gun away, to the far corner of the room.

"Rosie," she said, gently. "I know you're frightened, but I need you to listen to me."

Rosie's eyes snapped over to meet Lilian's. "Who are you what did you do and where's—where's my sister?"

"I want you to take a few deep breaths, okay? Deep breaths, Rosie."

Rosie shook her head, but took a breath as instructed, her eyes wide and panicky. "Where's Lilian you're not Lilian."

"I know," Lilian said, feeling the same old sorrow rise up inside her. The trembling in her hands increased, and for an instant, she could sense a panic attack starting.

Take your own pulse.

She did. And as she counted, her mind focused, laser sharp. The kind of focus she remembered from her days caring for critically ill children. A focus that allowed her to rapidly analyze the possible outcomes:

The neighbors would have heard the gunshots. They might have already called 911. She imagined police bursting into the apartment, loud and chaotic, handcuffing both Rosie and Lilian and hauling them off to jail.

Self-defense, Lilian thought. Surely it would be clear that Rosie had acted in self-defense.

But Michael had been unarmed. On several occasions in the hospital, there was documented evidence of Rosie screaming that he was an imposter. She might not go to prison, but she would likely end up in a secure psychiatric facility, possibly for the rest of her life.

Lilian couldn't let that happen.

"Rosie, I need you to try and stay focused. Okay?"

Rosie's chest rose and fell rapidly. "I shot him I shot him I shot Michael." A quick, curious glance at Lilian: "Is he dead?"

Lilian studied Michael's body. She didn't want to touch him, didn't want to go near him. For a moment she hoped he *was* dead.

But his chest was rising, his breaths shallow and rapid. Lilian heard a sucking sound, saw the blood bubbling around the wound. His lung had collapsed. She didn't remember much about her trauma surgery rotation back in med school, but she did remember the basics of a pneumothorax. Air was being sucked through the wound, filling the space between lung and rib cage, pressing his lung toward the center of his chest.

She needed to call 911, to make sure paramedics were on their way. She needed to cover the wound with something occlusive. That was the most she could do here, without chest tubes or decompression needles or any practical experience.

But even if she did everything right, he might not survive. And didn't he deserve to die? To bleed out on the floor of the apartment he had decorated with Rosie's artwork and belongings, where he had brought her under false pretenses and planned an unspeakably horrifying life for her?

Could she live with his death on her hands?

Michael stirred; lifted his head, just an inch. His face was pale, his eyes barely open, but he looked at Lilian. His mouth formed the word *help*.

She should help him. She had an obligation to do so. She imagined explaining to a judge and jury that she, Lilian Donaldson, MD, had stood by and allowed him to die. Without attempting any medical treatment, without calling 911. She could lose her license, be dragged into a criminal investigation. Her reputation would be even more damaged than it already was.

And she knew, from her experience with Dasha Nichols, that his death would leave a scar on her soul. Every death did. She wouldn't grieve for Michael, but she would mourn the loss of the man who had been her friend.

But even worse than that was how all this might affect Rosie. Michael was unarmed. If Lilian did nothing, Rosie's actions would look less like those of a confused, frightened, and abused woman with a brain injury, and more like the coordinated efforts of two sisters determined to seek revenge for the car crash.

And while part of Lilian did want revenge—she could taste it, coppery and sharp in her mouth—she had to do what was best for Rosie.

Or maybe she could do both.

Across the room, Rosie had wrapped her arms around herself. Her shoulders shook and tears ran down her face.

Lilian exhaled and decided.

She stepped around Michael's body, into the nearby kitchen. Using a dishcloth hung on the refrigerator handle, she pulled a knife from the butcher block on the counter. Then she returned to the bedroom and came around near Michael's head.

Michael shifted again. He caught sight of the knife in Lilian's hands, and his face drained of any remaining color. *Please,* he mouthed. *Please don't.*

Lilian knelt next to him. She picked up his right hand and pressed the handle of the knife into the palm of his hand—carefully, carefully, without touching any part of the knife herself.

Michael shook his head. Whispered, "Stop."

But he didn't resist as she curled each of his fingers against the wooden handle. He likely couldn't. His breaths were even more rapid and shallow now, his lips a dusky blue, his jugular veins distended. Hypoxic from lack of ventilation, bleeding out from his chest wound.

Lilian didn't break his gaze. "You deserve this."

She set the knife on the floor, a few feet from Michael's outstretched right hand, as if it had fallen there as he crumpled to the ground.

Then, and only then, did she get her phone and dial 911.

CHAPTER
FIFTY-ONE

SIX WEEKS LATER

Lilian stepped out the door of a slightly shabby office on the South Side of Chicago. Joe Segura, a friend from med school, followed her out, his jeans and faded T-shirt contrasting with the stethoscope slung around his neck.

"I'm so thrilled you're joining us," Joe said, holding out his arms for a hug. He'd always been a hugger. "You have no idea what a huge deal this is for our whole organization, Lilian."

Lilian squeezed back. "Thanks for giving me a chance."

She had just signed a contract to join Joe's mobile health clinic, providing medical care for the homeless and underserved in Chicago. The past few weeks, she'd felt the itch to start working again, but had balked at returning to the pediatrics clinic's endless charting and packed schedule. When the local news did a segment on Joe's initiative, it had piqued her interest. She'd called him. It turned out that he'd been wanting to add a pediatrician to the team. It would be only a couple days a week for now, and she'd be paid peanuts, but she'd be using her skills and doing something that mattered.

"See you next week," Joe said. "Come ready for a busy day."

"Can't wait," Lilian said, waving goodbye.

As she got into her car and shut the door, she glanced in the mirror. Her hazel eyes stared back at her, framed by a familiar whisper of fine lines. She had wondered, in the days following Michael's shooting, if she'd ever be able to look herself in the eye again.

Michael had been alive when the paramedics arrived, but he'd been pronounced dead on arrival at the nearest emergency department. There had been an immediate flurry of questions, with Rosie momentarily under suspicion. Lilian had spent those tense hours wondering if, despite all she'd done, her sister would be carted off to a facility, never to be free again.

But with the butcher knife near Michael's hands and Lilian's testimony that Michael had walked in to find them with the Indiana plates, the matter was resolved fairly quickly. Michael's car—a silver BMW 7 Series—was found in a used car lot in Skokie. The paint matched the smudge left behind on Rosie's Beetle. After that, there had been no more questions.

Lilian had no intention of telling anyone what had really happened—not even Caleb. She would have to carry that weight on her own.

But while she had made plenty of mistakes before and after the car crash—falling under Michael's manipulative spell, pulling away from her husband, not trusting her own judgment—she'd always done her best to take care of her sister. She would never regret that decision.

As she drove home, her phone rang. It was Caleb. She answered via her car's Bluetooth.

"How'd it go with Joe?" he asked.

"Good. Signed the contract—it's a done deal." She took a left turn, blinking in the early spring sunlight. Snow still clung to the shadowed areas of lawns and sidewalks, but a few brave shrubs had started to send green shoots toward the sky.

"I'm proud of you," Caleb said. She imagined him sitting in his office chair at work, pausing in the middle of his jam-packed day when his calendar alert pinged: *Call your wife.*

It wasn't entirely spontaneous, but that was okay. This was part of their homework from their new marriage therapist. *Check in daily with each other. Connection breeds connection.*

It hadn't been easy, exposing their secret wounds to each other. Caleb, it turned out, had felt intense pressure to perform at work once he became the sole breadwinner. The family's financial well-being depended on his two hands, literally, and on his ability to continue operating. With Rosie's injuries and the potential for a lifetime of expensive caregivers, that pressure had deepened. He'd been hurt, too, when he realized that Lilian was confiding in Daniel—*Michael*, she reminded herself—and not him.

Lilian, for her part, had explained to Caleb how his attempts to take care of her had degraded her sense of self. His distrust had fed into her own lack of faith in herself and had widened the gap between them. Even now, six weeks after Michael's death, she still instinctively picked up her phone to text *him* when she needed to talk. She had to relearn the habit of turning to her own husband, and Caleb had to relearn how to respond in a way that respected her autonomy rather than infantilizing her. It hadn't been easy, making these changes, but she hoped it would be worth it.

In last night's counseling session, though, they'd hit a rough patch. Their therapist had asked each of them to prepare a list of three pivotal memories that had shaped their early relationship. Lilian had carefully written hers ahead of time, describing an evening when they'd been caught in a thunderstorm together and Caleb had given her his coat; the time he switched his shifts at the hospital to attend her parents' thirtieth wedding anniversary; the look on his face when he'd proposed: tender, nervous, and hopeful.

After she'd finished, Caleb had looked at the ground and mumbled that he hadn't done his. She was still irritated with him. If he wasn't going to engage with therapy, there wasn't any point in going.

"How was Rosie this morning?" Caleb asked, bringing her back to the present.

They had decided to bring Rosie home to live with them. Together, they'd hired a series of aides in addition to the various therapists that came and went. Three days a week, Rosie went to a day program for cognitively impaired adults, and she seemed to enjoy it. Lilian, for her part, loved being able to see her sister multiple times each day.

"Great. Still sketching away." Lilian smiled, thinking of the most recent sketchbook Rosie had filled with various iterations of the *Two Sisters*. Sometimes from far away, sometimes close-up. Always with the older girl's eyes and the younger girl's hands drawn in exquisite detail.

Caleb chuckled. "And how are you feeling about Julia?"

Lilian weighed her answer as she made the turn into their neighborhood. Julia was the new part-time nanny they'd hired to help with Abigail—a fifty-five-year-old woman with a kind smile and competent hands. She had raised three girls of her own, and while Lilian still struggled to feel entirely comfortable having another person care for her daughter, she couldn't imagine anyone better than Julia.

"I think she's going to work out fine," she said, nodding to herself. "Your mom is having a harder time than I am, honestly."

Caleb laughed. Nancy had surprised them both by bursting into tears when they said they were hiring Julia; she had worried it was an indictment of her abilities. Once they explained things, though, she'd understood. And she'd quietly promised Lilian to pop in at random times to make sure Julia was taking good care of her granddaughter.

Lilian made the final turn into their driveway and pressed the garage door opener. As she pulled in, Caleb spoke.

"I need to tell you something," he said. "I didn't forget to do our therapy homework for last night."

She sighed, irritated all over again, and put the car in park. "Caleb! You made me feel like an idiot. Why didn't you say something?"

"Because after hearing yours, I was embarrassed to share what I'd written."

She rolled her eyes. "Let me guess. Your pivotal memories were things like 'The first time Lily gave me a blow job,' right?"

Caleb's burst of laughter filled the car. "No," he said, after catching his breath. "Although that was a damn good moment."

"What were they, then?" she asked, genuinely curious.

"If I tell you, you can't laugh—they're not as good as yours."

"I promise I won't laugh."

He paused, and she heard a rustling sound. Was he reading this off a piece of paper? The thought made her smile.

"First," he said, "not long after we'd started dating, I came into lecture and saw you sitting there. You didn't have any makeup on, your hair was in a messy ponytail. I looked at you, and I smiled."

He stopped.

"That's it?" she said, flatly.

"No, the second moment was after we'd moved in together and we both got food poisoning."

"From that sketchy taco stand outside the hospital," she said, hoping this was a better memory than the first one.

"We shared a two-liter bottle of ginger ale, remember? And a package of saltines. That's all we could keep down. When there was only one saltine left, I pulled it out and said, 'Who gets the last one?' You snatched it from my fingers and ate it, right in front of me."

"What? I have no recollection of that," Lilian said, shaking her head. *These* were his pivotal memories? Not only bizarre, but unflattering. She sighed. "Okay, what's the third one?"

"We were in our fourth year, doing our medicine sub-I, walking out after a long day. All of sudden you yelled, 'Dammit!' and ran back to the hospital. You'd promised your patient's daughter that you would call her with the results of some test, and you'd forgotten."

He finished and waited.

Lilian scratched her head, confused and a little disappointed. "Your most important memories from our early relationship include a day I came to lecture without showering, when we were sick and I stole food from you, and when I neglected my responsibilities at work?"

"I'm not great with words, Lily, give me a break." The vulnerability in his voice surprised her.

"I'm sorry," she said, softening. "But I'm not sure what I'm supposed to take from this."

He exhaled. "Number one: seeing you makes me happy. Number two: I'd rather feel like shit with you than by myself. Number three: you always keep your word. Those are important to me, but if they're not good enough—"

"They're perfect," she said, and her chest swelled with gratitude. For

Caleb. For their past together and the future they were working toward. "Thank you for sharing them with me."

He breathed what sounded like a sigh of relief. "I love you, Lil. I hope you know that."

"I do." She smiled. "I love you, too."

After hanging up, she put her phone in her purse and opened the car door. It rang again, and she answered without looking at the screen.

"What's up?" she said, assuming Caleb had forgotten to tell her something.

There was a long pause.

"This is Detective Berenson," a familiar voice said. "I need to speak with you right away."

CHAPTER
FIFTY-TWO

Thirty minutes later, when the nanny had gone home and Abigail was napping upstairs, a knock sounded on the front door. Lilian opened it to see a familiar short, bald man in a dark gray suit.

"Hi, Detective," she said.

"Nice to see you again," he said, extending a hand. "Thank you for agreeing to speak with me on such short notice."

"Of course." Lilian smiled and shook his hand, hoping she looked calm. Internally, however, she buzzed with anxiety. She couldn't imagine what he wanted, why he was here at her doorstep when everything was supposed to be settled. Not only the case with Michael and the car crash, but the issues with Ben Nichols. Detective Berenson had tracked him down in Florida, where he'd gone on a whim to visit a woman he'd met online. The detective had put the fear of God into him for stalking Lilian in the past, and he'd promised Lilian that she'd never see Nichols again.

It was all supposed to be over. But here Detective Berenson was, with news that couldn't wait, that couldn't be delivered over the phone. Lilian's stomach clenched into a tight knot as she offered him something to drink.

"Some water would be great," he said, settling on the sofa.

Lilian filled a glass for him at the refrigerator, spilling a few drops onto her shaking hands. Had he somehow discovered that she had planted the knife? Was he here to arrest her for being an accessory to murder?

She sat on the edge of the sectional. Detective Berenson took a long swallow, his Adam's apple bobbing, then set his glass on the coffee table.

"I'll cut to the chase here, ma'am. We have new information about Michael Sorenson."

"New information?" Lilian stuck her hands under her thighs to keep them from trembling. "I thought everything was closed out."

The detective sat forward, elbows on knees. "We did, too. But when we searched his apartment . . . You found the Indiana plates in a safe, correct?"

"Yes, along with the gun," Lilian said.

"There was another safe, hidden deeper in the closet. This one was full. Some of the items we were able to identify. For example, a dog collar, a braid of what appears to be your sister's hair, a half-filled package of birth control pills, and printed-out copies of negative reviews posted online—negative reviews about you, Dr. Donaldson."

Lilian sat back, stunned. "Michael posted those?"

"Not all of them," the detective said. "But the most recent ones: yes. We assume he was playing into your fears about Ben Nichols."

She shouldn't have been surprised—it was exactly the type of cruel, manipulative thing Michael would have done. Still, it felt like a punch to the gut, the wind knocked out of her.

"And that's not all," Detective Berenson said. "On his computer, we found pictures of you and your daughter. Looks like he captured them from the baby monitor."

The blood drained from Lilian's face. From the original investigation, she had known that Michael had been watching her, terrifying her with the baby monitor. He'd played the role of a trusted confidante, only to use her deepest fears again her. But hearing that he had kept mementos of it, knowing that he'd wanted a baby like Abigail for himself, made his actions seem even darker.

"He kept them to remember everything he did. Like souvenirs," she said, still stunned.

The detective nodded. "We believe so. But we found something else, too. Something we can't explain. That's why I'm here: I hope you can."

Lilian leaned forward, shaking herself. "Go on."

He reached into his inside suit-coat pocket and pulled out a stack of glossy, eight-by-ten-inch photographs. He set two of them on the coffee table in front of Lilian. "Can you identify these items?"

Lilian stared at the pictures. Then brought a hand to her mouth.

One picture was of her dad's White Sox World Series baseball, the surface covered in blurred ink autographs. The other was of her mother's engagement ring, the tiny diamond reflecting the light of the camera's flash.

"Those belonged to my parents," she said. "Michael stole them?"

It seemed like such a petty, cruel act. But then again, that was the kind of person he had been. A man who hurt the people Rosie loved.

"That's not all he took," the detective said. He pulled a third photograph out of the stack.

Lilian stared at it, confused. "Batteries?"

"Eight double A batteries, to be precise."

"I don't understand."

Again, the detective leaned forward, elbow on knees. "Your parents died of carbon monoxide poisoning, yes?"

Lilian nodded. "The power went out. They left the oven door open for heat. It was a gas oven, and the carbon monoxide detectors didn't go off because . . ." She stopped, realizing what he was saying. "You think Michael—what? Planted dead batteries in my parents' carbon monoxide detectors?"

"It's not only what *I* think," the detective said. "It's what your *sister* thought, too."

Lilian shook her head, dazed. "How do you know that?"

"We obtained copies of Rosie's sessions with her psychologist, I believe you knew that already? In Dr. Vasudevan's notes, she wrote that Rosie believed Michael had killed her parents. The doc didn't seem to put much stock in it, though. Dozens of people die every winter from carbon monoxide poisoning," the detective continued. "There was no reason to think it was a suspicious death, under the circumstances. To be honest, we didn't think much of it, either, until we found these. There are two sets of fingerprints on those batteries—Michael's and your father's."

Lilian ran her hands through her hair, reeling. She thought back to the image that haunted her: a cold winter night, the power out, her mother turning on their gas oven to warm the drafty old house. Not realizing that the vent wasn't open, that the carbon monoxide detectors weren't working. Her father, with his early-onset dementia. Her mother, who had always trusted him to take care of things.

A burst of rage lit her up from the inside. Her mind flashed to the image of Michael on the floor of his bedroom, blood pooling around his body, and she shuddered. *You deserve this*, she'd said. She'd been wrong. He'd deserved worse.

"There's no way of knowing exactly what happened," the detective said, "but Michael may have come into the house one day when your parents were out and put dead batteries in the carbon monoxide detector."

Lilian took a shaky breath, remembering the key under her parents' frog-shaped planter near the back door. Everyone knew where they kept that key. "And then what?"

"He may have let nature take its course," Detective Berenson said, hesitating. "Or he might have snuck in while your parents slept. Turned on the gas stove, left it cracked open."

Lilian nearly choked on the rush of grief. Her parents, stolen from her. They would never meet their grandchild, never have a chance to make amends for their shortcomings as parents. She put a hand to her mouth, unable to form words.

The detective let her sit, allowing it to sink in. "This is all speculative, you understand. The reason I came here was—"

Panic flashed inside Lilian. "Do you think Rosie *wanted* to kill Michael? Because I was there, and he had a knife, and—"

The detective held up a hand. "This doesn't change anything for Rosie, I want to make that clear. The case is closed. She was acting in self-defense. I came over here because I felt you deserved some closure.

You deserve to know the truth of what happened to your parents and how Michael Sorenson was involved. Between you and me, ma'am? I'm glad he's dead."

Lilian nodded, relieved. She picked up the photographs, fingering their sharp edges. "Can I keep these pictures?" she said.

"Oh, sure," Detective Berenson said. "In fact, you can come down to the station and claim your parents' belongings."

* * *

After the detective left, Lilian sat for a long while in her living room, staring at the photograph of the batteries. Had Rosie been planning to tell Lilian at the restaurant the night of the car crash? *This conversation is too important to have in a car. It's a matter of life and death, sis.*

And that afternoon in Michael's apartment, six weeks ago. *Michael did something bad*, Rosie had said, over and over again. She'd been frustrated when all Lilian could find was the license plates—she had wanted Lilian to keep searching.

Maybe that was why she had finally agreed to go home with Michael, even knowing that he wasn't Daniel. Somewhere in her healing brain, even though she couldn't explain it in words, she had sensed that the only way she could get the proof she needed was to be in his apartment.

Standing abruptly, Lilian grabbed the stack of photographs, then headed to the basement stairs. She and Caleb had only ever used the basement as a workout room and storage, but it was a lovely space. High ceilings, a walk-out to the backyard. Plenty of windows. Rosie seemed happy there.

As Lilian came into the wide family room, she saw Rosie sitting by the window with a sketch pad on her lap. She had gained back some weight, and her hair had grown long enough to tuck behind her ears.

"How's she doing today?" Lilian asked the aide, who was sitting nearby. Heather was a nursing student at the University of Chicago.

"She's doing great! We took a walk to the lake earlier, and now we're drawing again."

"Why don't you take your break," Lilian said. "I'll stay with her for a few minutes."

Heather nodded and headed upstairs. Lilian settled in a chair, slightly out of Rosie's line of sight. Rosie must have heard her, but she didn't look up from her sketchpad.

Over the past few weeks, Rosie had slowly settled into their home life. She loved Caleb and Abigail—she accepted both of them without question. Most of the time, she still believed Lilian was an imposter, but she'd recently started working with a neuropsychologist who had an innovative approach for treatment of Capgras syndrome. Someday, Lilian hoped, Rosie might recognize her.

Either way, it didn't bother Lilian as much. Before, Rosie's repeated questions had shaken Lilian to the core: *Who the fuck are you?* The words had echoed in her head, refusing to be silenced. But now Lilian took the question in stride.

Because Lilian knew exactly who she was. Her story might contain missteps, regrets, and failure, but it also spoke of grit and love, and persistence. From now on, Lilian was determined to own it all.

"Can I talk to you about something?" Lilian asked.

Rosie didn't look up from her pad of paper, but she nodded. The sketchpad seemed to be like a security blanket to her, a transitional object, a way to keep herself grounded and focused. Sometimes, when she was drawing, Lilian could sit outside her line of sight and watch her for an hour or more.

She yearned to *listen* to Rosie, though. To hear her thoughts. The therapy journal, even the day planner, were only a snapshot of her sister's past, and they had left her with more questions than answers. Including this new one: What had made Rosie believe Michael had killed their parents? Had her suspicions started when their dad's baseball and mom's ring went missing? Or had Michael admitted it to her later, after they'd gotten back together, perhaps using it as a way to punish or control her?

But like Dr. Vasudevan had said to Rosie, that sled was long gone, leaving only the snowy tracks of memory behind. There was no way to know what had really happened.

"The detectives found Mom's ring and Dad's baseball," Lilian said, setting the pictures on the coffee table. "They found the batteries, too."

Rosie glanced over at the photos. Lilian watched her face, looking for signs of interest, any spark in Rosie's eyes. But her expression didn't change; she could have been looking at pictures of trees or kitchen cutlery or any other random object. She certainly didn't appear to recognize their parents' prized possessions, let alone the batteries.

The pang of disappointment surprised Lilian. She'd been hoping for more, even though she knew that was unrealistic. Did she honestly think that her sister, after a severe brain injury, was capable of carrying out a plan to expose Michael for murdering their parents? It suddenly seemed ridiculous.

But at the very least, Lilian had been hoping that the pictures of the baseball and ring would trigger *something* in Rosie. A moment of connection, an acknowledgment of their shared past, as sisters. Their shared pain. She'd been yearning for that for two years. The chances of it happening seemed less likely than ever.

She should be grateful that Rosie was allowing her to sit here, Lilian told herself. This was a huge improvement. She shifted her weight, leaning forward so she could see Rosie's sketchpad. *Two Sisters*, once again. Today, Rosie had drawn the older girl's eyes in startling detail, as always, but she had altered the contours of the face, the jaw and nose, the shape of the eyes. It didn't look like the original painting, but it seemed familiar.

Lilian sucked in a quick breath. Rosie had drawn *Lilian's* face on the older girl, she realized. Lilian's wide-set eyes, Lilian's sharp chin.

But instead of the older sister's eyes gazing wistfully to the side, Rosie had drawn them looking downward, at the younger girl's hands. And, as usual, Rosie had drawn the younger sister's palms outstretched, cupping something.

Or rather, several small somethings. Lilian had never been able to figure out what they were; at one time she'd thought they were cigarettes; Caleb had suggested some kind of candy. Multiple small, cylindrical objects, with a stubby nose on one end.

"Batteries," Lilian whispered.

Rosie looked up sharply. Her eyes were clear and focused. Recognition sparked between them, and Lilian understood exactly what Rosie had been trying to communicate, all this time.

The same message, over and over, in the only way she knew how. *Look at this*, she'd been saying. *See what I am trying to show you. See me.*

"I see it now," Lilian whispered. "I understand."

Rosie tilted her head, assessing Lilian with her bright green eyes. "You look like—so much like my sister."

Lilian hesitated. This was usually her cue to leave, before Rosie's disorientation grew into agitation. But she longed to stay, if only for a moment longer.

"Tell me about her," Lilian said.

"Oh, my sister?" Rosie's face lit up in a smile. "She's my favorite person in the whole world and I'm trying to get better so I can see her again."

"What do you mean, get better?" She wondered if Rosie understood, on some level, that her brain injury was responsible for her confusion about Lilian's identity.

Rosie's smile faded. "I made so many mistakes I said terrible things. As soon as I'm better I'll apologize—I'll show her that I've changed but I need to be better, I need to be better first."

The sadness in Rosie's voice made Lilian ache. She remembered Rosie writing the same thing in her therapy journal.

I'm worried that she'll be disappointed in me.

I need to meet some kind of standard before I'm worthy of seeing her again.

"I don't think your sister needs you to be better," Lilian said, "or different in any way. I think she needs *you*, exactly as you are, no matter what happened in the past. She made mistakes, too. I bet she wishes she could apologize."

Rosie met Lilian's eyes, and there it was again: that spark of recognition. An invisible thread connecting them.

"You look *so* much like my—my sister," Rosie said, then whispered, "I miss you."

Lilian's lungs expanded as she sucked in a breath. "I miss you, too," she said.

But then Rosie blinked. And blinked again, hard. The spark vanished, replaced by an expression Lilian was oh-so-familiar with, that mixture of suspicion and confusion.

"You're not Lilian," she said, her voice tinged with distrust.

"I'll go." Lilian stood, not wanting to upset Rosie.

Such a cruel, unfair, confusing ordeal—loving someone with a brain injury. Why did her mind still refuse to acknowledge her own sister? The person who'd cared for her as a child, who'd been by her side since the car crash? Who had rearranged her own life to welcome Rosie into it?

Swallowing down her heartache, Lilian reminded herself that none of this was unexpected. Capgras syndrome nearly always involved those closest to the patient, but even though Lilian understood this, it still left her feeling hollow and hopeless.

Rosie turned back to her sketchpad and shook her head. "You can stay if you want," she said, picking up her pencil.

"Okay," Lilian said, carefully sitting back down. She held her breath; this had never happened before.

Rosie started to sketch, confidently filling in the background behind the two girls: a river, trees, a few boats. "This is a picture of us," she said, not looking at Lilian. "Remember we'd go to the Art Institute for hours and hours when I was little."

Rosie continued talking, and Lilian sat next to her sister, breathing in the moment, and listening.

ACKNOWLEDGMENTS

The seed for this story began when my agent, Amy Berkower, suggested I write something related to my profession as a physician, and I will always be grateful for that nudge. Amy has been a fierce advocate for this book through this long journey to publication and has guided my writing career with such care. I also owe a huge debt of gratitude to Genevieve Gagne-Hawes, who guided me through countless revisions of this story with such generosity, kindness, and skill. I feel lucky every day to have you both on my side, as well as Meridith Viguet and the entire team at Writers House.

I would also like to thank the team at Blackstone for all their enthusiasm and support for this story. Thank you to Rick Bleiweiss, Naomi Hynes, Megan Bixler, and Josie Woodbridge; to Samantha Bensor for the publicity; to Alenka Linaschke for the beautiful cover; to Kelley Lusk, Katrina Tan, Deirdre Curley, and Adrienne Roche. Special thanks to editor Sara O'Keefe for guiding me through a revision that made this story so much stronger.

My writing community has always been a source of strength and support. Thank you to the Women Physician Writers, especially Kristin Prentiss Ott, Lisa Preston-Hsu, and Kimmery Martin. Thank you to the 2022 Debuts, the International Thriller Writers, the Every Damn Day Writers, and the Women's Fiction Writers Association. To my dear friends in the Ink Tank: thanks for the spitballing, the commiseration, the check-ins.

Thank you to my beta readers for their feedback that helped make this story stronger: Kathleen West, Jill Atwood, Katy Bachman, Jessica Langer, and Angela Rehm. Shout out to the Murray Moms for the Marco Polos and support along this journey (Amanda Habel, Kellie Terry, Stephanie Higbee, Suzanne James, Erin Wiggins, and Amy Rex) and to everyone in my IRL book club for the conversations and laughs.

A massive thank you to Alison Hammer, my critique partner, one of my dearest friends, and now my coauthor in my other writing career. Thank you, Alison, for always being just a text message or phone call away during this long, challenging, and sometimes painful process of becoming published. I would not want to do any of this without you.

When writing a novel in a medical setting, it can be a challenge to accurately reflect medical information without becoming overwhelming with details. I did my best to portray recovery after a brain injury (both a severe injury like Rosie's, and a mild one like Lilian's) in an accurate and respectful manner. Much of this is based on my own professional experiences and training, and I am indebted to excellent attending physicians who taught me during residency, particularly John Speed, MBBS, and Toni Roberts, DO. I am very grateful to the nurses, social workers, pharmacists, respiratory therapists, physical therapists, occupational therapists, and speech-language pathologists that I have worked with and learned from over the years.

I also did my best to accurately and respectfully reflect the psychiatric and psychological elements of this story. While I have personally dealt with postpartum depression/anxiety, it was not to the extent that Lilian did in this novel, and I am grateful for several other women (who have asked to remain anonymous) who shared their experiences with postpartum mood disorders. I am grateful to Rebekah Stalker, MD (Psychiatry) and Nancy Nelson, MD (Obstetrics and Gynecology) for reading this manuscript and providing feedback. I am also very grateful to several women (who have also asked to remain anonymous) who discussed their experiences with intimate partner abuse, particularly the psychological and emotional aspects. I am in awe of your strength.

Nothing I write would ever matter if not for readers, bookstagrammers, book bloggers, booksellers, and librarians. I love the reading community! I will always have a special place in my heart for the bookstagram community, and I want to send a shout out to my many friends there, plus an extra special thanks to the Bookish Ladies Club and my co-hosts: Angela Rehm, Katy Bachman, Jill Atwood, Jessica Langer, Meirys Martinez, Brandi Jarrell, and Ketra Arcas. I love you ladies!

Thank you to my parents, Merrie and Jim Smithson, for instilling in me a love of reading and writing, and for teaching me that I could do anything I set my mind to. Thank you to my siblings, Ellie and McLean, for putting up with all my make-believe schemes during our childhood and beyond. My mom and my sister read early drafts of this manuscript and gave helpful feedback. Every one of my family members have listened to me talk ad nauseam about my writing for years, and I am so grateful for their support and love.

To my children (Isaac, Eliza, Everett, and Nora), thank you for celebrating with me every step of this journey. You are my dearest treasures. And of course, Nate. Without you and your endless supply of support, patience, and love, none of this would have happened.